Eternal

CASSANDRA THOMSON

This is a work of fiction. Names, characters, businesses, places, events, locales, and incidents are either the products of the author's imagination or used in a fictitious manner. Any resemblance to actual persons, living or dead, or actual events is purely coincidental.

Published by Fircrest Books
PO Box 1044
Freeland, WA 98249

Printed by CreateSpace
Charleston, SC USA

ISBN 978-1732567603
Library of Congress Control Number 2018908168

First Edition: August 2018

For my cherished grandparents,
Mary and Elmo, Judy and Walt, Cheri and Kirk.

"Ah how shameless – the way these mortals blame the gods. From us alone they say come all their miseries… but they themselves, with their own reckless ways, compound their pains beyond their proper share."

Homer, *Odyssey*

And ye shall be judged by the Titan Cronus, Father of Olympians, for entrance to the Isles of the Blessed.

Autumn 551 BCE
South of Corinth, Greece

1

When the soul arrived in the white, circular room, he probably thought he would be admitted to the Isles of the Blessed.

His smile was hideous. It struck Elysia as something between a grimace and a smirk, twisted up and gloating, teeth yellowing and cracked in places. Even if she had been inclined to, there would be no exchanging glances with her neighbors. They were engrossed by this man's presence, drinking in every detail.

The little man had crossed his arms when first he had been called upon, sneering beneath Khronos's booming voice. That simple immodesty told Elysia exactly where the soul thought he must be: the Underworld, or some version of it, just as the tales had told him. He had found himself in a rickety wooden chair, faced with a man and seven others who declared that a judgment would be made upon his soul. Elysia had heard the confusion from these souls so many times that she could nearly predict what would come next: an expectation of admission to the Isles of the Blessed.

The tales had the right of it, but not the whole truth.

Elysia's father sat in the tallest of chairs, a throne carved of a single piece of blue-black crystal. Khronos was the High Judge, the one who asked the questions and set the sentence, and the one who, according to so many, held the key to the lands of paradise.

Elysia had watched this scene play out almost every day since she'd turned twelve and been allowed to enter the chamber. The soul shivered and quaked, answering questions meekly until it recognized that the judges spoke of crimes it had committed during its life. Then it would sit up straight, as this little man had from the start, and spout tales of grandeur until Eris added the count of lies to the soul's tally of crimes. After that, there might be a protest, but then came blessed silence as each of her father's six councilors assessed the soul before them. Good souls appeared, too, ones who stayed honest and kept their integrity even beyond the grave. They were rarer, and although Elysia loved them best, the schemers were more memorable.

This soul was one of the few who refused to tell the truth. His opportunity to preface his judgment was not wasted; he smirked as soon as he was asked the highlights of his life.

"Rescued my employer's boy from his burning house," he rattled off, smile intact, as he ticked off his seventh "good deed" on fingers topped by black-bedded nails. "And saved his horses once the stables caught."

"And how many horses did your employer keep in the stables?" Khronos asked, looking up from the wax tablet he'd set on the arm of his chair. The ivory stylus in his hand clicked as he tapped it against his throne.

The little man balked, smile dissolving like salt left in the rain. He looked about him, counting the judges again. "Eight," he began, daring to make eye contact with Khronos once more. "One for each of the Judges of the Underworld, but how he knew they were eight, I don't know."

Sighing, Khronos sat back in his chair and nodded to Elysia over the little man's head. "How kind of him," she said, and the little man twisted in his seat to look at her. She rose from her throne. Where Khronos's was iridescent crystal, Elysia's was white marble, carved with all kinds of flowers: delicate apple blossoms, ash foliage, crocus blooms. Some flowers she had never seen in their true forms, like the large, proud dahlias that supported her arms. The roses that crowned the chair, however, Elysia knew.

Feeling the eyes of the little man as she skirted his chair, Elysia stood beside her father on the opposite side of the room. The man's smile returned, this time looking as though he'd pinned it to his face in his hurry to impress her. If he hadn't informed them that he'd been a farmer, Elysia would have thought him a merchant in life.

"He was a pious man. Me too."

Elysia gave the man a wan smile, flicking her eyes up to her father. Khronos clicked his stylus against his throne.

"Enough."

The voice belonged to Eris, Judge of Sin and Strife. She sat at Khronos's right in her obsidian throne. Standing, she looked to Khronos. "Let us judge this man a liar and be done with him, my lord. He is not worth any more of our time." Her fists balled in the skirt of her crimson gown, as if to keep herself from striking the soul before her.

The little man looked between Eris and Khronos, his arrogance palpable in the air. "I am no liar, my lord," he said, but Khronos held up a hand to silence him.

"List his crimes, Eris," Khronos said, voice firm. He put a warm hand on Elysia's shoulder.

"Lying to the Judges of the Afterlife," Eris began, "and compounding his lies extensively."

The smile slipped from the little man's face again.

"Stealing goods and crops from the residence and fields of his employer. Lying to those who were good to him. Beating the man Herod nearly to death over a toy meant for Herod's young daughter." Elysia felt her father squeeze her shoulder. "The rape of the women Neno and Theria. The murder of his wife Rhia. Other crimes which seem small when compared to rape and murder," Eris finished, placing one hand on her hip and letting her gown fall back into place, its pleats wrinkled. She wore a mask of triumph as she took her seat, as though speaking his sins had washed her clean of them.

The little man had gone nearly white as Eris listed his crimes. He looked as though he wanted to run but had found himself unable to move.

"Ares," said Khronos, and the man to his left rose from his throne.

"In both battle and valor, this man knew little, my lord," Ares said, brown curls bobbing with his words. "The only deed he ever committed was an act of sin, the beating of the man Herod over a toy. Never did he fight for a thing in his life, but instead used cunning or thievery to gain what he wanted."

Khronos nodded, and Ares reclaimed his seat. "Aphrodite."

The blond woman beside Ares stood. "In relationships, this man has committed sin after sin." Aphrodite raised her chin to look down at the little man, her golden mane swaying as she shook her head. "He murdered his wife Rhia after having been wed to her for nine days. He committed this act for desire of another, the woman Neno. When she spurned him, as she was wed to another man, this man raped her and her daughter Theria, a maid of sixteen years. None have loved him, and he has loved none, but done only harm." Aphrodite lowered herself back into her seat, still glowering. After another moment, she glanced to Khronos. "He did have a soft spot for his mother, though."

Shaking his head, Khronos moved on. "Hera."

"In the way of faith," said a woman crowned with braids, "there is little to tell. The man is faithless in gods and men, pretending to believe when it suited him, and only when he needed a favor. He was faithless in his marriage." She sank back into her chair.

"Athena."

Athena did not rise, her blue eyes frigid against olive skin. "There is no wisdom in this man. His decisions were cruel, self-serving, and led to his early demise at the hands of the man Meronus, husband of the woman Neno. Every decision he made only added to his sins."

"Apollo."

Golden-eyed and golden-haired, Apollo rose from his throne. "In the way of morality," he began, but simply shrugged. The corners of his lips hid a cross between a sardonic grin and a soft smile; he was ever stuck between the two. "I doubt that this man knows the meaning of the word."

The little man seemed to have given up trying to please the judges and fumed now, his face turning purple from the words he appeared to be holding in. Elysia strode to stand before him, arms crossed. "Thank you, Apollo, for that assessment," she said. The young man nodded and dropped into his cushioned seat. "As you have heard, the Six have little respect for you," she told the soul, uncrossing her arms to brace them against the little man's chair. "But we are in the practice of allowing repentance here, and I am the judge of that. Do you repent your crimes?"

The smile came back, an unadulterated smirk. Much to Elysia's surprise, he did not beg forgiveness or pledge penance for his sins, as most did. Instead, he laughed. It was a breathless laugh, as though he could not believe what he heard. When he must have realized that Elysia would not move, he stopped. "I won't be repenting to you, bitch," he replied, and Elysia felt her father's fury ignite in a vibration just beneath the threshold of hearing. The little man leaned forward until he and Elysia were almost nose to nose; he was done trying to woo the judges, it seemed. "I enjoyed every moment of those women, and that beating gave my muscles a stretch, the kind they don't get out in the fields. Even grappling with Meronus was a bit of fun until the bastard got his hands around my pretty neck. If I had it my way, I'd be enjoying you, too, but the expression on that titan says I won't be touching you."

Elysia did not glance back at her father. She knew what he must look like: face as red as his hair, fists pressed into the heads of the crystal hell hounds that supported the arms of his throne.

"A pity, that is," the soul finished. Leaning back in his simple chair, the little man grinned at her. "So, now that you righteous folk have finished judging me, am I free to go? The Isles of the Blessed await me, or so says the presence of that one there." The little man inclined his head toward her father. It was something Elysia had seen before; she had gathered, in the seven years she had been a judge, that her father was quite a figure to the Greeks. While the names of his six councilors elicited reactions of fearful fidgeting, Khronos's name received silent awe, stilling whatever anxiety the souls felt – until he spoke of their crimes.

"I am afraid not," Elysia said, standing up straight and releasing the arms of the soul's chair. "After the judging comes the sentencing, and the titan behind me holds that honor."

Returning to her throne, Elysia said, "Khronos," and the other judges rose from their seats. Her father had ticked off the little man's crimes one by one on his wax tablet, ivory stylus in hand. He held the tablet before him to study but put it down to stare at the soul, eyes unrelenting. Even from across the room, Elysia felt their searing glow warm her skin.

"You have committed crimes beyond count, atrocities beyond measure. You have caused suffering, pain, and death. Your soul can never be redeemed of these crimes, and you have not repented. I, Khronos the Creator and High Judge of the Afterlife, sentence you to an eternity of wandering the netherworld without reincarnation. You will have a chance to appeal this sentence in a millennium, at which time you will be judged by Elysia."

"…Without reincarnation? Who's Alysha?" the little man asked, and Elysia sighed. Eris, however, answered the question.

"*Elysia* is the woman who you would be 'enjoying,'" she said, her rasping voice harsh on the words. "You will not have a chance to live a better life or have closure on this one for a millennium. Enjoy your time in the netherworld," she added, and with a click of Khronos's stylus, the soul was gone.

The entire room exhaled relief.

"That is the kind of person that makes me feel unclean," said Aphrodite. Her hands rubbed up and down her arms, nails leaving light white scratches behind.

"I agree, for once," said Hera from across the room.

"Then we will be finished for the day, councilors." Khronos leaned back in his chair, rubbing his temples. One by one, the judges left the chamber, trailing through the open doorway hidden in the illusion of the round marble room. When Elysia and Khronos were alone in the chamber, she sat in Eris's throne.

Her father leaned his head against his cold crystal backboard. Moving his fingers to rub his eyes, he massaged them before turning his green-gold gaze on his daughter. "Let us hope that the next soul is as pure as spring water," he said.

"Clear and refreshing." The mantra was an old one, developed over Elysia's first year judging souls, when she had still been a child. Seven years had passed since then, judging day after day and sometimes into the night. Taking her father's arm, Elysia walked with him from the room. The torches snuffed themselves, casting the chamber into a windowless darkness.

Khronos paused before the tapestry in the hall that showed the first judgment of souls to take place in the chamber – the tapestry that he had made to weave the room into being. The great loom he'd used stood silent vigil in its own room down the hall.

"Elysia," he murmured, lifting her chin with hands warm and tough from years of labor at the loom and in the field. "You may already have a place in the chamber as a judge, but you were meant to share my duties as a High Judge. You are nearing twenty –"

"And I ought to claim my birthright," she finished for him. "Who knows it better than I, Father?" she asked, turning toward the tapestry. She must be worthy of her throne; it was not enough to just sit in it. The wool of the tapestry was soft beneath her fingers. Her father's throne stood at the head of a ring of six there, not seven. The cloth was older than her, older than even her mother, a woman gone seventeen years this summer. Her mother had begun anew with the rest whose vessels had died and gone to dust, reincarnated along with the souls who had been worthy of a new life. Elysia's memory of her mother included little more than a flash of blue-gray eyes and a phantom scent. But, like her mother, Elysia was human – and she had been given a choice. *Earn your place and your eternity, or fade into nothing with the rest of humanity.* The words still rang harsh in her ears, even after years of reliving them. The rest of her father's speech had faded from memory. The ultimatum remained.

"The requirements are few," Khronos said, his voice soft.

"You have only told me two." To claim her eternity and her throne in the chamber – to keep it forever – she had to pass two tests she knew and a third that would remain a mystery. The first requirement made the prospect of the second a little easier to bear, but Elysia still felt the weight of them. *To safely conduct yourself with humans, you must learn to defend yourself from harm. To judge the souls of humans, you must know what it is to live a human life*. The third requirement unsettled her, for it was the one she'd resigned herself to never knowing: she'd received a scolding for attempting to persuade each of the Six to tell her. She had no way to prepare for the test – no way to know if she had passed, failed, or even begun it. After meeting a soul like the little man, Elysia wasn't certain she could risk living a human life.

And yet, the longer she bemoaned the requirements, the less time she had to fulfill them – and she had no idea how long it might take. If she failed, the eternal cursed solitude of the netherworld awaited her, and she would never see her father again.

"I cannot allow you to go on like this much longer, Elysia," her father said, folding his hand over hers where it touched the tapestry. When he held her gaze once more, his brow furrowed. "You are not impartial, as the Six are, and you do not have the experience that comes with living with humans, as I do. You will not enter the chamber again until you know how they live their lives."

Elysia blanched. He had not laid out a rule since making it clear that he would not teach her to weave, claiming that he had neither the skill nor the time. Though she had been skeptical, his tone had brooked no argument. He spoke with the same tone now.

"We will depart for Corinth in two days, where you will live until you fulfill the requirements. It could be months or years, but you will go, and you will stay." His green-gold eyes darkened, his jaw set firm. She felt him dare her to argue, dare her to make him set down his cool control. His wrath was infamous. Though she had heard of the terror he unleashed upon the land, Elysia had never seen it firsthand. Her mother had talked him down when she had been alive, and after that, it had been Hera's job.

"There are days when I'd rather live a hundred years with you and die human than live a few months in the city, fearing that men like that last one will come knocking in the night," she muttered. "There are humans enough here."

Khronos shook his head, and her heart dropped. "The people here will never be strangers to you. The city will be different, so you will go, and you will stay," he said, but he softened. "To ease your fears, you will have an audience with a soul on the morrow. I have high hopes that it will placate you."

"Thank you, Father," she said, but the uneasiness lingered. What could this soul tell her that she had not already learned from the thousands she'd met?

Khronos loosened his hand from hers and stepped away. His eyes seemed distant, and disappointment shot through her gut.

"That is all, Elysia. I will leave you to begin packing. If all goes well tomorrow, you may wish to go sooner than you thought you would." Smiling his bright white smile, Khronos took his leave of his daughter and made for his weaving room.

Watching his red-gold head vanish from view, Elysia exhaled and leaned against the wall beside the tapestry.

And if I die in the city, he will be as silent about my death as he was about Mother's. Her spinning fingers rubbed together at the thought, yearning for the smooth-worn wooden weight and shaft. Her drop spindle, aged and probably too small to be truly practical, was the only thing that remained of Elysia's mother, aside from scant memories. She did not even know her name. Her father had forbidden anyone who lived on the compound from speaking of his wife, or else the residents were too intimidated to reminisce. It was as if her mother's presence had ended with her life. Only Elysia's room still held traces of her, in the few things she had not allowed to be thrown away when she was the tender age of three.

Even then, she had known that her father's grief was private. They had not spoken of her mother since the day Athena had wrapped her in a shroud and thanked her for her life, and Ares prayed that her battles would be over.

The pyre they lit had set flame to the valley, and the harvest had burned to ash while her father confined himself to his room. Not long after, Elysia saw the first snow of her life. It fell for days, smothering the fire and freshening the smoke-filled halls of the house. Hera had held her back from the snow, though Elysia did not remember wanting to play in it. It had filled her with a sense of awe as it fell, muffling the world and blanketing the blackened ground in a soft white quilt.

The snow melted a week later as they ate the first of the valley's rations. In the soil that had been hidden beneath it, new sprouts grew. The residents celebrated life returning to the valley, but Elysia had just been lonely. Isolation swallowed her, even when Hera held her hand.

Finally, Hera had taken her up the stairs to the highest floor in the house. She had stood in the hallway for what felt like hours, staring expectantly at the door to her parents' room. When it finally opened, she thought her mother would be standing there, with her father right behind, just as she had always greeted them in the morning.

Instead, it was her father alone. Instead of cupping her cheek and kissing her forehead, as he had always done before, Khronos swept her up in a hug and buried his face in her shoulder. In that moment, the void of loneliness had filled with joy. He'd carried her downstairs on his hip, Hera following a little bit behind. When he greeted all those celebrating spring's coming in the gardens below, Elysia's father had done it with hugs and claps on the shoulder, his grief seemingly forgotten. But it hung in the air around him, the pain of a soul who had known true loss and the fatigue of continuing every day when his heart belonged somewhere else.

Elysia still saw it in his heavy sighs, his tired eyes, his hands that had been seldom idle since he had emerged from his room that day. But because he had emerged, he had set her free: she was no longer alone in the world, frozen in time, waiting for his return. Her mother was lost to her, but her father kept her joy alive.

And unless she did what he asked – unless she completed her tasks – she would be cursed to that loneliness once more. This time, though, no one would open the door.

2

The white marble cooled as the afternoon sun sank below the hills, silhouetting rows of grapevines and olive trees. Nearer to the compound grew pomegranate, apple, and fig trees, some so close to the paths their roots peeked up for air between marble flagstones. The workers were out in the groves and rows, savoring the cool evening as they finished their day's work. The sun kissed the sky, making it blush a dusky pink, and as Elysia watched, the workers picked up their baskets and hauled their harvest back to the cellars.

Pushing off her wall, Elysia went to stand at the balustrade, a dainty rail carved with scrolls and supported by thin columns of marble. She could only imagine seeing the compound from above. It must be a great white glimmering thing, all that stone shining in the sunlight, set among fields of brown, green, and gold. Her father, in his vanity, had modeled it after the temples which were even now being built all over Greece. Beneath the shelter of the roof, Khronos had woven more rooms, floor after floor of brick and stone until the inner structure touched the ceiling. The judgment chamber stood on the third of four floors, taking its support from everything below it. Built in the northwestern corner, its corridor opened to the sun and air in the afternoon.

Standing in the remains of the sunlight, Elysia fidgeted with the end of her white-blond braid. The little man was still fresh in her mind, the horrors he'd committed even more so. Khronos wanted her to live with him forever in their valley. She wanted nothing more, and yet... Souls like that man's made her doubt humanity.

They cannot all be like that. Her head spoke reason, but her stomach and her heart were sick with worry. The valley was all she had known. The few humans she knew were good, wholesome; her father had made sure of that. She could identify most of them from above, the handful of harvesters and grooms who kept the crops and animals.

Philip stood down at the door of the warehouse, counting the day's harvest, his short pepper-and-salt hair distinguishing him from the young men and women who lined up before him, bearing baskets filled to brimming with bushels of grapes and olives. Though Philip was their overseer during the eternal harvest, he doubled as the valley's Master of Horse. Once, Elysia dreamed of marrying him, as her mother had married her father: for friendship, for necessity. Philip could show her a human life, but her father had put down the notion the moment she'd confided in him. If she was to marry, he told her, it would only be after she had seen the outside world and could truly comprehend what marriage meant.

Leaning around the column to her left, Elysia set out for her room. She knew who she would find within, as always. She lifted her gown's skirts as she descended the stair at the end of the hall, holding onto the rail and using her momentum to turn at the landing. Striding toward the curtain at the foot of the stair, Elysia put a smile on her face, but she thought of those yellow-brown teeth again and let the smile slip away.

"My lady." A hushed voice greeted her as she pushed aside the cerulean silk that veiled her room.

Falling into the mass of cushions that softened her wooden lounge, Elysia groaned. "You needn't call me that, Aliya."

Pottery and metal clinked together, and suddenly, a plate appeared beneath her nose. It was piled with fruit, cooked fowl, boiled barley; the warm scents overwhelmed her. Elysia took the plate from the older girl, who sat down at the end of the lounge with a plate of her own. "It would be improper to call you anything else, my lady. This household may know only one of the gods, but courtesy is something I will not surrender." Balancing a shred of meat on the blade of her knife, Aliya stared Elysia down with eyes the brown of ocher. Ever since she had been small, Elysia remembered an almost equally small Aliya begging her father to build an altar to Demeter, if to any of the gods. He had kindly shaken his head and done his best to explain to her that the gods were man's creation, but she had carried on believing, as stubborn as a child could be.

Ignoring her, Elysia gazed up at the ceiling. Her limbs were leaden; if dawn and her appointment with that soul came, she might not be able to move to meet them. "Father is sending me off to some city the day after next," she said.

Her words were met with silence. Elysia leaned up to look at her handmaiden. Aliya still gazed at her, holding her knife up, her food hovering in front of the glossy scar on her chest.

Sighing, Elysia sat up and leaned against the back of couch. She found her own knife in its sheath at her waist and took a bite of food.

Aliya followed suit, chewing daintily. "What city?"

"Corinth."

Aliya's eyes flicked to Elysia's before returning to her plate. "Your father found me in Corinth. My parents and theirs before them were born there."

"I thought he looked for refugees coming into the city," said Elysia, knife held aloft.

"Those in the city catch his attention, too. Corinth had had rough years. An earthquake brought all to their knees, and a frost not long after bit the toes and fingers and noses of the littlest ones. He helped all he could, Lord Khronos." Taking a deep breath, Aliya put her knife down on her plate and pushed a strand of curly, dark hair behind her ear. "My family was one of the poorest in the city, and we curled by the hearth at night to stay warm. Fire is treacherous in such a close space."

Elysia touched the girl's arm. "Father will choose the house. I'm sure it will be safe," she murmured.

"I am not afraid of an unsafe home, my lady, nor of fire," said Aliya. "Poseidon will protect me from flame, just as he has done before, or he will let your dear father bring me back home to be reunited with the ones I've lost."

"Hera will judge you strong in your faith, at least, when it's time for that."

Something mischievous twisted at the corner of Aliya's mouth, and she pulled Elysia's empty plate from her hands. "Corinth will be good for you. You will begin to understand what you've missed, growing up in this household."

"I think heresy requires more people to believe he's in the wrong, Aliya."

Aliya just shook her head, and her chocolate tresses swayed. Tiny misshapen scars freckled her shoulders, framing the rectangular patch of red skin on her chest. "It is not the heresy I speak of, my lady. Corinth is filled with all kinds of people that you could never meet here, sights you cannot imagine." Giving Elysia a little half smirk, Aliya put the plates on a shelf near the door. "You will see. It may take Corinth to make you appreciate your home, and it may take your return to appreciate Corinth."

Lying back on the lounge among the wool-stuffed pillows, Elysia considered Aliya's words. "Did you appreciate your first home after you left the city?"

Another pause came before Aliya spoke again. "I appreciated that, as poor and hungry as we were, our life was not all misery."

Elysia studied the girl, whose fingers fidgeted with the dinnerware on the shelf.

"Once it was gone, I missed it, but there was no getting it back," she added, her gaze falling to the tiny hills her toes made beneath the hem of her dress.

Quiet passed between them. *Perhaps I will appreciate the ability to start over,* she thought. Elysia cleared her throat. "I have a meeting with a soul in the morning," she said.

"What will you wear, my lady?" Aliya went to the trunk at the foot of Elysia's bed, her pensiveness left behind.

"I doubt the soul will care," she said, turning her gaze upward. Soft blue silk draped the ceiling above her. Her mother had pinned it there, to remind her of the cloudless sky outside when she feared the dark. It matched the color of her mother's eyes, or at least the way she remembered them. They were the single distinctive feature of her mother's that she'd inherited; everything else belonged to her father or to her mother's ancestors – her hair was such a trait. White-blond, it made her stand out among the rest of the household, who had dark hair and dark eyes.

The creak of hinges and clack of wood accompanied Aliya's rustling movements behind her. "The gray dress with the silver shoulder clasps? Given the right light, it would go well with your eyes."

"That will be fine, Aliya." It would be far from unrevealing its side slits, but a belt could put her worries to rest. The dress would near reach her toes, and holding the skirts from the ground would give her an excuse to hold them together. "Leave me, please. I would like to sleep." Her thoughts of her mother had her reeling off into her own world, and while sleep was not truly what she sought, solitude might just be it.

Dropping the lid of the trunk with a little *smack*, Aliya murmured, "My lady." She exited through the door in the back that would take her to her own chambers. Another trunk lid creaked, then a bed net.

Tomorrow marked the beginning of Elysia's rite of passage. The thought struck her strangely, as if the whole ordeal was unreal. That would change when she found herself on the road, she was sure. For now, the morrow seemed eons away, just as she saw her memories of her mother through the long distortions of time: blue-gray eyes; a slender woman with brush in hand, and then a drop spindle. White stone walls dripping honey and rose water. A handful of fluffy white wool pulled and twisted until only a long, thin strand remained. Elysia huffed and got to her feet, fully intent on burying herself in the pillows on her bed. The net beneath them squealed as she rolled across it, pulling blankets over herself.

Groping around on her bedside table, Elysia found her drop spindle. Her mother had taught her to use it before age three, but the memories of the lessons had escaped her. All that remained was the skill. The spindle was empty now, her last skein of wool spun to thread the day before. Her father had refused to give her more, and now she knew why: he preferred her packing to spinning. She turned the spindle in her hand. It was plain beige wood – pine, perhaps. The round weight at the bottom was carved of the same.

It was odd: her mother had been a skilled weaver and had taught her to spin. But her father would not teach her to weave, even after long years of begging. There was no use asking again. His shout of vehemence still rang in her ears. *I have no time, Elysia! You ought to know that by now.* He had thrown his hands up and left her in the hall at age fifteen, shoving aside the curtain of his weaving room as if it had been the one to offend him. She could not even follow him: the rules had been clear since she was small. *Do not interrupt Father when he is at his work, my dear*. It did not matter that she could not remember the voice that had spoken the words – she assumed it had been her mother. The voice of kindness, of reason and right.

And I can't even recall her face.

Scoffing at herself, Elysia let the spindle drop back onto her nightstand and blew out her candle. A long, sleepless night lay ahead of her.

3

Soft yellow-white clouds touched her face, followed by short-nailed, neat fingers. Eyes gazed down at her, the deep blue of a twilight sky, framed by jet lashes. Green-gold eyes, glowing bright, appeared beside them, and she fell into them.

Elysia's eyes snapped open.

Dreams had never been kind to her. She worked to slow her breathing, let her eyes drown in the ocean of billowing silk floating above.

When Elysia rose, she found her gray dress laid out on the couch, a belt of silver-studded charcoal leather set beside it. She pulled the gown over her head and slipped between the dress's shoulder clasps. The clasps held the garment together; a single piece of fabric unsewn, the dress split from shoulder to floor on her left side. The belt remedied any immodesty: overlapping the front and back of the dress closed the split down to her knee.

Cinching the belt into place, Elysia pushed aside her curtain. Dawn broke over the eastern hills, gilding the world. "Aliya, it's almost time," she called toward the adjoining room.

The young woman brushed aside the curtain that divided their rooms, poised with comb in hand. Her own hair shone with olive oil. "Have a seat, my lady," she said. Aliya combed smooth strokes through Elysia's white hair, fingers gentle when she began the braid at the nape of her neck. Her practiced hands took not even a minute to reach the end of Elysia's waist-length hair, tying it with a silvery ribbon. "Did you sleep well?"

"No," Elysia answered. "I was plagued by strange thoughts most of the night."

Aliya adjusted the shoulder clasps on Elysia's dress and arranged the gathered fabric about her waist. "Anyone else would have had the same. Where are you meeting this soul?" she asked, pausing her fiddling.

"I… I do not know. I suppose Father will fetch me," Elysia said, casting about for her sandals. They were where she'd left them after

Khronos had invited her to walk with him in the fields the day before last. It had seemed a sudden request at the time, but like so many other things now, it appeared deliberate. She strapped them on.

"Good, I see you are ready," rang his booming voice, and both she and Aliya jumped. Looking up, she found him standing in the doorway, the curtain balled in his hand and held out of the way.

Inhaling the air she'd lost when her heart leaped, Elysia stood. With a goodbye to Aliya and a nod of greeting to her father, she ducked under his arm. The cool morning air brushed her legs through the slit in her dress. "Is this soul similar to the judges?" she asked, following her father down the stairs.

"In a way. The Six and this one are good souls, but they are souls all the same," he replied. "They have the same desires as the others. Closure, a new life, to begin again. They begrudge me for compelling them to stay here and serve me instead of allowing their reincarnation, and they readily show it."

"They do not know you as I do, as a father."

"They know me better than you, in some ways," Khronos said, holding his hand out for hers. When he had it, he covered it, blanketing her fingers in warmth. "You know me to have leniency, but you are one of very few who know my leniency. Others see the unyielding High Judge, and some the removed landowner. You see all three and more, but the Six see the whole of the High Judge. They have known my wrath."

"Have I not seen the whole of the High Judge?" Elysia asked.

"Of course not, Lys. You are my daughter." He led her down the path, his tone dismissive.

The garden stood on the north side of the compound, where the plants could have sun and shade in turns. The sun rose over the pomegranate and fig trees that stood on the borders, between marble flagstones and rose beds. Despite the lateness of the season, the roses were in bloom; they were always in bloom. Part of living in the Lord Creator's household was the bounty that fell upon anything he touched, from flowers to crops.

Following the marble-set path toward the fountain tumbling at the heart of the garden, Elysia tensed. Her father still held her hand, but his fingers squeezed hers so tightly she felt the heat in her bones. His other hand hung relaxed at his side, but tension lingered in his jaw.

They had just passed the roses and stepped onto the flagging around the fountain when a scent met her nose.

Honey and rose water.

Elysia stopped, pulling her hand from her father's as he kept on. She wheeled, searching for the woman who should accompany that scent, those blue eyes of which she so often dreamed. But there was no one in the garden. None but her father, and he did not wear such a scent. He knew to whom it belonged. When they took breakfast together, the combination of honey for the bread and the rose water in the wash basin made his teeth clench.

Elysia's heart sped in her chest. Memories of deft hands at a loom spun behind her eyes, but the phantom scent was gone as soon as a breeze brushed by.

"Elysia?"

Her heart spasmed as she turned.

The woman who had spoken stood beside Khronos, her long-fingered hand clasped between his. His grip looked far more delicate on the woman's hand than it had been on her own. His gaze focused on Elysia. The woman regarded her with those eyes, shining brilliant blue in the sunlight and made even more vivid by an olive complexion. They studied her, curious and bright and perhaps a bit less kind than Elysia remembered.

"Come closer, Lys," Khronos said, beckoning. "This is the soul with whom you'll be speaking." His voice was soft, as though he were coaxing a feral puppy. Perhaps he knew the effect those eyes had on Elysia when he looked into them, himself.

"Who is she?" Elysia asked, taking another step. Only one flagstone remained between herself and the pair of them. The woman made no move to dip a curtsey or even her head.

"*She* is a soul who knows what it is to be an outsider in Corinth, my dear," the woman answered.

My dear. The voice – the one she had forgotten – rang familiar in her ears and Elysia took a deep breath. "Is there a name I should call you?" she asked.

The woman cocked her head, brows coming together. A smile pushed at the corners of her wide mouth. "Branimira is my name, but Mira will do." Petite as she was, Mira glanced up at Khronos before looking back to Elysia. "Shall I call you something formal, or may I use your name?"

Khronos looked down at her sharply, and Mira, to Elysia's surprise, reprimanded him for the look he gave her. "What? Do you expect me to go about 'my ladying' her all day if she hates it? If you think –"

"It's fine, Mira," Elysia murmured, her eyes on the color brightening beneath her father's skin. Ares had told her the tales: her mother could rile her father like no one else. One particular incident of parenting stood out. Apparently, her mother had wanted Elysia to learn the equestrian arts, and her father had been set against it. Horses might be gentle creatures, but they were also dangerous and unpredictable in moments of panic. Her mother asserted that riding was a skill she would need in emergencies, should she ever need to escape a situation. According to Ares, they had argued for weeks.

In the end, Elysia had learned to ride almost as well as her father. "You may call me by my name," she told Mira.

The woman's gaze flicked in Elysia's direction before turning back to Khronos. "Excellent. My Lord Creator, you may leave us," Mira commanded, and Elysia stiffened. Khronos, however, sighed and pulled Mira close to him, weaving his fingers and pressing his lips into the dark hair that curled only to the base of her neck. With one last long look, Khronos separated himself from the woman with a reluctance Elysia had not seen in him before; it did not even quite match the expression he wore upon entering the judgment chamber in the morning. He left with barely a nod of farewell to Elysia.

"You…" Elysia began but couldn't quite put into words her bewilderment. "He has never..."

That soft smile appeared on Mira's lips again. "I have a hold over him not many can boast," she replied. "Come, sit beside me." A soft rasp followed the edges of her words that Elysia did not recall with her memories of her mother.

Elysia took a seat on the rim of the fountain, the gray skirt of her dress rustling over the marble. Mira settled beside her. The woman looked at her with expectation once she had brushed out her skirts, but Elysia found she could barely choke out enough sound to make a coherent thought. "You are," she started, but her brows furrowed. "You were dead."

"Am dead," Branimira corrected. "Like your father's councilors, I'm a soul in corporeal form."

Something in Elysia fell away at her mother's words. "Why have you not seen me?" she asked.

Eyes that mirrored Elysia's softened. "You recognize me," Mira murmured, reaching out a hand toward Elysia's face.

She caught Branimira's wrist, hardly believing that warmth ran beneath her mother's skin. The last time Elysia had touched her, she had been cold. "How could I not?" asked Elysia, trying to ignore that her fingers were shaped like her mother's. "My eyes are all I had left of you, aside from my spindle. Father does not even speak your name." Her grip on her mother's wrist tightened. "I learned it today."

"There are many reasons for my not visiting and your ignorance of my name. The reasons for my absence are my own, but Khronos will tell you his reasons in his own time. They are his alone to explain and to understand." Mira's mouth quirked up. "I am still half certain that I don't quite understand him."

"But what are your reasons?" asked Elysia. She gestured to her mother's form. "If you can appear like this, why have you not?"

Letting out a slow breath, Branimira lowered her hand back into her lap as Elysia released her. Her eyes did not stray from her daughter's. "Death... it is not so final here," she said. "It should be. I wanted it to be. I wanted to know you, but you needed to know how the world works." Her expression pinched, pain filling the lines that had only just begun to deepen in her face. "I could not just die and appear a few moments later. You needed to understand that death is meant to be final."

"Not for every soul," she said, thinking of those who had reincarnated, of the Six. The Six had been given a second chance at life, but none had managed to earn the right to keep it. Pain remained in her mother's expression, so Elysia sighed and moved on.

"What do you mean to tell me?" she asked, studying her mother's face to commit it to memory. Branimira's eyes were the same deep cobalt as her gown, the color richer than the sky above. The wide planes of her cheekbones and forehead shone in the gray dawn light.

"What do you wish to know?"

"Everything."

Mira took all morning to explain the city beyond the valley. Dawn finished breaking and the sun rose, warming the world. As its rays fell over the garden, Elysia slipped her sandals off and dipped her feet in the fountain's bowl. A sculpture of a woman with water flowing from a pail in her hand stood in the center of the fountain. Her mother told her to expect little respect from the men of the city: they would not be accustomed to a woman with a mind of her own. They also wouldn't be ready to accept her place at the dinner table among them, or in the temple to pray beside them. It was simply the way of the Greek people, unlikely to change for another thousand years or more.

They spoke of the tests – and what they would ask of Elysia. "I have watched you since you were small. I asked your father to test you as the Six were tested," she said. "It was not enough for you to just sit in your throne – you must earn it." Her words echoed the ones Khronos had spoken so long ago, the same hard command.

"Why these tests? Why the secret one, why self-defense?" she asked as the sun beat down, turning the white marble of the garden paths into glowing walkways. Noon was almost upon them.

"The secret?" Mira cocked her head.

"Father has not told me the third. You must know that," Elysia protested, frowning.

Mira shifted in her seat, looking skyward. "The third test is secret because you should manage it naturally by completing the second test. It would be unusual to find a human who has not experienced what the third requires, and they never expect to experience it, either."

Elysia was silent. Even her mind was silent, blank as the marble paving. Finally, she spoke. "It must be something terrible or wonderful, then."

Her mother smiled. "It is both."

They talked another hour before the midday meal arrived in the hands of Hera. Elysia took a chunk of bread from the tray and dipped it in the bowl of honey before taking a bite of it. As souls, neither Hera nor Mira ate, but Hera scored the pomegranate and broke it open while Elysia chewed her bread. "Father ended the day early, I see," she observed.

"My Lord Creator lamented that the chamber was a melancholy place without your enlightening presence, my lady," she said, eyes scanning Mira curiously.

"Shut up, Hera."

Elysia stared at her mother, and Hera nearly dropped her knife. "My Lady Branimira, you – you cut your hair. I did not recognize you. It's been so long."

"Not long enough, if I say so," Mira said. "Last I checked, you didn't like me because my faith was flagging or some nonsense. But I suppose it doesn't matter now." Something flippant slipped into Mira's voice, high and uncareful.

Hera blinked. "My lady?"

"You took over my duties once I died? That would explain why you stole a plate from a servant to serve Elysia lunch. Are you her nurse?"

"I am noth-"

"It's fine, Hera," Elysia interjected, frowning at her mother's words. She turned to Mira, taking one half of the pomegranate in hand. She had half a mind to eat it, and the other half to let it drop flatly back onto the plate. "Mother, Hera has been my tutor. You could have continued your duties yourself, were you faithful in my comprehension of the darker aspects of the world."

"You were barely three," Mira replied, crossing her arms. "You would have remembered my death as some nightmare, if you remembered it at all."

"Why let death take you?" Elysia asked, putting the pomegranate back down. Hera took it up and scraped the seeds free, but Elysia gazed at her mother. "Father could surely have saved you."

"Your father commanded me to share my experience with you – nothing more. Do not be angry with him, my dear. He had his reasons, and they were mostly in submission to mine. I did not wish to be saved."

"I am not angry." She was dead calm, but beneath that was a seething confusion. Her gut had turned to a mass of slithering eels, quivering nervously.

"He does not wish for you to grow attached to any of us here, my lady," Hera said softly. Elysia looked at her bowl of pomegranate seeds, each a deep red and glistening in the sun. Some were torn from Hera's nails; the juice leaking from them was sweet, tangy. "It may be long years before you return home again, and if you are sorely missing us, it will be difficult for you."

"Of course," Elysia said, her insides slithering worse. The seeds looked wholly unappetizing now, their scent be damned. Mira was silent for once. "Did you truly love us?" She bit off the word *mother* at the last second. The word made her stomach twist – before today, it had been long years since she had last spoken it, and applying it to anyone, true mother or not, felt wrong. Her mother was dead.

Her mother had been dead sixteen years.

"I loved you more than anything, sweet one," said Branimira, "but even love is not always enough to drive away despair, and I thought I would drown in it."

"You did," she murmured, tearing her gaze from Branimira's. Elysia set the stone bowl back on Hera's plate and rose from her seat on the fountain's edge. Looking up at the maid with the pail, Elysia took a heartsick breath. Dipping her feet in the cool, clean water, Elysia stood and walked to the sculpture.

Hera protested, threatened to come in after her, proclaimed that this was far from proper and far from a private audience, but her words fell on deaf ears. Elysia circled to the maid's other side, where the pail was held in delicate hands. The water only rose to her knees, but her gray dress was soaked almost to the middle of her thighs, the chill water making the tiny hairs on her legs stand on end. The wet fabric clung, hindering her steps, so Elysia wrenched it up out of the water, holding it above her knees with one hand and bracing herself against the maid's marble dress with the other. The water splashed from the pail at eye level, and Elysia ducked her head in the stream.

All was quiet but for the splashing of water down her neck and into the pool. It blocked out her thoughts and rinsed her body until she stood shivering because she did not know if she could stand to turn back around and face the women waiting for her. Between the water rushing over her face and the concentration it took to breathe without inhaling that same water, she was numb. But even the numbness could not fill the growing hole that threatened to devour her.

She was going to leave behind everyone she loved for the sake of a test, a ridiculous test. *To judge the humans, you must know what it is to live a human life.*

A human life, she thought. *How can I live a human life if I cannot define it?* She had no idea of what to expect; her talk with Mira had done her no favors except to inform her that her life would be incredibly, unknowably different. She knew that she would be treated as her father's property, at least when she was there. She knew to expect little and less of men, and meekness from women. But nothing else. *What are the markets like? What is my* house *going to be like?* The urge to shriek crept into her lungs, but she fought it down like a cough.

And her mother. She had so many questions about the woman, not least of which was whether she had been so despondent in life, or if captivity in the netherworld had done that to her. She was supposed to have been reincarnated, but her presence told Elysia that that wish had not come to fruition.

A thousand leagues away, a deep voice asked if she was trying to drown herself standing up. Hera answered, her voice too quiet to distinguish words. Elysia would have stayed beneath the torrent of water forever, the sun beating down above her, if it meant that the week would go by and she could wash her hands of the entire business. She would have stayed under the fountain for an age if only it could wash away what was required of her. Instead, she was brought back to reality by the weight of fingers on her upper arm.

The hands that pulled her from the streaming water were rough and calloused from days spent handling crops and wrangling horseflesh. Elysia knew them almost as well as she knew her own, so many times had she held them and studied them, been led by them. When he pulled her into a forceful embrace in the middle of the fountain, his arms were covered in tiny round water droplets. They were all she could look at, pressed against his body with her head against his chest, his chin resting on top of her head.

"Behave, Lys, or your father will dock my pay for being unable to handle you." He smelled like horse, like earth and sweat and hay. His tunic was stained over his tanned square shoulders.

"Father does not pay you," she said, still pressed up against him, wrapped in his arms. The cold clinging fabric of her dress began to warm under his skin.

"Then perhaps he will finally put me to the sword," Philip said, steering her away from the maid. Reluctantly, he let her stagger out of his embrace and held her at arm's length. His brown eyes met her blue ones, and she looked away. The whole front of his tunic was water-stained, and her dress was stained with dirt and sweat where his clothing had rubbed against hers. The gray of her dress had gone charcoal under the water.

"Never. He would sooner let you go." *And he could never afford that.* Elysia felt his eyes on her, those honest eyes, lined around the edges from days in the sun. Suddenly she was aware that her dress clung to her body, the slit that she had tried so hard to close having slid open to her hip. She crossed her arms over her chest.

Philip opened his arms again and put one around her shoulder. "You should dry off. The day is not yet hot enough to accommodate such a thorough showering." There was the smile in his voice, the one that made her want to smile too, but the feeling never made it to her face – not with the weight of her mother's admissions like a stone in her chest. He guided her from the pool, sloshing with every step. She held her skirt stiffly in one hand.

Khronos arrived as Philip helped Elysia struggle over the rim of the fountain. "This wants explaining," he growled, looking from Hera to Philip, to the short-haired woman who was his wife, and finally to Elysia.

She looked up at him. That dead calm she had felt earlier had been traded for a quiet panic. "Pure as spring water, Father," she said, taking the hand that Philip offered her to step down from the rim of the fountain. “Clear and refreshing.” It was all she could do to catch her breath. Her dress *drip-dripped* on the flagging. Leaning in under Philip’s protective arm, she walked away, passing the first rose bushes before she turned back to her father. “We leave tomorrow.” She gave Branimira a tight nod and left all but Philip to stand gawking in the garden.

Better to leave now and be done with it sooner than to wait and whine like a spoilt child, she thought as she led Philip back to the house. She would not wait until an illness tried to take her and her father intervened – or did not intervene, as had been the case with her mother. She would not wait until she was so unhappy she would rather live in the netherworld than exist in this one. She would pass this test.

At any cost.

4

Elysia devoted the evening to saying goodbye to the only home she had ever known. Hera had followed Elysia and Philip back to the house, plate in one hand and the sandals she had retrieved from the fountain in the other. Aliya took both from the judge, shooed Philip away, and helped Elysia dry off and change. The handmaiden rebraided Elysia's hair; the torrent of water raining down upon it had pulled the morning's braid apart, wet white strands straggling down her neck. A tunic and slippers were laid out after Elysia declared that she would be riding through the fields and would not be persuaded otherwise.

Once dressed, Elysia strode down the three flights of stairs she had ascended not half an hour before. There was enough daylight left for a few hours' ride through the fields and hills. If she was leaving them behind in the morning, she would give her lands a long farewell. There was no proper way to do it, but if she was going to leave forever – if she died before she passed her test – there was no chance that she would leave the stables, her horses, her people… Not without farewells.

She found Philip with a pair of horses already in hand, saddled and bridled. Sometimes she feared he knew her moods too well, but it was good to have him at her side. He knew her every want before she could confide it, knew every desire she never spoke. Eight years older than Elysia, Philip had been her protector when her father was not around, had raised her as much as Hera had. And when she'd gotten older… Four years ago, he'd been the one she'd tried to kiss, not Apollo or Ares. The Six were her father's, but Philip was hers, he was *hers*, despite how he'd pushed her gently away. *Khronos will take my head if I let you do that again*, his whisper haunted her. *I will die long before your life has fledged.*

That was what she hated most. Whether she passed the test or not, those she loved would pass on long before she. Whether she claimed the eternity or left it to rot in the streets of Corinth, Philip was only human, and he would die with the rest. Aliya would vanish with time, as well. She could see them in the netherworld, but they would not be as they were, robust and bright. If she failed her tests, everyone would be lost to her, and she would be condemned to the gray nothingness of the netherworld.

Philip spared the bay beneath him as much of his weight as possible as he swung up, landing lightly in the leather of his saddle. Elysia watched him for a long time as he sat there, waiting for her in silence, his horse growing restless and shifting its weight a little beneath him.

At last, she swung herself into her own saddle, graceful from long years of practice. Mira had made it clear to her that she probably wouldn't so much as touch a horse in the city, so Elysia meant to take her time with her mare. Her father had made her promise to never name their animals; they were even shorter-lived than humans. Even so, she was one of the few things that Elysia had a claim on in the valley. The sorrel was hers, just as Philip was. She had been born for Elysia, trained by Philip, and bonded with her rider since they had both been the wild age of three.

The sorrel waited as Elysia rested her lips against the mare's soft neck, combing her fingers through the mane on the other side. Whispering nothings to the horse, she straightened in the saddle and took hold of the reins. Without a word to Philip, she clucked to the mare and nudged her with the heels of her riding sandals, setting off at a bouncing trot that set her braid to swinging. Outside, they passed Apollo at the entrance to the warehouse, his golden head nearly glowing in the sunlight. He gave them a cursory nod and returned to the counts of fruit he took in Philip's absence.

Philip's brown eyes studied her, knowing her inner workings like they always seemed to. "Follow me," he said, and he was gone before she could reply. Yards away already, the legs of the bay pumped under the pressure of Philip's heels.

With the sound of Elysia's kiss, the sorrel mare was off after him. They raced on the outskirts of the vineyards, and then the olive trees with their green fruit and green leaves whipped by. She knew where they were headed then: the place where she'd kissed him that time, up in the rocks among the scant trees that grew around the edge of their valley. Neither of them had been back since; something unanswered hung in the air around the place.

It was a while before they reached the rocks set high in the hills. Their horses slowed to a dogged walk as the terrain roughened, and finally they left the pair of them behind, hobbled to graze among the sparse grass. The hike was made easier for Elysia by her tunic; had she been wearing her usual dress, he would have had to help her over every boulder and ledge, her skirts hiked up over her knees. They found the tumble of rocks just as they'd left it, granite strewn over grass that grew emerald in its shade. The birds sang in the trees ahead of them, shrilling and whistling like the wind.

Philip sat her down on the highest rock in the tumble, a great boulder that thrust ten feet into the air with a wide, round top. He sat beside her, facing toward the trees and the setting sun. The universe seemed to open below Elysia: all she'd ever known lay before her in the valley between these high hills and the unexplored eastern ones. Leaning back on her elbows, she let the view envelop her, but Philip brought her back. "Growing up tears people away from their homes to conquer foreign things, just as you are being torn," he said, turning her gaze to his with a hand beneath her chin. "Young women are out there being married to men much older than them because that is the way the world works, whether they want it to or not. And yet, rather than go out there and explore as a free woman, if you were given the choice, you would rather stay here. You would subject yourself to the same fate when you have never known that life."

Elysia refused to meet his eyes.

"You have always been freer than any girl under her father's rule has a right to be, Lys. You are wild, and that will injure you someday. Your pride, maybe, but maybe your body, as well. The world is not made for women such as you just now."

"And what do you know of it?" She lifted her gaze to him. "You have lived here longer than I. You know the length of my leash, but how would you know that of women away from here? Hera has one as long as mine, and the rest of the Six and the field hands are given the same."

"*I* go with your father to the Corinthian agora whenever he ventures down from these godforsaken hills," he replied. "I see the women there. They're meek creatures unlike you. You have to tame that fire, or they'll put it out for you, and you and I both know that you would never deign to survive that." Elysia rubbed her fingers against the rough rock, trying to think of anything but what he said.

"Do you remember the last time we were up here?" she asked. Her gaze was sharp on him; she saw his shoulders tense, the set of his jaw harden as he gritted his teeth.

"Yes," was all he said. He wouldn't look at her, his mouth set in a firm line.

Elysia herself was at a loss for words to say next. She'd led herself over a cliff and into an abyss of the things they never talked about, territory they'd left uncharted. "How do I say goodbye to someone as close as you?" she murmured, sitting up.

"You don't," he said, voice rough with something she didn't quite recognize. His eyes met hers, bright around the bottom rim where shimmering saltwater had gathered. "You don't say it."

And then his lips were on hers. His mouth was soft, and she could tell he'd been stealing figs again. It was like the kiss of four years ago, but different, not some curious little thing. His mouth opened under hers and he wrapped his arms around her waist, pulling her closer. Her hands rose up to the back of his neck, fingers threading through pepper-and-salt hair. He was going gray too early, she decided. He was too young to be aging… And too old for her; she knew it, and he'd told her so. But she didn't care.

He was hers.

Every nerve ending tingled, and she pulled him closer, his warmth washing over her. His fingers pressed into the small of her back, their heat igniting her skin. She knew it had to end – they were going to get caught up in this net, the way Ares and Aphrodite stole fervent touches behind the stables, thinking that no one would see. Elysia pulled herself an inch away and put her hand over his lips, her breath fast and shallow. "You told me no last time. Weren't you afraid only today that your head might roll?" she asked.

He laughed, breathless as she. "I'm not worrying about that now," he said, eyes still trained on her lips. "That one kiss from so many years ago couldn't be the goodbye kiss I want to remember tomorrow, when you're gone off to that city that you dread. And I dread it for you. You need this as much as I do."

"Maybe." Elysia narrowed her eyes at him. "You only make it harder to leave you here," she replied, lowering her hand. He leaned into her again, so she kissed him, slowly, sweetly, until the sky grew darker. "I should have married you," she told him, and he laughed. She rested her head on his chest. He still wore his stained white tunic; the watermark she'd left on it from her dunk under the fountain had lightened the rest of the stains on the front. His tunic was longer than those of other men; he'd started requesting them from Athena after Elysia had skinned her knees as a toddler. Ever after, when she'd had a cut or a scrape, he'd torn a strip off the hem and wrapped her wounds until they could be properly cleaned.

"We should go," Elysia whispered, "or we'll have to lead the horses down the hills." Her gut had untwisted, her mind a pleasant haze.

Philip hummed a little but made no move to rise. "I want to see the stars in those blue eyes of yours."

She sat up, groaning. "Father really might kill you if he sees us return like this." She scooted over to the edge of their boulder, toeing the next one down. Both of them were a wreck, but she more so: her hair had been pulled from its braid, the ribbon dangling precariously at the very end. Her tunic was as wrinkled as his, stained from the saddle and the rock that lay beneath her. He caught her wrist.

"No goodbyes tomorrow, Lys," he warned, still lying on the boulder. "You don't say it."

"No goodbyes," she agreed, stepping down onto the next rock. He still had her wrist, and he got to his feet and followed close behind her, hand wrapped around hers. They found their horses as dusk fell, and Elysia gazed down at her lands. "Go home, Philip," she heard herself say. She pulled herself into her saddle, keeping the sorrel's reins in hand to prevent her from following the bay.

When she found Philip's eyes once more, he gave her a sharp look.

"I need to do something before I leave." Waving him off, Elysia set out along the bottom of the valley wall. Her sorrel picked her way down a faint path, one that only the pair of them had traveled since she'd been allowed to ride alone. Philip knew better than to follow her down this road.

The trail led past vineyards and groves of trees, around rocky outcroppings and over a tinkling brook whose waters irrigated the whole of the valley. After crossing the stream, they followed it to the cascade that brought it down into the valley. At its base, a pool rippled, waters glimmering under the moon. Elysia dismounted and let her mare drink, trusting her not to wander too far.

Touching the rock wall beside the waterfall, Elysia traced the poppy and butterfly that had been carved there by Ares. He had placed it here, where her mother would come to dangle her feet in the pool and scale the rocks. It had been her mother's most beloved place in the valley, Ares had told Elysia, for it had reminded her of her northern home.

"I met you today," Elysia murmured, brushing her fingers across the butterfly's wings. "You weren't what I wished for, but it was a good lesson. I know who you are now. Human, made with faults and virtues, just like every other creature. Even Father has them, acknowledged or not." She sat down beside the engraving, looking out across her lands. Blanketed in darkness, just a few things shone in the moonlight: the brook rippled like liquid silver, and apples, grapes, and pomegranates gave off a dull gleam. An owl hooted in the trees above her. Elysia filled her lungs with cool air, trying to imprint the scent of the valley at night on her memory. This place, filled with the memories she had of her mother before today, stilled her. This place let her breathe and asked nothing in return.

Elysia dozed beside the carving until the gray hours, then rose and collected her sorrel. The mare had slept standing up or else kept watch for the night. With one last long look at the carving and the pool beside it, Elysia mounted up and said a silent goodbye to the mother she had lost sixteen years ago.

She might never have existed at all.

5

The morning dawned golden once more, peach-and-cream clouds breaking across the valley as the sun rose below them. Elysia was already ahorse, having stolen through the house before sunrise to change into a new tunic and rebraid her hair. Her father reined his great black stallion around the wagons, examining their wheels. Carts of oxen pulled fruit and woven wares, as well as Elysia's belongings and the wagon guards. Charioteers drove the gilded cart that she and her father would take once they were a few leagues from the city. Elysia had thought it would be a quieter affair, just her and the usual fruit that her father hauled to the market at the end of the week, but no. They took near every one of their people with them, all sitting on the edges of the wagons.

When Philip walked to her, horseless, Elysia thought it was because her father had left him in charge of the household for the day. A stone dropped into her stomach when she saw him, but her father hailed him, boisterous as ever in the morning. "Ah, Phil, just in time. I was beginning to think you were going to make me send Aliya after you. Elysia, get down off that mare. Philip will be riding in front of you until we take up the chariot."

Elysia looked from Philip to her father. Her sorrel shifted beneath her to meet Philip's hand as he petted her long nose and neck. "You cannot be serious," she said, reins still firmly in hand. "He's not coming with us?" She glanced down at Philip, wondering if this was why he had forbidden her from speaking a goodbye to him: they were not being torn from one another, after all. *You don't say it*, his voice rang in her ears. She could still see his eyes shining bright, the sun lighting his graying head from behind. *No goodbyes tomorrow, Lys*.

She could throttle him for that, she thought, looking down at him. Her father would not hold it against her, she knew, once he learned what this man of hers had done. She had been ready to say goodbye, and now he might just be her undoing. Angry, hot tears filled her eyes and she tried to blink them back, remaining silent.

"Of course he's coming with us," Khronos said, reining up beside her as he rounded the closest cart, which was covered with white cloth to protect the fruit within from the harsh sun. It would beat down on them, unforgiving, in the dry mountain lands as they followed the long road to Corinth. "He is my Master of Horse, and we have every horse with us. We would be mad to leave him. Did you think I would make you leave him here this morning?"

Her father searched her gaze, but her eyes were on the boy – the *man*, she reminded herself – who stood at the head of her horse, stroking dirty, calloused hands down her sorrel's white blaze.

She had been a squalling infant when she'd met the stable boy of eight, not even old enough to remember his young face. Her first memory of him was that of a twelve-year-old guiding her down the front steps of the house and into the stables, where she met his horse. The gelding had been the bay who was still his companion, a gentle creature who hadn't minded when she'd tried to pull his forelock to bring his head closer to her. She'd been four, and Phil had already been her protector from all sorts of things. The monsters in the shadows, the monsters in the stories, her father when he made her cry.

Now, she could ride over him in a burning fury. The sorrel shifted uneasily beneath her, but Elysia's blood boiled. "We said our goodbyes last night for fear of such a fate."

She refused to look at her father after she spoke. There was something to be said for evading the Creator's wrath by ignoring him and playing innocent, at least in Elysia's experience, but he would seethe over sometime. Her lips were sore this morning, something her father had noticed when she'd kissed his cheek and groaned at the scrape of his stubble. Rather than sliding down from the saddle as her father had told her, she slid back over the cantle, reins held out in front of her. That stone seemed to reform in the pit of her stomach, her intestines squeezing uncomfortably beneath the weight of it.

Philip took the reins from her hands and vaulted into the saddle. Rather than put her arms around his waist, Elysia rested them on the back of the saddle between them. With the pair of them situated, Elysia looked to her father, who stared back at her for a long moment. His eyes were sharp on her hands, held carefully away from Philip's back where her fingers gripped the saddle. He clucked to his stallion, and the beast bore him to the head of the train, with Philip following behind.

"Deceiver," she muttered. If she had been any less conscious of who surrounded them, she might have spit.

Philip ignored her. "You'll fall off," he whispered as she jounced along, just in front of the sorrel's hips. Normally the mare had a comfortable, easy walk, but trying to keep up with the dark stallion's quick stride had turned her steps to jolting.

"I'd rather not touch you just now." It took all her concentration to avoid just that, to not sag in her strange position on her mare without her saddle, to not brush against his back or touch his dangling legs with her own. Her elbows felt all wrong, stuck out at her sides from her grasp on the cantle. She could feel his warmth radiating between them from under his white tunic, which appeared clean for once. In the cool air of the morning, it was like the heat of the sun on her skin, though the star was still low over the hills to their left. *I should have ridden over him when I had the chance*, she thought darkly. But he'd stood there staring innocently up at her, knowing full well the wrath she would rain down on him when they were in more private quarters, if they ever were again. "You took advantage."

"I may have. But if I had not, you would have forgotten me in the city. I could not bear that." He turned his head when he spoke to her, square jaw outlined in the dim light as they passed beneath the shadow of a grove of fruit trees. "It could have been done differently, but I didn't think on it very well at the time."

"Don't think on it again," she said, pulling down her tunic with one hand so it covered more of her leg. Riding astride like this bared her almost to mid-thigh. Her palms and fingers had cramped from their awkward position, so she stretched them out one at a time before resting them around his waist. "You infuriate me."

He repaid her with a smirk and laid his fingers across her clasped hands. She pulled one free and hit him hard across the back of his head, sending his short hair into disarray. With a grunt, he clapped the hand that had held hers to the spot she'd struck. "What was that for?" The ears of her father's stallion swiveled toward them.

"Those knowing eyes you gave me." She circled her arms back around his waist and could just barely tell that he had rolled his eyes at her. "Father!" she called, leaving Philip to hastily cover his ringing right ear.

He groaned something that sounded like "*Lys*" before jerking his hand back to the reins.

Khronos slowed his stallion's gait as the ill-tempered horse nearly shied at her shout. "Elysia, you'll get the three of us thrown," he said, brows drawing together over his golden-lashed eyes. "What is it?"

"Who did you leave at the head of the household in our absence?"

"Hera, of course."

Of course. Hera, the Judge of Faith herself, counselor and matriarch as one. She'd headed her own household once: she'd been the wife of some rich man, at least when riches had meant enough food to feed their children for five winters, rather than the gold, jewels, and olive oil that the Greeks prized now. She kept faith with her husband, kept faith with her children, and kept faith in life, but had never uttered a prayer to a presence above. *That's why it's hard for we Six*, she'd confided once. *We don't fit like we ought to. We are not faultless. But we believe* now, *despite the lives we led.*

The souls could not leave the compound, not even the judges; if they tried, they would find themselves trapped in the netherworld once more, wandering alone. Many had been warned, Hera had told her. Yet many had fled, hoping to see loved ones on the other side, but they found only the isolation and silence that was meant for considering the past life. It had been centuries before Khronos had his Six, millennia: most of the souls he chose had been lost back to the netherworld. Eris had been the first to stay, and Hera the last.

"Is that all you wished to ask of me?" Her father's gruff voice woke her from her thoughts as he struggled to keep his horse in hand. The beast was headstrong, and her father's forceful hand was not kind on its mouth, but the stallion finally relented when Khronos backed him between a pair of olive trees until his prancing stopped.

"That, and how long the road is," she replied as her father rode ahead of them once more, his horse's steps slowed.

"It may feel like minutes, hours, or centuries. The journey is different every time for everyone, just as reincarnation is different for every soul." Elysia glanced at the field hands and cart drivers, but they did not give any indication that they listened to the conversation. "This place has not yet settled on the same plane as the humans' Earth. Most of it exists only in legend, a tapestry on the wall, as it were. I alone – and you eventually – may travel the path without divine escort as we are, well… Divine." Her father's lip quirked up even as he reined in the stallion once more.

The white cloth of the chamber tapestry flashed behind her eyes, each throne worked in black or blue, gold or silver, white or red thread. "Our valley is a tapestry somewhere?"

"Woven by mine own hand."

They fell back a few yards again. Philip complained to her of his aching ear and bruised head, and she rested her forehead against his shoulder. The sorrel's brisk walk was easier to bear with something substantial to hold onto, her hands wrapped around Philip's waist. She was angry with him, but not the way she had been. Like a torch, her fury had been snuffed by a passing gust of wind; a rage as red as that was too difficult to sustain. This time, when he put his hand over hers, she didn't even protest to tell him to rein with both hands. It would have been futile, anyway: he had taught her to ride, he was Master of Horse, and he knew what he was doing on her gentle little sorrel far better than he had any right to.

All of him was warm against her face, her chest, her arms. The sun rose high enough to begin heating the rest of the world, rather than just the mountain peaks and bare hilltops surrounding them. Elysia breathed in the smell of him – horses, hay, earth, and the sweetness of figs on his breath. She memorized his scent while she still had time.

Just as Khronos had said, moments seemed to stretch on. With her head against Philip's shoulder, Elysia lost track of the seconds and minutes as she mentally counted them off. It must have been an hour before the sorrel stopped again, the sun beating down on Elysia's bare arms and legs. As she lifted her head, she felt the imprint of Philip's tunic on her forehead. Rubbing her face to soften the lines, she asked, "Have we arrived?" but when she looked around, she saw only rock and soil covered with a sparse layer of summer-dried grass. No great city, no statues, no homes. Just the road ahead of them, hoofprints and wagon ruts.

Philip shook his head in front of her. He had both hands on the long reins, their ends knotted together. Sore from the mare's unrelenting jouncing, Elysia searched for her father – and found no trace of him but the hoofprints his horse had left in the dust. "Where's Father?"

"Gone to get the chariot and give his horse to the driver, I imagine," Philip replied, sliding from the saddle. He held his arms up to catch her, reins still in his left hand.

"Can I not wait until he comes back?" Her knees ached from their awkward hanging behind Philip's, and she wasn't sure if she could stand if she dismounted. She didn't want to stumble into his arms, especially after his behavior in the last several hours.

"Now would be better than later, Lys." He looked down the line, eyes skimming over oxen and field hands to find her father, somewhere near the back of the train with the chariot. "Though the poor boy who has to ride that stallion may stall him."

Sighing, Elysia swung her leg behind her, slipping down from her horse. She landed hard and sucked in a breath as her knees jarred. Philip's hand came down on her waist, ready to hold her up if need be. She shook free of him. Moving to stand on the other side of her sweat-soaked mare, she rubbed the swirl of soft hair and skin beneath the sorrel's forelock, just as she liked. The mare bobbed her head happily against Elysia's palm.

Far back along the line, hoofbeats thundered on soil and *clack*ed across stones. A moment later, the chariot horses and the sorrel greeted each other with soft whickers. Rounding the three horses, Elysia looked back to Philip; unbidden, her mind flickered back to the setting sun as they searched for their horses among the boulders. The chariot creaked when she stepped in next to her father, balancing carefully. Feeling the gold-and-emerald discs of his eyes on her, Elysia cleared her throat and kept her eyes forward. Despite her attempts to right herself before Khronos urged the horses on, she still swayed precariously backward. "I'll see *you* in Corinth," she said to Philip, who smirked and waved at her.

The chariot was quicker, but no more comfortable. Already she missed the ragged gait of her sorrel, but it would not do for a lady to ride into town astride a saddle, let alone escorted by her horsemaster, or so she'd been told. With her father to her left standing in stony silence, Elysia braced herself against the jolts of rocks and potholes. She choked down the occasional rising curse. Even when she bit her cheek hard enough to taste coppery blood, she remained as silent as her sentinel father. Khronos looked down the road as though he were dying of thirst and a glittering fountain lay at the end of it.

Finally, Elysia saw the glare of sun on white marble ahead, a mass of short buildings in front of it. Khronos called them to a halt. From the tiny cabinet in the front of the chariot, he drew the gray dress she'd worn the day before, stains removed and scented with rosewater. "Put it on," he growled.

"Why?" she asked, but she took it from him and slipped it over her head. He handed her the belt next, and she secured it as tightly as she could, hoping the slit would not slip this time. If it did, however, the riding tunic beneath would save her the immodesty of showing so much skin.

Khronos shook his head. "A girl was slaughtered at the Games for disguising herself in the clothing of a man. Whether it was because she won and was revealed or simply because she wore a short dress, I will not risk my daughter being dealt the same." Lastly, he handed her a veil of blue silk. Familiar with this, as it was a fashion worn by all the women of the household when they headed toward town, Elysia pinned it into her hair with the jeweled combs fastened to the veil's edges. He clucked to the horses again, leaving Elysia to clutch at the edge of chariot.

They joined the press of farmers in line at Corinth's gates, still half a mile from the walls of the city itself. "Is it harvest season?" Elysia asked. In the valley, plants were picked one day and grew more fruit the next week. But here, the farmers seemed to have rigged up whatever they could to get their produce and wares into the city, some even pulling the carts themselves.

"It is. Our crops are not the only ones to bear fruit just now, but our fruit is of the highest quality. We do good business in Corinth."

As she looked around, Elysia's eyes felt drawn to everything at once. They approached the city and its statues of gilded marble, which stood over bleached-white shacks of mud brick and straw. Far to her left, looming over the city with buildings covering almost every square inch, stood a great, towering rock, thrusting hundreds of feet into the air. Her gaze caught on it and she could not tear her eyes away; on the highest of its rounded peaks stood a tiny, distant version of her house, complete with triangular roof and white pillars.

Khronos still spoke to her. "They call this the Merchants' Gauntlet," he said, gesturing at the shacks and alleys they approached. "This is the only gate on the south side, and thieves pilfer the carts and lose any pursuers among the hovels. The smart merchants put guards on their wagons, but some cannot afford to."

Elysia's eyes remained on the mountain. She had never seen such a huge boulder standing on its own, let alone one stable enough to hold so many homes and mansions. She pointed, interrupting him. "What is that?"

Khronos followed her gaze. "Acrocorinth, where the rich literally live above the poor. You will be seeing much of it, I fear, and not the luxurious parts."

"Oh?"

"The first part of your test will be passed there."

To safely conduct yourself among the humans, you must learn to defend yourself from harm. "Why not in the city?" she asked.

"The poorest people live on the lower skirts of Acrocorinth, and they were the only ones who would train your mother to protect herself when she wanted to learn." Elysia's eyes snapped to her father's. He laughed at her sudden attention. "Oh yes, she wanted to learn. Your teacher will be from the family who taught her. They call themselves Apocorinthians – and so do the rest of the Corinthians, though they do not use the term with pride, as the people do. The Apocorinthians treat their women with respect, even venerating them. They rely on their women as much as you and I rely on Philip and Aliya, so they treat them well."

"I see," she said.

"You will understand once you meet them," Khronos said, putting a warm hand on her arm. "But now we make for the Lechaion and the agora."

The white horses cut a path through the pedestrians and walked straight down the center of the marble-paved road. People moved out of the way slowly, casting confused glances at their fellows, who stumbled over themselves to get to the edge of the road and out of the way. Once they saw the gilded chariot, they moved quick enough – but not without heavy oaths. The oxcarts moved sluggishly, and in the end, Elysia and Khronos waited in the line behind twenty of them as they funneled into the city. Soon, though, they came upon the entrance: a checkpoint flanked by armed guards. Statues loomed twenty feet above those entering the city, one a man and the other a woman. The man was bearded, held a silver-tipped trident, and had been draped in a loosely fitting cloth of the same marble as he, which fell from his right shoulder, looped around his hips, and pooled at his feet. The woman was dressed in a gown, her hair loose to her hips, a tiara of shells on her brow. Creatures lay at her feet of which Elysia had only ever heard or seen sketches: miniature whales and dolphins, an octopus, a turtle. What could only be a seahorse was cradled in her delicate hands.

Both the man and the woman stood against dappled fans of marble that rippled outward. "Who are they?" Elysia asked, her voice small and quiet against the noise of the city.

Khronos looked up, his green-gold eyes translucent in the light of the sun. "Poseidon, god of the sea, and his consort, Amphitrite, enthroned in seafoam."

As he answered, Elysia noted the similarity between Poseidon's profile and her father's. Perhaps the souls remembered the giver of the sentence, after all. The long, straight nose, the full beard that hid a strong square chin – the eyes, though far above her, had nearly the same shape as her father's.

Amphitrite, on the other hand, looked more like Branimira and the fountain in the garden than any of the judges. While the statue looked like her mother in certain features, it was not her likeness. "She looks familiar."

Khronos shook his head, his mouth twisting downward into a grimace. "So say many. The faces of Greek statues are all somewhat similar."

The question, "Similar to whom?" flicked across her mind. There would be time to ask him later, when he would not be minding the road. The reins in his hands were slick with sweat, the leather shining in the sun as much as the flashing gold inlays in the chariot. People darted back and forth across the road ahead of them: thieves, taking advantage of the guards' turned backs as they checked the wagons and carts for hidden contraband and ill-meaning stowaways. Just what the contraband could be, Elysia didn't know, though she could imagine. Hera and the rest of the judges had raised her on tales of battles fought with brave steel and whizzing arrows… And the more ignoble battles fought with poisons and traitors who turned their cloaks.

As they passed the soldiers who stood in the shadow of the statues, Elysia and her father were stopped. One of the guards recognized her father, and her father him. His and the rest of the poor men's tunics, though covered in places with shiny leather armor, were already soaked through from the heat of the day.

"Adrastos!" her father boomed, a smile in his voice, and reached down to clap the man on a leather-clad shoulder. His hand *slapped* as it found leather, and Elysia saw the soldier wince. Beneath a bright halfhelm wrapped in white linen, the man's face was older, black-bearded but graying. He had a friendly mouth, and as Elysia watched, Adrastos smiled.

"Khronos! I didn't think to see you so soon. You were just here what, three days past? Must have some fine fruit up there in your valley." Adrastos's eyes found Elysia, and his smile turned rancid. That was a smile she recognized: it was a smile she'd seen just the day before last, on the wretched soul in the chamber. "And I see you've been hiding one such away."

Elysia drew away from him, into the side of the chariot, but from her other side came a hoot of agreement so loud and so close that her eardrums winced. Looking down to find the man she'd already marked as offensive, she instead found a boy as fair of face as Apollo, with silvery white hair and blue eyes, as tall as she even though the chariot put her half a foot off the ground. "A fine fruit indeed," he said, showing off fine white teeth, but his voice marked him to be much older than she'd thought at first. As she looked harder, Elysia realized that they could be of an age, but something betrayed him; whether it was the set of his jaw or some subtle line in his forehead, she was unsure, but he had to be at least a few years older than her. Three, possibly five. And something else about him unsettled her, sent a shot of high-pitched nerves ringing right through her stomach: he looked too much like her.

Beside her, a low rumble began in her father's throat like distant thunder. "You forget yourselves, men. I anticipated respect for my daughter and the business she has brought to the city. Especially from you, Zeus."

Half a moment later, Zeus's fair complexion turned paler, and he turned wide eyes on Elysia.

Adrastos laughed. "Your daughter? She looks more like some northern girl run down from the raiders, white hair and all. Zeus, your mother 'ave a sister birthing some little flaxen runts like yourself up there in the mountains?"

Elysia's heart thudded and her toes squirmed against the leather of her riding sandals. She could not speak for herself here. Instead, she dug her nails into the wood of the chariot.

"Mother's Corinthian," said Zeus, "and her sister is too old for Khronos." He leaned on the butt of his short spear, its head sunk into the ground. He studied Elysia like she was some queer creature – the same way she studied him.

"Eh. Khronos doesn't care who whelped you, anyway."

Turning her gaze from Zeus, Elysia found her father's face. It turned red with anger, the same way storm clouds turn black before they unleash their wrath on the world below. Reaching up, she clutched the back of his tunic, balling her fist in the fabric. The consequences of the wrath she'd never seen sang through her mind like so many little notes. Whole cities destroyed by earthquakes, volcanoes that erupted to shatter civilizations like slate dealt a blow by a hammer, seas that rose up to sweep villages into their waters.

"Let 'im through, then," Adrastos said, waving them off. "Nothing's different but the girl."

All six of the guards leered at her as they passed beneath the shadow of Amphitrite, but her father said not a thing more. Elysia let her hand fall, wrinkles etched into her skin from the bunching of the fabric beneath it, and took her first breath of Corinthian air.

It was not like mountain air at all.

There was nothing clean about it, nothing cool. It was hot cooking meat from the sides of the road, tiny animals spitted over tiny fires. It was waste and sickly-sweet rot and just a hint of something tangy, something salty. The rest was dust and heat. Grubby children looked up at her as they passed through the Merchants' Gauntlet, innocent-eyed and holding out hands in silent plea.

"Pay them no mind, Elysia. They do not starve here, poor though they may look."

"They live off the merchants?"

"They do. They know no other way until adulthood, when they are forced to choose their own lives."

Still, the children had bright, curious brown eyes. Only one or two had eyes of blue, but their hair was the same homogeneous brown as the rest. When she looked down the line, Elysia saw more resting in the cool shadow of Poseidon. Parents sat at the cookfires between their mud brick houses, turning the spits, and were else either unseen or gazing at the passing carts, staring daggers at the guards who sat among the fruit. Some of the women had bared the knives they'd been given to guard the wares, but they'd done it carefully: steel and stone were hidden amongst their skirts, only an edge or a point visible. The men had long-reaching spears with leaf-shaped, steel heads, the points glimmering in the sunlight. They'd borne them openly as they passed through the gates and the guards had not moved to stop them.

Farther down the line, Elysia found Philip on the black stallion, guarding the rear of the train from horseback with his own spear in hand. The stallion looked warily at the campfires and the children as he passed by them, as though the flickering flames and darting hands had spooked him before. A nervous boy rode Elysia's sorrel, his face pinched and wan as he rode beside Philip. Though the stallion was ill at ease, the sorrel was merely alert, ears flicking from sound to sound.

Elysia turned to the front of the cart. The journey quickened now that the carts ahead of them turned down side streets, each going its own way. “Isn’t the agora down the main road?”

Khronos nodded, glancing at her before turning back to the road with a smile. “It is, but some take shortcuts down to their stalls.”

The farther they got into the city, the cleaner it became. The plain mud brick houses were whitewashed, then became stone, then grew larger, and finally turned to marble, some boasting courtyards and gardens of their own. The road that had been dust and dirt outside of the gate became scuffed and cracked marble, then newly patched in places, and then immaculate as it joined with another road. “The Lechaion,” her father announced over the din of the city.

The Lechaion was the great white marble road that snaked through the city from the south, an unbroken paved path from a port on the Gulf of Corinth. From it branched two others, paved as well: one to the west and all Peloponnesus, and one to the east, diverging into two roads at the city’s edge. One kept on east, up through the isthmus and into mainland Greece, while the other went south, bending around Acrocorinth to fade into hundreds of dirt roads, each leading to some farm or temple in the mountains along the Saronic Gulf. It was one of those dirt roads that had brought them around the base of Acrocorinth and under the watch of Poseidon and his wife.

The main road was smooth marble, seams so well aligned they were near invisible. As Elysia looked down it, she could see a hundred yards of the road before it turned at some distant corner, and all of it swarmed with traffic. Pedestrians, wagons filled with bolts of cloth and crafts, sedan chairs and closed litters carried by slaves – each headed toward where the roads merged into a single street.

They turned the corner around a marble mansion whose walls spilled over with greenery and the sound of its own burbling fountain, and Elysia finally saw the heart of the city.

The road widened until it spanned at least twenty feet, and around them, marble rose. Small shops of weathered stone lined the road to the left and right. A few had their own banners – Elysia saw a white onion on emerald billowing on a pole above a vegetable farmer’s stand, a hammer on red over a smith’s, a length of unadulterated blue silk rippling from on high over a wealthy cloth merchant’s. Others had a ware or two thrust into the air on their poles: the leather worker had a saddle, the cordwainer a pair of sandals hanging from a hook.

Vibrant curtains of fabric hung from the marble walls that enclosed the agora, shielding the glare. Beneath each curtain sat a woman, spindle in hand and distaff under one arm, spinning bunches of wool into long, thin strains of yarn. "Do the women sell their fabrics?" she asked, studying each curtain. Some were dyed, either a single deep color or in patterns; others were the natural yellow-white of wool.

"Their fathers, sons, or husbands sell the fabrics they do not keep to clothe themselves. It is the way in Greece." His voice was sterner than she expected. When she looked up at Khronos, she found his gaze already upon her.

She held his stare. "Are you trying to make a point?"

"I am. It will not be easy, but you need to be submissive to survive in the agora, at least around men, just as those women are."

Elysia looked at the nearest ones as the horses picked their way through the crowd. She spotted a young woman with brown hair seated next to one of the stalls, silently working her yarn, but watching everything around her with hawklike eyes. When the man running the shop looked her way, she lowered her eyes and muttered something. The young woman stood and wrapped her yarn around her spindle when the man agreed.

Just as she watched the woman pick up a basket, the chariot jolted so suddenly that Elysia bit her lip. The wheels protested with shrieks and groans but held firm. Her father had driven the chariot off the road and over the curb that made the boundary, pulling up beside an empty shop.

"Are you *trying* to knock me out of the chariot?" She held a finger to her lip and found no blood, only soreness. She glared up at her father. "That has to be the third time today."

"Pay attention," he replied, voice gruff and gravelly. "We're here."

Here was an empty marble stall, bigger than some of the others around it, but by no means large. She could have crossed it in three strides. It had a dirt floor and a waist-high counter, but every surface and every wall was clean; some of the stones were old and some were new, but all gave a dim shine in the ambient light. *A stone cell in which to spend the day*, she thought ruefully. And it would be a long day – they would not leave for the house until the crowds dispersed in the hot afternoon.

With a deep breath, she turned and saw her father waiting on the ground beside the chariot to help her down. She took his hand.

When Elysia looked for the young woman who had traded spindle for basket, she had disappeared.

6

It took far less time than she expected to unpack the fruits and vegetables. The women helped, their hair and faces veiled against the morning sun and the eyes of others. The men handled the horses and the oxen, leading them along to the walled-in yard behind the stall. The chariot found its way between their stall and the neighbor's, its inlaid golden suns throwing yellow light onto the white walls surrounding it.

Philip emerged from the yard, hands black from rubbing down the horses. Elysia ignored him as she hauled another crate of pomegranates into the stall and set them against the back wall. It was to be a long, silent day for him; she'd decided to resolve their business when no one was listening, least of all her father's keen ears. A knot had tied itself in her gut since he'd ridden the stallion up outside the stall. She did not want him like she had when they were up on those boulders, watching the sun turn the valley gold and pink. She shouldn't – *couldn't* – want him after his deception. He had been built for someone else, someone who had the mind to play his game.

Elysia leaned against the counter, and as she watched, Philip unfurled their banner. Blue silk shimmering in the sunlight, it bore a burgundy pomegranate, wine-red grapes, and a deep purple fig encircled by a golden ring. As Philip tied its long tails to the cross brace at the top of the pole, onlookers headed toward their shop.

"Father, customers are coming," she called to the back of the shop, where her father sorted crates.

When Elysia turned, she found him next to her, putting a crate filled with figs on the floor beneath the counter. He hailed a homely woman from the back of the crowd. "Metrodora, good to see you."

The woman wove her way to stand on the other side of the counter, not even bothering to look at the produce on display. "You can lie all you want, Khronos." Her voice was crackly for a woman's, almost strained, as though she'd been sitting before a fire for endless days and nights. Her hair was charcoal and gray ash, her nose a beak. When her eyes found Elysia's, they were such a dark gray they were almost black, but they were rimmed with a shimmery silver that was near invisible in the shade. Metrodora might have been pretty once, but that had faded with age. "And this little wisp must be my granddaughter." Her voice sweetened, but it was still thin.

"Elysia, my daughter." Khronos put a hand on Elysia's shoulder and pulled her closer, so she stood almost in front of him. Metrodora looked her up and down. "Elysia, this is your grandmother, Metrodora. Your mother's mother." His tone spoke a hundred careful words. *The mother you did not know until yesterday, and this woman who cannot know.*

"It is good to meet you, Metrodora," she said softly.

"Please, child, call me Dora."

Elysia didn't think she would.

"Come out here so I can have a proper look at you." Metrodora beckoned with a plump hand. Her fingernails were neatly-shaped, clean ovals.

Looking up at her father, Elysia asked him silently for permission. When he nodded, he took his hand off her shoulder. "Behave," he murmured. "Remember what you've been told about the city."

She headed for the door and squeezed past Philip on his way in, slipping under the crate he held out of her way. When Elysia stepped out into the sunlight, Metrodora waited for her. She put her hands under both sides of Elysia's chin, palms warm against her skin. Metrodora pushed her head this way and that, then brushed away some of Elysia's white hair. Tiny strands had slipped from beneath her veil on the chariot ride. "You are a lovely girl, Elysia."

"Thank you." Her cheeks warmed, and not just from her grandmother's hands.

"You have your grandfather's hair, you know. Your uncle has it, too. You, he, and your mother all have his eyes... Your father's nose, though," she said, tapping Elysia lightly on the nose.

A hum escaped Elysia's throat. "Is my grandfather still alive?"

A shadow passed over Metrodora's face, as though the sun had decided to hide behind the clouds. "I'm afraid I don't know. He was a raider from the north." Her demeanor turned cold, and it seemed to pass through the air.

Horror sank through Elysia's skin and into her bones, a chill that wanted shivering. "I'm sorry." She rubbed her arms, trying to hide the goose prickles on them.

"It's alright. I don't think you could have known without your mother around to tell you. I doubt she told Khronos. She didn't have much of a stomach for the raiders, my Mira," said Metrodora, taking Elysia's hands in her own. "She near blinded her sire with a brand the last time we saw him, twenty-five years ago. Perhaps he's gone off and died." She gave Elysia a wry smile. "Now, what say you to a little fun?" Something glittered in Metrodora's eyes, which she recognized from spending too much time with Ares. Mischief.

"I should ask my father."

"Oh, come now, he won't even notice you're gone. Look at the crowd," she urged, letting go of one of Elysia's hands to gesture to the stall. The crowd grew closer to them as people gathered, expanding outward. At least twenty people congregated, asking prices and vying for attention.

"He's popular," she said, eyebrows raised. Philip had only just put their banner up; she could not imagine the attention it might draw by noon.

"He sells the best fruit in the agora and has the most loyal customers one could ask for, rich or poor. He treats them well."

A blond man leaned forward to speak, and as Khronos's deep laugh echoed from within the stall, Elysia nodded. "We can't be long, though," she warned, wondering what his reaction would be if he noticed she was gone. Her father trusted her to take care of herself; it was Philip who would worry.

"Perfect!" Taking Elysia's arm, Metrodora steered her toward the shop to their left, where a man sold raw wool, both creamy and jet. They stopped, and Metrodora reached down to touch the wool. "Now tell me, what do you know of spinning and weaving? My Mira told me that Khronos is quite the weaver himself, strange man."

"I spin well," Elysia began, then took a deep breath. "But I am not permitted to touch the loom."

"Not… Permitted?" Metrodora straightened, a tuft of wool held between two of her fingers. "What has he done, ruined you?"

"N-no," she said. Her spinning fingers rubbed together. "He did not have time to teach me and weave, too. His is taxing work."

"Mine is, as well, and I have taught many a girl to weave. How long will you be here? Just for the day?" The older woman bent down to pick up the bundle of wool, then offered a few coins to the man who'd watched her examine the wool. He counted the coins, nodding. Metrodora set off down the line of stalls again, wool under her arm.

Elysia hurried after her, trying not to trip on the edge of the road or her long gray skirts. "No, I will be staying in the city for some time. A month, at least." They headed back toward the end of the road that had brought Elysia and her father into the marketplace. "Where are we going?"

"I have to do my shopping before the crowds become too thick," Metrodora said, stopping at a larger stall. This one sold fish, from the smell of it, and after gazing at it, Metrodora moved on. "If your father installs you in his city house, we will be neighbors. If your days are free, I will teach you to weave at my loom, and perhaps we'll put those spinning skills to work." Metrodora turned and winked over her shoulder at Elysia. "What do you think of that?"

"That sounds divine," Elysia said, a ball of giddiness squirming into her stomach. Her curiosity had perked its insatiable ears. "How did you come to be his neighbor?" She clutched at her skirts as she followed in her grandmother's steps, so quickly did the woman walk. Metrodora had long strides for a short person, Elysia discovered, even with wool bundled under one arm.

"When your mother and the elders of our village sought refuge in Corinth, he met them at the gate. You will find that your father can sniff out the most invisible of weary travelers and bring them under his wings from the winds of the world." The next shop they stopped at was a basket maker's. His products almost sold themselves, from the look of the spare shelves. "Everyone forgets their baskets," Metrodora told Elysia after she handed over a pair of tiny silver coins for a boat of a basket, "but sometimes forgetting them is an excuse to buy more. You can never have enough baskets, can you, Petros?"

The basket maker shook his head. "Not you. You'd better be using them all." When Petros grinned, his smile was full of yellow-brown teeth, but it was not so hideous a smile as that of the last soul Elysia had met in the chamber. For once, she saw a friendly face. He might have even been handsome, given a bit of polishing up and a careful shave; his beard was uneven gray in places, a scraggly tangle around his chin. He had to be fifty at least but was lean despite his age. "This your youngest? She looks like your boy, with that fair hair."

"My granddaughter." When the basket maker squinted at her harder, Elysia shifted. "My daughter's daughter," Metrodora added.

"It's been an age since I saw Branimira." Petros looked up, as though his memories might be painted on the ceiling for his leisure. "Khronos chased her like a toddler after a cat. Married her and had you, did he, up in those hills?" Petros emanated gentleness, like Philip when he spoke to the shyest of the horses.

"Yes," Elysia said.

"You've got them blue eyes she had, temperamental as the sea. Clear one moment and moody the next… My girl has eyes like that, but not so light." He leaned over the counter and looked for something, then found it in the girl sitting beneath their banner pole. "Ianthe, come meet Metrodora's granddaughter."

The girl rose from her stool with the grace of a deer, long-legged and willowy under her red dress. With her she brought her spindle, spinning at knee-height as she fed it black wool from the distaff under her arm. "Hello," Ianthe said. She had a voice like her father's, soft and kind, but much higher and sweeter. Her eyes looked like the blue-black crystal of Khronos's throne, glimmering darkly in the sunlight. She looked from Metrodora to Elysia and dipped her head to them. "My father has told you my name, but I have not heard yours."

"I am Elysia," she said, nodding to Ianthe.

When the girl smiled, she showed white teeth so unlike her father's that Elysia felt a jolt. Her black mane was combed and plaited neatly, shining with olive oil. "Has Metrodora taken you up for a charge?" Ianthe asked. Even her breath was sweet, as though she had been drinking rosewater.

"I…" Elysia paused and looked at her grandmother, who gave her a wicked grin. Metrodora had offered her weaving lessons – did that make Elysia her charge? "I suppose so?"

"I was her charge not so long ago," Ianthe said, putting a hand on Metrodora's bare arm, pale against the tan of the old woman's skin. "I was sixteen, though my years now number closer to twenty-five."

"And she is married," Metrodora added, a proud smile undoing the years which had stolen the youth from her face. "Weaves and spins for her whole family, bringing customers into her father's store."

"Your doing, all," Ianthe replied, smiling graciously. "You taught me the ways of a Greek lady, and for that I will be ever grateful." The young woman turned back to Elysia. "You will forgive me, I pray, but I must return to my spinning. My son has outgrown his tunic and I must needs make him another before the old one becomes too short."

Elysia did not point out that Ianthe had never stopped spinning; her spindle had been spun and fed while they spoke. Metrodora took their leave of the shop, looped her new basket over her arm, and set off down the line of stalls.

When they were out of earshot of the girl who had retaken her seat and resumed spinning, Metrodora shook her head. "That one took my teachings too close to heart. Her father brought her to me with no idea how to raise a young woman. Motherless, you see, and all three brothers gone into the Guard. She was beautiful, though, and only needed some shining up and lessons in propriety, but…"

"But?"

"She became the perfect Greek wife." Metrodora slowed so they could walk side by side. "Quiet, faithful, yielding, excellent in her duties. And yet, her listening ear drove out the one thing the Greek wives are known for, behind doors and screens. Her bright personality was erased in her desire to please her father."

Metrodora handed a few coins to the baker for three rounds of pita. The smells of the shop near overwhelmed Elysia in their fantastic potency: the dry flour, the homey warmth of bread, the sweet, crystalline bowls of old honey on shelves behind the baker and his son. Metrodora put the flatbread in her basket, took Elysia's arm, and marched her across the street.

On the opposite side of the Lechaion, more luxurious things were sold. They passed silversmiths, goldsmiths, sculptors and spicers, a man selling exotic furs, and a lone shop of dyes, as pungent as it was huge. Within, slaves worked under a freeman, boiling fabrics in vats. Closer to her father's shop were several fabric stalls under that blue silk banner. Metrodora stopped there, Elysia out of breath beside her.

As her grandmother combed through bolts, Elysia leaned against a stone wall. "You said my father met my mother and your people at the gate when they sought refuge, but not how you came to be his neighbor," she observed.

Metrodora paused, her hand lingering over an orange silk. "He met me at the gate when I wandered in months later, heavy with child and near delirious. Corinth was my home, long before the village where your mother was born, and so I came back to it. I was the daughter of the foreman of a weaving room, and he thought my marriage to a shepherd would secure him a good supply of wool. It did for a year, but when winter came, the raiders came. They killed my husband, ate his sheep, and raped me."

Her eyes hardened as she stared at the next bolt, a deep green woolen with sharp yellow triangles at the edges. "They killed the babes in arms, the men they could find, the animals… They carried off little girls to raise among their women. And after that, new life was born in me: your mother. The elders couldn't understand my inability to leave her to freeze when she was born, but she was all I had. When the raiders came eighteen years later, I was dragged out to the woods as your mother and the elders fled south. It took me much longer to get here than it took them. I don't remember much, but he was at the gates. He seemed familiar to me, with his red-gold head and striking eyes. I thought I'd met him when I was young. He carried me to the house where he'd installed your mother and the elders, and there I remain. We were neighbors." Metrodora smiled at her and turned the next bolt to get a better look at the pattern.

Elysia blinked. Her grandmother's voice had never wavered, never broken, and she'd not shed a tear as she spoke, despite the frozen posture of her body. "My father still owns that house?" she asked, following Metrodora along as she flicked through the fabrics.

"He hasn't sold it. A servant cleans it from time to time."

Metrodora picked out a length of white linen with a single blue stripe. This time, she handed over larger coins, each stamped with a face on one side and a winged horse on the other. Elysia looked harder at them and scooted closer, but before she understood what she had seen, her grandmother had counted them and handed them to the man running the stall.

"What were those coins?" she asked as they crossed the street, dodging palanquins and the sweat-soaked, sun-browned men who carried them.

"The coins?" When Elysia nodded, Metrodora gave her a look that told her she was a newborn calf. "They are Corinthian stater. The horse is Pegasus, a winged steed who drank from the spring atop Acrocorinth." She waved her hands dramatically at the mountain that loomed over them. "The hero of our city captured him, and he became our emblem. Are you sure your father hasn't ruined you?"

Elysia laughed.

"I don't know what to think of him," Metrodora allowed as they reached the other side of the street. "I wasn't happy to hear that he wanted to marry my Mira when I made it back, and I did my best to scare him off. He's been wary of me since. But with you here, perhaps that can change." She gave Elysia a small smile.

"Perhaps," Elysia replied.

"Elysia!"

The voice belonged to Philip, who leaned out the doorway of the stall and beckoned her.

"I should go," Elysia said, looking back at him. He was only two stalls down, but she felt like she had been gone for hours.

Metrodora shooed her off after a goodbye kiss on the cheek.

When she swung around the corner and into the cramped space of the stall, she collided with Philip on his way out. "Finally!" he said, steadying her with a hand on her shoulder. "I thought that woman had stolen you."

Elysia caught her breath, shaking him off. "No, she just took me with her to shop the agora." She looked up at Philip and saw worry and something darker written in the lines of his face. "Were you truly so concerned?" Her hand reached out to touch the one still balanced at her shoulder.

He caught her hand and cleared his throat. "Not truly," he said, but she could feel the lie in her bones as he let her go. "But we should be going soon. Your father's near sold out of fruit."

Empty crates had been stacked neatly along the back wall, and Khronos stood at the counter trading coins for the last crate of figs. The second to last crate of pomegranates went for more, and the last of the pomegranates and grapes were set aside for themselves. "It's not even noon yet," Elysia protested. She had hoped to see more – to *do* more – in the agora before they went to the house.

"Corinth turning out better than you expected, Lys?" her father asked, grinning as he carried a stack of crates out the door and around the corner. Wagons had lined up in front of the chariot between their stall and the next.

She crossed her arms over her chest as she waited for him to return, but her father employed her to carry crates out to the wagons, as well. She could not carry near as many as Philip or her father, but she could carry two at a time. The women returned with the well-worn baskets they carried everywhere with them, now well-stocked with food, rather than the fruit they picked in the fields. Some balanced terra cotta vessels on their hips as if the pots were children, one arm wrapped around them while the other held a basket. The vessels had scenes painted on them, animals or heroes or fields abundant with different crops.

Once all the wagons were loaded with empty crates, Philip and another man walked the white horses around to the front of the chariot and harnessed them to it. Khronos drove the pair of horses into the street and helped Elysia into the chariot.

This time, she was prepared for the jolt from the horses' sudden acceleration and looked back as they wove their way through the crowd for the second time that day. She found Philip gazing silently back at her as he led one of the docile oxen into the traces. Quickly, she looked away and found the stall. She'd spent hardly more than half an hour in it.

"Are you ready to see your new home, Elysia?"

She turned back to the front of the chariot. The blue banner that stood before the fruit stall furled itself in her mind's eye, detached itself from its pole, and landed in the back of one of the wagons. Her first day in the agora, over quick as that. "I am."

And now my first day as a Corinthian will begin.

"Well, it should be just perfect for a pair of people then, shouldn't it?" Khronos asked her as she stepped down from the chariot. The horses stood quietly in the middle of the road, still harnessed to the chariot. Lined up in front of them were two oxen-less wagons, each filled with crafts and furniture and crates of clothes. "It's bigger on the inside."

"You'll be staying with me?" she asked, looking from the house to her father and back again. Something uncertain wriggled in her gut. If her father stayed with her... Would she be able to weave with her grandmother? Weaving had been forbidden to her since she was small, but the reason had always been that he would not have time to teach her. Surely if someone else taught her, the point would be moot?

Khronos nodded and pushed the wooden slab aside, and it swung inward on hinges. Elysia squeezed past him and into the house.

Within, men and women pulled sheets of white fabric off large pieces of furniture – a wide table, a wooden couch – and folded them into neat squares to keep dust from falling onto the floor. Khronos had been right about the size of the house; inside, it seemed much bigger. It was also much deeper than she would have thought, stretching forty feet back. A wall with a curtain in its doorway shielded the other half of the house from view. When she pushed her way past it, she found a door in the opposite wall, left open to air out the house. Beyond it, a wide courtyard opened, walled in with the same blue-gray stone. Twice the width of the house, almost all of it stretched out to the right. A rose garden bloomed in beds between the flagstone walks; a pomegranate tree, heavy with dusty red fruit, grew in the center in a ring of stones.

Home. It was a miniature version of her own yard, complete with a smaller version of the fountain and its statue of a maid. Leaning around the door frame, she saw that the back door of their neighbor's house also opened onto the courtyard, which could only be her grandmother's home.

Back inside the house, she found her father unpacking.

She took another look around – it was then that she noticed that near every wall was covered with woolen tapestries. A few she recognized, but one stood out to her. It hung on the wall in the front room of the house. Weaving her way around a pile of cushions, she touched the thick fabric. It was smooth beneath her fingers. "This is where you've been keeping it," she murmured.

The valley opened before her, sunlit and glowing golden. In the middle stood her home, a white marble temple amidst the browns and greens of rock and hill. The tapestries beside it beheld the valley from other angles, one from the end of the road, looking down the row of olive trees to see the shining pillars and rooms, another looking from one side of the valley across to the other, with the house far below. On the other walls, more tapestries looked in on the house, room by room, all except the judgment chamber. Some were bare, others furnished with the paraphernalia of each of the judges, but every room she recognized... Except one, though she knew its location immediately. The room was cold, shadowed, and empty but for a great loom. "The weaving room," she muttered, and moved down the line to brush her fingers over the beige-gray frame of the loom. The last time she had seen it, she had been a toddler. She had gotten just been a peek around the curtain that veiled the room before a warm hand pulled her away, engaging her with a chase through the hall. Her father had never known she was there, but from then on, it had been against the rules to look in on the weaving room. Mira's voice was the one that sang in her head now: *Don't disturb Father while he is at his work.*

"How long did it take you to make these?" she asked, looking over her shoulder to find her father bringing in another mountain of pillows and cushions to throw on the wooden lounge.

"Nigh on a year," came the reply, muffled behind the silk-and-down mountain. He dropped the pillows on the couch, sat down, and patted the ones beside him. Elysia took a seat and leaned her head on her father's shoulder, gazing at the tapestry that depicted the garden with its fountain. The roses were in bloom, their colors sunrise, scarlet, and snow. "I had been in the city for well-on thirty years already, and it was time to start somewhere new. It is tiresome to have to start all over again in a different city, so I built myself my own home." He gestured to the tapestries. "It was demanding work, but the judges helped, loathe though some of them were to do it. They like it here in the city, where they could mingle with others... In the hills, it is only isolation, for the most part. We kept the loom in the back room. Ares, Apollo, and I slept in this room, and the girls were next door in a third house. The servants and Philip's parents sheltered where your grandmother lives. We judged the souls in the garden."

"Sounds cramped," Elysia said. She could imagine sharing an entire house with three other women, but housing three men in one *room*? "I understand why you moved."

Her father chuckled. "Oh, but you don't quite. When the Albans – your grandmother's people – came down from the north, the judges, myself, and the loom all shared this house, and the fifteen of them all lived next door. The servants moved into the third house."

She lifted her head from her father's shoulder to look at him with wide eyes. "How?"

"We found the room. We all slept on the floor and did most of our chores in the garden when we weren't weaving. How the fifteen of *them* managed it… That I'll never know."

"But the pair of us will be living here?"

He looked down at her. "Would you like that?" Someone put a crate of clothes down next to him with a *thud*.

"I should be on my own. It is my test."

The smile he gave her was so earnest that she had to smile back. "I will be here until you pass the first test. *Then* you will be on your own." He held her at arm's length, green-gold eyes studying her in the dim light. "You're growing before my eyes, Lys." He rested a hand on her shoulder. Before she knew it, he was off to help one of the men bring in an armload of their things.

She sat there, thinking. He would be with her until she passed the first test. *To safely conduct yourself among the humans, you must learn to defend yourself from harm.* The mountain of Acrocorinth soared up in her mind, a thousand feet or more of rock, lichen, and marble manses. At the base lived the Apocorinthians… She imagined them as grubby, weathered people like those she'd seen in the Merchants' Gauntlet, roasting rats over meager fires, their children barely clothed and many not at all.

Her imagination steered her wrong.

The next morning, she and her father broke their fasts on honeyed bread and pomegranates she'd picked from the tree in the rose garden. Just like the ones in the valley, they were huge, with nearly a thousand and a half seeds hiding within, each protected by a shield of red flesh and juice. They were sweet as morning sunlight.

She'd slept on a miniature version of the bed she'd had back in the valley house: a strong net of fabric stretched over a wooden frame, covered in a mound of pillows, blankets, and furs. Her father had spent the night on the wooden lounge, much to his discontent, though he said not a word about it. The farmhands and Philip had slept either in the third house or outside on the flagstones, under the stars, surrounded by the roses – which, for the uncareful, meant getting stuck with thorns.

"We'll go to Acrocorinth as soon as we're done here," her father mumbled at his pomegranate as he tore a piece of white lining from the ruby seeds trapped inside. He shelled them out into a stone bowl with a fervor that said they'd offended him.

"Hard night?"

"Not near enough pillows."

He passed her the bowl, and she offered him a lump of bread drizzled with honey. They ate in silence and listened to the crows *caw*ing their morning greetings. Soon, Philip walked in from the garden, his arms tattooed with the grain of the stone and blades of grass he'd slept on. "Need the horses ready?"

"Please," Elysia replied before her father had looked up from his bread.

Before they went out the door, Khronos had her put her riding gown on beneath her dress. He gave Philip a string of chores to do for the day, and then they were off.

The journey back to the Lechaion seemed to take much less time, though the bumps and dips were no less jolting. When they passed the gates of Amphitrite and Poseidon, Elysia noticed that Adrastos and the white-blonde Zeus were in the Guard once more. She could hear them sniggering behind them as they passed, and Adrastos muttered a rough something about delicate ladies not being able to handle a real city. She shook her head, trying not to grin at the thought of proving them wrong.

Dust and grime covered her from face to sandaled feet before they reached the foot of Acrocorinth, where it was dryer than it had been on the road to the city. She could taste the dirt in her mouth, feel grit between her teeth. Her gray dress had gone beige from the waist up as dust billowed from beneath the horses' hooves – her father's beard had not fared much better. "Are we close?" she asked, coughing as another cloud of dirt found its way through her mouth and into her windpipe. Mansions seemed to grow out of the hill far above her, but they'd seen only a scattered few mud brick houses.

"Should be just around this bend."

As they followed the road around the curve of the mountain, three houses – huts, really, thatched with straw – came into view, then five, fifteen, thirty. Some were on the flat ground near the base, but more ventured up the slope, some sticking out of the hill at unnatural angles. The ones at the top leaned against the base of a sheer bare cliff that soared into the air another forty feet before it met another ledge. "See that one up there?"

Elysia followed Khronos's finger to the one at the very top, set in a niche away from the others. "That is Herod's house," her father explained. "He's the one who will teach you."

"Does he know we're coming?" The shadow of the mountain loomed over them as the sun rose.

"No."

Elysia looked sharply at her father, her brow creasing. *He'll probably throw us out on sight.* As they passed the first house, abuzz with activity despite the early hour, something prodded at Elysia's mind. "Beating the man Herod nearly to death over a toy meant for his young daughter," Elysia murmured.

"Yes, that Herod," Khronos answered.

"If he could not defend himself from that man, how will he teach me to defend myself from strangers?"

"If his daughter was young and playing with toys, the Herod I knew wasn't in good health when he was beaten. Their house had collapsed on him."

"*Collapsed* on him?" Her eyes found the mud brick hovel at the base of the cliff again. From afar, it looked sturdy enough.

Khronos only nodded in response.

Watching the people they passed, Elysia discovered that they were not the same as the homogeneous poor folk of the city; instead, these people appeared to be from everywhere. An ebon-skinned woman in yellow had a spindle in hand and a little girl in her lap. A blonde girl stood on a wooden ladder, patching a hole in a roof as an old man handed bundles of straw to her; a hook-nosed young man painted whitewash on the house next to them. Every child wore at least a belted length of cloth, if not something more complex.

"They are not as poor here as I'd thought," Elysia said.

"They own their clothes and the food they can find. The wealthiest here build furniture and houses for those who have neither, but none has money. They trade for what they need."

Khronos pulled the chariot up in front of a house with a wicker awning, which was decorated with the long canines of animals, each hanging on its own string and swaying in the breeze. "Delia," he called.

A woman came to the door, arms crossed. Though her face was wrinkled, her black hair was untouched by gray. "Aye, what do ya want?" she asked, but when she saw Khronos leaning out of the chariot, she lifted her arms to him and pulled his face down to kiss him on the cheek.

"Khronos, how long has it been? Ya've not aged a day. And is this your little daughter?" she asked when she saw Elysia peering around her father. "She's not much younger than my girls. But what've ya done with Branimira? Weren't you two married?"

"Mira passed sixteen years ago," Khronos replied, his mouth twisting. Elysia knew that look and the meaning behind it – it was an old pain, but not one unfelt. "I thought you had heard."

Delia let go of Khronos and stepped back a pace, the long-yellowed canines swaying and clinking above her. Elysia took an uneasy step down from the chariot.

"What killed her?" Delia asked, shadowed beneath the eaves of her house.

"She wasted away after Elysia's birth. Something took root while she was weakened." Khronos stepped down from the chariot and ducked beneath the teeth dangling down from the roof. They clicked together as he swept beneath them, turning about on their strings. Putting a hand on Delia's shoulder, he muttered something to her and pulled her back into the sunlight; her cheeks shone in the light as she swiped at them with dirty hands. "Elysia's here to meet Herod," said Khronos softly. "Do you mind holding our horses until we return?"

Delia looked up at Khronos and shook her head. The horses whickered faintly as she walked to the head of the chariot; she laid a hand against their necks and gave them a good rub, and the horses bobbed their heads in tandem. "Who are these, now?"

"Our whites," Elysia replied. "We do not name them." She went to stand beside the woman, who could only be a few years younger than Metrodora – and looked disturbingly like her.

"Aye, it is bad luck to name working horses." Delia looked up at the red-haired man standing beside her. "You want to see Herod?"

Khronos nodded. "I hear he's grown ancient."

She laughed, and the sound was so deep that Elysia jumped. "Aye, that's true. Walks with a certain tilt, but don't you go telling him that. His hair's as yellow as ever, though. Won't go white, neither, to hear him tell it." Waving them on, Delia began to untack the horses.

The trek up the hill had Elysia sweating. The grime from the chariot ride collected in little trails as it ran down her face. She loosened the sash on her dress until the side slit was past her midthigh; even in the cool shade of the mountain, the day had begun to warm. The climb felt nearly vertical, and she knew that if she fell, she would roll all the way back down the hill – if she didn't careen into a house first.

As she looked into the huts near the top of the hill, she saw berms of sand and stone built within to level them out. Through every door, a set of steep steps disappeared to an upper level. The houses were taller than they had appeared from below, each rising ten feet or more from the gray-brown dirt. Sparse yellow-green stubble of grass covered the ground between the houses. "Nothing – grows – here," she said between breaths. Dust and pebbles scraped in her sandals.

"They do not need it to." Unlike her, Khronos was as fresh as he had been at the bottom of the hill. "Most spend their days working in the city and bring home what they can. They don't live off their own land as we do; it is too steep and rocky for much to grow here."

When they reached Herod's house in its niche at the top of the hill, Elysia was exhausted. As he listened to her labored breathing, Khronos chuckled. "This is why you need to get out more. Earning immortality couldn't hurt, either."

She glared daggers at him as he called up into the house; there was no door to knock on.

"Who calls?" answered a feminine voice, guarded and abrupt. Another voice spoke up in the gloom, much deeper but indistinguishable.

As Elysia peered up the stairs, she saw a delicate pair of sandaled feet beneath a skirt of undyed linen. "Khronos and his daughter, Elysia," her father said, taking a step back as the woman, a girl in truth, swept down the rest of the stairs. "You must be Korinna."

"Aye, and who are you to know my name?" asked the girl, studying them with large brown eyes. She couldn't be more than sixteen, but her dress clung to her like a lover, the sash so loose that it bared her left leg almost to the hip and the front draped so severely that Elysia raised a brow just looking at her.

"A friend of your father's. He taught my wife to defend herself, and I'd like him to teach my daughter."

Elysia felt Korinna's eyes on her like needles tracing over her skin, raking over the gray of her dress and the silver clasps at the shoulders. "A highborn caller," Korinna observed. "We do not see those very often."

The scrape of leather on stone echoed out of the house behind her, and an older woman leaned under the eave of the doorway to gaze at them. When her eyes lit on Khronos, she stepped down further and around Korinna. By the brunette hair and the wide planes of their faces, the woman could only be Korinna's mother. "Khronos," she said. She watched him, her fingers mending a tear in the length of cloth she carried with her. "You'll find Herod down at the plateau. He's training the little boys for the Guard now."

"Thank you, ladies," Khronos said with a nod, and the women went back up into the house, though Korinna lingered. After a long stare at Elysia, she fled back up the steps.

"The plateau?" Elysia asked, watching the hem of Korinna's skirt disappear.

"Back down the hill. We passed it." Her father set off downward as she gaped at him.

"Wouldn't we have heard them if we passed them?" Her feet threatened to slide right out of her sandals as she scooted down the mountain one foot at a time.

"Herod's lessons hide amongst the houses."

Tramping downhill was much faster than the trek up, though far more dangerous. The houses clustered like bees around a honeycomb; one wrong move, one misplaced step, and Elysia would get stung.

Somewhere to her right, her father's voice boomed a greeting, and Elysia realized he'd disappeared. Ducking between a pair of houses, she followed the answering voice. She slipped past a nanny goat chewing at a wiry bush, then around another row of houses and onto a small ledge.

Before her, the ground leveled out on the hillside, its top left bare, though huts bordered every side. Boys formed a ring around the edge of what could only be the plateau, a sharpened stake in the hand of each. In the center stood three men, two tall and one hunched. Her father was one of the tall ones, but the other two were strangers.

Parting a pair of boys at the edge of the training ground, Elysia stepped into the empty space. "Father?" she called.

Khronos and his companions turned. One looked her age, and the other was so aged that his blond hair was going white above his hunched back. His gnarled hand clutched a wooden staff.

"This must be your get," growled the old man, and the younger put a hand on his shoulder. They had to be father and son, for though the father's blond was fading, the son's was sandy down to his shoulders.

"You're going to frighten her before we even get started," muttered the young man.

Khronos beckoned her forward. "Elysia, meet your instructors."

She crept out onto the plateau, sandals scuffing over the smooth surface. She lifted her skirt to avoid treading on it, and when she got to the three of them, she bowed her head in greeting.

"Enough of that." A hand darted under her chin and lifted it. Her gaze met the brown eyes of the old man as he dropped his hand. "We shake hands here. Lesson number one, never make yourself vulnerable." He held out a hand to her, the palm calloused and dark with dirt.

She regarded his hand. "If I shake your hand, you could pull me off my feet or hit me with that stick."

The old man chuckled and looked at Khronos. "Good instincts for a mountain girl," he said before shoving his hand at Elysia again. "'Tis true, I could pull you off your feet, but it would be much easier for you to pull me off mine."

She studied him for a moment, then clasped his arm above the wrist.

He smacked her on the top of the head with his stick.

The boys gathered around her giggled as she cried out, a few of the older ones laughing heartily. Even her father laughed, though the young man standing beside him kept a still face. Elysia rubbed her scalp, scandalized. "That was ill done, sir," she said.

"That is what you should expect from ill-doers," replied the old man, who let go of her arm. A red mark appeared there from her attempt to pull away. "I am Herod, and this is my son, Alexander."

Alexander nodded to her, blond hair brushing over his shoulders. Unlike his father, he had gray eyes. "My father's not as spry as he once was," he said, blocking Herod's attempt to club him over the head, "so I will be your sparring partner."

"I see," said Elysia. Her father nodded his approval.

"Today you will be watching and listening," Herod said. "Once you've watched and listened, we will see if Alexander can catch you unawares."

She looked to Alexander, and he gave her an encouraging smile. Surprisingly – it was not what she had begun to expect from Corinth – he had white teeth.

Khronos took her by the shoulder and steered her to the edge of the circle while Herod and Alexander stayed in the center. "Watch carefully, Elysia," he said. "Learn well. Once you pass this test, your life will be in your own hands."

Yes, she thought. *And I will be all alone in the city.*

8

Elysia's first lesson was a lesson for the boys, as well.

"Now, when ye're called for guard duty by the great Corinthians, what do you do?" Herod asked them.

"Shove a stick up their arses!" came the first reply, and Alexander laughed. Another boy called, "Run on over like a good boy!" More shouts went up after that, mostly unintelligible.

Herod banged his stick on the ground. "That first one will get you killed," he said, pointing at the boy who said it. "You don't get to fight today. Go stand over with the crone and her father."

Crone? When the little boy stood next to her, she crossed her arms and furiously brushed a strand of white hair out of her face.

"The boy who said to run on over has the right of it, I'm afraid," Herod continued. "But we do not run! We do not scramble! We are free men, aye?"

"Aye!" shouted the boys.

"And free men do not hurry to do as they are bid, no. We are not slaves. But we must be smart," said Herod, "for in the city, even free men are vulnerable. Even *guardsmen* are vulnerable. And so, we learn."

Alexander stepped forward. "We will play a game today," he said, clapping his hands together. "You know how to attack, you know how to defend, and now you will learn to creep. You will learn to sneak, to walk with steps unheard, and to hear steps unheard." Beckoning to a boy, he gestured to the stick in the child's hand. "Dion, I want you to sneak up on me and strike me." Alexander closed his gray eyes and waved the boy off. "Start from anywhere."

Dion wove his way around Alexander, past Herod, and to the far edge of the plateau before circling around to approach Alexander from the side. The boy jabbed out at his shoulder with the pointy end of the stick, but just as he did, Alexander dropped and swept the boy's feet out from under him. The stick flew from Dion's grasp. The boy blinked, stunned in the dirt, then retrieved his stick.

"Try again," said Alexander. "Walk like a cat." He closed his eyes.

This time, the boy went around to Alexander's front. He placed each bare foot deliberately on the dusty ground, rocking lightly from his heel to the ball of his foot with each stride. When he was within a bodylength of Alexander, Dion crouched and sprang forward, stick held out horizontally to rap the man in front of him sharply across the middle. Alexander caught the stick within inches of his belly, but when he opened his eyes, he smiled. "Better." Looking from Dion to the rest of the boys, he said, "Pair off. One of you will close his eyes while the other approaches. Both of you can have sticks, but for the love of Poseidon – use the *blunt* end."

Leaving the boys to gather in the center of the plateau and spar, Alexander came to stand between Elysia and the boy who had been forbidden from fighting. "Well, without Leon here, the boys are evenly numbered, and I have no partner to try," Alexander said, ruffling the boy's kinky black hair with hands yellow with callous.

When he turned to look at Elysia, she took a step away and bumped into her father. "You can't be serious."

"You watched. You listened." He blinked eyes as grey as her dress, framed by golden lashes.

"I'll trip over my dress." She put her hands on her hips and stared up at him.

"That can be remedied," he said.

He'd already crouched and grabbed her hem before she could protest. Grabbing him around the wrist, she pushed his hand away. "I brought a tunic, you don't have to go ripping my clothes apart."

The grin he gave her was more mischievous than she would have liked. "I was not going to rip your dress apart," he said, rising from his crouch. He stood nearly a head taller than her. "There's a much easier way to shorten your dress than you running to get one or tearing the bottom half off."

"And what is that?" She backed into her father in her haste to escape Alexander, who'd gone down on his haunches again, hands outstretched toward the bottom of her skirt. Khronos grunted as she rammed his side, catching her around the shoulders, and eyed the young man. Leon laughed as only a little boy could laugh – so hard and so high, he began to cough.

Her father cleared his throat, and Alexander got to his feet. "It's called girding, Elysia," began Khronos. "Pull your skirts up, back through your legs, and tie them in front of you."

Still glaring at Alexander, Elysia went around the back of an unoccupied hut. "This is ludicrous," she grumbled as she pulled her skirts in front of her legs. They made a couple of absurd triangles, the grey fabric wrapping around her calves. Huffing, she tried to do as her father told her, pulling her skirt above her knees and back through her legs, making loops around them. Just as she was about to tie her odd new pants in front of her hips, she felt the fabric of her riding tunic bunch uncomfortably around her thighs. Elysia felt a smirk form on her lips, and let her skirts drop.

When she came back around the hut, some of the boys were dispersing. A few talked in groups or played tag. Alexander, Herod, and her father stood in the center of the plateau, speaking with Leon.

Alexander was the first to notice her standing at the edge of the plateau again. She lingered there as a few little boys passed her and stuck out their tongues at her. She was about to repay them in kind, but Alexander cleared his throat. "The princess has returned from her clandestine mission," he said, bowing to her.

With a huff, Elysia strode toward the center. She shoved a ball of grey fabric into her father's chest; he instinctively reached up to hold it. Instead of girding up her dress, she'd taken it off and kept the riding tunic that had hidden beneath it; its length fell only to her knees. "At least I won't trip over my skirts." That had been the whole point – if they were to spar, she would not make a fool of herself by tangling herself in her own clothes.

"You will have to practice in your city clothes someday," said Alexander, his mouth turned downward in disapproval. It did not look good on him – his face was made for smiling, for laughter. He had a few lines to prove it, despite his young age.

"But not today," Herod said, and gave the back of her thighs a stinging slap with his walking stick. "Today you'll fight in yer wee little tunic, showing off those fine legs."

Elysia scowled at him and rubbed her legs, looking to her father, but Khronos only shrugged. "I've learned to let Herod have his little jabs," he said. "They'll make you angry at him, certainly. But they'll always have the effect he intends – to put the fight in you."

"If you wanted to put the fight in me, old man, all you had to do was call me a crone, and you've already done that," Elysia said.

Herod gave her a grin that she supposed was meant to be charming, but he was missing so many teeth that his face only became more grotesque: his nose had been broken so many times that its original shape was hardly conceivable, and he had so many scars that his face looked more a mask than anything else. One ran white from his right temple and through the eyebrow on the other side, a long pale line across his forehead.

"Elysia, your lesson for today will be a bit different from the one the boys had," Alexander said.

She faced him, arms crossed, though she tried to keep one eye on his father. "How so?"

"You will learn to sneak, but the primary lesson is to learn to trust your instincts. *I* will be sneaking up on you."

"If you move like a cat, how will I hear you? You spent an hour teaching the boys to do just that – you ought to be an expert." She hadn't moved from her spot, though Alexander crossed the plateau to where one of the boys had left a stick on the ground.

Picking it up, he said, "You get this. If you hear me coming, reach out with it. If you touch me before I close in on you, you win and get to sneak up on me. The lesson is not so much hearing as it is trusting your intuition. If you sense that something is wrong in one direction, jab that way. But use the blunt end, I beg you." He gave her a smile, and it was one that lit up his face, gray eyes sparkling as the sun drew farther across the bare plateau.

She took the stick from him. Rapping it against Herod's walking staff, Elysia shooed her father and Alexander's off to the side, then stood in the center by herself. When she closed her eyes, Alexander stood at the far end of the plateau.

But when she closed her eyes, of course, the world went black and Alexander was gone. The darkness was not complete, however, as moments went by – it soon faded from black to gray, then to dark red limned with pink.

Even so, she felt blind to the world, and not just by sight. She could hear no better than she had before, nor did the hot sun on her arms turn to anything else: no goose prickles, no chills, no hair-raising sense of dread. As time passed, though, that began to change, too.

"Listen to what your body tells you," said Alexander's voice, somewhere behind her. She turned, the dirt crunching and shifting beneath her sandals. "Everything you feel, hear, smell, taste is important. Trust your senses."

Warmth touched her shoulder, rough skin over the heat from the burning sun. Twisting, she brought the stick around – it whistled as it swung through the air, a deep *whoosh*ing sound – but Alexander was gone. He laughed off to her right.

Trust your senses, she thought, and stood still, no muscle but her heart moving. The stick in her hand was still held out to the side, a guard for that direction, at the very least.

A crow *caw*ed, and one of its fellows answered. To her left, her father murmured to Herod, and Herod shouted something to her, something meant to sting, but it didn't matter; it was not what she listened for. She listened for dirt whispering beneath leather, as it did beneath her own sandals. She listened for cloth rustling, for legs brushing together.

There. It was not a sound, but a scent: salt of sweat and something sweet, something she recognized as warm. *Rosewater*. Goose prickles raised along her arms. She tossed the stick into her other hand and swung backwards, but too high: a hand touched her ankle.

"Getting closer, Elysia," he taunted, "but still not close enough."

Her teeth gritted together. "You wear rosewater," she said.

"Very good," said Alexander's voice. He smiled; she could hear it. "You are beginning to see."

This time, when she listened, a chill went down her arms as air brushed against them. Movement. *Close* movement. The rosewater found her nose again. The stick darted outward, and the dull *thunk* of impact radiated up her arm.

Just inches to her left, Alexander grunted. "Good hit."

She grinned.

"Lucky hit."

She frowned. "What do you mean, lucky hit?" she asked. "I could smell you. I *felt* you."

"Open your eyes."

She found Alexander four inches from her. His hand reached for her shoulder again, not half an inch from her skin. "Lucky hit," she agreed.

He nodded. "Your instincts are far from sharp. You will need more training. But you have earned the chance to play this game from the other side." She grinned, but then he said, "Give me the stick."

Fear shot through her, and she clutched the stick to her chest. "No."

Alexander crossed his arms. "It's only a fair game if I get to use it, too."

"That may be true," said Elysia, "but you have the advantage of skill over me."

"Aye," called Herod. "Play without the stick. Let 'er feel the sting of yer hands, son." When Elysia scowled at him, she saw her father doing the same.

"Very well," said Alexander. He held out a hand to Elysia. "We play without the stick."

She handed it over.

He may not have had the reach on her, but that did not stop Alexander from nearly knocking her to the ground every time she got remotely close to him. The first thing she tried was exactly what Dion had: standing before him as he closed his eyes, then skirting around and approaching from behind. She tried to walk as the boy had, too – like a cat, delicately, though Dion had had bare feet where she had sandals. His feet had been nearly muted where hers scuffed over the sand. Despite her efforts, Alexander darted out to smack her squarely on the top of the head when she got within a yard of him. "Sneak better," were the only words he offered her.

Biting her lip in concentration, she circled around – and Herod shoved her in the hip with the end of his walking staff, sending her sprawling. "Unfair," she cried, but he shrugged. Her father nudged him in the shoulder, but the old man just grinned. Huffing, she got to her feet, checking her newly bloodied knees. The skin was torn on one, white and flaking on the other.

Having lost the element of surprise, Elysia did her best to make some noise as she feinted to the right, and then attacked from the front – and he shoved her to the ground with both hands. At her scandalized cry, he chuckled. "Ready to surrender?"

"Never." Getting up, she brushed the dirt off and sucked the blood from her lip, which she'd bitten as she had hit the ground. Pulling the skirt of her tunic down, she thought up her next plan.

This time, she tiptoed forward until she stood in front of him, just beyond his reach. She lingered there for more than a minute, standing with her arms crossed beneath the glare of the sun. "Elysia?" he called, and she struck as he spoke, stretching out a leg to tap his knee.

"Clever," he said as he opened his eyes, "but were you an attacker, your prey would be long gone by now."

"I am not learning to attack," argued Elysia, "but to defend."

"So it may be," Herod chimed in, "but to defend, you must be able to think like an attacker. Where will he attack from? What will he do to subdue you?"

Elysia turned to look at her instructor.

Herod shook his head. "I think ye need a different lesson than this one. Ye've got it partly right – you *are* learning to defend rather than attack, but there're some subtleties ye're missing here. Get back in the center and close yer eyes, and Alexander'll have one last go at you. Then we'll send you on a little outing."

Frowning, Elysia traded places with Alexander and closed her eyes. It was just as it had been before: immediate darkness, lightening as the seconds passed and she remained under the sunlight. Unlike that first time, though, she listened from the moment her lashes brushed her cheeks, and she was already aware of Alexander's position: right in front of her, though he would not attack from there. His scent hung in the air all around her, salt mingled with rosewater. *And if it were honey instead of sweat, I would think my mother stood before me.* Putting one hand out, she spun in a quick circle. The air shivered over her outstretched hand. No skin, no body heat.

She waited. He had to get close sometime.

After a minute or more – it felt like an hour – Elysia felt something, a brush of wind, breath on the back of her neck. One hand out, she whirled, and her wrist was enveloped in rough heat.

When she opened her eyes, he stood over her, so close that his shoulder-length blond hair hung in her face. He held her wrist next to his neck; if he had failed to catch it, she would have caught him in the throat. His eyes were the gray of storm clouds becalmed in the sky, just waiting to loose their rains.

"Who wins?" she asked.

"This match goes to Elysia," her father answered, much to her surprise. Herod nodded beside Khronos. "If you were the prey, you would have had a fighting chance to get yourself away."

"Now, that outing," Alexander said, dropping her wrist. "If we're to tune your instincts, I know just the place."

9

Alone, Elysia and Alexander hiked back to his house. The sun had risen high over Acrocorinth, but Alexander led them under the shade of the huts, each taller than the last. Still, Elysia was sweating by the time they reached the niche where Herod's family lived. "I'll be back in a moment," said Alexander, and before she could protest his leaving her outside in the sun, he climbed the stone stairs. Elysia couldn't tell just how high they went, but the house was nearly fifteen feet tall and the stairs were dangerously steep.

He was back in less than a minute, but what he brought with him was a surprise: Korinna, dark hair shining in the sunlight, her arms laden with some kind of harness. "Alexander says you're going climbing," she said, dumping the harness – two of them, she saw now – into Elysia's arms.

"First I've heard of it," Elysia replied.

Korinna and Alexander both studied her before shrugging. "We're going to visit the Highs," Alexander said.

Korinna groaned, and Elysia raised an eyebrow at Alexander. "Highs?"

"Higher Acrocorinthians. We call them Highs, and high they are." He pointed upward.

The cliff soared almost fifty feet – far higher than it had looked from their approach, and far steeper. "We're to climb *that*?" It rose nearly vertical, bluish stone pitted with age and weather, growing sparse gray moss in places. It sported loose sand where ledges had formed, and she could just imagine what that would do to her grip.

"We are," replied Alexander. Korinna gave her a grin that was almost cruel.

They led Elysia around their house, where the hut had been squeezed uncomfortably close to the cliff. A rope dangled forlornly from the cliff face, one end on the ground, coiled in a way that suggested it might reach up and strike her.

Alexander put his harness on. "We're going to climb in *those*?" she asked. The harness was a contraption made of tied ropes with a metal buckle here or there, some spotted with rust. "They look unsafe."

"They will serve, and have long done so," Alexander replied, tightening a buckle. The skirt of his tunic rode up until he pulled it down along the rope that he rode like a saddle – in the end, the tunic's skirt overlapped in a makeshift breechclout. Korinna tied his harness to the rope that dangled, feeding it through a loop and leaving a few feet at the end.

After that, it was Elysia's turn to struggle with a harness. Korinna showed her how to arrange her skirt while Alexander laughed, much to her chagrin. She berated him for making fun of her a few times before she gave up and tried not to laugh at herself.

In the end, both she and Alexander were tied to the end of the same rope through loops on the fronts of their harnesses. "Korinna will keep control of the rope and give us as much slack as we need," he explained as the girl put on her own harness. Korinna's looked far sturdier than their own, complete with a few more buckles. The most notable thing about it, however, was that it was anchored to a rock which stood in the space between the house and the cliff face. Korinna uncoiled the rope and fed it through a loop in her harness, until the dangling end of the rope – the one that Alexander and Elysia were tied to – was taut.

"Go on up now," Korinna said. She gave Elysia a little wave and jiggled the rope. "My job is to make sure you don't hit the ground before the rope goes taut. It usually works."

"*Usually*?" But Alexander tugged her rope, and she followed him to stand before the cliff.

"There are a couple of bodylengths between us. Stay close enough that you can see where I put my hands and feet, but not close enough to brush the soles of my feet."

It was then that she realized that Alexander had come out of his house without shoes on, his bare feet brown with pale nails. She looked down at her own feet, shod in riding sandals that had covered toes and heels. "Should I take my sandals off?"

Alexander looked down at her feet and grimaced. "That would be a definite yes. You won't be able to find toeholds with those."

Quickly, she unlaced her sandals and kicked them off. Korinna gave her a nod, and then she and Alexander found their first handhold, a shallow dip in the rock.

"Put your hand in this," he said. "Most of them are going to be like this, shallow and smooth, barely enough to hold onto. That's why we'll go fast until we find the ones we can really sink our hands into, the ones with lips or ledges to rest on." When she nodded, he smiled. "Good. Don't look down."

And he was off, crawling up the cliff face like a spider. It was all she could do to remember where he'd put his feet as he took off, and then find the handhold she needed to pull herself up.

By the time they were five feet from the ground, she had disregarded his advice and looked down. She had her hands in a pair of shallow bowls, their curves deep enough to hold onto; her feet were far apart, but she reached for her next toehold as she looked. Korinna made a face at her and she made one in return, squinching up her brows and wrinkling her nose. She was of a height with Herod's roof. It was thatched with what had once been yellow straw, now going gray in places and black in others.

The rope went taut on her hips. "What did I tell you about looking down?"

She looked up, and found Alexander scowling down. "It's only five feet, and *you're* looking down." He was at fifteen feet himself.

"That may be, but I have done this many more times than you have," he said. "Look down, and you'll get vertigo and panic. My poor sister will have to hold your weight when you fall." Frowning, he took another step up the wall. "You're holding us up."

How strict, she thought, but when she got up to fifteen feet, she found out why – the handholds were far too shallow to hold onto for more than a few seconds. Alexander was five feet above her, taking his rest on a ledge.

And she couldn't find the next foothold.

"I'm stuck," she muttered. "I'm stuck, I'm stuck, I'm stuck." Groaning, she looked up. His feet dangled over the edge, the rope taut above him.

"What's that?" Alexander called, not budging.

"I'm stuck!"

He said nothing.

She scanned the wall, looking for a handhold, but didn't see one. The bright sun shone on the wall, eliminating the shadows that had told her where to look. Her steady leg was sore now, her arms trembling from strain. Korinna was silent below. Uncertain, Elysia reached out with her dangling leg, toe against the wall, looking for a foothold in the rough stone, and found only pain as her toe scraped over a groove in the rock. The farther apart her legs got, the farther up the weakness traveled; soon, they shook with her arms. "I'm going to fall, Alexander." Fear shot through her stomach, breathed into her lungs.

Alexander leaned over the ledge. "Find a toehold."

She looked down. She regretted it. She had been staring at the rock in front of her, searching out a ledge by feel, but now she drew in a sharp breath laced with panic. She knew it wasn't as far as it looked – they weren't even halfway there yet – but all the same, it looked far. If she fell, she was sure she would break at least one leg. As she looked down, Korinna was not in her line of sight, though the rope above her and the one beside her were taut. *She must be there*. Anxiety gnawed at her.

All at once, her leg gave way and she gasped. She held to the wall with one hand and scrambled for the rope with the other. But her remaining hand slipped, and she dropped like a stone with a scream – but only a foot and a half.

She hung in the air, the harness pinching at her thighs and around her hips. The breeze spun her, turning her about as she sat in her harness, holding onto the rope to keep herself upright. Her first breath was the sweetest she'd ever tasted.

"Hey, you up there!" Looking down, Elysia saw Korinna, both hands clutched tight around her end of the rope. "Get back on the wall, or you'll pull Alexander off too."

Above her, she saw Alexander leaning over his ledge, the rope that connected her to him held tight in his hands. "Sooner would be better than later," he admitted.

Scrambling to find holds on the wall with Alexander's guidance, Elysia pulled herself from the grips of the wind. And then she was off, as he had been, wriggling up the wall as fast as she could tow her body up it.

At the ledge, she took her first breath free of panic. Alexander turned to her as she heaved in air. "Did you have that feeling, the fear that gripped you?"

She nodded.

"Those are your instincts. You need to awaken to them, to hear them whispering to you, or shouting at you. Without them, you are prey so ignorant that anyone could catch you unawares. *Pay attention to what your body tells you*. Do you understand?"

Something nudged at the back of her mind. "You want me to be afraid all the time?"

"Not afraid, aware. There is a difference."

"Is that so? And, pray tell, what is the difference?"

"You will feel it, I'm certain," Alexander replied, standing up. "It is the difference between knowing your rope is sound and thinking you might die today." He offered her his hand.

She took it and let him heave her to her feet. The sun beat down, and Elysia's fingers were slippery with sweat, but she wiped them on the rocks. He showed her the first handholds and they set off towards the top again.

And now, she was free.

The wind was at her hair, cool on the tingle that made her nerve endings feel alive. The foot-and-a-half plummet had her wanting to spin the way nothing else had before, had her wanting to take a deep breath of coastal salt air. She wanted to breathe in the wind as it fled from her lungs, and maybe if she climbed high enough, she would be able to taste starlight. All was exhilaration. It was like that the rest of the climb, up and up and up against blue-gray stone and brushes of falling sands, every muscle stronger than it had been before.

Alexander pulled her onto the top of the mountain, and she let out a whoop so wild it felt like a fleeing animal escaped from her mouth. *This is the roof of the world.* From their vantage point, Corinth stretched out before them, the Lechaion a long white snake starting at one end of the city that disappeared toward the coast. The wind ripped at her tunic, still held down by her harness. Alexander slipped his own off, the rope and buckles clinking as they hit the ground. "Should I take my harness off too?" she asked.

He looked at her and smiled. "I doubt we'd ever get it back on you. No, here." He slipped the rope from the front of her harness and coiled it on the ground near his own. "Just pretend you aren't shaped oddly for a time."

She laughed, then tried adjusting the harness. "This is ridiculous." It looked as though an angry cat clung to the front of her dress.

She heard Alexander laugh, too, a sound as rough as his hands and deep, but the sound came not from where she had last seen him, standing beside her. Instead, she found him with legs dangling over the edge, looking down at his house fifty feet below.

"Isn't it dangerous to sit there?" Elysia asked, taking a single step closer. The wind screamed over the ledge, pushing and pulling at her until she went to her knees behind the shelter of his back.

"My brother and I once frequented this place," he replied. "It's not as dangerous as it seems, but it's good that you're paying attention to your fear." He scooted back from the edge to sit beside her. "Now this is just a training method. The magic is almost gone for me." Leaning back on his elbows, Alexander looked up at the sky. "Once, we were gulls on the winds that rush up over this cliff. Korinna still comes up here to fly."

"Fly?" she asked, though her mind still focused on the mention of a brother. Had that been the voice she'd heard, up in the house? Neither Alexander nor Herod had been home at the time of their visit, yet there had been a man's voice in the eaves.

"We call it flying, but it's letting the wind hold you up as you lean over the cliff."

Elysia blinked. "That sounds more terrifying than magical." Despite the rush she'd just had, she didn't want to *fall* back down the mountain – she wanted to go down the way she'd gone up: safely.

"I'll show you sometime," Alexander said.

She paused, then asked the question that had bothered her since she'd met him. "How did you learn to speak so well?"

He turned to look at her, brows arched. "You noticed?"

"There's a marked difference between you and your father."

"There is." He scratched behind one ear thoughtfully. "When a girl named Branimira learned to defend herself from my father, her mother Metrodora repaid us with lessons in Greek courtesy."

Understanding clicked in Elysia's mind. "And so you learned."

"And so we learned."

But Korinna as is as spunky as any girl I've met. The teachings must not have taken as deep a root as they had in Ianthe. "Herod did not learn, though."

Alexander laughed so loudly the sound must have carried to the bottom of Acrocorinth. "*Herod* thought the lessons were worthless. Mother thought we must needs have a weapon more than our strength, for the Corinthians fight with intrigue."

Elysia nodded. "I've been told."

They sat at the top of the cliff for a few moments more, looking out over the world. Hills and valleys rose and fell to the south, and blue-green water winked at them in the sunlight in the north. Eventually, Korinna called up at them, her voice a high phantom on the wind.

Elysia let Alexander tie her back on the line. He stood over her as he had during their match, his face shadowed by long blond hair as he tied the knot on her harness. He smelled more of sweat than rosewater now, though she supposed she did, as well: climbing the hill, climbing the cliff, their battle... All had had her sweating – and at the start of all of that, she had been caked with the dust of the road. *I must look disgusting and smell worse.* Alexander made no comment.

They rappelled down the mountain most of the way, but it was up to Elysia to lead: once again, she was on the bottom of the rope, and on the way down, that meant she went first. The hardest part was climbing off the ledge next to the anchor, for Alexander had to hold onto the rope that connected them as she went over; finding handholds without looking all the way down was no easy task. Once she and Alexander had made it over the edge, however, Korinna quickly lowered them.

At the bottom, Elysia shook hands with the younger girl. "Thank you."

Korinna merely shrugged. "Thank Father and Alexander. I do this every day."

Alexander stepped out of his harness beside her. Undoing her buckles herself this time, Elysia let her harness drop and stepped out of its many loops. "Thank you, Alexander," she said, and offered him her hand.

He looked more surprised at her gesture than expected, but gently shook her hand.

"You're welcome," said Korinna with a roll of her eyes. Arms crossed, the dark-haired girl lead them to the front of the house. "Is Elysia staying for dinner, Alexander?" she asked, and Elysia felt Korinna's probing eyes. "We'll have to dump a vat of rosewater over her head to get her clean and fresh."

Elysia reddened. "She certainly doesn't sound like a student of Metrodora's," she said to Alexander.

He shook his head. "She can when she wants to. She just doesn't want to." To Korinna he said, "Not unless her father says she is. Have you seen him?"

"No."

"Then I suppose she won't be staying."

Korinna nodded and turned on her heel, flying up the steps and into the tall house.

Alexander walked her back to their fathers on the plateau. "Tomorrow we'll play that game again," he told her, "but we'll start you on your first round of techniques, too, and see how well you learn those."

They found Herod and Khronos sheltering in the shade between a few huts. "Light her torch, Alexander?" Herod asked. The grin the old man gave her *felt* dirty.

"The torch of her instincts is what I'm certain you meant, Father," Alexander replied. He put a warm hand on her shoulder, his skin scoured clean by the rocks, despite the dirt beneath his nails. "It's good and lit, wouldn't you agree, Elysia?"

"I would." Following her father's eyes, she found them locked on Alexander's hand on her shoulder. She ducked out from beneath it and stood beside her father. "If that's the lesson for today, I would like to go home and clean myself up. Will you excuse us?" she asked.

"Of course," Alexander replied, though Herod crossed his arms and looked at her with suspicion. "I'll see you tomorrow."

Exhaustion set in as Elysia and Khronos walked down the hill. "I'll be red as a pomegranate in the morning," she complained as they reached the chariot. "Did you know they were going to send me up the mountain?"

"I had an inkling," her father said, giving her a sly half-smile. "Telling your mother she'd have to climb the hillside was Herod's favorite threat when she didn't perform to his satisfaction. I thought he might say the same to you, but... His sons are old enough to escort others up now, so he can follow through with it."

The horses greeted them with whinnies when they heard Khronos's voice. Delia slipped out from behind the curtain in her doorway; the teeth dangling from the awning rattled against the bone pins in her hair. With one look at Elysia and her soiled tunic, Delia smirked. "Herod put you through the grinder on your first day, did he?"

Elysia shook her head. "His son, Alexander."

Delia quirked a brow as Khronos harnessed the horses once more, but the woman said nothing. Elysia donned her gray dress at her father's behest – he wouldn't have her stoned by a passing Higher Acrocorinthian before they even reached the city. The fabric was smooth and cool on her scraped hands, wrinkled from being balled up in his arms. The air was too hot to wear the dress over her tunic, however, so Elysia asked Delia if she might change in her house.

The horses were fully harnessed when she came out, and quick as she stepped into the cart, they headed back to the city.

Something about the journey away from Acrocorinth was different to Elysia than the journey there, as though she breathed new air. Everything seemed more real: the gulls and crows wheeling above her, the horses trotting in tandem, the jingling of the harnesses' buckles. *Awareness*, she thought.

My instincts are awoken.

10

The next day, every jolt and bounce of the chariot drove a hot iron through her muscles.

She had stretched as Philip had shown her when they returned to the house, but she did not do it soon enough; her muscles had stiffened long before they'd made it back to the gates. Adrastos had leered at her and Zeus had frowned when they saw her in Khronos's chariot, but neither had delayed them. A bath had waited for her after she'd stretched, much to her relief. Aliya and the other ladies kept the doors and windows veiled, barring anyone else from entering the back room while she bathed in the pottery tub her father had procured. They doused her in rosewater and rebraided her hair.

They had been silent through the whole ritual. Aliya had frowned at her scraped palms, hip, and knees, but kept her disapproval to herself.

Now, her second day of training was upon her, and each muscle was sore from the day before. Her scratches and scrapes had turned a healing pink. Her bruises, on the other hand, had deepened to dark purple; she had two on her chest, where the heels of Alexander's hands had slammed into the space just below her collarbone. No matter what she tried, they remained, two shadows glaring out above her neckline. Her toes were sore in their sandals, her hips bruised near to the bone: one from Herod's staff and the other from the fall that followed. *All* of her was sunburned, but it was not enough to dissuade her (or her father) from getting in the chariot.

Every bruise was a beacon that would tell Alexander where she was weak, and her sore muscles and sunburns made her slow.

It will be a wonder if I survive this day.

Acrocorinth loomed high above them, staring down as they approached. Elysia climbed the hillside after they turned the horses over to Delia, resigned to the beating she would receive today. They stopped halfway up, where they found Alexander waiting to lead them to the hidden plateau.

When he and Elysia stood in the center of the barren ground, once again in the shadow of the mountain and the morning, the lesson began.

"Today, you will learn techniques to release you from three holds," Alexander said. He circled her with hands clasped behind his back, a hawk surveying his prey. "My father will judge how well you're doing before we move onto the next technique."

Herod nodded from the shadow of a house, resting his chin on the end of his walking staff. His brown eyes glinted in the dim light; Khronos stood beside him, leaning against the whitewashed mud brick of a hut.

"First," Alexander began, "Getting out of a chokehold." He took a big step toward her and reached for her.

Though she backed away as quickly as she could, he caught her around the neck, his hands hot on her sunburn. The pressure made it sear, but he did not squeeze – just held her firmly enough that she could not slip away. "Now that I've caught you," he said, gazing down at her, "Put your hand up and sweep it back, like you're pushing your hair out of your eyes. You have to raise your arm *inside* the circle of mine, else you're only fixing your hair."

She swept her elbow under the arm that held her throat, forcing her upper arm into his wrist.

"Good. Now, turn – no, not that way. The *other* way," he said as she turned toward the hand that still held her. "If you turn this way, the fact that you have loosened my grip means nothing, and you lose the element of surprise. Try again."

This time, she spun out of his grasp and into the sweet arms of freedom. "I did it!" she exclaimed, grinning.

Her father chuckled from the edge of the plateau and Herod clapped slowly. "You did," said Alexander. "Do it again."

She spun out of his hands so many times she became dizzy, first going one way and then the other, his fingers always finding her neck again. They went faster and faster until the world was a blur as she whirled away from him, the skirt of her tunic flaring out with every turn. She tasted dirt from the dust she'd kicked up.

At last, Herod stopped them. "Yer done with this one," he said. "Find the girl some water 'fore she wilts, then do the chokehold from behind."

The water they found was in a jug, which Korinna brought down from the eaves of the house: sweet, clear, and cool. When they finished ladling it out and each had their share, they thanked her, but she followed them back to the plateau, hauling the heavy jug along with her.

"You don't have to come with us, Kor," said Alexander to his younger sister, but mischief flickered in his eyes just as it did in Korinna's.

"Yes, I do," she replied. "I'm certain that Father and Khronos will be wanting refreshment... Although Father would doubtless prefer wine." Her dry humor did not seem lost on her brother, but Alexander did not laugh.

Both men were grateful for the water, but Khronos frowned when he realized he'd been offered water instead of wine. "You do not mean to poison us, I'm sure," said he, "but isn't it dangerous to drink this?" He took a hesitant sip from the ladle, eyes on his daughter. "How much did you drink, Elysia?"

"A few spoonfuls."

Herod shook his head. "Korinna fetches water from the spring at the summit every day. It's clean." He growled the words, threatening Khronos to give offense, but Elysia's father said nothing.

Korinna found a perch on a boulder between two huts. And from her perch, she jeered Elysia and cheered her older brother once they began again. "She'll swoon like a rose once you get your hands around her neck, brother," she said, smirking at Elysia as she squared off against Alexander.

I'll show you what a rose I am, she thought. *A rose wild enough to have thorns.*

"The second hold you'll escape is a chokehold from behind," Alexander said. He circled her again, his hands in front of him this time. "Stay still."

She stopped turning with him, and he disappeared from her peripheral vision. Suddenly, there were fingers on her throat again. When he spoke, his voice was right above her ear; she felt the warmth of his breath, and the scent of roses was in the air again. It took a deep breath to calm the nerves in the pit of her stomach. *My instincts don't like this*, she thought, but another feeling tied her stomach in knots, too – a shivery, tingly feeling that she hadn't felt before. "Now," he said, voice soft, "put your arms straight up and twist."

It worked like magic.

She threw her arms into the air and jerked away. Her arms collided with Alexander's wrists, and like a flash, she was free of his grip. When she looked back at him, surprise was written on his face and his arms hung in midair. Even Korinna's mouth was agape.

"That was fast," said the younger girl.

"It was fast," agreed Herod, "but it's also easy. Do it a few more times and move on."

By the time they finished, she was dizzy again, and Alexander shook the ache from his wrists.

"Last one will get a bit more into your personal space, crone," said Herod from the sidelines. Elysia crossed her arms, glaring at him.

When Alexander had stretched the last of the soreness from his wrists, he circled her once more. The sun peeked up over the top of Acrocorinth now, washing them in golden light. "Be still," he said, and she lost him in the glare of the sunlight.

Then his arms were around her, trapping her arms to her sides in a flash of heat. Flinching away, she tried to escape his grasp, but he held her tight.

"You're doing it wrong, princess," called Korinna from her rock.

"Drop your weight," said Alexander. He followed her every move, inch for inch, skin to skin. "Don't let me lift you."

She did as she was told, but she must have done it wrong; he lifted her as if she were a child with her arms around his neck. Setting her back down on the ground, he said, "Drop it further. You've decided you want to take a seat on the ground."

Biting her lip, she let herself fall toward the ground as he lifted her, and they were suddenly frozen, neither able to move. "Good," he said.

"How do I get out of this?" she asked. He still held her, arms tight around her waist.

"That is a lesson for tomorrow," Alexander said. "For now, it is eno-"

"Bah, let 'er do it," rasped Herod. Elysia looked to him, craning her neck around Alexander's side. "Just make sure she doesn't make contact. You've got my nose, I want ye to keep it."

Eyes wide, Elysia glanced up at Alexander. "Your nose?"

He sighed, then shook his head. "This is a bad idea." He reaffirmed his grip on her. "Drop your weight like I showed you. When you've done that, whip your head back to hit my face, but twist away at the same time. On the count of three."

She nodded.

"One. Two. Three."

She dropped like a stone. Alexander leaned forward, and she tipped her head back – and met only air. She felt his breath on the side of her neck where he'd dodged to the left. Spinning away from him, Elysia ripped out of his grasp. Her arms stung, her sunburns ached where his hands scrabbled at her. *More bruises.* She whirled uncontrolled and landed in the dirt, front first. The heels of her hands tore open for the second time in two days when she caught herself, and her knees skinned their scars anew. Her chin and her bottom lip hit the ground hard. Breath heaving in her chest, she sat up little by little, using her fingers to push herself up. She leaned back on her freshly bloodied knees.

Nobody rushed to her side. Not her father, not Alexander, not Herod, not Korinna. They stared at her; not a single foot or sandal scuffed in the dirt. Straightening her short skirt to cover her legs, Elysia spat out a mouthful of blood and wiped more from her face, then got to her feet and surveyed her knees. Well and truly scraped, they had black sand embedded in red flesh. She did her best to brush it out, ignoring the shards of pain sent up her legs; her hands burned most. They had larger chunks of rock in them. "Well," she said, turning to face her teachers, her father, and her little jeerer. "Shall we do it again?"

They did it again, and again and again. She fell twice more as she ripped away from him, his fingers still clutching at her elbows. Exasperated, she said, "There must be a cleaner way to do this."

"There is," said Alexander, "but you'll learn that later."

When she went home, she was more sunburned, bruised, and thoroughly beaten than she had been the day before. When they passed Adrastos and Zeus, they wore open stares, but she smirked at them as they had to her. The chariot and the red dress she wore over her tunic covered her knees, but her scratched face and swollen lip were evident enough. "You beating your precious, respected daughter, Khronos?" Adrastos asked.

Defiant glee flashed through her.

"She's been taking it upon herself to find new ways to get beaten," her father replied, and Elysia grinned a bloody grin, certain her teeth were stained red.

When Philip saw her, though, he was none too happy. "Yesterday she went rock climbing, and if that weren't dangerous enough, now they're beating her?" His voice rose, irate, brazen, and painful to Elysia's ears.

Sitting on the cushioned couch in the back room, Elysia pulled the leather strap from the end of her hair and unbraided it. "The *ground* beat her, Phil," she said, scowling. Khronos had his arms crossed but hadn't taken the bait. Philip had lungs of iron and could outlast anyone in a shouting match; he'd proven it when he'd gotten into whinnying matches with the horses.

"The ground." He rolled his eyes at her. "So says every woman who's ever been beaten. *I fell.*" She felt his disgust in her marrow.

"*Look* at where my scrapes are, Philip!" Getting to her feet, she shoved her hands at him. "Palms." Ripping her hem aside, she showed him her raw knees. "Knees." She pointed at her face. "Chin. How many times did I fall as a girl and have these same scrapes? *How many?* And now you would blame the same injuries on my tutors. Should I blame all the falls I had as a toddler on you?" Heat rose up her neck. She finished quietly, retaking her seat. "I don't think so. If you can't handle watching me get beat up, or even seeing the scrapes and bruises, you should go somewhere where the sight of me won't offend you."

"The sight of you could never offend me," said Philip.

"But the idea of me being hurt offends you."

"Shouldn't it? You're more to me than anything I've ever known." He took a step toward her, skirting the tub.

Khronos, who stood in the doorway, took a step forward as well, though his appeared slightly more threatening.

"You've known that I would have to pass this test since before I could speak. How can I learn to defend myself if not by practicing? Wounds heal, bruises fade."

Philip's jaw clenched, his teeth gritting as his muscles tightened. "Wounds fester, and no man should have the right to beat you. These *teachers* of yours, why can't they *tell* you how to defend yourself instead of pounding it into you?"

She wanted to scream at him, speak reason to him until he understood, but what could she say that had not already been said? "No man *has* the right to beat me. If you must, you may come and see how these teachers of mine *teach* me. It will be a lesson for you, and if you cannot learn, I will see the back of you as you walk out that door. Do you understand?"

The muscles in his arms flexed as he crossed them tighter. "I will not promise to hold my tongue, but I will be there."

"Good. You will ride the sorrel on the morrow. Leave us," she said. The tightness in her throat burned.

Philip swallowed the command, but only just. Bowing, he said, "My lord, my lady," and went back into the front room, avoiding Khronos. The curtain swirled angrily as he passed.

Elysia's eyes closed, and she covered her face with a hand. "What have I done?"

A deep voice answered, so close she jumped – her father had remained so quiet that she had expected him to meet this episode with silence. "Encouraged him, I assume."

She groaned into her hand, but her father pulled it away from her face. "He has loved you for so long, Lys. If he thinks you feel the same way about him, he will do anything to keep you safe. You've become his. Be careful, and don't break him, please." Khronos smiled at her. "He's the best horsemaster I've had in a long time."

With a frustrated sigh, Elysia nodded acquiescence. As she finished unbraiding her hair, Aliya came from the garden and ushered Khronos from the room. She lifted pails of cool water into the tub. Undoing her belt, Elysia slipped her dress over her head and dropped it on the floor. She took a step into the tub and sat, letting the water wash over her battered body. The welcome chill soothed her sunburns and fiery scrapes. *I shouldn't have scolded him*, she thought, but at the same time, it felt right. *He should not have jumped to those conclusions so quickly, and what else could he think was going to happen?* Philip knew exactly what she had to do, knew of the tests; he probably knew the third but had been sworn to secrecy.

It will never work. Not between us. The evidence had presented itself: Philip was made to take care of horses, not a woman, cruel though the thought might be. At least, he was not made to take care of *her*. She was a child that he loved, become a woman. She did not need taking care of.

And had he the choice, he would keep her caged. "Under his protection," he would call it. She would be locked away in some dim house, spinning and weaving – once she knew how – for the rest of her days and only adventuring with *him* for the rest of her life.

She had been raised to be free.

Aliya poured rosewater over her hair. Scrubbing at it with her fingers, Elysia dunked her head in the water. *I am not some idle Greek girl to stay in one place forever.* Though she had spent her life in the house in her valley, she'd been free to roam, free to ride her sorrel and explore the hills, free to do as she pleased. The humans, with their lewdness and violence, were the reason she had stayed there.

Dirt and sweat unfurled through the water, swirling in the current of her splashing. The morning would see her dressed in her tattered tunic, but for now, she wore only rosewater. In the morning, she'd square off against Alexander, but for now, her thoughts squared off against him.

She had felt something today. It was a strange feeling, halfway between the soaring, heart-wrenching panic she'd had when she fell off the mountain and the giddy ball of nerves she'd been when she'd run her sorrel the first time. It also hadn't been the anxious anticipation that he would attack her. *Something else*, she thought. *It was something else.*

That feeling had risen whenever his skin brushed hers, a flash of heat that wasn't sunburn. Splashing out her frustrations like a child, Elysia managed to shower nearly the whole room with water. Aliya held up a sheet to shield herself from flying droplets; she was far from inexperienced when it came to Elysia's moods.

When she'd toweled off, pulled a new dress over her head, and slid back into her sandals, Elysia found her father sitting in the garden. Alone, sitting on a marble bench beside a rose bush, he looked as content as she'd ever seen him.

She could hardly bear to interrupt his peace. "Father," she murmured. He looked at her, and something wistful danced in the soft lines around his eyes.

"Elysia." He beckoned her, patting the bench. "Have I told you enough about your mother and I?"

She sat beside him, holding a saffron rose out of the way and arranging its stem on the bush so it wouldn't jump back at her. "Her name has never passed your lips that I can recall." She tried to extract the bitterness from her words, but her father's face told her she'd failed.

"I suppose that is so. But do you know why?"

Because it hurts, because she is gone, and you live. A voice in the back of her mind whispered, *He is the Creator, warden of the veil. He could bring her back.* Elysia shook her head. "No."

"It is because, when we were in the valley, she was not lost to me." Taking one of her hands from their resting place in her lap, he kissed her knuckles, his red-gold whiskers scratching over her fingers. "I had you, and your mother and I spoke almost every night. Our story had not ended. Nothing was in the past when I could see her, hear her voice... And so, because our story went on, I could not tell it. I could not say where it ended." He set her hand back in her lap. "But now it has."

Brows furrowed, she asked, "It has?"

"When we left, I said goodbye to her for the final time. She had wanted for so long to see you off, to send you on your way. Once she had, she begged my leave to go." Melancholy permeated her father's voice, a sadness Elysia had not heard before.

She understood. "You let her have new life."

He nodded. "And now it is time to tell our tale."

11

"We met at the end of the harshest Corinthian winter in memory," Khronos began. Reverence echoed in his voice, and Elysia imagined that he relived everything. "Raiders had put her village to the torch, made off with everything they could carry and destroyed everything they couldn't. Metrodora had disguised her as an old woman – she pinned a skein of wool over Branimira's hair, if either of them are to be believed. She and the elders were chased from the village with whips."

He'd met them at the gate, Metrodora had said. "How did you know they were coming?" she asked.

"I'm always on the lookout for the weary traveler, and the Greeks have not named me 'god of time' without reason," he said. "My sight is a gift, but it comes with a price; it stings like a face full of smoke and bestows upon me a grand headache. But when I mean to use it, I see what could pass. Some days, I would go to a gate and watch for a while, see the shadows of oxcarts and farmers go by, but occasionally, there would be a group of ragged people, refugees.

"When your mother's people came, Poseidon and Amphitrite were glazed with frost, all their creatures iced over, the ground hard and cold. I knew of their coming the autumn before they arrived. On every frosty morning, I stood beside Amphitrite to wait, and as spring neared, one day they finally staggered into the city. Some of the elders had lost fingers, toes, and noses to frostbite, but they had been determined to keep Branimira safe – she was the last of their young people. Cherished, but also the only bargaining chip they had once they came to the city."

"They meant to *sell* her?" asked Elysia.

"For a bride price, yes, if that was what it took to find and keep a roof over their heads. I managed to stall that for a while; I installed them in the house next to ours. I bought them a loom so they could continue their trade – they were weavers and spinners, and they felt that was the only way they could repay me for room and board." Khronos shook his head.

"Just being around them was enough for me. It's quite a lonely thing, living without friends in a city. You will find that neighbors help – Metrodora told you she lives next to us, did she not?"

Elysia nodded.

"Good," Khronos said, and smiled. "She will teach you many things I could not."

Like how to weave, for example, thought Elysia, and smiled back at her father.

"Once they moved in, I spent a lot of time around them, especially Branimira. The elders were determined to marry us once I moved them into my house, but Branimira would not hear of it; she wanted nothing to do with men. During the village raid... She saw her friends raped, her people killed. She wanted nothing to do with me, either, until I told her of a certain group of people who could teach her to protect herself."

"Herod and the Apocorinthians," Elysia supplied. That was how their love story began? With him finding her a teacher to help her militarize herself against men?

"Herod was stubborn as a mule, of course," said Khronos, chuckling. "And he remains so. He didn't think some outsider girl from the north would be able to go through with the demands of the training, but she was the most determined person I've met. She had a fire, your mother, somewhere deep within her. She knocked him spinning a good few times, and finally, he declared her ready to be finished with her training. After that, she was still wary of me, but she had all the weapons she needed in her own control. She did not fear me, as she had before, and she started to become fond of me."

"What about your adventures? Was that all she did, weave and learn to protect herself?"

Khronos laughed, the walled courtyard ringing with the sound. "No, that wasn't *all* she did. We went all over the city, exploring and hunting down craftsman's shops. We prayed at a few of the temples, climbed Acrocorinth... But only on the days she tore herself away from weaving. Or rather, on the days that *I* tore her away from weaving. When she needed new wool to spin, or had thread to dye, I would find some excuse to keep her out the rest of the day. Her elders were half scandalized and half looking forward to our marriage, but..."

"You wouldn't marry her." *We are property*, her mother had said. "She did not want to become yours."

"She wanted to be her own, and that was something I respected," he agreed. "But when the elders tried to marry her to Adrastos, I intervened. I offered a bride price worth far more than any other man would have paid for a high-strung, foreign wife, and forced their hands. We were married then, and she hated me for it."

"*Why?*"

"Because I did not ask her first. Quite a fickle thing, your mother. But that only lasted a few days. I told her I would gladly be her husband, but only in name, if that was what she wished. I loved her, but I would have been her friend if that was what she wanted. It wasn't, though. She loved me as much as I loved her – she just hadn't wanted to show it."

"Then what?" asked Elysia, sitting forward in her seat a little.

"Then it was much the same," said Khronos. "We wove, she lived in the house with me, and we went on our little adventures... But mostly, we wove. I had already been working on the tapestries in the house – I had begun them when I first saw the refugees, so they might have a home when they came to the city. Alas, I spent too many days waiting for them, once the frosts began, and it took your mother and I another few years to finish them. It was a greater project than I had first envisioned. But between our marriage and our finishing the tapestries, Metrodora had wandered in, nearly a year behind the rest of her people, with a son on the way. We remained only long enough for the birth; Branimira wanted to drown the boy, but her mother would not allow it. They parted on poor terms, but part they did, and we left for the valley, where you were born." Khronos picked a blushing rose and slid it into her braid. "You were our bright light."

"But she died," Elysia murmured.

"Not because of you, sweet one," Khronos said, lifting her chin with a warm hand. "It was her own choice. She could have lived with us for eternity, but she did not wish to. I gave her the same choice you have been given, though hers did not come with tests; she would have been too ill to complete them. She chose death over immortality, and she did so every time I offered it to her. More than anything, she wanted to have new life, to forget the things she had heard, seen. And at last, when she thought she finally had her new life, I, in my bitterness, stole it away from her."

"But she loved you," Elysia said. "She loved me."

"I made her choose between love and release. As long as I had the ability to keep her with me, she was torn. When I told her of your leaving, she knew it was her time for new life. She needed to say goodbye."

Mira's words rang through her ears: *I have a hold over him not many can boast*. "Father," Elysia said, and put a hand on his arm.

Khronos looked at her, tearing himself away from what must have been the reminiscence in his mind's eye.

The desperation, a tightness in her chest, melted into a smile. It was the kind of smile that made her eyes glaze with tears and emotions rise in her chest. "I'm glad I got to meet her."

Khronos watched her and smirked, then clapped her on the back. "I miss seeing that smile." Standing, he offered his hand and pulled her to her feet. Above the blue-gray stones of the courtyard, the sky had turned to vermilion brindled with gold, the clouds blushing around their edges. "But now it's time to sleep."

Sleep did not come easily for her that night, despite the comfort of her pillows and soft warm woolens. Instead, her mind was alive with anxious thoughts, speculations about the morning to come. If Philip picked a fight, he would lose. Where Alexander moved like a cat, Philip was like a bull in a fight: he charged with his head down, beating his assailant with brute force. He and Ares had sparred in the warehouse when she was little. She'd snuck down to watch them when no one watched her, eyes wide as they batted at each other with padded mitts.

If Alexander moved like a cat and Philip like a bull, Philip had no chance if he wanted a fight. Even Herod was fearsome with his walking stick, and her father would no doubt beat Philip into the ground should he raise a hand against her tutors. She could not, however, see Philip doing anything else if Alexander even laid a hand on her on the morrow; he had proected her his whole life.

Rolling over under her furs, Elysia took a deep breath and let it out. Tomorrow would come and pass, and at the end of the day, she would have learned something.

Whether that something would be about Philip or Alexander, she was not certain.

12

The day dawned bright and clear, though Elysia had prayed for rain.

If it had rained, they might not have been able to take the chariot, and her lesson would have been canceled.

With a sigh, she slipped on her blue dress and tunic. Aliya had worked her magic overnight; the undyed wool of the tunic was clean of blood, mud, and sweat. Philip wandered in from the courtyard. Khronos was already up at the front of the house, pulling bread from a basket and laying it out on the table. Philip rubbed his eyes. "It's hardly dawn," he yawned.

"You awoke *before* dawn in the valley," she said, taking her seat on a stool.

Philip ate his bread and honey standing up. "The city tires me," he complained.

In truth, the sounds of the city kept her awake at night, as well. People walked by the windows at odd hours, their feet scuffing on the road; cats yowled, and occasionally, a scream in the night chilled her bones. She had never missed her room so much, with the silent press of sun-warmed marble walls surrounding her. Never had she tried to sleep through the sounds of another in the same room; here, she shared a room with her father, and his rhythmic breathing was worse than the snores that came noisily out of his throat at any hour of darkness.

"Would you rather not go?" she asked, but she knew it was a fool's hope. She was as stuck to him today as a snail was stuck to its shell.

"Of course I'm going," said Philip, roughing up her hair. She felt the stickiness of honey as he pulled his hand away.

She shoved back at him with a bit of vengeance in mind, but Philip backed out of reach and headed out the door.

Once the white horses were harnessed to the chariot, Philip saddled the sorrel; all four horses had been stabled in the deserted house next to them. It was not ideal, but it kept the animals warm, and the house's courtyard had a fountain with clean water and sweet grasses for grazing.

The house, of the same grayish blue stone as the others, had been so long abandoned that Khronos said thieves didn't bother checking it anymore – it had been picked clean.

Though she had wanted to spend time with her sorrel, Philip was so quick in readying the mare that they were under way before Elysia had looked twice at her. Calm as ever, the sorrel followed them at a jaunty pace, her forelock bouncing as she tried to keep up with the white racers harnessed to the chariot.

The journey from the city sped by as they rattled over holes, cobbles, and marble. When they passed the guards, the now-familiar white-blond Zeus and the graying Adrastos, the pair were too busy watching the incoming farmers' carts and oxen to notice them.

Once clear of the city, they drew nearer and nearer to the cool shadow that Acrocorinth cast in the morn. Vast and thirsty, it drank in light like a horse sucking down water after a long ride. Soon, they were beneath it, part of it, and for a moment she wondered if that made her part of the mountain – if, for a moment, she was an Acrocorinthian, or if she would one day be counted among its peoples.

When they met Alexander halfway up the hill, Philip was surprised. "I thought Herod tutored you," he whispered as Alexander took the lead and wove between mud brick hovels, most of them emptied as their residents headed for work in the city. "Does this young man spar with you?"

"Yes."

That inflamed him, but so did her bare legs when she handed her dress to her father, revealing the knee-length tunic underneath. "You spar in *that*?" he asked, all incredulity. "And you let him touch you? That's just indecent."

"I don't *let* him touch me. We spar. It's required to some extent."

"I wouldn't expect you to have an opinion on my daughter's wardrobe, Philip," Khronos said, folding the blue gown in his arms.

Elysia's glare and Khronos's words put down further protests.

"Today," Alexander said as she joined him in the center of the plateau, "you will learn techniques that require cupping the hand." He held out his own hand. The way he held it reminded Elysia of a dish.

"Like this?" She mimicked him, holding her hand the same way, fingers bent at each knuckle.

"Not quite. Come here." He pulled her toward him by her outstretched arm, and somewhere behind them, Philip cleared his throat. Elysia tried to listen to Alexander, but the uncomfortable awareness that Philip watched her colored her every move. "They should be a little less bent," Alexander said, shaping each of her fingers until the curve of her hand looked more like the bowing of an overstuffed pillow than a deep bowl. His touched warmed her, and something high and nervous shot through her gut.

She took a deep breath to calm the feeling, and that was when she realized Alexander had stopped talking. She found him gazing down at her, gray eyes dancing in the dim light. "All right?" he asked.

"Fine," she murmured, then glanced at Philip. He stood with arms crossed, leaning against a hut. Turning back to Alexander, she added, "Just not accustomed to having more than our fathers for an audience."

He laughed, a short sharp bark. "Get used to it. Korinna has threatened to bring our mother and sundry others to spectate," he warned, his hand still wrapped around her fingers.

She laughed, but it came out breathless from the heat she felt wherever their skin met. "I suppose I'll have to get used to it, then." *And to feeling like this, whatever* this *is.* But Alexander's touch was only half the problem.

Philip's eyes raked across her skin like fingers clutching at her sides, hungry for her. Something had changed in him since his deception on the rocks, since coming to the city, and it made her uneasy. Maybe it was the sight of her bruised and bloody, maybe it was that a man who was not him touched her, but suddenly, he had turned from her gentle, caring protector into someone she had never met who wanted to know her. The way he watched her… Like he was an eagle and she a rabbit, and he waited for the best opportunity to catch her.

Tearing herself away from her thoughts – they served only to make her more anxious – Elysia focused on Alexander. Her hand cupped the way he'd shaped it, she held it up. "Now what?" she asked.

"Now," he said, "you hit me on the shoulder."

She gave him a critical eye. "How would that stop an attacker? It'd be like hitting them with a cushion."

Smirking at her, Alexander shook his head. "This is practice for the techniques. Now do it."

Shaking her head and feeling ridiculous, she swung her hand at his shoulder as he turned it toward her. "How was that?" she asked as he straightened.

Running a hand through his blond hair, Alexander took her hand again. Once she cupped it, he said, "You did this," and splayed warm, rough fingers across hers to flatten her hand. "Keep it cupped, loosen your arm. Try again."

She swung at his shoulder, hand cupped all the way through; the edges of her fingers stung where she'd struck him. "Better," he said, "but now you're swinging from back here." He pulled her arm past her hip, where it stuck out at an angle behind her body. "You need surprise. If an attacker sees your hand back here, he will know where you will strike him, when, and how. Try to keep your hand right at your side." He turned his shoulder to her, and she hesitated, forcing herself not to reach back behind her at the start of the swing.

When she did hit him, her arm was tight. "Loosen my arm," she said as he made to straighten. This time, she gave him no cause to touch her or criticize her technique. *No cause to tingle but for the sting of my hand on his shoulder, and yet still I do.* Every time she looked at him, something buzzed, but every time she looked at Philip, something angry roared.

They kept at it for half an hour, first one side and then the other, until Elysia thought she had a pair of limp leather straps where once her arms had been. "Teach 'er the moves now she's good and sore," said Herod from the shade of a hut. The sun had peeked out over the mountain, sending sunbeams to land among the mud brick houses and beat the dry brown earth into submission. The earth needed rain, and Elysia needed water. "Maybe she'll go gentle on you."

Alexander shrugged. "Gentle or not, we are sparring." He looked at Elysia. "This is a mock fight, remember, not the real thing. Try to land a hit, and the odds are that I will dodge. You're not trying to hurt me, but you're learning to hurt an attacker – so if you get close, try to stop before you make contact, especially on this technique." He gave her a crooked smile. "I would rather keep my hearing."

He held her arm again, though this time, he brought it up toward his ear. "This is called the ear slap, and it's just what it sounds like," said Alexander, "Whip your hand around just like you've been doing and aim for my ear."

"Ever been slapped in the ear, crone?" Herod asked. "Leaves ya ringing for a good week, throws off yer balance, and hurts to beat all the gods."

Elysia let Philip seethe at the *crone* comment and squared off against Alexander.

"As you're just learning these today," he said, "I won't fight back, but a day will come when I will. Prepare yourself by practicing well."

She jumped at him, leaping inside his guard. He caught her right arm before it reached his elbow, caught her left as it brushed his shoulder. He held her, his hands warming her wrists to the bone. "You swung like you were trying to throw your hands off their wrists," he said, pushing her away from him. The heels of her sandals skidded and crunched in the dirt. "Again."

Somewhere, Philip whispered something furious to her father, but she made her next attack, hands up before she got to him, her elbows between them – but she ran out of room to swing, his hands around her wrists before she could reach sideways and get her power back. "That's the beginning of another technique." He shoved her back. "Again."

Lips pressed together, she stayed in one place until something clicked. "You should be coming at me," she said. "I won't be attacking, I'll be attacked. You have to come into my space." She beckoned him with both hands.

Alexander ran at her on light feet, hands reaching for her shoulders. Once he got hold of them, she put her elbow to her ear and twisted. Whipping all the way around, she swung her arm toward his ear – and stopped. Her hand was so close to his head that only his soft blond hair separated her palm from his ear.

Still shocked that she'd gotten past his defenses, Elysia grinned, her hand remaining right where it had stopped. "I did it," she said.

Alexander pulled her arm down, smiling a broad white smile. "You did."

And then he was on her again, in her space, this time with one hand on her left arm. Breathless and surprised, she whipped her right hand around, until it nearly connected with his other ear.

"Good," said Herod as they stood frozen once more. "Yer instincts 're awake. Next move, Alexander."

Elysia leaned around Alexander's shoulder. Herod looked more awake than he had yesterday, watching them and standing as straight as he was able. "But we've only done this one a few times," she said.

"It's in yer arsenal now, crone," he said, stamping his staff into the ground. "That's what ya want. Don't need any more 'n that."

Alexander nodded. "The next one is simpler," he said, but Elysia held up a hand.

"Water."

Alexander's brow furrowed. "This will only take a few minutes," he said. "After that, we can get water."

Backing out of his space with a sigh, Elysia put her hands on her hips. "Fine."

But Philip was less than acquiescent, standing in his shady corner, surliness rising from him in waves. "She asked for water, *Alex*," he said, and Elysia stiffened; animosity kept his words afloat in the air. "If the Lady Elysia says she wants water, she gets water."

Alexander stood silently, then turned. "I didn't catch your name earlier," he said. His tone was cool, but Elysia sensed his readiness to spring into action against Philip should the opportunity present itself. "What was it, again? If I might beg your pardon."

"Philip." He pushed himself off the brown brick wall of the house he leaned against. "And you may not beg my pardon, young man, as I have none to give to a man who beats a lady."

Beside her, Alexander bristled. Elysia put a hand on his arm, but he brushed her off. "Philip and I have already had this conversation," she said, but the men paid her no mind. Philip had at least five years on Alexander and the bulk to prove it, though Alexander was no stripling boy. Caught in the middle, Elysia's heart sped – and she realized that as soon as she had taken off her long dress, Philip had ached for this. *You have always been freer than any girl under her father's rule has a right to be*. "He knows that I did the beating myself."

"Does he?" asked Alexander.

Don't goad him. Don't.

"He does not seem to, does he, *Phil*?"

"Stand down, Philip," Khronos said, and then, "You started this."

Philip charged them.

Still standing behind Alexander, Elysia froze. *He's not supposed to be like this*, she thought, mind in a panic. Her thoughts collided with each other and wrecked. *He's not. He's my protector, not some savage dog.* When Alexander glanced back and saw her still standing behind him, he grabbed her by the wrist and shoved her out of the way.

Then, Philip bearing down on him, Alexander ducked.

Elysia's hands went to her mouth as Philip flew over Alexander's back, his sandaled feet ramming the younger man in the side as he flipped, fell, and hit the dirt. On his back, Philip groaned, while Alexander rose to his feet, graceful as a panther.

Stiff with shock, Elysia made her hands fall to her side as Philip sat up. Her chest was numb, but somewhere in there, the piece of her heart occupied by him tore a little. One by one, she relaxed her muscles, shoulders first, and took a deep breath. *I made a threat.*

When he stood, he looked to her. She almost lost her resolve. "Philip," she said, and her voice quavered. She cleared her throat. "Leave. Take the sorrel and go."

Her horsemaster spit blood; his teeth were crimson where his bitten lip had smeared. "I will not leave you," he said.

"You attacked my instructor when I brought you to learn that he had not hurt me. You have shamed yourself, my father, and me." Swallowing hard, she forced the next words out. "Leave. Find yourself new lodgings. When you understand how you have erred, you may return, and you will apologize to Alexander and I."

Looking like a seething bull still contemplating a fight, Philip left the plateau, but he first stopped to spit blood at Alexander's feet. "That is what I say to your training," he said, and left the way they'd come, disappearing dusty and bloody behind a house.

Quiet descended on the training ground, and Elysia ran a hand over her braid. Alexander kicked dirt over the new bloodstains on the ground. "Water?" she asked.

"Water," Alexander agreed. Khronos and Herod looked on as they left.

The walk to the house in the niche was mostly silent; Alexander rubbed the new bruise on his side, and Elysia tried not to think about what she'd just done. The thoughts harried her all the same. She'd made her best friend homeless – or at least, he would be until Khronos went back to the valley and took Philip with him. *But I had no choice.*

"I'm sorry you had to see him like that," she said as they passed the last row of hovels. "He has been... overprotective lately."

"I would expect nothing less," said Alexander, though he gave her a curious look. "It is not really my place to pry, but is your father planning to wed you to him? Or are you already married?"

Elysia shook her head. "It's nothing like that," she said, waving a hand. "He's been watching over me since before I could walk. He's my protector. Every bruise worries him."

Alexander made a noise like he understood. Though Elysia was unsure if he did, she decided to leave the rest unsaid. Philip had already done his damage. She was not going to stop her training – and her tests – because one man was unreasonably jealous.

Alexander left her at the threshold of the house to fetch his sister and the water.

When Korinna came down the steps, she glared murder at Elysia, and before Elysia greeted her, the girl upended the jug in her hands over Elysia's head. Elysia screeched, water splashing down her neck and chilling her as it followed the path of her spine.

"What was that for?" she shrieked, trying to back out of the cascade, but Korinna followed her until only a rivulet flowed from the jug.

"That," said Korinna, setting the jug on the ground. A solemn *bong* echoed from its teardrop-shaped mouth. "Was for bringing your dog to practice and setting him on my brother."

Alexander came down the steps, water jug in hand. He spotted Elysia wiping at the water streaming down her face and looked to his sister. "Korinna, apologize."

"No. Not everyone is going to grovel at her feet." She crossed her arms. "I won't."

Sliding her fingers across her nose to scoop off the water dripping down it, Elysia flicked the droplets from her hand. "Philip is his own person," she said. Rubbing as much of the water from her eyes as she could, she tried to dry her fingers on her tunic – but that was wet, too. "I would not ask him or anyone else to attack your brother, and besides, I like this training." She put her hands on her hips over the sodden wool of her tunic.

The brunette looked entirely unconvinced. "I will not apologize," she said, and took the second water jug from Alexander's hands. Striding past Elysia, Korinna walked down the hill, passing out of Elysia's sight around the edge of a house. "Is that all the water I should expect?" asked Elysia, coughing. Finding the end of her braid, she squeezed more water from its end. It still smelled of honey from Philip's fingers mussing it. *I'll attract dirt like oxen attract flies.*

Alexander sighed and shook his head. "I'm sorry. I understood what happened with Philip, but when I told Korinna, she was furious. She doesn't like being around those who would tell her how to act."

"I wouldn't tell her how to act."

"I know," said Alexander, "but anyone she sees as an outsider or highborn – she doesn't treat them with respect, as they so often give her none."

I understand that, thought Elysia. Adrastos and his scraggly beard came to mind, with his leers and guttural words.

"We should return before my father says something unseemly to yours," Alexander said, starting down the hill.

Following with scuffing feet, Elysia wondered what "unseemly" thing Herod might say to get her father fired up. Some innuendo, probably. She'd already swallowed her reaction to the first – she didn't want to have to do it again. Hurrying to keep up with Alexander, she asked, "What's the next technique, then?"

"Ear pull. Much less complicated than the slap."

Korinna held the water jug for Khronos when they got there; as he ladled water into his mouth, it sparkled in the red hair of his beard. "Took you long enough," said Korinna. "What were you two doing up there by yourselves?"

"Talking about you," Alexander replied. When Korinna stuck her tongue out at him, he repaid her in kind.

Herod cleared his throat. "Children, there's a student to be taught." He rapped Korinna over the thighs with his stick. "Teach 'er."

The ear pull was just as Alexander had said – less complicated, but no less difficult. All she had to do was reach up into his guard, hook her fingers around her ear, and pull… If he didn't push her off him or put her in a hold first. *So much for not fighting back*, she thought as she landed on a bruised hip for the second time. "Won't whoever's attacking me be surprised if I fight back?" she asked from the ground.

"Only if they don't know you," Alexander said, offering her his hand. Clasping it around her wrist, he pulled her to her feet. Elysia ignored the heat that flashed up her arm and the goosebumps that followed.

"Why would someone I know attack me?"

Alexander shrugged, but the set of his mouth told her he held something back.

Herod spoke up. "Sometimes, the ones we know best we know not at all," said the old man, his words gentler than she was used to, as if he told her some hard truth that would sound better spoken softly. "And they're the most dangerous because of it." He waved her off with his stick. "You lot can be done for the day."

Wiping dirt and sweat from her brow, Elysia frowned. "We hardly practiced." She brushed her fingers off on her damp tunic.

Alexander shook his head. "The idea is that you shouldn't need much practice. We want you to be able to defend yourself as quickly as possible.

Every day we send you home without a full arsenal is another day you're in danger." Pushing his own damp hair from his face, Alexander smiled at her. "You're doing well for a High, though."

She smacked his arm. "I'm no High. But why don't you just teach me everything in one day?"

"You think you could learn everything in one day, with the sparring too?" he asked, raising a brow.

Elysia paused. "What if I could?"

"Korinna would probably kill you for breaking her record."

Elysia glanced at the girl who sat on her rock, lounging in the sun with the water jug beside her, eyes closed. "Korinna learned all this in a day?"

"Two days," said Alexander. "She had an incident with a High that left her less than pleased with her ability to protect her own person."

"*What*?" The word came out louder than she'd meant, high with disbelief, and Korinna twitched on her rock, one leg dangling over the edge.

Alexander's hand darted over her mouth. "She'll realize we're talking about her. Anyway, she clawed her way free." Taking his hand from her mouth, Alexander crossed his arms. Gazing across the plateau, he kept a careful eye on his sunbathing sister. "She doesn't get out of the house much when I'm outside – our mother keeps her busy when I'm not home – so she loves the sun." Admiration was written in the lines of his smile. "We're being left behind, though."

Looking away from Korinna, Elysia realized they were alone on the plateau with the girl; their fathers had gone back to the main path. "I should go," Elysia said, but Alexander caught her wrist.

"You know," he began, eyes finding hers. "I go into the city almost every day. If your father would agree, I could teach you in Corinth. He could stop wearying his horses and suffering the bumps of the road, and you would be able to do more with your day than come out here," he finished.

"I will ask him," she said. "But I should go before he comes back to find me." *Spending time with a nice boy in the city. What could go wrong?*

As she waved to him and called a goodbye to Korinna, she answered the question herself.

Everything.

13

The ride home was squeaky and jolting, the horses' harnesses jingling as ever. And, for a time, that was all it was – Khronos remained silent after they said their goodbyes to Herod and Delia.

A quarter-mile from the gates, Khronos spoke. His voice was soft, so quiet Elysia strained to hear it over the hoofbeats. "You've dismissed my Master of Horse."

"He attacked my tutor." She didn't look at him; she didn't want to look up into his green eyes with their unearthly gold rims and see something dangerous lurking in the corners, where she was accustomed to seeing a smile.

"I remember a time when you would have done anything for his attention. And yet when he acts on the same desire toward you, he is shunned and shamed. He will not be happy. Did I not say to be careful with him?"

"You did," Elysia said, staring down the statue of Poseidon that seemed to grow a foot taller every second. "But he left me no choice. I made a threat, a promise to him, a demand for respect, for him to *listen*, and he did exactly what he was told not to." Her hand curled into a fist on the edge of the chariot. "When I pass my tests, I will be more than a girl that he taught to ride a horse, more than his friend. I will be the lady of the valley, and he will be my subordinate. He will have to listen. Better he learns now than I have to teach him later."

"It sounds like you've thought about this," her father said. "But remember to practice mercy. Mercy is as divine as justice."

He let the issue rest. Their way through the gate went without remark, though Adrastos looked Elysia up and down and asked if she hadn't earned herself a beating today.

No, she wanted to reply, *but someone else earned one.*

More bruised than she had been the day before, Elysia was stiff when she sank into her cool bath, and nearly as sore when she stepped out. She'd thought about Alexander's offer – about his coming to the city to teach her. *It couldn't hurt,* she decided, *and it would save the horses a tiring and Father time that he could spend in the agora.*

When she'd robed herself in a new dress, Elysia found Khronos in the garden on the bench where he'd been the night before. Sitting down on the sun-warmed marble, Elysia put a hand on his.

"Father, if I could learn to defend myself in the city, would you allow it?" The words rushed out, so fast that she couldn't stop herself or lose her will to ask. *It's about training and practicality, nothing more.*

Leaning back, Khronos gazed at Elysia, his red-gold hair shimmering in the afternoon sun; the beams of light barely broke over the garden wall now. Gold had been a part of him for as long as she could remember. The gilded rim and spires amidst the moss green of his eyes, the flame of his hair limned with gold, the sun-kissed cast to his skin. His possessions, excepting his throne, had a golden sheen: the chariot, his bedposts, every curtain, pillow, and furnishing in his room. *It was the first color*, he'd told her once, when she'd asked why it was his favorite. *The first that I remember, a bright star staring down at me.*

His eyes shone with that first color, as though she looked back through the tunnel of time itself to look at that star through the green-gold portal of his eyes. "Why would I disallow it?" he asked, and he studied her, hunting for something.

"Because…" Elysia choked on her words and reddened.

"Because he is a man and you are a woman, yes?"

"Yes."

"But if he is the man who is teaching you how to protect your womanhood, who am I to say where he can teach you, as long as you are taught?"

She stared at him for a long moment. "You mean this?" she asked.

He gave her the smile he gave only to her, a sly one, like a joke shared between them. "The horses have been running for a week. Who am I to tell them they cannot rest?"

Elysia nudged him with an elbow. He leaned to nudge her back –

And a hinge creaked to their left.

A white-blond man stood in the doorway to their neighbor's house. His voice, familiar, was muffled as he called back into the house: "When did we get neighbors?"

The sound of pottery clattering from within Metrodora's house was audible in the courtyard. Her voice echoed out of her house, something unintelligible, and then the woman herself appeared in the doorway. With her black hair braided – though tendrils were loose near the top – Metrodora looked robust as ever, a spindle hovering below her slightly doughy middle. Wrapping the thread around its shaft, Metrodora said, "Elysia! I apologize for not visiting." She swept into the courtyard on wide, flat feet. "It slipped my mind. We did not get to see each other very long, you know, and this mind wanders." Elysia's grandmother planted a kiss on each of her granddaughter's cheeks.

"It's good to see you," Elysia said with a grin, but she remembered the man standing in the doorway behind Metrodora. "Is this my uncle?"

Looking over her shoulder, Metrodora nodded. "Yes, you've not yet met… Zeus, come here." She beckoned him with a wave, and as he got closer, Elysia's eyes widened.

"*Zeus?*"

He had the same surprise in his eyes, eyes as stormy blue as her own. "*Khronos's daughter* is Elysia?" he asked his mother. Up close, she noticed how closely matched they were: he had hair like hers, though his had a hint of a silvery sheen. He had freckles too, smattered over the bridge of his nose and across his cheeks; from afar, they'd been almost enough to make him look a mismatched tan, as if half his face had been shadowed while he'd stood beneath the statues at the gates he guarded. His nose looked far more like Metrodora's than her own, curved outward and hooked like the noses of other Greeks she'd seen.

Metrodora scowled at him. "Of course – he married your sister. I have no other grandchildren, do I?" The raised eyebrow she gave him made Elysia stifle a laugh, but Metrodora turned her gaze on Elysia next. "And no great-grandchildren from you, hm? You are still young, though. We may find you a husband yet."

"A husband?" The thought struck a chord that made her heart race, its chambers filling with panic. "I'm not here to find a husband. I'm here to learn about the city."

"And why not have a husband for a guide?" Metrodora asked, smiling sweetly, though Elysia sensed edges on the question.

"I'm not ready to marry," Elysia tried. She felt her father's hand on her shoulder, warm and steadying over the shoulder clasp of her dress.

"No one is ever ready to marry," said Metrodora, and she took Elysia's hand to draw her to her feet. Khronos's comforting hand fell from her shoulder. "Your mother never was, but when she did, she found love."

Fabric rustled behind Elysia as her father stood. "Branimira found love before she was married," he said, "and that is how it will be with Elysia. She will be married when I say she will be married. I am her father, and I have that right."

Something shivered through the air between their locked gazes, unbridled and wild as an untamed horse. "I am her grandmother. I have the right to find her suitors."

Elysia slipped her hand free of Metrodora's grasp to wrap it in the folds of her dress. "I don't want suitors."

The pushing smile that had lit the woman's face shrank. "Then come by soon so I might teach you to weave," she said. Her hand came to rest on Elysia's cheek, as if it could not stand being without her touch.

"It may be a few days," Elysia said, "but I will." *If I can find the time between training and nursing my hurts.* The place where Alexander had grabbed her wrist to get her out of Philip's way was already purpling, though it was hidden in her skirts.

"Good! Now, you should get to know your uncle better." Grabbing Elysia's shoulder and pushing her back down onto the marble bench where she'd sat moments before, Metrodora smiled so deviously that Elysia thought perhaps she meant for Zeus to be her suitor. *Surely that's forbidden in Greece.* But she was wary as her grandmother seated her uncle – who looked to be only a few years older than Elysia – down beside her. "We will leave you to it." And with that, the woman took Khronos's arm and towed him off to the far end of the garden.

"She's so pushy," said Zeus. He sighed, looked at her, and laughed. "You can wipe that bewildered look off your face, niece. I am not the men with whom I keep company."

"You mean the guardsmen?"

"I mean Adrastos. He'd frighten any girl newly come to the city."

She crossed her arms in front of her. "*You* called me a fine fruit. Did you forget that Mira married my father?"

He shook his head. "I see Khronos every week. I didn't realize you were his daughter. It sounds stupid now, but I thought you were a nymph."

"A nymph."

For some reason, Zeus reddened, folded, and refolded his hands in his lap. "He's always telling people in the agora that a nymph blesses his crops, so he can grow them year-round. So… I thought you were the nymph, finally come to see the city. And then he introduced you as his daughter, and, well…"

"You went along with what Adrastos said." When he nodded, she laughed. "I can't believe my father didn't tell you he expected better of you."

"He did, in his way. Demanding respect." One corner of his mouth twitched up.

"So how old are you?" asked Elysia. "Three-and-twenty?"

"Not quite yet. I will be come spring, though. You're nineteen. I remember when your father came to the agora and gave fruit to the poor, he was so pleased by your birth. I got a whole pomegranate." Now the other corner of his mouth twitched up, and white teeth showed through.

"Good teeth must run in the family," she observed, and smiled back at him.

"It must."

Following her father and Metrodora with her eyes, Elysia watched as they stopped by the fountain. Metrodora whispered something in Khronos's ear and he shook his head, and then the pair of them looked back at Elysia. Hurrying to look away, she asked, "So, what are you named for?"

He looked so incredulous she thought she had breached a social convention. "What?" she asked.

"What do you mean, 'what?' You don't know?"

"Know what?"

"Who Zeus is."

Shaking her head, she crossed her arms tighter. Her skin went white around the edges of her fingers. "Zeus is a person?"

"Zeus is a god." Her uncle looked past her, his gaze focused on her father. "Strange, I had your father pegged for a godly man."

Elysia snorted. "That he is, but we keep with Hera and Apollo," she said, using what little knowledge she had of the gods. *And, of course, we keep with Khronos.* "Which god is Zeus?"

"Zeus is the king of the gods." Tilting his head at her, Zeus scratched behind an ear. "You didn't know that?"

"No."

"Then I suppose you did come to learn about the city," said Zeus. His hand found her shoulder and his blue eyes found hers. They drew her gaze the way Acrocorinth had when she'd first seen it, two deep pools drawing her into their cool embrace. Her arms loosened a little, the white marks fading from her sunburned arms. "I will teach you about the gods when I am free from guard duty. If your father has not taken up that mantle of responsibility, it's only right that I do." An earnest crease appeared in his forehead, and it made Elysia smile.

"All right," she agreed.

He clapped his hands together and got to his feet. "First will be Apollo's temple, since something tells me you've not seen a proper temple, no matter the patron gods of your family. Did you see it when you were at the agora? It would've looked like this." He drew a rectangle in the air with a triangle on top.

I lived in one of those four days ago. "I didn't see it," she said. She'd been busy looking at all the banners and watching people.

Shading his eyes, Zeus looked at the sky. The sun had not quite set, though the clouds' undersides blushed against the brilliant blue sky. "We still have time to see it, if you wish."

"You're taking this very seriously," she replied, gripping the edge of the bench.

The impassivity of his face broke and a grin gave him wrinkles in all the right places, framing his eyes, the laugh lines around his mouth, the dimple in his left cheek. Zeus moved faster than she could say, grabbing her and spinning her in a wide circle, dress swirling around her legs and whipping in the wind. She let out an exhilarated shriek.

When he set her down, Elysia laughed, breathless. "Father," she called, eyes not leaving Zeus's. "May Zeus and I go to the temple of Apollo?"

Khronos's voice was near when he spoke, and she found him and Metrodora on the other side of the rose bush. "You may," he answered, "but be quick. When darkness falls in the city, it is not safe to roam the streets. Only those who conceal themselves in darkness will be out once the sun sets." His eyes were sharp on Zeus. "Do not let her stray from your side."

"I won't." Zeus nodded to Khronos and offered Elysia his arm. "Khronos. Mother." Giving his mother a nod of respect, Zeus swept Elysia out of the courtyard.

They tramped through Metrodora's house to reach the street, and though Elysia didn't have time to study the tapestries on the walls, she *did* have time to ogle the loom in the back room. A half-finished, richly woven pattern of blue and green ended at shoulder height; the shuttle that ferried the weft threads through the loom rested on the heddle that held the warp apart. Clay weights hung at the bottom of the warp threads, keeping the thin, strong cords from floating on each updraft.

As soon as she'd absorbed that much, they ducked around the curtain that separated the rooms, wove around pottery and furnishings, and stepped out the door. In the middle of the unpaved street, Elysia looked around, but there was not a soul in sight. Zeus practically dragged her down the street in his enthusiasm; her fingers slipped from the bend in his elbow to take his hand. Her bruised wrist was out in the open, cool air gliding over it, but her uncle either didn't see it or didn't remark of it.

The leather soles of their sandals tapped against hard-packed dirt as they ran through the streets, sending echoes against the houses' plaster and marble walls to ring back at them. Zeus led her down narrow streets – the chariot had limited Elysia to main roads and tributaries, but on foot, they followed alleys between houses, and more than once, he helped her over a low fence.

Despite the lateness of the hour, the agora bustled: it was filled with shopkeepers putting leftover wares in their carts and the pious going to their evening prayers at the temples. The banners and poles had come down, but the curtains of cloth hung on the walls billowed as people, carts, and animals trundled by. The sun shone through them and threw splashes of vivid color on the walls behind them, painting the marble bright hues of scarlet, cerulean, and gold. Meat cooked nearby, the rich, hot scent drifting on the wind with the spice of cloves and nutmeg.

Zeus led her up the stairs where the Lechaion ended – and entered a whole new agora. A few shops stood on her left, but to her right, a square of white-paved space opened, lined with roofed and colonnaded sidewalks. People milled and soaked up the sun, with skin and dyed clothing of every color she could imagine. In the center, a fountain spouted water, a great carved thing of Poseidon and a wild-eyed horse. At the far end stood the biggest buildings Elysia had seen in the city, each of the same design: a rectangle with fluted columns supporting triangular roofs. Within, statues bathed in shadow.

Taking a deep breath, she stepped off the last stair and into the crowd behind Zeus. "I've never seen so many people," Elysia murmured.

He squeezed her hand, and the scrapes on her palm burned. "There will be more at the temples. They're offering the gods an evening meal." Pulling her along, Zeus navigated the crowd, stopping and starting to avoid colliding with passersby.

When they reached the temples, Elysia was jostled at every turn, her bruises poked painfully by an elbow or knee. She tripped up marble steps and out of the crowd, which gathered around an altar. It had been hidden before by the press of bodies. On it lay a seared, dripping lamb, skin crackling and bubbling juices. Spices had been sprinkled over the meat to stifle the scent of charring.

At the head of the altar stood a man dressed in a long, white tunic and a cloth-of-gold cloak, a belt of rubies and topaz at his waist. His voice rang clear and deep through the chatter of the crowd, though Elysia only heard snatches. She raced up the steps after her uncle. "*...and we offer to you this lamb, that you might be pleased with us and bless us still...*" The words rang off the marble pillars at the top of the stairs, but once past them, the world quieted.

People crowded under the shelter of the building, but here, there was silence. Elysia's eyes followed the gazes of the men – and *only* men, she noticed – who knelt, faces raised to beseech their gods in prayer. Some mouthed words; others simply gazed toward the statue that rose to the ceiling of the temple.

It was a young man of gilt and marble, standing tall with a sheet of cloth hanging across his waist. His hair and eyes had been painted gold, and Elysia knew his clean-shaven face.

Apollo. The humans had brought him to their world, too, and made him their god. *The Judge of Morality, sent to languish among the humans.* She wondered if, somewhere, there was a little boy named Apollo, not unlike her uncle, who dreamed of one day growing up to be as handsome as the statue before her.

Zeus led her to a pillar on the side of the building. They stood there together, looking up at the statue of the man whom Elysia had thought was just another soul, albeit a powerful one. "So this is Apollo," she whispered, but her voice carried over the marble floor and heads turned.

Her uncle nodded and leaned in to cup his hand over her ear, breath hot on her skin. "There's a room for women to pray in the back, but we'll leave in a moment. You look highborn enough to be ignored, for now."

She looked at him sharply, but Zeus shrugged and leaned toward her again. "You've never been to a temple before, so I figured you wouldn't know about the division. Men and women pray separately, just as they're supposed to eat separately, though I doubt your father practices that."

Shaking her head, Elysia leaned against the pillar and looked up at Apollo. An instrument hung from his hand, golden with silver strings. She recognized his lyre, which had been his constant companion in the valley. The sweet notes that had accompanied his duets with Aliya still made Elysia shiver.

Shielding his eyes, Zeus looked at the sky. The sun sank lower every moment, its rays no longer warming her sunburned skin. Zeus pulled her down the steps to the street that ran between Apollo's temple and the one beside it. "We should return home." He held out his hand to her.

Rather than head back through the agora, Zeus led her down the street behind the temples, and they took an even more complex route back to the house – without him, Elysia would have been lost. Halfway there, as dusk fell and light drained from the streets, a group of men emerged from the shadows at a crossroads.

Zeus pulled her beneath the shelter of his arm. A man stood on each side of them; one appeared in a doorway behind them. A fourth, the only one whose face was visible, leaned against a low wall ahead – and his face was familiar.

The scraggly black-and-gray beard, flinty eyes beneath heavy brows, the sour mouth. "Adrastos," Zeus said lightly, though his muscles stiffened. "This is an odd place for you. I've never found you here before." The houses were dark around them: quiet, tiny, mud-brick hovels.

"I say the same to you, my friend," said Adrastos. His voice made Elysia shrink under Zeus's arm, wishing to disappear into the dust, as if she had never been there.

He's Zeus's friend. As for the three other men around them, Elysia could not say whose friends they were.

"We've missed each other before, then." Zeus's smile was bright in the gathering dusk, but his hand dampened with sweat. "This is the way I come home from the temples."

"I missed that girl there, too. Is that Khronos's daughter? Quick of him to marry her off."

I am no one's wife.

"She is my niece," said Zeus. "Turns out *I* had a sister whelping blond runts in the hills." His words were easy, yet they struck a blow to Elysia's heart.

He says it so carelessly, like she is nothing. Like I am nothing.

Something in her seethed, an anthill in her gut. She regarded the tan-skinned man across from her with a wary eye.

"Her father waits for her return." Zeus's voice had an edge on it, an urgency. "I'm sure you wouldn't want to keep him waiting, my friend. Khronos is renowned for undoing the careers of guardsmen with a whisper."

Adrastos pulled at his beard, looking Elysia up and down. She felt his eyes at her neckline, her bare arms, peering around the slit in her skirt; it had slid halfway up her thigh. She leaned into her uncle and closed her eyes against his wool tunic, listening. She would not deign to watch Adrastos undress her with his eyes. No one took a step; the streets were silent excepting a barking dog somewhere across the city.

Finally, Adrastos sighed. "I'm sure I wouldn't want that either," he said, and Elysia opened her eyes. The man had not moved, his gaze hungrier than ever, but he held out a hand behind him. "Please, if you must."

Zeus led her past the man, but Elysia's skin crawled.

Fingers groped through her dress, squeezing the back of her thigh and upward, into territory that no one had the right to touch, digging into her with ragged fingernails.

Elysia swung without hesitation, and swung *hard*, the shallow bowl of her hand finding Adrastos's ear and clapping it so hard the street rang. Her screech of rage echoed off the buildings around them, dogged by his pained shout.

"Run," said Zeus as Adrastos staggered backward. The man held his ear with his mouth agape; the men lurking in the side streets rushed to his side.

An arm around her shoulders propelled Elysia forward. "Run!"

She hiked her skirts up to her knees and followed Zeus around blind corners, crashing through gaps left in his wake when he pushed through crowds. She didn't look back – she *couldn't* look back; one misstep, one stumble, and she'd hit the ground or break an ankle on a loose cobble. Her breath came in bursts, lungs burning like they'd been set on fire.

They turned a corner, and Elysia saw the blue-gray stone of their houses. She paused, but Zeus grabbed her hand and dragged her across the street, slamming open the door of her house. Elysia sprawled on the floor, but Zeus was up and at the door to stop it from banging against the frame as it shut.

Her father yelled something from the back room, then threw the curtain out of the way and demanded to know what had happened, but she couldn't tell him; she couldn't breathe, couldn't think. Something silenced him, though, because then, her father was on the ground beside her, hands in her hair, under her chin, pulling her against his chest. His thumb wiped at her face, under her eyes, and she realized there were tears there.

Her words hiccupped into the front of his tunic. "I-I-I ne-never-er…" What did she never? She forgot. "A-Adrast-stos, h-he… We ra-an." Her breath was shallow, hitches and fits.

"Adrastos attacked you?" Khronos rocked her, smoothing her long white hair; she must have lost her veil as she ran, for her hair clung in a windswept mess around her shoulders.

She managed a nod and knew her father would turn purple with fury. She clutched at his wrist. Her muscles clenched and unclenched, squeezing so hard her abdomen hurt. Her throat was raw. Elysia dashed at her tears, but she felt the pressure of Adrastos's fingers on her, felt his touch, the roughness of the fabric between his skin and hers, and a fresh wave fell. "Bath," she said, using her father's shoulder to push herself to her feet. "I nee-eed a bath." Her hands shook, her body shuddering. Her hair was still damp from the bath she'd taken just hours ago, but she needed another one – she needed to scrub herself clean, to douse herself in rosewater.

Anything to get his hands off me.

14

The water was gray when she stepped out, her sunburned skin bleeding and raw from scrubbing. The longer Elysia had waited for bathwater to be drawn, the dirtier she'd felt; by the time she'd stepped into the water, the shiver that had started in her thighs had crawled down her legs and up her torso to her neck.

And even now that she was out, now that she was scrubbed down, now that she was cleaner than clean, she felt dirty. It was like those thick, gnarled fingers had found their way beneath her skin to burrow in her muscles.

The olive oil lamps burned in the front room when she emerged. She'd wrapped in a gown and woolen blanket despite the hot night. Khronos alone remained in the house; Aliya had gone to sleep in the courtyard and Zeus must have gone home. Her father waited on his couch, but she found a seat on her own bed, pulling pillows, cushions, and blankets over herself until she was swaddled in bedding.

Her padded shield did not stop her father's words from jolting her, though his voice was soft as a whisper. "Do you want me to bring him down?"

I want to be the one to bring him down. "I want you to take his job, his home, his slaves," she growled. "I want him to feel spiders crawling across his skin in every waking moment, and I want him to feel talons in him when he sleeps. I want him to die sunburned and blistered in the street, driven mad by hunger. I want my face to be the last thing he sees." Her hand clenched around a pillow, her fingers a claw. Her bruised wrist was the color of midnight, deep indigo and green. "But more than anything, I want to sleep." *And not to dream.*

A frown on his face, Khronos blew out the lamp on the table beside him. She heard him rustle on his blankets, but he said not another word.

Darkness did not make it easier to sleep.

Even with her body hidden beneath the weight of cushions and blankets, shadowy fingers ran over her, caressing her skin. She laid awake, listening, waiting for someone to come through the front door or pass the window, but the night was eerily silent. She didn't know which would have been worse: the silence or a night penetrated with footsteps.

Morning came eventually, though, and when it did, her eyes were dry and her head pounding. They broke their fast on bread, honey, and pomegranate seeds; every day they remained, the fruit hanging from the courtyard tree diminished. Their water came from the courtyard, as well: from the fountain, a spring of freshwater as sweet as the water of the valley, though here, they drank it with wine.

The chariot ride was as silent as their breakfast. Elysia ducked as they passed under the statues, but the guard had changed; the shifts must have been different, as Zeus had helped her father harness the horses. She had half expected Philip to walk through the door when it creaked open, but then she'd remembered banishing him. The thought had surprised her. She had not thought to regret it, after what he'd done – she had not expected to miss his presence at the breakfast table, or to walk next door and assume he'd be there, petting the sorrel mare he'd taught her to ride.

She had been right to dismiss him. If she was to continue her training – if she was to reign in the valley beside her father and become eternal – she had to finish her tests. And if Philip attacked Alexander because he was training her, Philip would only stall her progress. She couldn't afford him: she'd been in Corinth less than a week, but she'd already been attacked once and leered at countless times. Still, she missed his presence.

Acrocorinth was breezy and shady for the first hour. Delia greeted them, cheerful as ever, and took the horses in hand. Alexander met them halfway up the hill and walked them to the training ground. Something felt different to Elysia, and not on the outside. Something had snapped off inside her, some delicate vessel shattered by the hands that haunted her dreams.

Herod waited for them at the edge of the plateau, beating out seconds in the dirt with his staff. As Elysia took off the gown that hid her tunic from unwelcome eyes, the old man began the lesson. "Today's the ankle stomp. Easy enough, quick enough, should keep you out of the sun. Doesn't look like yer skin can handle much more of it today."

Elysia looked down at her raw red shoulder. "I'm fine," she said, but across from her, Alexander's arms crossed, and he studied her. His gaze wasn't the same as Adrastos's; it was gentle, and he regarded the red splotches where she'd scrubbed hard enough to scour away her old skin and reveal the new, pink skin beneath.

"That is not sunburn. I know those marks," he said softly. "Korinna did the same."

Elysia imagined the younger girl dumping pots of water over her head, depleting the family's stores of rosewater, scrubbing herself down with a rough brush, and doing it again. "Just show me the technique," she said. Her hands almost made it to her hips, but she felt too open, too exposed. She let them hang in front of her body, hands clasped together.

Herod still watched them, Khronos standing beside him with arms folded. "I don't think so," said Herod, and for the first time in four days, he walked into the middle of the plateau, leaning heavily on his stick. "I want to know more about this attack my boy suspects, crone." He stood beside her, peering up at her – hunched though he was, Elysia thought he must have once been a mountain of a man. He still had the intimidating air.

"I did not come here to be interrogated. Teach me."

"You *were* attacked." The grin he gave her was animalistic, sneering. "You must've gotten away, else you wouldn't be 'ere. How'd you do it?"

"With an ear slap," she answered. "He… grabbed me… from behind, so I turned around and hit him. And then I ran."

"Good," said Herod. "And how did yer instincts feel?"

"Sick." They still felt sick, knotted and nauseous in her belly, like an inconsolable child.

"Good." Herod wove unsteadily to his spot at the edge of the training ground. "Carry on."

Alexander sighed and uncrossed his arms. "Ankle stomp, then." Beckoning her closer, he held out one leg that ended in a sandaled foot. He leaned down and pointed at his ankle. "Stomp right there. You might break bone, you might make him pull a muscle, but it will hobble him for a good moment so you can get away. Sound all right so far?"

She nodded when he looked up at her, his gray eyes dancing with light. Straightening, Alexander brushed his hands together. "Then we'll practice stomping, because I'm not about to let you try this on me." His smile was so earnest that she couldn't help but half-smile back.

The stomping seemed just like any other stomping, but Alexander frowned and sighed and tried to tell her how she was doing it wrong until Herod laughed from the sidelines. "Let's try something else," Alexander finally said.

When he took her hand, tingles danced along the rawness of her skin. He led her over to a hut. "Stand here," he said, pointing in front of him.

As she inched into the narrow space between Alexander and the wall, he put his arms out and trapped her there. "What," asked Elysia, "are you doing?" His breath was roses, his arms casting warmth onto her skin.

"Teaching you." He looked down at their feet, and Elysia followed his gaze. "See how I'm standing?" His feet were in front of her and to either side, lined up with his shoulders. "You've been stomping straight down, but that is not where an attacker's foot will be. They will be where mine are. Try stomping here," he said, digging a mark in the dirt with the toe of his sandal before moving his foot out of the way.

It took her a moment to recover from his closeness, but when she struck, she struck hard, her foot coming down with a *thud* that sent vibrations up to her thigh and dull pain into her heel. "Perfect," said Alexander. "Now, do it again."

Again and again and again the drill went, and all the time his hands were on either side of her shoulders, searing into her sunburned, scratched skin. Her legs had gone numb by the end of it, but finally, Herod called for a stop. The sun had crawled over Acrocorinth, peering down from the heights like a child hiding from its friends. As Khronos and Herod walked back to the main path, Elysia caught Alexander's arm; solid and strong beneath her hand, it was corded with muscle from years of labor and training. "My father gave permission for practice in Corinth."

A sideways smile tugged up one corner of his mouth. "Then I will see you tomorrow before daybreak."

She dropped her hand from his arm, alarmed. "How will you find me?"

His head tilted in confusion. "Metrodora? We see each other in the agora, and she has told me you live next to her." His smile widened. "She's quite thrilled. Her son and I are friends, too."

Somewhere ahead, her father's voice called her name. "I'll see you tomorrow, then," Elysia said, excusing herself with a wave and plucking her gown from a rock.

As she walked under the shade of the houses, she spun a little. What would tomorrow bring? Undoubtedly sparring, but would it be different, with no one watching them? Without their fathers studying them, without his little sister to jeer at her and cheer him on?

Only tomorrow will tell.

15

"I'm going to the agora today," said Khronos, scooping hummus onto his flatbread. An olive oil lamp shimmered in the center of the table, casting a smoky glow into the predawn house. "I doubt you'll be home before me, but if I'm not here when you return, keep Metrodora or Aliya company. I don't want you to be alone."

Nodding, Elysia hurried about the house, a piece of flatbread coated in honey hanging from her mouth as she braided her hair. She couldn't find the dress she wanted, and none of her gowns gave her as much freedom as that one, with the style's side slits.

A knock rattled at the door. She made to answer it, but Khronos held up a hand to stop her. Rising from his seat, her father put down his half-eaten triangle of pita and went to the door. It creaked as it opened. "Alexander," he said, and Elysia peered around her father's shoulder.

"Khronos." Alexander nodded his greeting, and when his eyes met Elysia's, he gave her a short wave. "It is not my place to suggest what you do with your home, but you need a better door if your goal is to protect your daughter and your belongings."

To her surprise, Khronos did not stiffen or scowl, but moved aside to let Alexander into the house. "I mean to buy a set of bars today," he replied. "Metrodora's house will need some, too, if we're to have them – our houses adjoin."

Elysia felt her eyebrows rise as Alexander said, "Well, keep thinking about it."

She didn't know if she believed it. Her father was twice his age – many thousands of years twice his age – and she'd never *heard* of Alexander before coming to Corinth. "How…" she began and swallowed as they looked at her. Pointing first at Alexander, then at her father and back, she asked, "How do you two know each other?"

"The agora," said Alexander.

Khronos sat down on his stool, taking a bite of the pita he'd left. "His family are my most loyal customers," he said after swallowing.

Alexander laughed. "There is a reason we are loyal, you know. It has to do with good business and better produce."

Elysia crossed her arms but regretted it as her healing skin burned at her own touch. "You never spoke to each other when we were at Acrocorinth," she pointed out, wondering if she had missed the signs of camaraderie.

They exchanged a glance, and her tutor shrugged. "I was training you," said Alexander. "It would have been unprofessional to strike up a conversation with your father."

"And it's not now?"

He paused. "This is the first time I've been here. Usually, I come to see Zeus and Metrodora, so this is half professional and half social. Shall we go?"

Hands on her hips, Elysia gave him a quizzical look and made for the door, her blue skirt sweeping across the slate floor. "I'll see you when I come home, Father," she called.

Alexander followed her out after a moment, but the windows didn't much muffle her father's words to him: "Don't let her beat herself up too badly."

As if he needs telling, she found herself thinking. Alexander had done his best to keep their sparring wound-free since they had begun; her own inelegance had caused the most injury.

"Ready to go?" Alexander asked, and when she nodded, he led the way.

The rough stone buildings gave way to the homes of the poor, and Elysia noticed that they were eerily like Alexander's, though they were notably shorter. The mud brick houses seemed to stretch on as she followed him. "Where *are* we going?" she asked. The streets grew more and more devoid of signs of civilization; the pottery set outside for collecting rainwater was whole against one house, but farther down the line, a few once-fat vessels had been shattered around their wide middles. Soon, small bits of pottery were strewn in the streets, crackling underfoot with every step.

"An abandoned part of the city near the outskirts where we can practice," he said, waving for her to catch up.

Trotting to keep up with him, she thought, *This isn't abandoned enough?* How many hundreds of people must have lived here once, before the pottery was broken? "We're not there yet?"

Alexander looked around. "Oh, there are people here, but they will not rise before dawn. Or noon."

Peering closer at the houses – many of which had no door, nor a curtain for privacy – Elysia frowned. The world turned from dark blue to grayish yellow just as the sun was about to rise, and the innards of the houses, once steeped in shadow, lightened. She saw a form here or there, one slumped on a stool with head resting on a table, another laid out on a couch like a doll. Elysia moved closer to Alexander, his arm brushing warmth onto hers. "Do they know we're here?" she whispered.

He shook his head. "No. They might dream of us if we disturb their sleep, though."

The shards and coin-sized pottery pieces in the street disappeared and were traded for chunks of crumbling brick. Houses sagged; some had completely toppled, spilling mud, straw, and roof tiles into the middle of the unpaved road. Everything had been picked clean. The houses that still had doorways were dark voids: no edges of furniture within, nothing hanging on the walls, no movement except the occasional scurrying shadow and skittering of a rat scrambling for cover as they walked by.

At last, Alexander stopped in the middle of the road and held out his hands. "Here we are."

This training ground looked just like the other, but the land here was being retaken by nature. A pomegranate tree grew wild and unpruned in the center of what had once been a square, its trunk ringed with stones that were spattered with cracked and overripe fruit. The sickly-sweet aroma of rot and the tang of juice hung in the air. A wall surrounded the houses, though it was chinked and missing segments in some places, collapsed in others, and crumbling like it had seen far too much rain. The houses set against the wall had been devastated; some were no more than a pile of bricks with terracotta tiles on top, grass peeking from beneath them. Elysia had never seen such destruction. "What happened here?"

Nudging stray bricks out of the middle of the square, Alexander said, "The gods shook the earth and Corinth trembled beneath their wrath. The poorest were hit the hardest." He looked at her with a curious gaze. "Haven't you wondered why my father is hunched?"

Elysia shrugged. "I thought it was part of his charm."

Alexander cracked a smile. "That," he said, pointing at her, "is why training here will be better than on the mountain. No one to scold or cane us."

The image of him trapping her against the wall yesterday burned in her mind. "Speak for yourself," she replied, but grinned at him anyway. "So your father and his hunch."

"Right." He walked to her and put his hands on her shoulders. "When the earth shook, the mountain near bucked us off its back. The house landed on top of him." Pushing on her shoulders, he said, "You're supposed to escape, not stand there taking in the story I'm spinning."

Her eyes widened. She'd let him approach without even a queer feeling – aside from the one she had now, where his palms rested against her shoulders, hot against her sunburned, raw flesh. "That was stupid of me," she said.

She stuck her arms up and whirled away from him, landing squarely on her rear when her skirt wrapped around her legs.

Alexander's mirth was far from over when she managed to untangle herself, her skirt already stained with dust. Hands on her hips, she stared him down. "I suppose today will be my first lesson in real clothes."

"I suppose so," said Alexander. "We're also going to try combinations, because just one technique might not disable an opponent." Crossing his arms, he traced an analytical eye down her body.

Her nerves stood on end as she noted each pause – which weren't in the places she'd realized men looked first. His eyes stopped at her shoulders, her knees, her feet, but he never gave her bosom a second glance. *He is here to train you*, she told herself, but her face heated and she crossed her arms before she could fidget. *His gaze shouldn't stop there.*

"We'll practice techniques you've already learned, now that you're wearing that skirt. What are they?" His voice was hard, drilling her.

"Ear slap, ear pull, ankle stomp, and the three to get out of holds."

Nodding, Alexander walked toward her and stopped almost uncomfortably close, but not quite. Her nerves jumped. "First things first," he said, "I'll try to keep you in a hold, but you will be able to fight back this time. *Try* to avoid injuring me."

Without a second's warning, he wrapped his hands around her neck; she couldn't draw a breath before the pressure made breathing uncomfortable. Throwing an elbow up and turning out of his grasp, Elysia whipped around and ran – but he grabbed her braid, and a jet of hot pain shot up her scalp. "*Combinations,*" Alexander said. Her braid thumped against her back as he let it go. She faced him, rubbing the sting from her nape. "Fight back."

Gritting her teeth, Elysia let him come at her again, despite the instincts that told her not to. At the last moment, just before his hands found her neck or her shoulders, she thought, *Trust your instincts.*

And she struck, her hand cupped a hair's breadth from his ear. He flinched sideways as her hand almost connected. He stumbled only a step, brows raised beneath long hair. "You wanted me to wake up my instincts," said Elysia. "Hard for them to sleep when you're running at me, trying to throttle me."

"Good point," he replied. And then he circled around behind her, vanishing beyond her line of sight. She froze.

His arms wrapped around her waist, squeezing her tight against him. She dropped so fast he flipped over her head, arms swiveling him forward. A puff of dust rose around him as he hit the ground. Alexander wheezed for air as he rolled onto his stomach. "What… did I say… about injuring me?" he asked as she crouched beside him.

"Sorry," she said. She felt the horror on her face, mouth agape and eyes wide. "I didn't know that could happen."

Even as he gasped for breath, he crooked a smile. "A jape, Elysia." Righting himself to kneel in front of her, he said, "That would certainly… stop an opponent." Alexander heaved himself to his feet and offered her a hand up.

Taking it, Elysia stood, her mouth twisted in a frown. "It's going to be hard to do this well if we only go for a few seconds at a time."

"That may be, but it should only take a few seconds for you to get away."

One hand on her hip, Elysia looked up at the sky, now bright blue; the sun crawled over the wall. "I need to learn more techniques."

She felt his eyes, and when she found his gaze, he gave her the queerest look. "What?"

"You need to let go of my hand first."

Eyes darting downward, Elysia found her fingers still wrapped in his from helping her up. "I think *you're* holding *my* hand," she said, glancing back at him. His eyes danced again, like they did every time he smiled, but he let her hand drop.

"If you say so." Turning, he gave her a sideways look and made for the pomegranate tree. "Come here."

The closer she got to the rotting, overripe fruit, the more cloying its scent became; the sound of flies' buzzing wings was heavy in the air. The slender trunk dripped with the juice of cracked pomegranates, seeds spilling onto the ground. Elysia was struck by the solitary tree.

"This tree was the heart of its community, once," said Alexander. "They raised it from a seed to feed themselves. There were other trees, but they died." Crouching down next to the ring of stones, he picked up a nearby fruit and bashed it against a stone until its innards spread over the rock. He waved a hand at the seeds. "If these seeds were the women in Corinth, Acrocorinth, or even Greece, only one or two a year will learn what you're learning." He looked at her. "Only one or two will become seedlings and then trees, strong enough to survive harsh conditions."

"It takes a long time for a seed to become a tree," Elysia pointed out, thinking of some of the newer seedlings in the garden at home, in their terracotta pots beneath heavy rose blooms. They'd been waiting to mature for years, it always seemed to her, but they grew taller every year.

"That is where you are different. You will learn to survive harsh conditions in a week's time."

Her eyes widened. "A week?"

"It will be much faster, since we will have more time and fewer distractions." Standing, he wiped his juice-stained hands on his tunic, leaving purple stains.

One of Elysia's eyebrows quirked in disbelief. "What're the techniques for today, then?" she asked, hands on her hips.

"Techniques for breaking noses and making an attacker cry," replied Alexander, his smile growing. "And won't that be something to brag about."

The first technique was a modified punch to the face – not a straight-on punch, but one with the bottom of her fist, bringing it down right on top of the nose. The second time she tried it, she didn't stop soon enough; her hand came down hard enough that his eyes watered, and he bent over, one hand on his knee while the other rubbed pain from his face. "Do you remember what my father said?" he asked after he announced that the pain had gone, though his voice was thick with congestion. "I have his nose, and he wants me to keep it. This is probably the most dangerous day for my nose that there will ever be." He'd laughed, and Elysia breathed relief.

The second technique, Alexander warned her, was said to be lethal – this time, he took the heel of her hand and put it against the bottom of her jaw. "It has the potential to break teeth, knock someone unconscious, or kill, if you do it hard enough," he said. "So you only need to know the theory of it. This is one that you should only use in the direst of situations, all right?"

"All right," she replied. *Life and death in the palm of my hand, just as it will be when I have earned my eternity.*

The rest of the lesson was sparring. They sparred until her arms were numb, her elbows and knees scraped, and her body so tired that her only desire was to crawl into bed. Her dress had become more brown than blue. No water could be found in the abandoned neighborhood; the well had long since been polluted, and the tiny shed that housed it had collapsed.

"Tomorrow we're bringing our own water," Elysia told him with the sternest look she could manage, but he was so quick to smile that it was difficult to be serious.

"You will have to carry your own jug," he said, but then thought better of it and added, "And perhaps mine, too."

She picked up the end of her skirt and whapped his arm. "That would be funnier if I emptied your jug before I picked it up."

"Then you would have to share."

When they walked back through the ramshackle neighborhood, it was mid-afternoon, and the shadowy figures in the houses moved sluggishly, as if still asleep. Some lifted cups to their lips, while others turned rodents on spits over dim smoky fires; still others, women mostly, sat outside their houses on chairs in the shade, spinning fluffy, carded wool into knobby thread. None looked up as Elysia and Alexander passed by, deaf to any world but their own.

Alexander took her hand, pulling her along quickly after him. "These are not people to stare at," he said. Once they'd crunched through the bits of pottery in the street and found the whole vessels again, he explained. "They like to pick fights, they like to drink, and they hate outsiders."

She hesitated to judge them on their appearances or Alexander's words; when she spent time in the chamber, she had learned that often, good folk lived poorly, but she had also learned that some were best judged by appearances, like the little man. *These are the people Father would say I'm protecting myself from.*

Even the Apocorinthians, in their poverty, lived better than the people she had just seen. Herod, despite his injuries, had not stopped working to turn to drink or let his wife take over in his stead.

That thought made Elysia stop. "What is your mother's name?" she asked; she had met the woman, but never been introduced. The conversation had been too quick.

Blinking back at her, Alexander said, "Ligeia. Have you met?"

"Briefly."

"She would like you." His smile returned in its radiance, and it was then that Elysia noticed that, perhaps, he was handsome beyond the smile, the hair, and the clean hands – he had the aquiline nose of the Greeks, some shadow of Herod's nose, which had been lost to its brokenness. The features he shared with his mother captured her attention: gray eyes attracting sunlight, high cheekbones casting shadows down his face, brows set to shade his eyes unless hit by the right light. "You have the same spirit," he added, squeezing her hand.

Warmth flooded up her arm from their twined fingers and filled her with a nervous giddiness she'd only felt inklings of before. *What* is *this?* The heat spread under her skin up her neck, brightening her cheeks with blush. Her heart beat time against her rib cage, a bird beating the rhythm of flight.

Fifteen minutes later, Alexander still held her hand, and her blush had barely faded; when they found the front door of her house, Elysia blinked. Four beams of wood were propped against the outside of the house, raw and whorled with huge knots, which stared at her like great brown eyes. She towed Alexander over to one and touched it; the wood was rough under her hand, but not quite splintery. "What is this for?"

"The doors," he said. "Khronos meant it when he said he was after bars."

"But… they don't look like bars."

The door to their right creaked open, and her father's red gold head peeked out. "They're not bars yet," Khronos said, stepping down from the threshold. One hand shielding his eyes from the lowering sun, he added, "They have to be cut, shaped, and sanded, and then installed."

The words meant nothing to Elysia, but the gaze he cast down on her hand holding Alexander's did. She dropped his hand as if it had stung her and clasped her hands in front of herself. *He knows what I get up to.*

Alexander looked at her as his hand fell to his side, startled, but said nothing. Instead, he turned back to her father. "Are they going in tomorrow?" he asked, crossing his arms now that his other hand was free.

Khronos nodded. "It might take a bit longer, as Elysia's dismissed my best set of hands, but I'll make do." The wry smile her father gave her made her blush so hot she thought she would melt in the street. *Maybe it was a mistake to banish him, after all.*

"I'll pray to Hephaestus for your good luck, then." To Elysia he nodded, patted her shoulder, and smiled. "I'll see you in the morning."

The jarring of his hand on her sunburned shoulder sent a flutter of breathlessness and a wave of pain through her; it was all she could do to nod. With a wave to Khronos, he started off down the street, his hair jaunting along over his shoulders.

When she turned around, Khronos leaned against the door frame, studying her. "Have another man wrapped around your finger, Lys?" he asked, and she gaped at him.

"What?"

Smiling with a shrug, he pushed the door out of his way and went back into the house. "Come eat!" he called, his voice muffled behind the window coverings.

Elysia stood in the street, contemplating his words. Running her fingers over a groove in the wood beams, she frowned. *Or does* he *have* me *wrapped around his finger?* Confusion flitted through her mind, thoughts turning to the way her skin heated at his touch, the way Alexander's smiles matched her own.

Shaking her head, she walked into the house and sat down at the table, eyeing the fish, fruit, and bread. *The easiest thing would be to sleep and forget this until tomorrow.*

But awake or asleep, tomorrow would still come.

16

Elysia woke to metal grinding against wood. It was still predawn as she donned her gray dress. Peering around the edge of a curtain, she saw her father outside with a beam propped up on the kitchen table – which, she realized, was missing from the kitchen itself. He held an instrument in his hand: it had teeth like a comb, spotted with rust.

As she pushed open the door, it creaked, announcing her presence. Khronos did not look up, focused on his work. “Morning, Lys,” he said. A sleepy rasp coated his voice.

“Father.” Swiping a strand of hair from her face, Elysia ran her hand over the flat of the blade in his hand. It was smooth, thin metal. “What is this?”

“A saw,” he replied. “And hard labor. Metrodora’s like to kill me when she realizes that it’s me out here and not another neighbor. I’ve been at it for a good half hour. See how it works?” He waved to bits of wood on the ground. The angles on the smaller pieces matched the straight cuts on the beam.

“It cuts the edges off,” she observed. The beam had an inch-long cut in it where Khronos had begun to saw off another side. A piece of charcoal lay beside the beam; a thin line had been drawn on the wood, presumably a guide for the saw.

Khronos nodded and was about to reply, but distant whistling cut him off. He and Elysia listened to it, silent.

When a blond head appeared around the corner, Elysia’s heart jumped into her throat.

“Morning,” called Alexander with a wave.

Elysia almost answered back, but Khronos beat her to it. “You get an early start, don’t you?” he asked as Elysia waved to the blond man approaching.

"My mother, sister, and I wake up for chores hours before dawn." Running a hand across the wood laid out on the kitchen table, Alexander tilted his head. "Almost done, are you?"

Khronos nodded. "This is the last to be cut. Next will be hammering them into place." He pointed with the saw at the other wooden beams leaning against the house, all the same length. "And then I'll be done."

"We'll look when we come back," Elysia said, grabbing Alexander by the wrist. "I have learning to do, and he has to teach me." Dragging Alexander down the street, she waved to her father, who waved back at her with the saw, a single eyebrow arched.

"You're in a hurry today," said Alexander, but Elysia just shrugged.

She had decided the night before, as she tried to sleep, that she would watch him – and only watch him, not act on the same impulses that had ruined her relationship with Philip. She would not make the same mistake twice.

While she did not drop his wrist, her resolution *did* keep her from indulging the urge to slide her fingers down to twine with his, where they had fit the day before.

Silent, they passed the dilapidated part of the city, with its strange, shadowy people and its predawn silence. Her grip tightened on his wrist, and she kept close to him as they passed naked doorways. The uneasiness that something lurked in them went deep into her bones, into the pit of her stomach, like a predator stalked her. It was as if the gray before the sun had become twilight, and shadowy men with clawed hands surrounded her again, reaching for her.

"Are you all right?" asked a voice from above her, and she jumped away from it, closer to the gaping dark doorways. It was Alexander's voice, of course; deep and low, concerned. He gazed down at her with shadowed eyes; the so-far-sunless morning had robbed them of light.

"Fine," Elysia replied. Shivers ran along her arms, and she felt cold – not because the morning was chilly, but for the sudden absence of heat; she had leaned into him without thinking about it. "Apologies – this place makes my skin crawl."

Alexander shook free of her hand and wrapped his fingers around hers, enveloping them in dry heat. "Then we'll begin the lesson now," he said, stopping. A groan echoed from the depths of a house; Elysia felt it like it had licked across her body, raising goosebumps as it went.

"I don't want to *stay* here."

"We're not." He loosened the comfort of his grip from her hand. "You can walk quietly, but can you *run* quietly?" His smile hid in his voice.

Elysia took off, pottery crackling and dust flying beneath her feet. Alexander made an *ah* sound –

– And rounded in front of her, stopping in her path. He put his arms out to catch her, the heels of his hands butting against her shoulders as she stopped herself from running into him. "You run like a three-year-old stomping a tantrum."

"And you run like a panther," she replied, twisting out of his grip. As she turned, a woman came out of a house, her eyes so red and baggy that her lower lids sagged like a hound's. Elysia took Alexander's hand and pulled him along, away from the woman whose eyes looked a hundred years older than the rest of her body. "This is no fit place to learn this, before the eyes of others," she murmured to him, glancing around. A few other eyes probed at them from windows: dead stares, dully curious, or glassy.

"Perhaps," said Alexander, his stride outmatching hers once again; she trotted to keep up with him. "But these people would hardly be capable of stoning you."

I doubt that. Their homes were built of crumbling mud bricks – how many of those thrown would it take to beat her into a proper Greek girl?

Probably more than it would take to kill me.

They left the slums for the uninhabited outskirts near the southwest corner of the city. They found the tiny neighborhood as it had been: dusty, heavy with the scent of rotting and ripe pomegranates, and reduced to piles of rubble. The fruit Alexander had smashed on the rock was gone; only a splash of color on stone remained to tell that seeds and a shell had been there.

Alexander clapped his hands together and snapped her to attention. "As you've nixed running from today's lesson – we can't do that here," he said, gesturing to the crumbling walls that enclosed them, "we'll work on the eye rake and the eye jab."

"Those sound painful," said Elysia, stifling the urge to run a hand over her eyelids.

"They're meant to be," Alexander replied. He beckoned her to the wall he stood beside, his hand braced against it.

He's going to trap me again, she thought, and when she leaned against the lumpy brown bricks, he did just that, closing her in. "This is cozy," she said, fighting a shudder.

Alexander smirked. “Don’t move.” He took his hands from the wall and let them hover over her face, thumbs pointed toward her like daggers. Though his nails were short, they threatened pain, and Elysia held her breath. Her gaze locked on them, waiting for them to move.

“This is *not* cozy,” she whispered, and behind his hands, Alexander’s smile grew.

“First is the eye rake.” His hands came at her, and were she not already pressed against the wall, she would have flinched backward. Careful fingers hooked around her ears, and his thumbs came so close to her eyes that they blurred. “Close your eyes,” he said.

She closed her eyelids, and the heat of his thumbs warmed her skin at the inner corners of her eyes. Her breath left her, abandoning ship as his skin touched hers. His nails glided over her eyelids, with enough pressure to make her suck in a breath. The warmth of his hand dissipated from her face, but another warmth spread across her cheeks as she opened her eyes.

Somehow, he seemed closer than he had been when she’d closed her eyes, so close she felt his breath on her skin. This close, she saw lines of charcoal drawn in the light gray of his eyes, the blond ends of his lashes, the exact angle of the nose his father claimed to have given him. “That’s the eye rake,” he said.

The scent of figs rode on his breath, and the sweetness grounded her in reality. Figs belonged to Philip, and she did not want to think about him while standing before Alexander. “My turn?” she asked, voice quiet as she spoke from beneath the pressing weight the scent of Philip had left in her chest. She held up her own hands.

Alexander closed his eyes. As Elysia raised her thumbs to his face, hooked her fingers around his ears, and gently pulled her thumbs across his eyelids, she pushed Philip out of her head. He had no claim on her; she had made that clear days ago.

She let her hands drop. When Alexander opened his eyes, she saw them again, raincloud gray threaded with black, and some spell was broken.

I belong to no one.

The rest of the lesson was straightforward. Where the eye rake used two hands, the jab used one; Elysia cupped her hand and swiped the ends of her fingers across Alexander’s eye. Since she’d mastered cupping her hand on the second day, remembering was easy; the hard part was getting under his guard when they sparred.

Though each touch distracted her, sent her to some misty land where she was free to study him, Elysia distanced herself from Alexander. As they sparred, she kept him an arm's length away with what he'd taught her.

But now he was closer again, and she was trapped – to her left was a pile of brick and tile, and at her back and right was the wall that encircled the broken neighborhood.

Worst of all, he was close enough that she felt his warmth, and the warmth made her forget what he had taught her. Sweat shone on his forehead, in lines trailing around his eyes; his blond hair stuck to his neck. Elysia was certain she looked the same – most of her hair had been pulled from her braid. Sweat and heat washed over her in sticky waves.

Trying to calm her heart and chest that heaved with exertion, Elysia backed into the cool shadow of the wall. "We forgot water," she breathed.

Alexander closed in, trapping her as he had before, his own breath heavy as he put a hand on each side of her shoulders. "And whose fault was that?" he asked, staring down at her.

She gazed up at him. "Mine, probably." Something in her fluttered, told her to lean forward, to meet his lips as she'd met Philip's.

It wasn't the part of her that acted.

Mocking an ankle stomp, Elysia darted out from under his arms as he faked pain. She ran to the shade of the pomegranate tree. Her breathing still came heavy, but the fluttering had become something else, anxiety roiling in the pit of her stomach, telling her to be careful how she stepped around this man who captivated her so easily… Because if she stepped badly, she might find herself tangled in his arms, and she was none too certain about what her body would do then. It had already betrayed her with Philip.

"Ready to go home?" asked Alexander from where he leaned against the wall, an arm flung across his forehead to shade his eyes.

Home. The word sang sweetly across her mind, bringing the pomegranate trees she'd grown up with to dance in her mind's eye, but that was not the home he meant. Elysia nodded.

Pushing himself off the brick wall, Alexander reached for her hand as he passed her, and Elysia let him take it.

When they found the house, linked hands swinging between them, they found Khronos and Zeus lifting a new-made beam off the kitchen table to lean against the side of the house. The beams from earlier had vanished, presumably already in place.

"They look like a good fit," said Alexander, his voice stirring her from observation. He glanced between the door frame and the bar that Khronos and Zeus had set beside it.

Her father and uncle looked up as one. Khronos brushed his hands together, a grin spreading over his face at the sight of Alexander and Elysia. Much to Elysia's astonishment, his grin did not drain away when his gaze flitted over their clasped hands – if anything, it grew. Zeus's expression, on the other hand, was one of confusion.

"They look like a good fit because they're measured to be a good fit," replied Khronos, coming forward with a hand held out for shaking. Alexander dropped hers and moved forward to meet him, and Elysia felt the sudden chill of open air on her palm, as distinct as the sudden pang at the lack of his touch. Trying to hide the blush that crept over her face at her reaction, she crossed her arms, trying to get some warmth back.

As her father and Alexander clasped hands, Zeus came forward with his hand held out as well, though his eyes were on Elysia, scanning her. His eyes stopped around her hips and knees, and Elysia looked down. Her lower half was coated with a thin layer of dust, beige over the blue of her dress. Hastily, she brushed at it; tiny puffs rose from her dress, but she was left with faint dirt stains and a sigh.

"And how fares my daughter's training?" Khronos's voice, directed at her, made her look up from her skirt. His green-gold eyes laughed at her, apparently finding her comical.

"Well enough, I think," Alexander answered, looking at her over his shoulder. His right hand, thoroughly shaken by her father and uncle, dropped to his side again. After a moment, though, he held it out to Elysia.

Her insides shivered as she took it and he drew her forward to stand beside him. It was all she could do not to grin; she maintained her composure in front of her father. Propriety stared her in the face. Still, though, Alexander's fingers found their way to twine between hers, and Elysia breathed deeply as warmth shot up her arm. "I learned to pop and scratch eyes today, Father," she said brightly, and the words sounded so odd coming out of her mouth that she paused after saying them.

Behind Khronos, Zeus burst into laughter as he bent to pick up a saw. The propriety she'd tried to remember disappeared as a grin found its way back to her mouth and Alexander squeezed her hand. She glanced up at him and saw an answering smile.

"That does sound useful," said Khronos to Alexander. "If she had known that the other night, she might have done some real damage."

Zeus laid the saw on the table. “She did do some real damage,” he said, his laughter traded for a frown. “Adrastos said his head rang like a bell, when last he deigned to talk to me. He’s been discharged from the Guard, as well. Apparently, we’re overmanned, but it’s news to me.” He tilted his head at Khronos.

Khronos just shrugged. “I heard, I inquired, and it turned out there was a man too many on the gate.” He picked up the beam and began toward the door.

Zeus hurried ahead of him and opened it, gesturing for Elysia and Alexander to follow. “Is there some way I can help?” Elysia asked, but she knew what the answer would be.

Khronos looked at her. He was already inside the doorway, and Zeus closed the door behind him. “We’re done.” Turning to the door, he set the bar down in newly-set iron brackets. One was set in the wall on each side of the door, along with two in the door itself. “Shall we have lunch?” he asked, raising his eyebrows at the pair of them.

Twenty minutes later, Elysia and Aliya had food laid out in the backyard. The maid had been spending her days with Metrodora and seemed to glow in the sunlight; the city that had once been her home, in poorer times, did her good. When they were done, Elysia fetched the men, who had undoubtedly been gossiping instead of putting away tools – the kitchen table remained in the street, a pair of saws and three charcoal sticks atop it.

Alexander stopped her on their way through the back room; Khronos and Zeus kept on through the door in search of food. “What is this?” he asked quietly, one hand hovering over the hardened clay rim of the tub.

Elysia’s brows furrowed. “It’s a bathtub,” she said, taking his hand that hovered in midair and tracing it along the rim. “You fill it with water and bathe in it.” The tub still had a dark ring around it from her bath the night before, where the water had not yet dried.

Alexander frowned but didn’t take his hand away. “Like the bathhouses, but at home?” His gaze traced the contours of the tub, and finally, his eyes landed on her hand and his. “Where does the water go?”

“There’s a plug in the bottom,” she said, waving at the round, wooden block fitted into the floor of the tub. “It drains from there. It runs down a ditch and out to the gardens.”

“Interesting,” he said, voice filled with wonder. The hand not trapped by hers ran through his hair. His eyes turned to her, and for a moment,

Alexander just looked at her. His gaze shifted, and she felt it on her lips. Her breath caught in her lungs.

"Elysia!"

She groaned, and her gaze fell back to their hands on the edge of the tub. "Father calls," she muttered, and when she glanced up at Alexander, he wore a sheepish smile.

"That he does," he replied, and his thumb brushed over Elysia's cheek. Then he was gone off past her into the garden, leaving her reeling. Heat spread across her face where he had touched her, and she steadied herself on the tub. Her heart raced in her chest.

He's doing this on purpose.

What other explanation was there? Every time he touched her, it had a purpose: to train her, to teach her, to make her hurry along as they walked... But this time, she saw no purpose for that touch. He wasn't teaching her anything; she taught *him* about that bathtub. He wasn't towing her along after him. That left only one reason – he *wanted* to touch her. And the way he had looked at her...

Her face heated again, and she shakily made her way around the tub.

It would take a week to train her, he had said. She stopped, dread swallowing her. A week, perhaps a day or two longer, and she might never see him again.

We were doomed from the start. The thought ran through her like wildfire, eating up every other thought in its path. *But there is no "we,"* reasoned the rest of her, and she took another step forward. What had she been thinking, letting him hold her hand, letting him lead her around? Elysia would not be like her father, pining for years after losing Mira, keeping her hostage. She would not let it get far enough that she pined. She couldn't afford that.

And worse, if Alexander learned who she was – *what* she was – because he became closer to her, nothing good would come of it. If he realized that her father hadn't *just* been named after the god of time, Elysia did not know what would happen. Surely, her father would be forced to do something to keep word from spreading. His presence in Corinth was not something he would want revealed, if his hiding in plain sight as a fruit merchant told her anything.

But when she stood in the open doorway and looked at Khronos, Zeus, and Alexander, Alexander gave her a smile that took her breath away.

Snap out of it.

Watching as Zeus and Khronos dug into the food and fruit, Elysia stood beside Alexander, despite the waging war in her mind. “Are you all right?” he asked, and his hand brushed down her arm, tracing its way down to her hand.

She folded her arms before his hand reached her wrist. “Fine,” she murmured, but it was all denial.

17

Alexander paused, and though he didn't reach for her hand, she felt his urge. It wasn't an urge she was immune to, either. For all her misery over their relationship, her body seemed to have an idea that her mind didn't share. It made the arm closest to him prickle with goosebumps.

He gazed down at her, and something deep in his eyes told Elysia that he was hurt, but he looked away when their eyes met.

Bread, bowls of honey, pomegranates, olives, and cheese sat in neat bunches in a row on the bench. Satisfied, Elysia settled down on a stool she'd pulled from the house, a piece of bread in one hand and a pomegranate in her lap.

They dug into the meal with fervor, a round of muttered thanks going up as she chewed on her own bread. Zeus's enthusiastic chewing made her want to giggle, but Elysia hid her smile behind her bread.

Something wasn't right here, though, and the way her father looked at her… His gaze was pointed – so pointed that he ignored Zeus when spoken to, and then asked if Zeus and Alexander might excuse a father and his daughter.

Wary glances came her way before Zeus and Alexander started their own nervous conversation; Alexander helped Zeus to his feet and they wandered across the garden. Picking up her stool, Elysia took it to where her father sat at the end of the bench. "What is it?" she hissed, following Alexander with her eyes.

"He wants to see you." Her father's tone told her everything she needed to know; disdain dripped from it like pomegranate juice from her fingers. The man he spoke of was one he needed, but not one he necessarily wanted.

"It has been three days. He hasn't learned his lesson yet." If anyone knew Philip, it was Elysia, and she knew everything *but* his reason would speak to her, given the chance. It would be desperation, loneliness, and jealousy, and she needed none of it.

"He begged," said Khronos, wincing. "On his knees."

Elysia rubbed her eyes with a sigh. Her father had warned her of this, but she had not listened. "Tell him he can speak to me in another three days." *Mercy is as divine as justice.*

A roughly calloused hand lighted on her knee, and Khronos pulled her to his chest with an arm around her shoulder, planting a kiss on top of her head. "Good," he murmured, but he did not let her go. "Now, might we talk about this other man in your life, the one who wraps his fingers around yours at every opportunity?"

"There's nothing to talk about." Her voice came out far more solemn than she meant it to, and she pushed out of his grip.

"I know what you get up to," he warned, an echo of a week ago about a different man.

"I know," she said, raising her eyes to meet his. They shone at her, green and gold galaxies. "But this time, there is nothing to know."

Khronos gazed at her, then smoothed a hand over her pale braid. "Then I will pretend I believe you." His hand traced down her jaw to lift her chin. "And watch over you as you do what you will." The smile he kept just for her tugged at his lips – she could see it in the lines around his lips.

The combination of his faint smile and his words warmed Elysia. "I love you, Father," she said, covering his hand with hers.

"And I you, sweet one." Rising from his seat on the bench, Khronos beckoned to Alexander and Zeus. "Now Zeus, before your mother finds out..."

With wide eyes, Elysia listened as her father revealed her self-defense training, and was promptly met with outrage and confusion from Zeus. Alexander spoke in defense of her training, but before her uncle put their closeness together with her training, Elysia made herself scarce.

She spent the rest of the afternoon with spindle in hand, at first balancing on the edge of her bed as she spun new yarn. After a time, Elysia retired to the backyard, where she found that the men had moved elsewhere and been replaced with Metrodora. Like her granddaughter, the woman had a spindle in hand.

"Grandchild," she said without looking up from the wool she added to her thread. There was a smile in her voice and warmth in her tone that was so like Khronos's that Elysia wondered if her father had, after all, learned something from the woman. "Come, sit beside me."

Her spindle clutched in her hand, Elysia took a seat on the bench. The wool that Metrodora spun was the jet she had picked up at the market, black as midnight and newly washed and carded. It looked so fluffy that Elysia imagined it would be like touching a cloud, soft, delicate, and yielding. "A new project?" she asked.

"Quite."

The silence stretched between them as Metrodora continued her work, so long a silence that Elysia almost set her own spindle to spinning again. Her grandmother spoke just as she made to move. "You have not come to my house for your lessons in weaving yet." The way she said it was not ungentle, but probed Elysia for a reason.

"I have been otherwise occupied, I'm afraid."

"Will you be otherwise occupied tomorrow?"

Elysia's eyes widened. She was not prepared for this question, though she should have seen it a while ago.

"The other girls have gone home for the day," Metrodora continued, eyes never leaving her work, "and I think it would be good for you to begin your lessons with them, if you do not mind waiting until the morrow." Just for a moment, she flashed a smile at Elysia, and then she was focused again.

"That would be fine," Elysia replied hastily, and then her daily routine flashed through her mind. "I do have chores and… duties... that need attending to in the hours after dawn." Though she tried to match her grandmother's formality, it was difficult; Hera had been a good teacher, but in Corinth, the quality of her instruction did not matter. Nothing stuck.

"That will be fine." Pinching the thread and holding the spindle to pause it, Metrodora looked at Elysia. And in that moment, Elysia was struck by her eyes.

They looked just like her father's. Granted, they were that dark gray of a Greek, but they had the spires and bright lines that Elysia had come to recognize as belonging *only* to her father – and so to a god. Metrodora's spires and lines differed in that they were silver against her gray eyes, but still, they shined with a light of their own. At the market, in the bustle and the bright light, she had not noticed just how they shone.

"Child, are you all right?"

Elysia nodded, but she was still lost in those eyes as she cleared her throat and said, "Yes, fine… Only a little bit startled." Tearing her gaze away, Elysia looked down at the spindle in her lap. Had she stared for too long? Probably. But the implications… Unless eyes like those were more common than she had always assumed, there was more than one god walking the earth. Her mind spun, disoriented.

"Please excuse me," she said, and then scrambled for an actual excuse. "I ought to check on my father." Giving a wan smile to the grandmother about whom she knew so little, Elysia got to her feet and made for the door, her spindle and wool clutched against her chest. Pulling the back door open, she gave Metrodora a little wave, and ducked into the safety of her house.

Was she descended from two gods? How was that possible, if her father was supposed to be the only god? He was Khronos the Creator, Father Time, Judge of the Afterlife, and, as she would someday be, eternal. It had to be a mistake – her grandmother had to be a human with a god's eyes, or at least ones strikingly similar. Perhaps her first thoughts were right; perhaps eyes like her father's were simply less rare than she had first thought.

Whatever the answer, the question floated in her mind, bouncing off other thoughts.

Slapping the curtain out of the way, Elysia walked into the front room and eyed the men sitting at the kitchen table, which had been brought back into the house, along with the stool she had taken to the garden. Setting her spindle and wool on her bed, untouched since she had left for the courtyard, Elysia crossed her arms.

"How is my mother?" asked Zeus, leaning an elbow on the table and raking his hand through his hair.

"She was... well," was all she could really say.

"Elysia?"

Alexander's voice stilled her, and her eyes skated to where he sat at the table, picking apart a near-clean pomegranate. Soon, he would be unoccupied. When Alexander was done with that fruit... He would be free to do whatever he pleased with his evening. Elysia wasn't sure which would be worse: his leaving or his sticking around for whatever was next.

Nodding to him briefly, Elysia took up her spindle again, but merely toyed with it. Alexander went back to his pomegranate, and Zeus and her father fell into hushed conversation.

"Done." Her eyes found Alexander as he sat back against his chair; his hair swayed into his face and he swiped it back. He wasn't looking at her. The shell of the pomegranate sat barren on the table before him.

"Good," replied Zeus, "because I have something planned."

Elysia looked sharply at Zeus and found his blue eyes alight with mischief. Her father sat on his stool and leaned against the wall, one elbow propped up on the table. Though he hid it behind his hand, Elysia thought she saw the edge of a smile, even in the shadowy light of the room. Well, if her father found it amusing, it might be worth seeing exactly what Zeus had hidden up his sleeve. "Oh?"

"A visit to the temple of Poseidon," he announced, grinning at her. "To give thanks for what you have seen of our lovely city so far."

At the word *temple*, Elysia's knuckles went white around her spindle. Could she go back, even to a different temple? Phantom fingers swept chills down her body. "I think I oughtn't go," she muttered, fingers spreading a smooth hank of wool over her thigh. It was warm and soothing against her raw nerves, a touch she had felt every day since a time before memories.

Zeus frowned, concern etched in the lines of his mouth. Rising from his chair with a bounce only he could manage with concern on his face, he sat on his heels before her. One piece at a time, he wrestled the spindle and wool out of her hands, and then enveloped her hands with the warmth of his. "Your father told me you came to the city to learn to defend yourself." His blue eyes met hers, beseeching and questioning. They were lighter than Elysia's, like the sky on a cloudless day, bright and earnest. "What good is that training if it does not have a chance to be used? Staying away from the temples will only make others curious about you."

Her hands fidgeted nervously between Zeus's, but Elysia knew her uncle had a point. The second test reminded her of that as it rang soundly in her ears. *To judge the humans well, you must know what it is to live a human life.* "All right," she whispered, and Zeus's whole body relaxed, his mouth turning up into his infectious grin again.

Pulling her to her feet, Zeus gestured for Khronos to join them as he towed her toward the door. "I hear that they'll be butchering a cow tonight, which means the gods will be left with only a few choice bits by the time the crowd is done with it," he said wickedly, and stepped over Alexander's legs where they crossed the doorway. "And *you*," he added, reaching down to pull Alexander up from his seat with his free hand. "You are going, too. We'll get you some meat to take home. Walking with the most influential man in Corinth ought to warrant that."

The three of them steered Elysia through the doorway.

She scanned the streets for any sign of men lurking in the shadows. There were several, but none jumped out at her; she was protected by the company of the men who surrounded her.

If only her mother could see her now.

18

The way to temple of Poseidon was much the same as the way to the temple of Apollo: Zeus led them through narrow alleys, winding streets, and over low fences. This time, though, Khronos helped Elysia over the fences; after all, he was her father, and the most appropriate one to touch her. Though Zeus was her uncle, Khronos outranked him – and Alexander was not even in the same roster, no matter what her body seemed to think.

Just as before, the Lechaion was still crowded when they reached it. Most of the traffic was headed toward the square, but a few carts pushed home for the night. Her father held her arm gently the whole time, holding her back at one moment and guiding her forward the next. *Maybe Zeus told him of my clumsiness,* she thought, and felt a grim smile on her face. Alexander, slowly but surely, guided her toward some semblance of elegance; every day, she recovered more readily from her falls, and sometimes she even managed to catch herself with a bit of grace.

The glow of the setting sun over the Saronic Gulf cast the agora in the same light as it had nights earlier. The dyed silks floated on the breeze, throwing vermilion, gold, and azure onto white marble pillars and walls, bathing the otherwise stark structures in warm color. The silks were not the only things drifting on the breeze; from somewhere up ahead, Elysia caught the scent of roasted, spiced meat and couldn't help but hum in appreciation.

From the stairs, Elysia heard a priest's voice – something that caught her off guard. The agora hardly had room enough for the four of them to squeeze in, but still she heard the voice, the prayer, the burbling of the fountain.

Every person was silent.

The hush over the agora felt like it permeated the entire world, so complete was it. If the priest's voice hadn't echoed so, Elysia would have heard the breathing of those around her. His was the only voice. Unlike the night she had visited the temple of Apollo and seen the prayer dedicated to him, no one spoke, not even at the back. Everything had stopped for this prayer, and she thought she knew why: Poseidon was the patron god of the city, the one whose blessings they asked for above all others.

As he edged forward, Khronos put a light hand on the shoulder of the man standing beside him. Nodding, the man stepped aside, and Khronos moved on to the next person, clasping him on the shoulder. Everyone moved aside for him; Elysia followed in his wake with Alexander and Zeus.

This time, Alexander's guiding hand was at her elbow. Her body tensed instinctively at his touch, but she said nothing. Not here, not in this place of silence and reverence. His hand gripped tighter around her arm when she flinched, and she felt him pull her back, pull her closer to him – and then he let her walk freely again, his hand loosening a bit. Relief washed through her. She wasn't alone in her uncertainty.

Soon, Khronos had led them through the ranks of the poor, and Elysia realized there was an order in the square: the impoverished stood at the back, the wealthy toward the front, and those of the merchant class somewhere in the middle. The sailors, rank with the smells of the docks, of fish and sharp salty water, stood just ahead of the poor and the slaves, between the bakers and the basket maker's family – Elysia recognized Ianthe and her father among them, and next to Ianthe stood a child who held hands with her and a man who had to be his father. The family brought a smile to her face.

They kept on forward and passed the fountain. Poseidon stood stoic as ever, the white, wild-eyed horse reined in by his touch; it seemed to Elysia that perhaps the beast feared the water that surrounded the pair of them. At the base of the fountain, people knelt. Some knelt only on their knees, while others touched their foreheads to the ground. Though the press of bodies around them was almost suffocating, somehow none were stepped on… There was an air of practice about the square, as if each man knew where he was to stand. And still the prayer went on, the priest's voice rising and falling with his fervor: *Corinth asks for your forgiveness for her wrongs, and she prays that you will lead her through the storms of autumn. She prays that you will lend her sailors a guiding hand while they are at sea, that they may not be led astray from their purposes, whatever they may be…*

The closer they grew to the front of the agora, the richer the garb became: while the poor had worn undyed, too-many-times-patched woolens, the middle class had richly woven clothes, dyed in blues, greens, reds – but the clothes of the wealthy made Elysia's jaw go slack.

There were airy, silken confections of a yellow so bright it seemed to battle the sun for its share of attention, and patterns so well imagined that Elysia could not dream the hours the weaver must have spent laboring over it. Some wore simple stripes, but others preferred patterns more complex: zigzags, angular and harsh; florals picked out with pearls… One man appeared to have bright red flames licking up the end of his brilliantly orange cloak. One woman wore a gown embellished with rare needlework; another wore a dress with shoulder clasps encrusted with sapphires, emeralds, and crystals that threw rainbows where the light touched them.

Up here, among the wealthy, the scent of cooking meat was stronger. It hung in the air, warming it with peppers, dill, spiced wine, and the hot smell of the meat itself, which called to some primal part within Elysia and made her mouth water. The crowd grew thin; it seemed the rich were afforded more personal space – and it was then that she saw the few wearing purple.

She couldn't help it. She stopped in her tracks. These were the first people in Corinth she had seen wearing the color, and there was a reason she noticed them: purple was a color she had only ever seen in her father's tapestries, and how he had gone about getting that dye was still unknown to her. The only tapestry that bore the color in prominence was the one he had woven of two spiraled, pale pink sea shells side by side on a violet field. It hung from a wall in his bedroom, where he could marvel at it, or so he had said – why he wanted to look at shells still mystified her, but she wondered now if it was the background he looked at. That rich violet so rarely appeared in everyday life that it was a shock to see it here, and worn so openly… But only by a few.

She counted three men and one woman fully clothed in the color, and another two women with sashes and cloaks patterned in it. They could only be Corinth's elite, praying among the masses. The only difference in their prayer was their proximity to the priest and the meat, which had at last come into view: a cow, skinned, portioned, spitted, and turned by young, clean boys clothed in white. The four who wore purple shone with vibrancy and confidence, even in the vulnerability of prayer. One woman had her head lowered and eyes closed, but her posture was straight-backed and elegant. The other two women could only be her daughters; they stood beside her, enraptured by the priest. The men were more enigmatic – one seemed to listen to the priest, another looking past him, his gaze on something in the distance, and the third simply looked heavenward.

Elysia looked down at her own clothes, eyes catching on the dull blue of her skirt and the dust stains on her knees, the unadorned sash at her waist. Her father, on the other hand, possessed the bearing to stand among the richest of the wealthy. His clothes were his own impossible design, crafted on the great loom at home: a tunic the lush green of the garden after rain, with cloth-of-gold trim and a cloak of the same, patterned with swirls that moved under her eyes. The only sign the tunic had seen a day's work was a thin line of sweat at the collar and a few specks of sawdust. It made him fit in, while Elysia knew that she and the men behind her did not. They did not have godliness to give them radiance, like Khronos, or the clothes to match: like Elysia, Zeus favored a plain, dull blue. Alexander was worst off, in his tunic of undyed, yellowing wool.

Perhaps we will only be perceived as guests, Elysia thought. *Or foreigners. We look the part.* The four of them had the fairest hair in the agora; though a few others shared Alexander's sandy blond, and perhaps one or two Khronos's red, not one other had the same soft white-silver as she and Zeus. Again, she wondered if perhaps some would think them brother and sister.

"*Poseidon!* We humbly offer this meal in your name to feed the people of Corinth, the last of it to be given to you in great gratitude, for without your providence, we would starve." The priest's voice rang down from on high; the dais upon which he stood rose to shoulder height. As if on cue, the boys stopped turning the spits. Grease popped and hissed in the fire as it gathered on the underside of the portioned meat and dripped into the flames.

Three boys circled behind the dais, retrieving flat stone plates, while the fourth carved into the meat, portioning out smaller pieces to the boys who held plates. "*People!*" the priest called out, "Feed yourselves in the name of Corinth, so you might receive Poseidon's blessings. Let him provide this food as he provides guidance for our ships and horses." The boys handed the first few plates to the six who wore purple, who passed them into the crowd behind them. "Eat, drink, and live long lives in his name."

Murmurs spread through the crowd and it began to move; some found friends and broke off into groups. Others left the square, forging ahead between temples or returning down the Lechaion, while a silent few climbed the steps into the temples for silent prayer. Soon, Elysia had a plate in hand. She passed it back, then another and another, until everyone around her had a plate and no one remained to pass it to. Alexander had three helpings crowded on a plate, but none said anything. Everyone ate, though Zeus looked at her with that grin of his again, a piece of meat sitting untouched on his plate.

"Not all bad, I hope?" he asked, drawing close. The crowd grew louder, though the press of bodies lessened. Khronos stood with a man in purple, beside the woman and her daughters.

"No." Even if the prayer had been difficult for her to appreciate, something about the gathering made her comfortable – maybe comfortable enough to feel safe, if her instincts would stop blasting out warnings whenever anyone stood close enough to brush her. The only person standing close to her was Alexander, mute and out of place, separating the meat on his plate into five small portions. He ate one, but the other four went untouched. "The priest was well-spoken."

"The words vary little each week," said Zeus, picking up a piece of meat; strips tore away between his teeth. Chewing and swallowing, he added, "But his enthusiasm is easy to listen to."

Elysia was halfway through her nod when a hand touched her elbow. Her instincts zapped her, making her flinch and look up at Alexander, who had gently tapped her. "Are you going to eat that?" he asked, nodding to her food. His words were cold, impersonal, but the lines of his eyes had wariness written in them.

Elysia glanced at her plate and swallowed. The beef smelled so rich she wanted to lift the plate to her nose and sniff it, but hunger gnawed at her. "Yes," she said, finding his gaze. She felt him searching her face the same way she searched his, looking for *something,* anything.

If he found it, he said nothing. Shrugging, Alexander clapped Zeus on the shoulder. "I will see you soon, my friend," he said, and before turning away, he said to Elysia, "and you on the morrow." And then he was gone, disappearing into the crowd toward the Lechaion.

Glee and misery bubbled through her. *Tomorrow, we leave propriety behind again.* Half of her smiled inwardly. The other half shook her head, praying he wouldn't want to talk. If they talked, she was bound to reveal something, and she wasn't sure what her father would do. *He knows what I get up to.* If something happened to Alexander because of her own foolishness – if her father took drastic measures to keep their secret safe – she would never forgive herself.

There could be no coming back from that.

19

The evening passed quickly: Elysia hurriedly ate bites of beef between lulls in conversation with Zeus, wishing she had time to savor each one. Rich and juicy, the flavor invaded her mouth; she tasted the spices, dill, the olive oil and wine, strong as the flavor of the meat itself, as its scent had promised. Her father brought the family in purple to meet her. She stared overlong at their clothes, but the people were as beautiful as their clothes were rich. The older man and his wife and daughters had the dark, curly hair of Greeks, though his and his wife's hair were threaded through with enough gray to make them regal. The daughters were with their husbands, self-made men of the sea, retired early on fortunes enough to support them for a century. Elysia was informed that many other wealthy families kept altars in their homes, praying and sacrificing there.

As the gathering dispersed, the boys in white dismantled the spits and let the near-bare skeleton of the cow fall into the fire. The priest, still standing on the dais, proclaimed that it was Poseidon's meal and thanked them for their piety. The family in purple said goodnight as darkness fell on Corinth.

Zeus led Khronos and Elysia between temples and around the back, just as he had led Elysia nights before. Though Elysia looked furtively around at every crossroad, no men emerged from the shadows. They reached their doors without seeing a soul; between the close buildings in the poor sections of the city, the darkness was complete, and everyone was abed.

After bidding Zeus goodnight, Khronos held the door open for Elysia. "I'm going to have a bath before bed," he said as the door swung shut behind them. Pulling flint and steel from a metal box between tapestries, Khronos struck a spark to light two candles. "You can bathe after."

"No, that's all right." She sat down on her bed, moving her spindle and wool into a basket. "It's been a long day – I would rather just sleep. I'll bathe tomorrow. Thank you, Father."

No matter how she professed to sleep, though, Elysia could not. Her body was tired, bruised, and sore, but her mind was awake. Tomorrow would bring the unknown, as Alexander had said nothing about the content of the lesson. He'd given nothing away, save little signs of affection earlier in the day. And, now that she'd steered them into confusion, he was more severe than he had been that second day, when he had told her all the ways she was doing wrong.

Eventually, Elysia fell asleep, but only after her father returned, clean and smelling of rosewater. She fell asleep to the rhythm of his breath, beating out soft music from his couch.

A gentle hand on her shoulder woke her from a confused dream of phantom hands and Alexander's grey eyes.

She blinked up at the kind brown eyes of Aliya.

"Your bath is ready, my lady," she murmured. Her hand remained on Elysia's shoulder, warm and delicate, despite her callouses.

Elysia blinked at her again before shifting upright, her mind weighed down by the fog of dreamland. She had been at home again, her head under the fountain, but she had been drowning. Alexander had stood behind her but hadn't pulled her out. "Thank you, Aliya," she said, pulling the blankets off herself. Padding into the back room, she disrobed and stepped into the water. The chill woke her and set her body back on edge; goosebumps rose on her arms as she sank into the tub, slouching so the water reached up to her shoulders. She pulled the tie from her hair and raked her fingers through it. It was dirty, knotted, stubborn. Her muscles and bruises ached; a greenish purple was embedded in the skin over her hips, and her knees were midnight blue.

After dunking her head and combing through her hair with her fingers, Elysia scrubbed all over, but gingerly. The skin of her thighs was still dotted with red rawness. She had scrubbed hardest there, for that was where Adrastos's fingers had been. When she got out, the water was dirty, but she felt clean.

Her dove gray dress went over her head once her hair was braided again, and then she was ready for her day of training.

Half an hour later, Alexander appeared. He was his jaunty morning self when Khronos greeted him, but when his eyes met Elysia's, she felt iciness in his gaze. Cool professionalism radiated from him as it never had before, and a lump formed in her throat.

"Ready to go?" he asked, breaking the silence that stretched between them.

Swallowing, Elysia nodded. She pushed past Khronos and waved goodbye, and then the door closed behind her. "Hello," she said, glancing up at Alexander. The impassivity on his face made her flinch.

"Good morning," he replied, and began walking, hands clasped behind his back. His pace was slower this morning, casual, though his back was rigid; Elysia thought perhaps he dreaded reaching the training ground as much as she did.

They passed through the sleeping, broken down neighborhood in the gray light before dawn. Everything was still, and Elysia could not bring herself to speak into the silence.

When they reached the training grounds, not a word was spoken between them. Alexander's hands rested at the small of his back as he walked away from her. He stopped, leaning against the chinked wall across the square, gazing at her from the shadows. His arms crossed over his chest. "Now that we have left propriety behind, might we talk?"

Elysia stopped by the pomegranate tree. The scent of sweet, overripe fruit filled her senses. She steeled herself.

"We're not training until we talk, Elysia."

"Why?" she blurted, one hand fisting in the fabric of her skirt.

"Because," he said, pushing off his wall and stepping forward a few paces. Stopping abruptly, he ran a hand through his hair. "Today's lesson might go badly for me, and I need to make sure of a few things before we begin."

"Like what?" She mirrored him, arms folded in front of her chest. Her skirt fell back into place, wrinkled.

Alexander sighed and stood before her. The inches of height he had on her made her feel small; the way he stared down at her did nothing to help. Goosebumps rose on her skin as he took her wrist. "This, to start with. You've closed yourself off. Why?" The light did not dance in his eyes, even as the sun rose behind them.

Her voice was a whisper. "There are things I could say." She swallowed, trying to wet her dry throat, and stared at his chest. She couldn't look into his eyes anymore. "Things I might let slip, things you shouldn't know. The more I know you, the more I want to talk to you, but I can't. I *cannot*," she added for emphasis. Khronos's wrath might come down on them if Alexander found out who Elysia and her father really were – and what that meant for the gods: there was only one, soon to be joined by a second. Would Alexander believe her if she told him? He might scoff and call her a barbarian heretic from the hills. "My father is a powerful man, and he would not be pleased."

Alexander remained taut, though his hand loosened on her wrist. "So you're protecting us with distance."

Elysia nodded.

He let out a steadying breath and released her but didn't step away. "All right. We'll concentrate on your training, then." He raised her chin with a knuckle, running it along her jaw, and gave her a small smile. "As much as I would like to know you, I won't pry."

When he backed away, Elysia was breathless and frustrated by her reaction to his touch.

Alexander clapped his hands, bringing her to attention. "As I said, today could go badly for me, depending on if you can stop your momentum in time not to hit me."

Elysia frowned. "You've been fine before." *Except for the day I almost broke your nose.*

His grin was sheepish. "Today is different from before," he said. "You'll be learning theory, as with the jaw strike. You'll learn today what men call *dirty tricks*, but they're your best weapons against male assailants – or any person, really."

"All right," Elysia said.

Alexander just looked at her. "Your best weapons are against the groin area of the body."

Elysia stared right back. And then it clicked – and her whole body flushed. "Oh."

"Oh," Alexander said back to her, crossing his arms. The light sparked in his eyes at last, a smile tugging at his lips. "As I said, it could be a painful day for me, once we're sparring."

Her face turned as red as the dawn, humiliation washing over her. This day would go down in her memory as the most embarrassing. The only acquaintance she'd made with anyone's groin had been accidental, when she had whipped around during a game of tag with Philip and smacked him. He'd howled.

"So, theory," she whispered. The quicker she finished, the quicker she could go home – and her afternoon was planned, she remembered. Metrodora would drag her away from Alexander or Elysia's own house, whichever held her attention, should she tarry too long. It would not do if the woman found out what she was doing, off alone with a man in a deserted neighborhood. The training, the isolation with Alexander…

Neither were things of which proper Greek women would partake, she was certain. Either would set her grandmother against her father – and if Metrodora *was* a goddess, it would be a clash very few would survive.

Alexander held up a cupped hand. "Remember this?" he asked, and at her nod, continued. "This time, we use it for a groin slap." He swung his arm forward in an underhand motion, bringing his cupped hand to a stop beside his leg. "Just like that, straight into the groin. It radiates intense pain through almost the entire body."

"That should be easy enough to remember," Elysia murmured. She mirrored his movement, swinging her cupped hand from behind her hip and straight forward.

"Next is the knee ram – ram your knee into the attacker's groin." He ventured closer, standing beside her to show her the proper way to hold her leg: heel as close to the buttocks as she could manage, her knee at a right angle to her body. "This works best if you're in close quarters and can jam your knee into him – you can only lean forward so far on one foot."

After adjusting her knee into the right position, Elysia had him check to make sure the position was correct. With a nod, Alexander moved onto the last so-called dirty trick: the scoop kick. "This is less a kick than in a class of its own," he warned. "It takes balance, a bit of precision, and needs to be done quickly. This one is better if you are out of range for a knee ram." Demonstrating, he lifted his foot off the ground, past knee height, and pulled back. "It's easy to fall over if you lose your balance." Alexander looked her square in the eye. "Don't. Your attacker may fall on you, and that is the last thing you want. Slam your leg into the groin, lock your foot, and pull back as hard as you can. That ought to disable him – and if he falls to his knees, he will be at your level: go for an ear slap. Got it?" he asked, and his eyes blazed, intense.

He needs you to know this. It's his job. If Alexander cared more than he ought to, Elysia wouldn't protest. He was a good teacher, and his vehemence made it stick. "Yes," she replied.

"Good," he replied, and his face lit up in a grin. "Then it's time to spar. Go easy on me?"

She grinned back, uncrossing her arms and putting them on her hips. "Only if you go easy on me."

The grin slipped from his face. "Never." And then he came for her.

Sparring came with just as many near-hits as it had before, but Elysia surprised herself: every time but twice, she got out of his hold with only breakaways. Of course, holding him off once he let go was completely different. When she tried an ear slap, he pretended to stumble disorientedly after her as she backed away. “Not enough!” he growled. “Combinations.”

“Fine!” she yelled, her voice louder than she had meant; with exertion came a lack of volume control. She mocked a scoop kick, stopping her leg at his knees before pulling back – and she discovered what he meant about balance. As she fell with the force of her momentum, he came right after her, landing on her. Elysia’s breath vanished as his weight struck her chest, and then she was wheezing, gasping for air as he rolled off her. Turning on her side, she pulled in as much air as she could without inhaling the dust she had stirred up, too.

“That was what I meant about a fall being the last thing you want,” he muttered, getting to his feet and brushing the grit from his scraped knees.

“Looks like… We’re both going… Home with bruises tonight,” she said between breaths, and took the hand he offered, standing. It was hot around her wrist, callouses rough on her skin.

“Want to rest a while?” he asked, and Elysia looked up, shielding her eyes with her free hand; Alexander still had her other one.

“I can’t.” Her voice was hoarse and small as she tried to breathe – getting the wind knocked from her and the exertion of sparring had her lungs afire. “Metrodora is teaching me to weave today. I should head back.”

Alexander’s hand slipped down from her wrist to close over her fingers. Warmth flooded through her. “Stay just a little longer. We can eat, if we can find a pomegranate that’s still good.”

“All right.” High-pitched nerves rang in her as she realized they were back to how they had been yesterday morning – only now, she had his promise that he wouldn’t pry, given freely.

Finding a pomegranate that was not overripe proved to be more difficult than Elysia would have thought: the fruit had ripened under the hot sun for weeks. Only the fruit closest to the middle, the most sheltered, were still good, and they required a climb. Alexander managed the tree as well as he handled the cliff behind his house, with agility she marveled at. He found a shard of tile and stabbed the poor fruit with it, splitting it open.

Taking the half he offered, Elysia pulled the seeds out a few at a time, as she always had. The white skin separating the groups of seeds was delicate, the arils sweet; she savored each one, watching Alexander eat his own. He took his time, picking at it.

They sat there, teeth crunching on the seeds and sucking the juice from each. Finally, Alexander spoke. "There was another question I wanted to ask you," he said, almost childlike in his uncertainty. Elysia turned to him, but he stared into the pomegranate cupped in his hands. His brows were drawn together, expression almost pained; beyond that, she couldn't read him, and the pause stretched on. Elysia's pomegranate was half-eaten in her hands, as her appetite had disappeared: the solemnity of his tone had taken it away.

A full minute later, Alexander spoke again, turning to study her. His eyes held a wariness she had not yet seen. Yesterday had been confusion, hurt, complete distance – now, only wariness. Anxiety rushed through Elysia's body. "Is there a part of you that wants me to be more than just your trainer?"

Her thoughts stopped in their tracks.

And then her mind exploded with so many fragments of thoughts, and she crashed through the chaos to find her answer – one which dissatisfied her and wrenched her heart, along with his, if he asked for the reason she thought he might. "Yes," she began, but her voice broke, her words cramming against the lump in her throat. Alexander brightened, sitting up straighter, but didn't move toward her. Tears built behind her eyes. Blinking back her emotion – she could not afford to dissolve here, not now – Elysia took a deep breath and continued.

"But I can't indulge that part of me." Alexander's face fell, and his downtrodden expression made her heart splinter. "My father has plans for me. They don't include marriage or romance – I cannot afford it," she whispered. His eyes found hers again. "I wish I could," she finished. Wiping furiously the corners of her eyes, Elysia set her half of the pomegranate on the ground.

Gray eyes gazed at her before looking into the distance. With a nod, he sighed. "And I said I would not pry, so I will not ask you about those plans." He gave her a sideways glance. "Come on. Let's get you home." Offering her his hand, Alexander helped her to her feet.

The way back was near as quiet as the way there, but their hands remained linked. He didn't let her go, and Elysia decided that it was up to her to pull away. Despite what she had just told him, she didn't let go, either. *Holding hands is not romance*, she reasoned against common sense. Still, deep in her heart, she knew she was wrong and going against everything that was supposed to happen here. *You will leave, you will never see him again, your heart will be broken, and all of it your doing.*

But, she thought, *what is a human life without vulnerability?*

20

Khronos was gone when they returned, as were Aliya and the others. Elysia said a brief goodbye to Alexander and watched him round the corner, his whistling echoing in her ears. When he was out of sight, she lingered by the door, biting her lip until his tune faded. She went to collect her spindle and wool.

When she knocked on Metrodora's back door, it opened to reveal a young woman. Elysia had seen her the night before with her toddler and husband: Ianthe, the basket maker's daughter. Her black hair was braided over her crown, shining in the dim light of the room beyond. The laughter and the clacking of women at work echoed, and she gave Ianthe a smile. "Come in!" said Ianthe, though she gave Elysia no choice in the matter, finding the hand that was free of spindle and wool and pulling her into the room. "We have been anticipating you."

Five women waited in the room; one or two glanced at Elysia when she came in, but the rest continued their work. Three stood at the loom in the center of the room, and two sat side by side on a bench with spindles in hand. Metrodora came toward Elysia with open arms, planting a kiss on each of her cheeks. "I was going to send someone to search the city for you, sweet one."

The pet name jolted Elysia – her father had called her that only yesterday. Had he learned that from Metrodora? "I had other lessons to attend," Elysia said, and at Metrodora's probing look, she added, "One in my father's employ is giving me tours of the city."

Metrodora nodded. "Good, but you ought to be careful. Some places are less refined than others," she said, her voice scolding as she squeezed Elysia's shoulder.

"I know." *I spend most of my time in those places.*

Eyes of silver light searched her face before Metrodora turned, apparently satisfied. "Let me introduce you," she said, waving a hand to the ladies. They rose as one, and Elysia realized they had watched her the whole time, but not directly – their eyes had focused on their work, mouths continuing their conversations… But their ears had been well-tuned to her. Ianthe sat alone on a bench. "You know Ianthe, of course," Metrodora said, gesturing to the woman who had just taken her seat and picked up her spindle. She had black thread on her spindle and black wool on her distaff, just as she had in the agora. Elysia nodded and turned her gaze to the two women at the loom – both of whom she recognized. They had worn purple sashes at the prayer the night before, though they dressed more plainly now, in orange and red gowns. "These are Roxane and Theodora, sisters long graduated from my care." Roxane wore the red gown and Theodora the orange, the colors as brilliant against their dark hair as the rich purple had been. Elysia nodded to them, wondering if they would remember her the way she had been last night, in her dusty blue dress. Today's clothes were not much better, but the dove gray fabric hid some of the less obvious dust stains.

Turning at last to the two who sat on the bench opposite Ianthe, Elysia was surprised by the youth of the girl on the left. She had to be Metrodora's charge. After all, the woman had a reputation, and three of her previous students had already been introduced. Metrodora held out a hand to the girl, whose red hair was braided like a trail of flame against her black gown. Rising with a grace Elysia had never seen in one so young, the girl pinched the thread of her spindle, then reached for Metrodora's hand. "This is Khloe," Metrodora said softly, as though she, too, was astounded by the child. "My newest charge." Silently, Khloe nodded to Elysia with a smile and returned to her seat – but Elysia thought she saw a flush of color in the girl's cheeks. "Her mother is Khrysanthe, who was once a charge of mine, as well." The last woman was golden blond and blue-eyed, with skin almost as fair as her daughter's. Elysia was reminded of a much, much gentler Aphrodite when Khrysanthe adjusted her daughter's braid over her shoulder.

"It's lovely to meet you," said Elysia. She truly felt like a girl from the hills, ill-mannered, feisty, and trained in things that would be inappropriate for any Greek woman to learn – and she wondered if this was how Korinna felt. She had seen her seldom since she had met Alexander, but that girl was fiery enough that the thought of her made Elysia crack a smile, here in this house of cultured women.

"Shall we get to work?" Metrodora asked her, squeezing her shoulder and heading to the loom.

Elysia looked up at the great warp along with the blue-green project still being worked upon it… But three feet behind the large loom was a smaller one. "Today," Metrodora began, turning to grin back at her, "you will begin stringing the loom. This is the hardest part, but once you have managed it, everything else will seem simple."

Swallowing, Elysia nodded.

"Now," Metrodora said, going through a basket in the corner of the room. From it she pulled a spool of long, tight thread. "First, you will cut each cord to length; after that, you will tie them onto the weights."

Looking back at the other loom, Elysia recalled how the weights at the bottom had swayed in the breeze. If it had been any other way, the threads would have moved at even the slightest draft, and she imagined the consequences. "This will take you all afternoon, so you will just be doing this today."

Elysia's eyes snapped to her grandmother. All afternoon to cut thread and string it? How many threads were they going to hang?

It turned out to be nigh on three hundred threads – and if anything was difficult, it was cutting the thread. She had to stand on a footstool and drape thread over the loom, then add a bit of length to account for the knots that would be tied on either end. In all, each thread was fourteen feet; how Metrodora and her ladies spun that much thread and found places to store it was a mystery to her. It came out of baskets, and Elysia understood why her grandmother was the basket maker's best customer: she needed baskets in which to put the thread, wool, spindles, weights, and other paraphernalia she had scattered around her weaving room. Baskets were stacked to the ceiling in corners, their wicker an assortment of browns. Some had hinged lids, others simpler ones, and some were completely without lids. A few only had handles.

After she measured the first thread and cut it, Elysia had to cut all the rest, using the first as a template. And indeed, the rest of her afternoon was spent cutting threads and conversing with six other women. Elysia learned what Metrodora had meant when she had told her that Ianthe had taken her teaching too much to heart: while Theodora and Roxane made jokes and laughed raucously, Khrysanthe blushed prettily, and Khloe giggled as small girls were wont to do, Ianthe was serious to the point of stoicism. She rarely glanced up from her spindle, and when she spoke, it was only to speak of her son or to weigh in on discussions about cloth. The rest of Metrodora's once-charges were spunky. Roxane and Theodora spent their days running their husbands' households, just as their mother had run their father's before them, and Khrysanthe did the same with hers.

Eventually, the sun sank, and the women went home. The goodbyes were brief, as they would see each other again on the morrow, but Roxane and Theodora stopped on their way out the door. "Elysia," said Roxane, resting a hand on her shoulder. "If you can, convince your father to remarry. Khronos is a wealthy man, and he would do some girl's family good."

Elysia frowned, wondering if she ought to be offended that Roxane was suggesting he marry again so soon after he had lost her mother. *But it's not soon,* she realized. *To Corinth, Mira has been dead sixteen years.* She sucked in a breath.

And to me, too.

Metrodora cut in before Elysia could reply. "Believe me, dear, I have tried. He will have none of it. This one is his world now." A warm, soft palm patted Elysia's cheek.

With a nod, Roxane followed her sister out the door. Metrodora pulled it closed behind them. "How was that?" she asked softly, a kind smile on her lips.

Elysia gave her a weak smile, looking at the bundle of thread she had cut so painstakingly. "Wearisome work, stimulating conversation," she answered honestly. Tomorrow would be real work; she had not quite gotten the number of threads she needed, even after counting and recounting. She imagined the ache that would settle into her shoulders after her defense training *and* hanging three hundred threads from the loom – not to mention tying the weights on the ends.

"As it should be, for now." The silver in Metrodora's eyes shimmered at her through the dim light in the house. "Now, tell me something."

"Yes?"

"Khronos does not beat you, does he?" Metrodora asked, her expression bleak. The smile was gone from her mouth, her lips pressed into a firm line.

Her eyes widened. "No!" Her voice came out unexpectedly loud, unexpectedly breathless; Elysia flinched at the sound of it. "Why would you think such a thing?"

"You are always covered in bruises, Elysia." Metrodora reached down and widened the slit in Elysia's skirt until her thigh showed. The upper half of her thigh was a greenish purple. "I see them when you shift, and you had a bruise in the shape of a hand on your wrist." Her grandmother pointed to the yellowing skin on Elysia's wrist where Alexander had shoved her out of Philip's way.

Taking a deep breath, Elysia tried to think of what to say. Finally, it filtered through the cloud of harried, panicked thoughts. The truth would have to suffice. "There is another explanation," she said slowly, "but I doubt you will approve."

Crossing her arms, Metrodora pointedly raised a brow at Elysia.

"My mother wished for me to learn to defend myself. I was only allowed to come to the city if I learned." The rest – the tests, the details of the training – was unspeakable

"Your mother has been dead for sixteen years, my dear," said Metrodora, her eyes narrowing.

"My father upholds her wishes, and I admit, I am grateful for the training, no matter the bruises or the pain. I have already needed it." *Please don't ask.*

But ask Metrodora did, and so Elysia explained Adrastos's attack, though her grandmother wanted much more detail than her father or Herod had. While they had asked only what had happened, her grandmother wanted to know where Adrastos's hand had clutched at her, but also if she had dreams. At the question, Elysia's heart sped. *Have I been screaming in my sleep, through stone walls?*

And then her stomach twisted, and revulsion flew through her. For the second time that day, tears stung in her eyes. Branimira and Zeus were both children of rape. Her grandmother knew trauma, though wildly more severe.

Mute, Elysia nodded. Metrodora's hand patted her cheek again, but whatever words she would have spoken were cut off by the front door swinging open.

Zeus entered, breathless, but his face lit up when he saw Elysia. Despite her threatening tears, Elysia could not help but return his smile.

"Just the person I was going to search for next," said Zeus, leaning in to kiss his mother's cheek. Seeing them together was jarring; they were so distinctly different. Zeus was light where Metrodora was dark, blue eyes and fair hair against her charcoal-and-silver. "Are you ready to go see Athena and Hera?"

"What?" she asked, voice high and panicked. *They're here?*

The odd look Zeus gave her confused her, and then he spoke, and her excited thoughts shriveled up and died. "The temples?" he said, raising an eyebrow. "Just as we saw Poseidon last night and Apollo before him?"

"Right," Elysia muttered, wondering if she ought to go. Her chest had begun to bruise. Her ribs ached where Alexander had landed atop her – along with everywhere else that had taken a hit or a fall today. Her shoulders ached from leaning over spools and spools of thread, but that smile… Her uncle's exuberance was hard to resist. Nodding her acquiescence, Elysia held out her hand, and they were out the door as fast as he had burst in, with only a cursory smile to Metrodora as they left.

Although it was her third night through the Lechaion at dusk, Elysia still could not get over the beauty that the setting sun washed across the walls. Tonight, however, Elysia had no time to stop to admire it; Zeus pulled her along at a breakneck pace, pushing past carts and darting through crowds. The square was nowhere near as crowded as it had been the night before. A priest spoke an evening prayer, but the sacrifice was smaller than the one to Poseidon – a goat, barely spiced at all, from the scent. Still, the smell of roasting meat was undeniable, and Elysia's stomach rumbled. *When did I last eat?* The answering memory was heavy in her mind: Alexander cracking open a pomegranate and sharing it with her, but both halves had gone barely eaten, left to rot beside the tree.

The temples of Athena and Hera were combined and much the same as Apollo's had been, but only a few men prayed before each statue, which stood side by side in the front of the temple. Once she had seen the statues (which looked extraordinarily like their counterparts among Khronos's judges), Zeus showed her the back of the temple – and when she saw it, Elysia felt her lips part in surprise.

Ten times as many women were crammed into the back as there were men in the front. *Wisdom and faith,* she thought. *Two things any woman would pray for.* Before she knew what she was doing, Elysia was on her knees before the miniature statues behind the screen that hid the women from the men. Zeus's silence told her she had surprised him; after all, the last time they had been in a temple, he had been in such a hurry that he had not even *shown* her the back, and she had gone along. And yet, now she knelt before the much simpler statues of the women she had known since a time before remembering.

And she prayed.

Would Hera and Athena hear her prayers? They had always seemed to know when humans prayed to them, though as far as Elysia knew, they were powerless to answer the prayers they received. Part of her hoped they wouldn't hear her, but another part wished they would. At first, she closed her eyes and folded her hands in her lap, but it didn't feel right;

instead, she met the eyes of the statues and let her hands rest on her throbbing knees. Marble floors did not compliment her bruises, but she had to do this. Elysia took a deep breath. *I need guidance*, she thought. *I know you would give it to me if I were at home, or if you were here. Give me an inkling. Are these feelings of desperation, of passion part of a human life? Are they my test?* Exhaling, she gave the statues a last long look and got to her feet. There was nothing for her to ask about the third test; she did not know it, and no one would tell her, no matter how much she begged. Turning to Zeus, she took a step forward, but then glanced back. The painted blue of Athena's irises gazed at her, but the statue gave nothing away. One last prayer flitted through her mind. *Tell me it needs ending if it does, and if it doesn't...*

If it doesn't, help me understand it.

21

When Zeus and Elysia returned, her father and the women ate their dinner in the backyard with Metrodora. Until he looked up and saw her, something haunted lurked around Khronos's eyes, but it disappeared as soon as he saw her. Metrodora gave them a little wave and returned to her fish.

Her father rose to greet her and gestured to the seat beside him, where two extra plates of fish sat, fried in olive oil and drenched in tangy marinade. Handing the first plate to Zeus, Elysia took up her own, sat down beside her father, and dug in. She had eaten three bites when his voice was at her ear, deep despite his near-whisper. "Your grandmother is none too thrilled with your training, Elysia."

Elysia almost choked on her fish. Swallowing quickly, she looked into her father's tanned, weathered face. Though his human body grew slowly older, his eyes were ageless. They stared her down like she was a doe in the wilderness and he had a mind to eat venison on the morrow. "I didn't mean to tell her," she whispered fiercely, glad that Metrodora was caught in conversation with Zeus and Aliya. "She dragged it out of me." She swallowed, though there was no food in her mouth. "She thought you were beating me."

The frown and haunted look about his face loosened at her words, and he sat back. "How –" Shaking his head, Khronos cut himself off. "It doesn't matter. If she had thought that, she would have saved the tongue-lashing and boiled me alive."

The severity of her father's words made Elysia's eyebrows rise, and she glanced at her grandmother, who grinned wickedly at her over her conversation. "Thank you for delaying my time over the fire," Khronos muttered, and returned to his food.

After the meal was done and goodbyes had been said, Aliya drew Elysia a bath. Morning came swiftly after a night surprisingly dreamless. For the first time in days, Elysia woke without memories of Adrastos's face or his shadowy hands. She awoke before dawn, and so had Khronos. Her father tore chunks off a round of pita at the table.

Sitting down on the stool opposite him, Elysia pulled a strip of bread toward her before he could eat the whole round by himself. She dipped the piece into the bowl of honey beside his arm. "Save some for me," she scolded. Chewing the end of her pita, she reached for an olive.

A knock sounded from the doorway, interrupting her before she picked one.

"You had better dress," Khronos murmured, and Elysia looked down at herself. She wore a tunic so soft it felt like a warm breath against her skin – but it was merely knee-length. It would never do in Corinth, even if she had practiced in a tunic nearly the same on Acrocorinth. In the city, she had been told, she was likely to be stoned before she got halfway to the training ground.

"Right." Picking up a green dress from her bed, Elysia made for the back room. Hiding behind the wall beside the curtain, she pulled the tunic over her head and listened for voices in the next room but heard nothing. After she had thrown her dress over her head and adjusted the clasps and belt, she flew back into the room, but stopped on the other side of the curtain.

The room was empty.

Frowning, Elysia pulled the front door open. No one lingered outside. Her father was gone, too; whoever had knocked had taken him with them. He had not said goodbye.

The sound of soft whistling echoed down the street, though, and distracted her from her father's disappearance. *He'll be fine,* she reasoned as she looked for Alexander, who would surely come around the corner at any moment. *Father created the universe; he can take care of himself.*

Alexander rounded the corner, bright as ever, blond hair swaying as he walked. He waved a carefree hand as he approached, and she met him in the middle of the road. "No Khronos to see us off this morning?" he asked, craning his neck toward the doorway, like he expected her father's red-gold head to peer around it.

"No." Anxiety raced through her, but she quashed it down. "He went somewhere."

A hum of thought came from Alexander's throat, but he shrugged. "Well, he will know where we have gone," he said and offered Elysia his hand.

Will he? Puzzling over that, she let Alexander lead her down the street. The thought struck her as unwelcome. If her father came to watch them – if he could at any time – he might find them in any number of compromising positions. Then again, she was learning to defend herself; he ought to expect to find her in compromising positions. A blush fanned over her cheeks as she remembered yesterday's training and Alexander landing on her. *The world would have shaken if he had appeared then.*

When they reached the training grounds, Alexander got right to it. "Today, we will focus on techniques you can use should you get taken to the ground or be attacked in your sleep, when you are most vulnerable. We will practice what's left tomorrow, and after that, you will have two days of practice before your test."

"My test?" she squeaked.

"Yes. My father and I test each of our students to make sure they're ready." He gave her a confused look. "Did your father not tell you that he was bringing in an opponent for you?"

"No." *But I know now.* She cleared her throat. If her father was bringing someone to the city for her, she needed to be ready. "Ground moves?"

"Right." Alexander clapped his hands together. "A few techniques can be done from the ground – the ear slap, eye rake, ear pull. You can do any move that requires close quarters from the ground." He gestured to the ground expectantly.

Trepidation struck Elysia like a blow to the chest. If she laid down, she would be completely vulnerable, completely under control that wasn't her own. With a breath, she steeled herself. Hadn't he just told her what moves she could use to her advantage once she was on the ground?

Elysia lowered herself to the hard-packed ground, trying to mute her reservations. Those shadowy hands were in her mind, making her nerves tingle. She pictured Aliya trying to get the dirt stains from her dresses after the last few days of training. Elysia sat in the cool dust, legs outstretched, and exhaled. "All right," she said shakily, and Alexander knelt beside her.

He put a hand under her chin, lifting it with gentle fingers. "I know this might be hard for you," he murmured. "If anyone but me had taught Korinna, she would have outright refused to learn this – to put herself in this position again. If it makes you uncomfortable, you do not have to learn it, but if you refuse, understand that you'll be at a disadvantage against not only your opponent during the test, but anyone who attacks you and means you *actual* harm."

When Elysia swallowed, she felt the warmth of Alexander's fingers against her windpipe. "I can do it." Her words came out hoarse, but she meant them. His face, his gray eyes, were so close she could study his eyelashes; she saw where they turned from black to blond at the ends, the way they brushed his cheeks when he blinked.

"Good." His hand fell from beneath her chin. "Lean back."

Elysia did as she was told, but Alexander made no move to touch her. He stayed where he was. The ground was hard beneath her back – the leather tie at the end of her braid bit into her spine. Elysia adjusted herself one final time, mentally checking where she felt open air to make sure the slit of her dress had not slid too far up. "Comfortable?" he asked.

"As I'll ever be," she muttered.

He dove into the theory of the day's lesson. "The first thing you will learn is how to slam your elbow into your attacker's face."

A short laugh ratcheted up her throat, and she sat up on her elbows. "Sounds simple enough. Are you sure I don't already know how to do that?"

He grinned at her but shook his head. "If you do, good for you, but I will teach you either way. Now," he said, and moved. Elysia froze, wary again, her laughter forgotten. Getting up on his knees, Alexander leaned over her, putting a knee on either side of her legs. He rested what was left of his weight on his palms on either side of her shoulders. His face was mere inches from hers, but he kept distance between their bodies. Elysia's skin prickled beneath her dress, and her breath shallowed. "Is this alright?" he murmured, and his breath washed over her: roses and pomegranates. No figs today, it seemed.

She nodded, and his eyes hardened. "I need you to tell me if you're comfortable or uncomfortable, Lys."

His use of her nickname burned, and her brows furrowed. "I'm fine," she said, her voice clipped, as tense as she felt.

Alexander frowned but continued. "Elbow strike. Lean back."

Carefully, Elysia took her weight off her elbows, moving her braid out of the way before lying down. Her air was tight in her chest, and she forced herself to breathe in and then out, conscious of each move she made and how it might affect the man hovering over her.

"Now," he said, "if your hands are free, an elbow strike is simple." Balancing, he took Elysia's hand and pulled it across her chest until her arm straightened out. "Bend your elbow, lift it, and pull it back across your body. If you can, roll your body with it – it will give you more force. You can break a nose, break bone, damage eyes, and knock out teeth, depending on where you land the hit." He drew back, removing his face from most of her reach. "Try it, but carefully. You know what my father would say if I come home with a bloody nose."

Herod's rough voice played in her head. *He has my nose, and I want him to keep it.* A smile tugged at her mouth, and slowly, she bent her arm, dragging the tip of her elbow across his face. Alexander didn't move, just watched her. When her elbow returned to her side, Elysia let out a breath. "How was that?" she asked, some of the tightness gone from her voice.

"Fine," he breathed. His gaze nailed her to the ground, as though his hands had closed over her arms and pinned her there.

"What?" Voice barely more than a whisper, Elysia searched his face. Her muscles protested their stillness; her hands wanted to run through his hair, pull him closer. Her lips wanted to feel the warmth of his. Panic flitted through her mind, down to her stomach to brush against her lungs, where it made her breath speed. She couldn't give in. Alexander was too close to her; if she gave in, she wouldn't learn anything. Her body would be too distracted, betraying her mind with every move.

Alexander blinked and broke whatever spell bound him. "Sorry." Readjusting his hands on the ground beside her shoulders, he took a deep breath and spoke again. "You can do the same thing with a knee if an attacker is farther down." Scooting backward until his knees were at her feet and his hands at her thighs, he gestured to her knees.

Easing her right leg out from beneath the slit in her dress, Elysia bent her leg at the knee and passed it over his face – but when it was almost all the way across her body, he caught her with a hand in the crook of her knee. His eyes focused on the deep stain of color on her thigh, revealed as she had moved. "Is this from our practices?"

"Yes." What else could she say? To say no would be to lie, and the question of her father beating her might come up again. Still, Elysia felt her face heat. "You are a good teacher, but even you will find teaching me to be graceful an impossible task."

"We'll have to work on that," he muttered, and released her. Cool air hit the back of her knee where his hand had been, and she sucked in a breath. The sun rose, the sky yellowing with the new day.

"What's next?" Elysia asked, her stomach twisting as he drew back up to her torso and closer to her face.

His wry smile made her tilt her head. "Another move or two of which you will learn only theory."

Oh. There seemed to be a few of those.

"The first is called the claw twist. Give me a clawed hand."

Elysia held up her hand for inspection, her fingers bent and rigid, nails all pointing inward. He shifted her fingers around, moving them further apart, but it looked like she had the right form. "Good. Now," he said, and here he winced, "for the part you are not allowed to practice on me."

She raised an eyebrow at him, and he raised his eyes to the sky before forcing himself to continue. "To say this as quickly as I can: if your attacker has you on the ground, grab his testicles, pull, and twist."

Eyes widening, Elysia flattened her hand on the ground beside her. Her skin shivered with revulsion. "Another dirty trick?"

Alexander laughed. "A very dirty trick," he replied, and moved on – sort of. "Another dirty trick is a knee strike from behind, which is just what it sounds like. It does the same thing as the scoop kick. Bend your knee and ram it into your attacker's groin." He looked nervously behind him, but Elysia kept her legs still. She would not do him that unkindness.

"All right," she said, sitting up on her elbows again. Her face couldn't be more than an inch from his, and she instantly regretted moving. *Self-control. Maintain your self-control.*

"Last is the eye rake. It's really more useful when you're lying on the ground." With a gentle hand on her shoulder, Alexander pushed her back down. His delicacy stopped her breath; he even moved her braid onto her shoulder to keep it from straying beneath her. "You know what to do?" he asked, gray eyes boring into her.

Elysia nodded and lifted her hands to his face. Her fingers hooked behind his ears, and his eyes closed as she ran her thumbnails across his lids. Her thumbs stopped at the outer corners of his eyes, resting there as he opened his eyes again. *It would only take a little pull...* "I need to get up," she murmured.

Alexander blinked at her, puzzlement crossing his face, but moved aside. Getting to his own feet, he offered her a hand.

Elysia took her time. Relief washed over her when he was out of her reach, out of range to pull his face to hers, and she took a moment to let relaxation sweep back over her. A deep breath filled her lungs, and she let it out. Then, she gripped his wrist and hauled herself to her feet, not bothering to hide her gracelessness. "What's left for today?" she asked, her eyes on the pomegranate tree. The halves they had left beneath it yesterday were gone, and Elysia imagined some rodent carrying them off to feed itself and its family. *Feasting on our sorrows. If only they could disappear, too.*

"Sparring," he said shortly, and a hand closed over her shoulder.

As automatic as her heartbeat, Elysia twisted from his grip. The more she practiced, the better her combinations got; she could mock an ear slap, an eye jab, and a knee ram almost at once when she managed to get out of his hold. She no longer fell as she spun away from him. It was only when he pushed her away or pulled her down that she fell, and it was only then that she won her bruises; the things she had learned today were already put to use. He pulled her down three times, and she escaped him within seconds. Though she had not much choice but to use her dirty tricks, he seemed to sense them before she had barely shifted, and mocked pain as well as he could for every other kind of move. The last time she scrambled out from beneath him, he called a stop for the day. "Your body knows what it's doing before your mind has even registered something is happening," he said, "which is how it should be."

The walk home was quiet, his hand warming hers, fingers fitted together. They could not have left the house more than an hour or two before; the sun was not much higher than it had been when he had taught her those very dirty tricks. When they got to the house, Khronos was just sending the women out to the agora. Alexander left with a wave, heading off toward the agora with the women, and Elysia sat down on her bed, taking up her spindle.

Khronos ran a hand through his red-gold hair once the last woman had left. Sitting on the bench opposite her, he rested his elbows on his knees, hands folded under his chin. "Philip showed up this morning."

Her whole body froze, the wool she pulled from a new skein stopping halfway to the join she was trying to make. Khronos's eyes were steady on her, gauging her reaction. "And that was why you disappeared this morning?" she asked, maintaining her composure.

"I escorted him from the premises. It's been only two days. He's sleeping in the shop, you know."

"The *fruit* shop?" Incredulity strayed into her voice. *Where else would he sleep? You banished him from the only house he could stay in in Corinth.* Her heart tugged for him, a pang deep beneath her ribs.

"Yes." Her father sighed. "Will you be ready to see him tomorrow?"

Elysia wrestled with the question. Philip had been her best friend. He was probably her first love, the one who knew her – and her weaknesses

– best. Avoiding him was pointless. Determined and desperate, he might just sneak into the backyard if she abandoned him tomorrow. “As ready as I can be,” she said, returning to her spindle and joining the new wool.

The rest of her morning was spent spinning. Halfway through, she moved to the bench in the garden, surrounded by the scent of roses. They brought Alexander to mind. Frustrated, she pushed thoughts of him aside. She would know what to do once tomorrow had come and gone.

As the afternoon drew nearer, Elysia ate a small meal and waited for Metrodora to call her for her weaving lesson. Her spinning grew mindless, simple busywork; her hands knew exactly how much wool to feed her spindle, when to wrap thread around the base, and when to add new wool. Her thoughts went nowhere, for she spent most of the time staring at a spot among the rosebushes, trying not to think. It would do no good to worry about tomorrow, because she could not prepare herself. As far as she could foresee, Philip would approach her one of two ways, different from each other as the sun from the moon. He would either be enraged she had traded him for another, or else he would quietly cling and ask to be brought back into the fold. She thought of him as a friend who had betrayed her, no matter his true intentions, and that stung. Was a week enough time away to grant forgiveness? Alexander was still around, and if Philip went after him again, Alexander might not simply dodge. He might *fight back*, and if that happened, Philip had no chance.

Metrodora found her just as Khloe and Khrysanthe arrived, Theodora and Roxane close behind. Before Elysia could protest, her grandmother pinched her spinning thread and took it, holding it close for study. “You’re near as fine a spinner as your mother,” she said, a hint of surprise riding her voice.

“I was taught to be her legacy,” murmured Elysia. Her grandmother’s expression clouded with both pride and dismay, and she handed Elysia’s spindle back.

“You are your own woman, sweet granddaughter. Do not forget.”

The weaving lesson was much the same as the last, begun with cutting warp threads to length. Chatter rose and fell as the afternoon wore on. An hour after she had begun cutting the threads, though, Elysia had as many as she needed, and it was time to tie on the weights: rounded stones with hollow centers. The most difficult part was tying them at the right length: if she tied them too short, she would have to untie them once she reached a certain point, let out the inch or so she had missed, and then retie them. Trying to retie them at this moment would be impractical; she had so many to tie already and stopping to undo a knot and retie it meant it would take her that much longer to get to the actual *weaving* part. Neither Khloe nor Khrysanthe, who spun quietly on their bench, moved to help her – Elysia was on her own with the loom. She felt the emptiness in the wooden frame glare at her, impatient for her to fill it with cloth.

When she finished tying weights to the bundles of warp threads, Metrodora informed her that she had to tie still more to the *other* ends of each of the bundles. Elysia stared at her grandmother, aghast. "Does it always take so long?"

"Only for unskilled fingers, but you will become faster as you learn," she replied, patting Elysia on the shoulder before returning to the larger loom where Roxane and Theodora stood, passing the shuttle back and forth. Metrodora shifted the heddle and pushed the thread up to tighten the weave.

The rest of Elysia's afternoon passed as slowly as a chilled snail. Her fingers were sore from securing knots, but when she finished, she was *finished*, and she knew she had accomplished a feat. "Excellent work," Metrodora said as Elysia headed out the back door. "Tomorrow, you will get to arrange them on the loom, and after that, I'll set you loose with a shuttle." With a wink, her grandmother shut the door behind her, and Elysia headed into her own house.

Her father and the ladies had dinner ready when she walked in. The rest of her evening was spent like any other night in the valley, and indeed, it felt like she was home; the tapestries that had shaped the valley hung on every wall around her, ferrying her back to the judges and nights spent laughing until her sides were sore. *I'll be back soon,* she thought, mind turning to the test that she was sure to pass in a few days. After that, it would be living a human life – and she was, slowly, learning what that was. A human life was vulnerability, normalcy, a routine, socializing. *And,* she reminded herself, thinking of Korinna, *beautiful, beautiful spirit.*

22

Another night free of Adrastos flew past, but instead, she dreamed of Philip. They sat on the rocks in the valley, the sun setting fire to the sky behind them. She gazed at the trees, at him, her hands dangling by her sides. She waited for him to take them, to run his thumb across her skin, but he never did. When her father's wrath came, they tumbled separately into the valley below, alone.

Dread filled her when she woke. She instinctively searched for Philip to make sure he was alright, but Elysia found only her father, sleeping on his couch. Something twisted in her gut and told her sleep would not find her again, so she set out breakfast. She found pita in a basket beside the table and honey in a container not far from it; for pomegranates, she slipped past her father and into the garden. Careful not to disturb the women sleeping on the grass, Elysia relieved the tree of a few fruits and tiptoed back inside.

Khronos was up and at the table when Elysia pushed past the curtain, already working on the pita she had laid out. He'd torn the round in half, folded the piece he'd taken, dipped it in honey, and started eating – and he reached for the other half. "Oh, no you don't!" Elysia pulled *her* half of pita out of his reach and replaced it with a pomegranate. "Eat some fruit."

Her father was so scandalized, she had to laugh.

"Corinth has changed my appetite," he muttered, picking up the dagger from the tabletop and stabbing the fruit with it.

"Has it?" First Philip and his fatigue, her own dreams, and now her father's hunger…

"The city does strange things to those who are not used to it." Wrenching the fruit open, Khronos pulled a bunch of seeds and popped them into his mouth. "Especially to those like us, who are accustomed to a paradise on another plane."

Elysia took a seat on the stool opposite her father, tearing a strip off her flatbread and dipping it in honey. She watched Khronos carefully, but he didn't look at her, absorbed with his breakfast. Finally, she steeled herself to ask the question that needed to be asked. "When will Philip be here?"

Green-gold eyes flicked to hers before returning to the pomegranate. "He will be here when you return from your training," he answered between the crunch and grind of the seeds he chewed. "I ought to tell you – your first test will be on the third day hence. After you have passed it, I will be gone from the city, excepting the days I come to the agora. On those days, I will check in on you. Aliya has asked to stay with you, and I told her she may."

Elysia smiled, chewing and swallowing a piece of pita. She contemplated asking who he was bringing to face her during her test but decided against it. If her father had not told her, she was likely not supposed to know, and getting Alexander in trouble wasn't on her to-do list.

She had just changed into a dress of pale rose when she heard whistling filter through the windows in the front room, heralding his arrival. Part of her wondered if he whistled to let them know he was there, so they could hide the things he shouldn't see. The other part of her thought it was habit – a habit that sent anticipation shivering across her skin. Tamping down the feelings that gave her goosebumps, Elysia said goodbye to her father and joined Alexander in the street before he reached the door.

The eyebrow he raised communicated his surprise. "Eager to go this morning?" he asked, offering his hand.

Slipping her palm into his, Elysia shook her head. "Eager for today to be over."

Though Alexander gave her a questioning look, she remained silent, and true to his word, he didn't pry. *He will be here when you return,* her father had said.

And if he makes me regret my decision to hear him out, he will never be home again. She was certain of that much. If Philip could not see her in the right light – if he could not afford her the respect a person deserved, or at least the deference he ought to show a soon-to-be goddess – then he would sew discontent among her people. She already worked hard to earn respect from the ones who had watched her grow up; to have him sabotage her would make it that much harder, and she could not allow that. Change would come to their household very soon, and if Philip did not keep up, he would be left behind.

"What will I be learning today?" she asked, trying to distract herself, and let Alexander's voice wash over her as they walked.

By the time they got to the training grounds, Elysia was well-prepared for what she would learn: more ground work and one last technique she could use no matter her position. The first thing he showed her was a throat chop: slamming the narrow side of her hand into an attacker's throat. Practicing it was easy when compared to her discomfiture yesterday, for she wasn't nearly as much at his mercy as she had been on the ground.

Soon, though, she mastered the move. Alexander gestured pointedly at the ground, and with a deep breath, she took a seat in the dust. The sun peeked over the wall, and it sent glare into her eyes whenever she looked up at him; he stood over her, towering, his blond hair glowing in the light behind him. "This one is easy, too," he said, and as Elysia squinted up at him, she saw his little smirk. "Grounded knee and ankle strike. If you are on the ground and your attacker is standing, smash a kick into the side of his knee or ankle." Moving to stand beside her knees, he turned his body to the side. "This is the best position for it, but hitting an attacker from *any* angle in those joints will disable them, at least for a moment. If you land it right, and with enough force, you can tear muscles, ligaments, tendons, and break bone. You can be just as dangerous as any weapon."

Pride glowed in Elysia's chest, and very slowly, she lifted a sandaled foot and placed it against the side of his knee. Sliding her foot down his shin, she let it stop at his ankle. "Here?" she asked, still trying to see him, but the light of the sun behind him and the shadow it cast on his face made it impossible to see anything aside from that trace of a grin playing around his mouth.

"Yes." Suddenly, Alexander dropped down, and Elysia blinked in the sunlight before she found him again – sitting on his haunches beside her hip, gazing at her. "Biting is last."

"Biting?" Her voice was higher than she'd meant, squeaky.

He cracked a crooked, white smile at her. "Yes, biting. Bite hard, bite deep, and don't let go until they *really* want free. It's a last resort, though," he warned – and then he hovered over her, forcing her to lean back or else smack their skulls together. His legs clamped hers together, and hands pinned her arms to the ground below her elbows.

Elysia lost her breath.

"If you are immobilized, use your teeth. They are your last weapons. You can try a headbutt, but that will disorient you as much as your attacker. So. Teeth." Alexander leaned his neck to the side, revealing the vulnerable places on his neck. His pulse twitched beneath the skin of his throat. "Aim for a vein. You might end up with a mouthful of blood – but if you don't have any other options, blood will be your last concern. Got it?"

Breathing in and letting out a slow breath, Elysia nodded. Though her skin still prickled at his closeness, her mind didn't spin as it had yesterday. She didn't feel quite safe, but she also wasn't *uncomfortable*. His hands held her arms to the ground, but he was not threatening; Alexander stayed where he was, still and studying her. "Ready to get up?" he asked at last, and at her nod, he rocked back and pulled her to her feet.

"Is that really all that's left for me to learn?" she asked, frowning. What had it been, half an hour since they had left? She wasn't ready to go back yet. *Just another hour in paradise*, her mind thought, and the furrow between her brows grew deeper. She scolded herself – she could not use him to avoid Philip.

Alexander nodded but held up a hand. "There's still sparring to be done, if you would like, but it sounds like you might have too much on your mind to be any good today."

Elysia shook her head. "I might have a lot on my mind when I am attacked. I should be training for any kind of situation, right?"

"Right," he said, but sighed. Running a hand through his hair, he looked up at the sky, like it might have a better way to explain whatever he was about to say. The brilliant blue blankness seemed to offer him nothing, though, as he turned back to Elysia. "The thing about sparring is you *expect* to be attacked. It just helps your body remember what it is supposed to do in a dire situation. With luck, it will react the way it's supposed to when you are attacked, especially when you are not expecting it. Sparring when you're preoccupied might be detrimental. You have to be paying attention," he said, and grabbed her chin to turn her wandering eyes back to him, "and right now, you're not."

"I'm sorry," she said, and fidgeted, wondering if she ought to offer an explanation. He had wanted one earlier, but he hadn't asked. "There is something waiting for me, and I have to handle it. Sooner would be better than later. The more I think about it, the worse it will seem, until I never want to face it."

Alexander nodded and tucked a strand of long hair behind his ear. “We had better get you back, then.” Without another word, Alexander offered his hand, and they set off toward home.

Walking back with Alexander beside her made Elysia relax, even if only for a moment. Out of curiosity and habit, she peered into the darkness of the run-down homes, but her eyes were unseeing; she could not have said which houses were awake, asleep, or even inhabited. Her whole being concentrated on the warmth in the palm of her hand, threaded between her fingers, and that was fine with her – because after her talk with Philip, she might never feel it again.

When they reached the house, Elysia lingered outside and pretended she didn’t see the corner of a curtain move. Alexander squeezed her hand. Before she knew what he was doing, he leaned in to murmur in her ear, breath warm against her ear. “You have to face it, Lys,” he said, and she froze at the nickname. Then he was gone, her hand cooling as he went back down the street the way they had come, heading toward the agora.

Behind her, the door opened, and a familiarly rough hand pulled her into the house.

23

Philip was livid.

He said nothing to reveal it, but Elysia knew the look he gave her – a look that told her she was in trouble, the same look he had given her when she had run her sorrel before she was prepared. His forehead was creased, skin red with the breath he held, his arms crossed. "Hello," she said carefully, closing the door without turning from him. Dread settled into her skin, and she knew if she broke eye contact with him, the danger lurking beneath his skin might come unleashed.

Philip said nothing, but his arms pulled tighter together. His deep brown eyes studied her, calculating every movement, and finally, he lifted his chin and leveled with her. "Holding his hand now, are you?"

Elysia bristled. "It's not about him, Phil," she said. "We're here to talk about you."

"And you expect me to want to talk about *me* when I have to watch *you* walk yourself right into injury?"

Part of her wanted to huff and walk past him, but she beat it down. *He wants to keep you safe.* "Believe me, I have crushed any hopes we had to get involved." Still, the image of Alexander's hand in hers would not flee her mind.

Something stricken crossed Philip's face. "You had hopes to get involved?" A silent question hung in the air after his words, unspoken but hurt all the same.

Elysia put her hands on her hips. "That depends on you."

"Does it?" he said, and his voice transformed from a tightly controlled creature to a slinky little snake determined to worm under her defenses. Philip took a step toward her. "And what part of me would that be?"

"Your wisdom," Elysia said through gritted teeth, "and your faith in me."

Philip's eyebrows shot up. "You do not seriously think I lack faith in you."

The statement set Elysia's teeth on edge. She crossed her arms. "You think you know me so well, and yet you treat me like a child who cannot defend herself." Her fingers dug into her arms, burning against sore muscle. "Someday – someday *soon* – I will be the lady of the valley. You will be under my command more than you are already. I will not allow you to behave like I'm some student when I am as eternal as my father." Elysia suddenly wondered just *where* her father was. He would never leave them alone to wage this war unchaperoned. Philip's eyes lit with new fury. *You're safe,* Elysia told herself. Even if Khronos wasn't in the garden, she was safe; her nerves prickled. Her body was ready to act should she need to. She hoped.

"You think I treat you like a *child,*" said Philip, scorn hard in his voice. He leaned down, eyes level with hers. "And what do you call trading tongues on those boulders? Did I treat you like a child *then*?"

Barely containing a scream, Elysia pushed him back with a sharp rap on the chest. She had to get out from beneath his stare, out of the space between his body and the door. But still she did not look away, and as she pushed him, she spat, "*You* kissed *me*. You made that decision for me."

He caught her hand and refused to move any further than three steps back. "Did I, now?" His chest heaved beneath his tunic, its fabric as stained as the one he had worn that evening on the rocks with her. "I recall you seemed to rather enjoy yourself."

Something vicious dripped from his tone, cold, dangerous, and chilling Elysia to the bone. "I might have," she conceded, nowhere near cowed. *I love you, but you are a poison. You are mine, but you will kill me.* "That does not change that we are not equal in your eyes."

"You are a woman."

The clamor, the din, the chaos in her mind silenced all at once. Elysia stared at the man who had been her teacher, her mentor, her best friend, her lover – in the most chaste sense of the word. When she had been small, her world had begun and ended with *him*. And whatever happy world that had been, he had just ended it with four words. *Four words.* Fighting with herself, she struggled to speak, to make sure she had heard him incorrectly. "What?"

"This equality you want, that your father has given since you could speak," he said, wrenching her toward him, "it will never become a woman. You are to be protected, cherished, and with every breath you take near men who have no right to your presence, you put yourself in danger. I must keep you safe, and if you insist on this notion of equality, I cannot do that."

The pedestal she put him on crumbled, and their happy little world stopped turning. Upon it fell a wrath as terrible as she imagined her father's to be. *Destroy him*, some part of her screamed, but even as she pulled her hand violently back into her own space, she felt hollow. She could not hurt him, even now. "The world is not made for women such as me just now," she whispered, hoarse. "And neither are you."

Philip's eyes darkened, and he took a step toward her. Clutching the hand he'd held against her chest, she held out her other one to stop him. "No," he said, frustration in the short word. "No, no, that wasn't what I meant."

"You have to tame that fire, or they'll put it out for you," she said, recalling his words. "I have always been freer than any girl under her father's rule has a right to be." Her chest heaved with every remembrance, every word she knew she had misinterpreted.

"You have been." He took another step forward and her hand brushed against his chest. Elysia felt his beating heart through the wool, and his familiarity made her shiver. "Your recent behavior proves it."

"I would have married you." Her voice broke, and she pulled her hand back to her chest as if it had been burned by him, too.

"And I would have protected you. I will still protect you," he said, stepping closer to her, his chest only inches from hers. The scent of figs on his breath made tears hard to deny.

"I have *loved* you," she said, but she spoke only to herself now. Her eyes found his again. They were so plain, so honest, so deep, but they had hidden a snake in her nest, in her father's nest. "But I am wild, and I have only injured myself."

Philip stared at her, silent, one hand suspended as he reached to brush a tear from her face. His face changed, the set of his jaw. "That is not what I meant," he said, voice a low growl.

"Isn't it?" Elysia's own voice was a cry, far louder than she had intended. "Everything you've said to me has been deception." She slapped his hand away from her cheek, leaving her tears to fall. "Even if you protected me, who would protect me from you?"

The anger Philip had carefully concealed freed itself, and his face became terrifying – nostrils flared, mouth a hard line, eyes narrowed. Elysia moved to back away –

He grabbed her arm with bruising force.

Her breath caught in her throat. Eyes flicking to his hand and then his face, Elysia stared at him. She could not hide her fear. He'd never touched her before, not in a way she objected to, not like this. He was not allowed to, not even to give her a swat when she misbehaved as a child. Her hand itched to slap him, to send him ringing out the door, but she lost her element of surprise with her hesitation.

"That boy is putting thoughts in your head, and he will regret it," said Philip.

"Make no mistake, Philip." She calmed her shaking voice. Eyes locked on his, she wrenched out of his grip. "If you do anything to harm Alexander, you will not be given mercy. Leave this place, and never come back. And do not think to say goodbye, Philip," she said. Her mind was a deafening rainstorm as she tried to see her way to the end of this. "You don't say it."

"I will never leave you, Lys," he said, glowering. "I'm in your heart, as you are in mine.'

"Get out!" she shouted, pushing him with flat palms. Open surprise crossed his features, and at last, Philip reached for the door handle.

"Don't forget that I know you, Elysia," he said. "Better than you know yourself. This won't last."

"Out!" She moved forward again, intent on shoving him out the door, but instead, he opened it and slipped through. He watched her until he passed out of sight.

Her body found its way to the floor, numb in the dirt, tears turning to mud on her cheeks. She cried until pain made her stop, though her first attempts were halting; her sobs wrung her out, turning the muscles under her ribs and in her abdomen to a tight pit of flame, burning her whenever she took a breath. Finally, she lay there on the floor, breathing shaky breaths without a sob to follow each of them, and she realized she was shivering, her body cold from the exertion of all the tears that had escaped her.

Sitting up before standing – her legs felt like slugs beneath her, weak, wobbly, and gelatinous – Elysia took a blanket from her bed and wrapped it around herself. She wiped at the crust of salt and mud forming on her cheeks, on her chin. She wanted to sleep, but it was not even noon yet; still, her body was exhausted. It would be a miracle if she stayed awake until sundown.

She made her way into the garden in an unthinking blur; suddenly her father appeared, his eyes emerald pools of concern. Elysia let him guide her to the garden bench, and slowly, carefully, she laid down on it, her muscles groaning a creaky protest. Khronos sat down at the end of the bench and eased her head onto his thigh, smoothing her hair away from the places where it stuck to her face with drying tears. "I still need him, Lys."

Elysia closed her eyes and pulled the blanket closer. "I know," she muttered.

"I cannot bring him down like I did Adrastos."

"I would not ask it of you, Father," she replied, pressing her cheek into his leg. It wasn't a very comfortable pillow, all strong corded muscle, but then, neither was the marble bench a good mattress. Elysia was beyond caring. "Wake me up when it is time for my weaving lesson."

"You still want to go?" he asked, and she almost felt his eyebrows rise.

"Yes." Curling her legs underneath the warmth of the blanket, Elysia got as comfortable as she thought she was like to get. "I will not be absent. Not for this."

Her sleep was the kind of deep, dark dreamlessness that came only with complete exhaustion. She awoke four hours later, her father's thigh still burning beneath her cheek, his hand still smoothing her hair. The sun shone high above them now, beginning its descent into the west. While she had slept, Khronos had pulled the blanket over her face to block the sun; the fabric felt foreign on her salt-stained skin, too warm against her breath. Pushing it off, Elysia groaned. Sleeping on marble had done nothing to soothe her sore muscles, and her ribs ached.

"Easy there, Lys," her father said, helping her sit up with a hand on her shoulder. Concern glowed once more in his eyes, searching her face. "Feel better now?"

Elysia rolled her shoulders. Something in her chest felt broken, and her throat was still tight with tears. Her words to Philip rang through her. *You don't say it.* They were the most vicious thing she could have said to him, and she must have hit the mark. He had just *left*. Nineteen years of enchantment broken in four words.

"No, Father," she answered, rising with whatever strength she could muster. Making her way to the fountain, Elysia leaned down and splashed water on her face. It was cool and clean. Grime ran down her face and between her fingers. Her last day in the chamber came back to her, so long ago. Had it been only two weeks?

Closing her eyes, Elysia let her mind take her home, back to Hera's arms on bad days and her father's on good days. Now they'd switched: her father comforted her bad days, and whenever she saw Hera, it would be her best day, the happiest day she would see in a long time.

She splashed another wave of water onto her face. The water ran down her neck and she wished she could breathe it in, that it could purify her inside and out. *But it is all done with,* she thought. She no longer answered to Philip; no matter how he felt about her, she had made her decision about where they were headed – which was nowhere. *Once, I thought he was mine, but he wanted me only to be his.* Elysia belonged to only herself.

Wiping her face on a clean corner of blanket, Elysia headed for her grandmother's door, but turned back just before she got there. "Pure as spring water, Father," she said, trying to reassure him. "Clean and refreshing."

His answering smile was weak, his wave half-hearted. He would pretend that he believed her and watch over her anyway.

The weaving lesson with her grandmother and the girls passed Elysia in a blur. She followed her grandmother's instructions in arranging the warp threads on the loom and tied on the heddle, but at the end of the night, she could not have said how she had done it. Though she said not a word in conversation, the others didn't seem to mind; they let her go quietly about her work. Elysia lost herself in tedium, focused on spacing the warp evenly, tying the heddle to certain threads with careful fingers. At the end of the lesson, her loom was set up in the wooden frame; yellow-white threads hung innocently where there had been glaringly empty space yesterday. Metrodora declared that tomorrow, she would be given a shuttle and a comb and set to work, and then Elysia returned to her own house once more.

She sat on the edge of her bed, with the strangest feeling that everything around her was about to combust, as if her molecules tried to hold themselves together, but they really wanted to fly apart. Her mind set thoughts back on their halted courses once more, floating through her head like tiny ships, colliding occasionally.

When the light outside the windows grew dimmer, Khronos walked through the front door, a covered platter in his hands. He saw her sitting on her bed, hands holding onto the edge with white knuckles, and shook his head. "Come, eat," he said, sliding the wooden plate onto the table. When she didn't move, his voice was a little sharper. "Lys. You must eat."

The name burned her, but her father had been using it long before Philip had, and she could say nothing to him that would make him stop; a habit nearing twenty years old would be difficult to break. Taking a breath as she got to her feet, Elysia watched as he pulled the cloth from the platter. Beneath it lay four skewers, thick with dark roasted beef and chicken dripping honey and juices. And even though she wasn't hungry, she would eat it, because it was just what her body needed: something hot, hearty, and comforting.

She found herself on her stool without knowing how she got there; her eyes were drawn to the food, and suddenly, Elysia thought maybe she *was* hungry – hungrier than she knew. What had she eaten today? Pita? She'd eaten pita bread and drunk tears.

Tearing a chunk of meat from the skewer, Elysia dropped it on the table. *It's hot, idiot,* her common sense told her, and she couldn't help it – she grinned. Food *was* what she needed, because even now, she was returning to the person she had been hours ago, when she had left the training grounds with Alexander by her side.

The prospect of getting through another day as she had gotten through this one didn't seem so bad, because that blond man with gray eyes and an infectious smile would be there – and he would teach her to protect herself. He respected her enough to teach her and care about her, and did not do the protecting for her… Maybe that was better than nineteen years of possessing someone and being a possession.

"What's that smile for?" asked Khronos as she picked up the meat that had landed on the table. She looked up and saw the smile he kept just for her, crinkling his eyes at the corners.

"Good food," she answered.

24

The high walls of a dim, narrow alley surrounded her, pottery tripping her every few steps. She was on her way home from training, but Elysia had never been this way before. Alexander's hand was in hers, warm and strong. When they were halfway down the alley, though, she stopped to adjust her dress – and when she reached for Alexander's hand again, the air was empty. She turned around.

She was alone.

Alexander was gone, but it didn't make sense: there were no open doorways, not here. Just the end of the alley, far ahead of her, and the beginning, behind her. The wall she leaned on was cold against her hand, but she kept going. If she got home, she would see him tomorrow.

The farther she walked, the narrower the alley got, and more and more pottery seemed to be in her way. They were not whole vessels anymore, either; they were shattered, some half-broken, shards rising halfway to her knees. Soon she stepped on them – and the next time she looked up, a wall stood in front of her. Elysia frowned. That hadn't been there a moment ago, and this was the only way out of the alley.

But then her feet were on solid ground again, and there were *hands* on her, uninvited hands clawing at her, trying to find the edge of her dress and rip it away. Shrieking, she turned – and her scream stopped in her throat. It was not Adrastos. Instead, brown eyes she had once known to hold warmth stared into her; the hands she knew better than her own shoved her against the wall, tore at her clothes. The chest she had leaned against so many times pressed against hers, pushed the air out of her. And then Philip's fingers found the shoulder clasp on her dress and tore it off; his hand held her clothes together, digging so hard into her shoulder that she felt it bruise.

"No," she whispered, and his mouth was on hers, slamming her head into the wall and muting her. His hands pinned hers above her head, where they were useless. Frigid air slid against her skin as one side of her dress fell, no longer supported by his hand. And then, so slowly that she screamed into his mouth, one of his hands groped its way down her body while the other held her wrists together. It pinched and squeezed her, *hurt* her, and slid under her dress to wrap around one of her cheeks and press her close to him.

Fight back! Her mind screamed at her, trying to make her act, trying to move her muscles on its own, but she was paralyzed beneath Philip's hands, beneath his mouth. *No, not like this, not like this, I don't* want *this.* His tongue tasted like figs, breath loud in her ears.

Finally, when she thought he would never stop, when she thought *he'd never let her go*, his mouth moved to her ear. His voice was rough and low, and he bit her ear as he spoke, sending a lance of pain into her throbbing skull where it ground against the brick. "This is love, Lys," he growled. "Don't you want love? Don't you want to pass your test?"

Elysia woke screaming and flailing, her body half off her bed, her shoulder pressed into the corner of the frame and her head on the floor. She tried to figure out where she was, tried to fight off the phantom that no longer pressed on her. "No, no no no." Her voice came out a whimper, and suddenly her father was there, cradling her head and pulling her upright onto her bed. Khronos hugged her tight to him, rocked her.

"It was a dream, sweet one," he murmured, strong arms wrapped around her. Elysia buried her face in the hollow where his neck met his shoulder, resting her eyelids against warm skin as she tried to erase the images from her mind. "Only a dream."

"It felt like more than a dream," she whispered into his tunic, trying not to slobber on him – her nose ran from the crying fit she must have begun in her sleep, and tears flooded like a wave had burst through a levy. Her sore muscles wracked all over again, and part of her sobbed from the pain more than from the hands she still felt pressing into her skin.

"I was about to wake you for breakfast. You don't have to go back to sleep – dawn is almost here."

Taking a deep, shaky breath to calm the muscles around her lungs, Elysia nodded but didn't extricate herself from her father. Not yet.

"Do you want a bath?"

The question caught her off guard, but it was a welcome one. "Please."

The cool water of the bath erased the mess she had made of herself, the hot stickiness of sweat and tears and panic. She splashed water over her skin, letting it wash away the dirtiness she felt, rather than trying to scrub it out. She had done that before, and it had yet to work – somehow, though, she felt stronger. Her body was sore, but her muscles had tightened into something more substantial than they had known before. She had survived her fight with Philip. One of her worlds might have stopped turning, but it was the world meant for the little girl she had once been.

She wasn't a little girl anymore.

Washed and robed in her sky-blue dress with a belly full of pita, honey, and olives, Elysia waited by the windows for Alexander's whistling. She was eager to get going, to leave yesterday and her nightmare behind her. Though the day's training didn't sound particularly promising – they would only be sparring – the prospect was more exciting than any of the earlier days combined. It had her on the edge of her seat, a knee bouncing to keep her busy, counting the seconds until her day would begin.

When Elysia heard the whistling, she near jumped for the door. *As soon as the door closes behind me, it will close on Philip, too,* she promised herself. Over the din of her thoughts, she heard her father call a goodbye, and she gave him a wave as she closed the door behind her.

It didn't make her feel nearly as free as she had hoped, but something in her fluttered at the sight of Alexander. This time, instead of waiting for him, Elysia reached out. "Good morning?" he said, slowing nearly to a stop as he took her hand, wrapping her fingers in warmth. Tingles and heat shot up her arm as he fitted his fingers between hers.

"Good morning," she replied, giving him a proud smile – for once, she felt like the goddess she would be. The weight lifted from her shoulders when he smiled at her, and each of those smiles came back to her: when she did well in training, when some ridiculous move she tried made him laugh. Suddenly the nervous girl returned, shivering at his touch and trying to catch her breath. They still walked, just getting to the place where the pottery was merely chipped, and he asked her another question.

"Did you handle yesterday's issue?"

Elysia's stride paused for a beat. "Yes." For a second, she darkened; Philip had haunted her before, but she would have none of it. No guilt. He undermined her, betrayed all she had believed about him, and in doing so, set her free. She reveled in the sunlight, liberated from her chains.

You are your own woman, my sweet granddaughter, Metrodora had said. *Do not forget.*

On its own, her right hand began swinging Alexander's. She felt his eyes on her face, searching her, gray eyes that seemed to absorb her whole self when she looked into them. Soon, their hands had enough momentum that she saw him crack that bright white smile. Her own cheeks burned with a grin; nothing held her back but herself, and she was done with *that.* It had led her nowhere but regret before, when she had wasted her time waiting for Philip to decide where she was headed. She had already told Alexander what she felt. She had told him part of her wanted him to be more than her mentor – but she could not afford to indulge that part of her.

Well, she supposed, *that could change*.

When they reached the training grounds, Elysia released him, their hands flying apart at the apex of a swing.

Alexander clapped his hands together, though he still wore that grin. "So. Sparring."

"Sparring," she echoed, but held up a hand. "I had a nightmare last night."

Alexander's brow furrowed, his grin disappeared. "What kind of a nightmare?" His voice was soft, careful velvet on her ears.

"A… An attack," Elysia replied, and frowned. "You told me to tell you when I was comfortable or uncomfortable."

"Yes," he said, reaching for her and running his thumb over her hand – whether or not he meant to, it made her shiver.

"I don't think I'll be comfortable with groundwork or getting pushed against a wall today." Her voice shrank down to a whisper, but Alexander heard her: he nodded.

"You know how to handle yourself in those situations, anyway." He pulled her hand to him, cupped it in his. His fingers traced hers, drew the lines of her palm.

Elysia stopped breathing. "What does this mean?" The words escaped her before they registered – and his confusion was obvious by the crease in his brow as he glanced up. "We hold hands, even after I said we couldn't be together," she added, clarifying.

Alexander's head tilted to the side as he looked at her. "Were we supposed to stop?"

"I don't know."

His hand reached to touch her chin, and instinctively, she followed it closer to him, letting him draw her in. "If it bothers you, Lys, we can stop," he said, and put a hand on her shoulder.

Alarm shot through her. *We're going to spar* and *have this conversation?* Rolling her shoulder out of his grasp, Elysia took a step back – and he followed her. "My name is Elysia," she said. She stepped forward, fingers hooking in the neckline of his tunic, hauling him closer.

Alexander's eyes widened with the same astonishment she felt toward herself. "Elysia," he offered warily, warning in his voice, but she ignored it. She fought her own battle inside her head, staring up at him.

If she moved forward, if she *leaned* forward like her body wanted her to, would she hurt him? There was so much she could never tell him – more than just Philip stood between them.

The shallowness of her breath filled her ears, mirrored by his. He stared at her, waiting for her to move.

And she did.

She pulled him closer, until she could chastely kiss his lips – lips soft and warm beneath hers, carefully still. Pulling back half an inch, she searched his eyes. He did not pull at her; he did not ask her for more, made no move to take more than she had given. Instead, he reached a hand up to her cheek and brushed his thumb across her skin, raising a blush. His fingers rested against her neck, and Elysia's pulse raced beneath the pressure of his skin. "I thought part of you did not want this." Alexander's voice was merely a murmur, eyes level with hers, head bowed to her height.

"I am learning," Elysia breathed, "that that part does not govern all of me."

Alexander's brows drew together. "That part wanted to protect me, did it not?"

"You can protect yourself." *Not from my father, maybe, but that can be* my *job.*

The corners of Alexander's mouth pulled up in a smile, and relief flooded through Elysia, a rush of soothing air on her nerves. "I would probably be a less-than-adequate teacher if I could not protect *myself*," said Alexander.

"Probably," Elysia agreed, gazing at his lips, moving forward. He met her halfway. She wove her fingers in his hair, and the scent of rosewater surrounded her; his lips were honey and pita and *home*. An arm looped about her waist and pulled her closer. Elysia gasped, breathing in the warmth between them. After the deep-digging pressure of Philip's fingers in her dream, Alexander's hands were featherlight, gentle, cradling her like a bird. Something in her fluttered at his touch, ready to take off. His lips sent heat running from her mouth to her belly to her toes, and Elysia shivered.

I am free.

When they parted, she rested her forehead against his. Her hands still clutched his silky hair, holding him close. Alexander's breath was as fast as hers, half a laugh, his eyes closed. Sliding her hand down his neck and back up, Elysia hummed.

His smile erased the lines around his eyes and replaced them with the happy crinkles that he wore so well. He brushed his thumbs over her cheeks, leaving a trail of heat, and opened his eyes. Pressing his lips to her forehead, he murmured, "There is someone you should meet."

"Oh?"

"He has wanted to meet you for some time, but once you stopped coming to the mountain, there were no opportunities. It's quite a walk."

Quite a walk it was: half an hour passed before they reached her house again. After that, it was fifteen minutes to the Gate of Poseidon, and by that time, she was certain of their destination.

Acrocorinth.

They passed Zeus at the gate. It seemed the city had stood by its decision to remove the "extra" man from the gate; Adrastos wasn't even lurking in the shadows of the statues, and Zeus let them pass with an exuberant wave and a hoot.

Just as they had walked to the training grounds, Elysia and Alexander walked with hands linked, but the doubt was gone. She held his hand and swung it – and occasionally, he brought her hand to his mouth and brushed his lips over her knuckles, and tingles shot through her.

It took them the best part of an hour to reach Acrocorinth. By the time they got to the base of the mountain, the sun was low in the east, rising with the morning, and their silence had turned to conversation. Pointing at the top of the mountain, Alexander told her about the temple of Aphrodite, the goddess of love. "Beside it is a fountain, the Peirene, where Korinna and my mother fetch water every morning. There are springs all over the mountain, most of them lower than that one. But up there, a hero of Corinth tamed Pegasus while he drank from the fountain. The Acrocorinthians have been blessed since."

"Pegasus?"

"A flying horse. He graces our coinage to this day."

Elysia gaped at him as her mind raced back to the day she had spent in the agora with her grandmother. She'd seen the horse on the coins

Metrodora had handed out with every purchase. *Pegasus, the winged horse.* Had her father created him with the rest of Earth's creatures? Or was he another fantastic myth the humans had concocted?

It didn't matter, she decided. He was real to them.

The rest of the walk passed as Alexander told her about his people. Those who lived on the low slopes were more a community than she had realized, cobbling together money, meals, and materials whenever a neighbor needed it, and getting by on almost nothing when they did not. Every two weeks, they sent the able to a forest fifteen miles away to hunt game for the whole village. Delia had come to them after her husband died and her father's businesses had collapsed, paving the way for ex-Highs to find a life outside the Merchants' Gauntlet and the broken-down neighborhoods in the city – and brought them her unknown talent with a spear.

"Why does she no longer hunt?" Elysia asked. The teeth hung from strings outside her door had long since bleached or yellowed, turned brittle in the Corinthian sun.

"She tore something in her leg. She can walk well, but running is another matter."

"She is Metrodora's sister, you know."

"I do," Alexander said, nodding. They drew closer to the mountain, rounding the corner – the first huts of the lower slope appeared around the bend, whitewashed mud and thatch that were dotted with mold and mildew. Once again, Elysia saw the dark-skinned woman with the little girl in her lap, wearing the same yellow dress she had worn when Elysia had seen her near two weeks ago. "They are not fond of each other," he elaborated, "so Delia does not deign to speak of her, and Dora would rather see Zeus off to war than think about the sister who chose to abandon the city in favor of us."

Elysia raised a brow at him. "And yet she taught you Greek manners."

He nodded. "And yet she taught me Greek manners," he murmured, quieting before flashing her a smirk. "I was quite an irresistible child, though."

Elysia laughed. "You're still an irresistible child," she shot back.

"Who's an irresistible child, now?" came a deep, throaty voice. Elysia jumped, expecting her grandmother to lurk in the shadows of the house they had come upon – a house with the canines of animals clinking in the breeze. *No,* she thought. *They just have many more similarities than I had noticed before.* The smoky voice, the thick black hair, the dark gray eyes. *The eyes. I must check her eyes.*

"Alexander," Elysia replied, and in the shadow of the roof's overhang, a form came forward. Something snarky played about Delia's lips.

"See now, my guess would've been his father," said Delia, and the snarkiness lurking around her lips became a full smirk as she stepped into the dim light cast by the dawn. "Good to see you again, 'Lysia."

"And you, Delia," she said. Stepping closer, Elysia reeled, thankful she did not have to say anything more.

Delia's eyes were plain.

No silver spirals, no rims or spires of gold or any other color. They were simply gray flecked with black. Whoever their parents had been, those remarkable eyes had passed only to one child… And only one other person bore them: her father. Even Elysia did not have them; she had her mother's and grandfather's blue eyes. Neither did Zeus have them, for his were the same as hers, given by the same ancestor. And to Elysia, that meant one thing: Metrodora had not told her whole story. There was divinity in her, a divinity Elysia had found in only her father.

Something rang her back to the present. A question had been asked. Blinking, she looked from Alexander to Delia.

"What are we up to, Elysia?" Alexander provided, squeezing her hand, and that was when she noticed Delia's gaze on their hands.

"We're… we're to meet someone," she muttered.

"And who's that yer meeting?" Delia asked, one eyebrow raised.

Silently, she prayed word of this wouldn't get back to her father; they were supposed to be *training.* She had a test to pass in… Could it only be two days? A day and a half? Elysia's eyes widened. She had learned all the techniques, but her sparring was far from graceful, her combinations unthoughtful.

"My brother," Alexander said, and Elysia's eyes shot to him. "Elysia has not met him yet, and he dearly wants to be introduced."

That's right, he has a brother. Metrodora had taught him, too; he and Alexander had flown together on top of the mountain once.

"You'd better hurry, then, 'fore Herod returns from training the boys. He'll want to test her if yer not done by then."

Nodding, Alexander bid Delia goodbye, and Elysia trudged up the hill behind him. "Your brother?" she said quietly, trying to remember if his name had been mentioned, but she could not find it, not when he had spoken of the lessons or flying on Acrocorinth.

"Euthymios," he supplied. "Older by three years. I should let him introduce himself, though," he added, turning a small smile on her as they walked. "He has insisted on meeting you since my father said Khronos was back – he had quite a liking for your mother when he was tiny. She took care of him when she spent the day up here."

"Do you remember her?" Incredulity colored her voice, and she could not keep it out of her tone; it seemed everyone *but* Elysia had known her mother.

"No," Alexander said with a shrug. "I couldn't have been more than one when her training finished. But oh, Euthymios loved her. A bright spot in his shadowy little world."

Elysia frowned. *Shadowy little world? For a* four-year-old*?*

Finally, they reached the top of the hill and the house in the niche. It seemed taller than Elysia remembered, but that was the distortion of memory. It was a proud moment when Elysia realized she was neither sweaty nor out of breath from the climb – her body was stronger, growing fitter with every walk and every blow landed – or missed.

Halooing into the house, Alexander pulled Elysia up the stairs right after him. She had never been beyond the doorway before, and yet here she was, traipsing into their home, holding the hand of Ligeia's youngest son. She followed him up the stairs, keeping her eyes downcast. She would *not* trip on a stair before she even made it into the house proper; if Korinna was in the room above, Elysia would never hear the end of it.

The stairs were steep and led high into the house, a good ten feet; at the top, she realized the house's foundation was just as tall. The stairs were cut into it, the stairwell opening fenced off, so no one would mistakenly step into it. When she got to the top, she found that the house was one room, though a clothesline draped across the middle of it, a white sheet hung to hide what Elysia could only assume was the sleeping area. In the cramped space between the sheet and the rounded wall, furniture and a loom vied for space. The furniture was spare: a wooden lounge like her father's, though this one had no cushions; flat wooden benches along the walls; a table and five stools beneath a window in the back; and lastly, that loom. It was grander than the looms in Metrodora's house, wide and proud with pale, whorled wood. The cloth woven upon it was as plain as the tunic Alexander wore. Just as in Metrodora's house, baskets filled with wool, thread, and supplies were stacked everywhere, but they were not so crowded – these had an order, and all were the same kind of basket, pale gold wicker. They stood against the walls where there was empty space and hugged the fence of the stairwell, blocking it further. *No accidents in this house,* Elysia thought.

Her survey of the room was broken by the realization that, though there was furniture and supplies aplenty in the main room, there were no *people.* Frowning, she turned to Alexander. "Wait here," he said, bringing her hand to his lips before letting go. Pushing past the sheet, Alexander disappeared behind it.

She heard low, muffled voices – from what she could tell, they belonged to Alexander and Korinna. The sheet was pulled to bunch further down the line. Behind it were three people, two of whom she recognized, and a third who looked strikingly familiar.

"Hello, Elysia."

25

The man who greeted Elysia looked so like Alexander that Elysia took a step back. His answering smile was bright enough to pull a weak smile to the corners of her mouth in return; he had as much boyish charm as Alexander. His eyes were rimmed in red with deep, dark circles beneath his eyes; his hair hung limp and stringy from his skull, in want of washing. He differed most from Alexander, though, in his thinness. Where Alexander was muscled, this man seemed to be skin and bone. Above the sweat-stained neckline of his tunic, his collarbone and ribs were so pronounced Elysia feared they might break through his skin at any moment. With his brother standing beside him, he looked a wraith.

"Elysia," Alexander said softly, "this is my brother."

Korinna shifted on the end of Euthymios's bed, her body between Elysia and her oldest brother. A thin hand rose up to light on her shoulder, and the girl looked at him. Something silent communicated between them; Korinna scooted to the side, leaning against the wall to sit with her knees up. A spindle sat abandoned on the bed, a distaff wound with fluffy wool just beside it. *Keeping him company,* Elysia thought, *in his dark little world.*

"Please, come closer," Euthymios said. He held a hand out to her, and though Elysia took a step closer, she did not take it. She was still human; she could get sick. Euthymios beckoned her with his fingers. "It is all right." His voice wheezed, constricted and rasping. "I have been wasting since I was a boy, and neither of these two have gotten sick, nor have my parents."

Taking a step toward him, Elysia caught the scent of sickness: sweat and sourness, the same scent her mother had tried to wipe out with honey and rosewater. Her hand landed in his and she sat beside him. His hand was cold, fingertips blushing a faint blue. The skin was damp with a chill, and all Elysia wanted to do was warm it. She clasped his hand between hers.

"I'm Euthymios, the older brother," he said, and though his eyes were shadowy, they were the same gray as Alexander's, dancing in the dim light from the window beside the bed. In the bottom of his right eye, Elysia spotted a dot of brown. *More of his father in him.*

"I know," she replied. "And you know who I am."

"*Yes*," came Korinna's voice from the end of the bed, and Elysia heard the scowl in it. "Because we talk about you all the time."

"Korinna," Euthymios scolded, but there was a smile in his voice. Even Elysia couldn't help a little smirk; Korinna was so much herself. Addressing Elysia once more, Euthymios nodded. "I know who your parents are. Branimira and Khronos? However, I don't know who *you* are, and that is what matters. What have you done to enchant him, so he speaks only of you?"

Elysia's cheeks burned red, so hot she felt her face might catch fire and burn the house down with it. Looking to Alexander, she found him giving her a tiny smile, arms crossed as he stood in the narrow space between Euthymios's bed and the sheet that divided the house. "Bested him, once or twice," she managed, flustered.

The smile on Euthymios's face grew into something wide and spectacular, even in the hollow shadows of his cheeks. Someone had taught Herod and Ligeia's children how to care for their teeth, she thought in passing, because all three had bright whites. Even Euthymios in his sick bed had them, a jarring sight beneath thin, cracking lips and the jaundiced skin of his face. "It might have something to do with *that*," said Euthymios, and Elysia blushed harder. "Confidence, modesty, and confusion all at the same time. Do you not agree, sister?"

"Mostly confusion," Korinna muttered.

One corner of Euthymios's mouth went higher than the other, and Elysia recognized Alexander's crooked grin. "Maybe so," he said, eyes never leaving Elysia's, "but there is something about you that is different from the rest."

"Maybe it's that she knows nothing."

"Korinna!" Rough, true scoldings came from both Alexander and Euthymios in the same moment, and Elysia flinched. Frowning, she looked back at the brunette girl, who pouted against the wall – but she did not quiet.

"It's either that or her hair."

Though Alexander seethed and Euthymios was silent, Elysia shook her head. *I am a crone here*, she thought. Korinna's eyes seared dangerously into her.

"I can leave, if you'd like," Elysia said.

Korinna held a hand toward the door, but Euthymios cut her off as she opened her mouth. "That will not be necessary." His eyes locked with his sister's, and Elysia wasn't sure what to do. Her hands, clasped around Euthymios's, lay on the blanket covering his legs; he sat up against a headboard, propped up but slumped, though the way he held his head was as proud as the way Alexander held his. "If Korinna would truly like to be away from you, she can leave. She has legs with which to walk," he added coolly, but Korinna did not budge. She huffed and picked up her spindle and distaff. Dropping it over the edge of the bed, she set the spindle to spinning and went to work.

"She is headstrong," Alexander said. Elysia flicked her gaze to Korinna, but the girl gave no indication she had heard except to sit up straighter.

Cold fingers brushed against her chin, and Elysia turned to Euthymios; the hand not trapped between hers steadied her to look at him. "How many years are you?"

"Nineteen."

Euthymios nodded and glanced between her and his younger brother. "Do you have such a skill with wool as your mother did?"

You are your own woman, my sweet granddaughter. Elysia took a deep breath. "With wool and a spindle. At the loom, I have yet to be taught."

Euthymios's eyebrows went up, and even Alexander looked surprised. "No one taught you?" asked Alexander, his voice soft.

"After my mother died, there was no one who could." *A lie.* Her father could have taught her, Hera could have, or any other female judge; even the ladies of the household, the fieldhands – they could have taught her. *Aliya* could have taught her, but no one had been allowed to. Her father didn't want her in the presence of a loom, which she had never understood. He wanted her to be eternal, like him, but he did not want her to weave like him: he did not want her to create. But when she had set up that loom, nothing special, nothing magical had happened. Even if she had felt something, Elysia wouldn't have known what to do with it; what did she know of creation? "My grandmother is teaching me now."

Alexander nodded and put a hand on her shoulder, seemingly reassured.

"You know, our mother taught all three of us to spin and weave," Euthymios said, eyes sparkling mischievously. "I still spin. It cuts Mother's and Korinna's workload in half when they have no need to both spin *and* weave."

Elysia looked at Alexander, eyebrows raised questioningly. He held his hands up. "I'm best at switching the warp."

"He would rather repair the roof than take up a spindle again, and he's more likely to fall through the roof than repair it."

"I am not!" Alexander's arms tightened across his chest, but he wore a grin.

Euthymios shook his head, but he leaned forward to speak as secretly to Elysia as he could. "Someday, I will want to ask questions of you, but today is not that day."

Swallowing hard, Elysia nodded. *What kind of questions?* She wanted to ask, but he seemed to dismiss them. Withdrawing her hands from Euthymios's, she got to her feet. Alexander's fingers found her hands, and out of the corner of her eye, Elysia saw Korinna glaring at the way their fingers fitted together.

"It was good to meet you at last, Elysia," said Euthymios, and after she said her goodbye, Alexander drew her from behind the sheet and into the main room. He did not stop walking until they summited the hill behind the house, where they had once climbed the cliffs. Pulling her close, he bent to kiss her, his warmth fanning out over her skin until Elysia shivered and ran a hand through his hair, smooth and soft beneath her fingers. The tingles that shot through her with every touch turned into flames licking over her, but Alexander's kiss was so sweet, so light that Elysia could not move.

Finally, he broke away and leaned his forehead against hers, his gray eyes melting her beneath the earnestness in his gaze. "He likes you," he said. His hands cradled her face with heat.

"Did he like no one else you brought home?"

A sad smile found his lips. "There has been no one else."

Elysia frowned. Her hand wrapped around his wrist as she tried to distract herself from his touch. "Why has there been no one else?"

Alexander sighed, sending roses washing over her, and closed his eyes. "Twenty years ago, there was an earthquake. Mother and I had gone to get water up at the fountain – up there, there was nothing to fall on us.

Father and Euthymios were in the house. The walls fell in. You've already seen my father. Euthymios's legs healed badly, and his lungs have never been the same… Other houses were not so lucky. We were some of the only children who survived." Gray eyes opened again, and Elysia swore she saw too much shininess before he blinked, and then it was gone. "Only two ladies close to my age live here, both now married. My father will not have me marry a girl from the city, either. You know how he feels about Corinthians," he finished wryly, and Elysia thought back to that first lesson, when Herod had trained the boys for the Guard. *The great Corinthians.*

"I do," she replied.

Something lit in Alexander's eyes, erasing his somberness. "You are the first," he murmured.

"I am the first," Elysia echoed. *If only you were mine* flitted through her head, but the pang did not stop the grin spreading across her face, nor the glee jolting through her. Her hand remained in his hair, curled in the warmth at the base of his neck. She closed her eyes.

When she opened them, she found him studying her. As loath as she was to interrupt him, there was still something she must do: practice. Only a day and a half remained before the test that would determine if eternity was even within her grasp. The anxiety she'd felt earlier blossomed again into a flower of dread. "Will we practice here today?"

Alexander's eyes widened. "We can go to the plateau, if you like."

"I think so," she said, pulling his hand down from her face. Leading him along, Elysia found the path that would take her to the training ground where she had begun her lessons. Just as Delia had said, Herod was there with the boys. As she and Alexander stood at the edge of the plateau, she searched among the boys for the two whose names she knew: Leon and Dion. Though she remembered their names, recognizing them among thirty bodies whirling sticks and dodging was another matter. Herod stood on the other end of plateau, leaning on his stick; the sun had risen over the mountain, and he was in just the right place to bathe in its warmth. His eyes were closed, but Elysia could tell by the way he stood that he listened to his surroundings.

When a boy paused to salute Alexander, he earned a rap across his thighs from his partner, and Herod's eyes snapped open. "Who's landed a hit?" he barked. The little boy who had saluted Alexander kept silent as his partner raised his hand so eagerly he jumped. "And how did he land a hit?" Herod asked the boy who had been hit.

"I waved to Alexander," the boy muttered, rubbing his thighs and glaring up at Alexander, who held up his hands.

Herod shook his head. "If you were in the middle of a battle and yer general walked onto the field, and ya stopped to acknowledge him, what d'you think would happen?" He waved a hand across the plateau, giving the question to all of them.

A few answered at once, but the rest shifted uncomfortably. The boy who landed the hit piped up, and he did so as proudly as a lioness standing over her kill. "You would die!"

Herod's nod was solemn. "You would. Don't let yer enemies gut ya over courtesies," he growled. His stick thumped the ground. "They won't show you any. Back to work." And just like that, the boys were back at it, sticks clacking together so loudly Elysia's ear drums throbbed.

Pulling her with him, Alexander made a careful circle around the field of sparring boys, sticking as close as he could to the huts at the edge. When they stood before his father, Elysia watched Herod with wary eyes.

Herod proved his danger – he rapped them smartly across the knuckles with his stick, and though Elysia wanted so badly to tug away and rub the pain from her knuckles, Alexander held on. "What's this now?" asked Herod, and the stick darted out again, making Elysia flinch. It stopped just close enough to point at their joined hands.

Steady as the mountain itself, Alexander gazed at his father and, slowly, grinned.

"Aren't you two just spectacular," grumbled Herod. "This is what I get for training a girl from the mountains."

Herod's stick whipped out again, this time aimed at Elysia's knees.

Her body reacted instincts-first, leaping backward and pulling Alexander with her. He was far from prepared – he stumbled over himself as he fell back with her. "Father," he growled, his hand clutching Elysia's so hard it felt like her bones rubbed together.

"Alexander," said Herod, and the stick came at Elysia again, this time for her stomach.

Falling back, Elysia flexed her hand to get Alexander to let go. Pulling her stomach in and taking another step back, Elysia barely managed to dodge as the stick *whooshed* in front of her. Vaguely, she was aware that the clacking of sticks had stopped; boys parted ways for her and the man attached to the swinging stick. Ducking, she missed a blow meant for her head.

"Good, you've learned," shouted Herod.

Elysia stared at the man assailing her, jumping as the stick aimed for her ankles. After he aimed one more blow at her hip, Herod stopped as suddenly as he'd begun. Distantly, as she calmed her breathing and eyed Herod, Elysia heard Alexander clapping. The boys joined him, and Herod rested his stick on the ground. Her mind whirled, wondering how she had offended Herod by holding hands with his son. They had gotten halfway across the plateau; she must have given that much ground to get away from him, but her mind had been on the spinning stick.

"You see, boys," Herod began, "once you learn to trust yer instincts and ya get some skills under yer belt, you can save yerself in unforeseen situations."

Anger lit in Elysia's gut. It had been a lesson taught without warning. Crossing her arms, Elysia gave Herod her best glare.

Alexander's father addressed her next, inclining his walking stick toward her, thankfully not enough to make her flinch again. "You are capable of more than you think."

Elysia shook her head, exasperated. Alexander stood at the edge of the plateau. Though his arms were crossed, the grin returned his face. "Had enough practice for the day, Elysia?" he called.

Hearing her name on his lips brought a smirk to her own. "It's not even noon yet," she replied.

Alexander picked up a stick and brought it to her. Herod and the boys all but disappeared. Closing in like the panther he was, Alexander stopped within inches of her. When she reached for the stick he held, he pulled her in and kissed her. *Ooooo*s and *eeeeeew*s echoed around them, and she blushed hotly, considering their audience. *Is this even done in Greece?*

No, but neither is teaching women to defend themselves.

"Spar with the boys," said Alexander. "They'll teach you some things I can't."

Elysia frowned – and gasped as someone dealt a stinging slap to her hamstrings. Whirling, she looked for the culprit, but the boys grinned in equal measure, eyes sparkling with innocence. Alexander laughed. "Like that."

"Fine," Elysia said, swinging the stick at the boys, who jumped back as one. "But if they will not play fair, do not expect me to."

A boy at the end of her arc parried her, and Elysia swung into action. They stopped an hour later with the sun overhead; Elysia's body trembled. Sweat ran stinging into her eyes, but she had fought every boy twice. At last, Alexander stepped forward again, a stick in his hands.

Too fatigued to deceive him, Elysia swung down hard, aiming her stick at his head. He blocked her easily, a hand on each end of his staff, arms spread strong above her as the blow landed with a sharp *clack.* Panting, Elysia gazed into his eyes. *Let me be done.* Thirst turned her throat to fire, breath ripping like claws across the roof of her mouth.

But Alexander pushed her away.

Elysia ran forward with a screech, dropping her stick and ramming both hands into his chest. He stumbled and fell – and then they were on the ground, still but for breathing. Elysia's elbows scraped against the ground between his arms and ribs. "I'm done," she rasped, wincing and leaning up to stare him down. "No more practice today."

Alexander nodded, trying to catch his breath; letting his head fall against the hard-packed dirt, he closed his eyes. Carefully moving off him, Elysia sat at his side, focusing her own breath. The boys swung their weapons around but kept a measured distance. It would not do, after all, if one of them came too close to poking out Alexander's eye. Elysia smirked and adjusted her skirt, glad it hadn't come loose and shown more skin than appropriate. Getting up, she offered Alexander her hand. "We should get back."

Opening one eye, Alexander assessed her, ignoring her hand. "You're a right mess."

Pushing at a straying lock of hair, Elysia shrugged. "So are you." His tunic, which had been a clean yellow-white, was stained brown wherever he'd hit the ground: one hip and an entire side were coated with dust. Elysia imagined what his back looked like, proud that she had even managed to knock him down. He hadn't expected her to come at him *without* a weapon. She pushed her hand at him again.

Reaching up, Alexander clasped his hand around her wrist, making her skin tingle with warmth, but suddenly she was on the ground again, yanked down on top of him, her arm stretched out across his chest. "Let's not go just yet," he said, grinning wickedly. The clacking and yells of the boys seemed to dull, and they were hidden by the crowd of small, sun-browned feet – and Alexander knew they were, too. He stared at her with his eyes dark as storm clouds, pouring fire across her skin.

"Alexander!"

Elysia closed her eyes and groaned, dropping her head onto his chest. Alexander shifted beneath her, though, leaning up to see Korinna, who was certainly behind them, waiting to reprimand them.

"Mother," he said.

Elysia's eyes snapped open.

Above her stood the small woman – though she stood much taller now, standing over Elysia with hands on hips – Elysia had seen on her first day on the mountain. They had not been introduced, but Alexander had told her his mother's name: Ligeia. And now she stood over them, fury in the deep gray eyes she shared with her sons, her brunette hair wild, as if she had run down the mountain to find them. At her feet sat a jug of water, still trembling and swishing from its journey. "Alexander," she said again, and Elysia felt herself shrink down into the ground. The little boys around them had long since stilled, watching the woman with wary eyes.

"How could you behave like this in public?" Ligeia asked, and Alexander tensed beside Elysia; the hand that had been wrapped around her waist dropped to the ground in a fist. "You will ruin her honor, her prospects, any hopes she might have of a good marriage if this is found out. You know that, don't you?" She snapped her fingers. "Up."

Alexander scrambled to his feet, but Elysia could not follow, for Ligeia's gaze found her next. "And you," she hissed, "letting him treat you this way, as if he has a chance and your father won't kill him. Have you no sense?"

Anger lit in Elysia, a liquid fire. With careful measure and grace, she got to her feet, then stood tall before Alexander's mother. "I have sense," she replied, voice quiet and hands folded. Raising her chin with as much pride as she could muster despite her dirty, sweat-stained clothes, Elysia met Ligeia's eyes. "Sense enough to know that marriage is not on the table for us."

Beside his mother, Alexander crossed his arms, but he did not look hurt. For that, Elysia was grateful. Ligeia crossed her own arms, mirroring her son. "If that is true, then you ought to stop leading him along. He is my son, and I will stand for him if he will not stand for himself."

"Mother," Alexander said quietly, but she held up a hand to silence him. His eyes turned to Elysia, his shoulders shrugged.

With a sigh, Elysia nodded. "Marriage to me is not on the table for *any* man. My father will not have it. Alexander knows this."

"Does he?" Ligeia raised her eyebrows to her son, who nodded. "And Khronos does not mind you cavorting around with men you hardly know?" she asked, voice and eyes sharp on Elysia.

"I know him better than I know anyone else in this place," she replied. "I know him better than the man I thought was my best friend, I know him better than my uncle, I know him better than I know my *grandmother*."

Voice as low as she could manage, Elysia kept as much as she could from the listening ears of the boys. With every word she spoke, they seemed to lean closer, until Elysia could barely breathe. Finally, she threw her hands up, and they jumped back. "Alexander is not a stranger," she said, eyes drifting to him. His eyes held an emotion she had not seen before, soft and kind, something that told Elysia he looked at her with new eyes. "He has not been since we climbed the mountain together." Holding out her hand to him, Elysia finished. "And because he is a stranger to neither my father nor to me, I think it would be appropriate, even in the eyes of the Corinthians, if I asked for him to please escort me home."

When Elysia was done, Alexander wore that crooked half-smile of his – the one that always came right before that all-out boyish, white-toothed grin that she so enjoyed. "I would be happy to," he said, wrapping his hand around hers.

Warmth enveloped her skin, swirled up her arm, and Elysia's heart thudded. "Thank you," she said, and turned back to his mother. "And thank you, Ligeia, for being so concerned for my honor. It means more than I can say." Ligeia's concern was well-placed. After all, if her grandmother wanted to find her a match just after meeting her, and if Philip had been concerned about the length of her *dress*... Holding hands or doing anything more where others could see could only label her a harlot in Corinthian eyes.

Raising her hand above the crowd to wave to the man she had all but forgotten, Elysia called, "Good evening, Herod!"

His answer was a grunt of, "Crone."

Shaking her head, Elysia squeezed Alexander's hand. His grin had found its way up to the corners of his lips, sneaking in, despite the presence of his mother. With a nod to Ligeia, she said her goodbyes to the little boys; Alexander kissed his mother's cheek, and they were off back home, albeit a bit dirtier and far more sweat-stained than they had been when they set off. All the same, Elysia could not stop herself from sharing Alexander's smile.

She had learned to fight off an attacker with a long reach without issue – indeed, it was one of very few things during which Alexander had not stopped her because she did wrong. All it had taken was dodging a stick, something she had been honing her instincts for since the very first day of training, apparently. And now that she had done that, there was just one day left.

One more day, and she would be given her first test for immortality, for the eternity she would spend by her father's side. Taking a deep breath, Elysia looked to Alexander, who looked at her with those eyes sparkling in the light.

Clarity struck her. She stopped.

"What?" asked Alexander, frowning. They passed through the cool shadow of the mountain; the teeth dangling from the roof of Delia's hut nearby *click*ed in the breeze.

"Nothing," Elysia replied, smiling at him and hugging him around the waist. He wrapped his arms around her shoulders. Most of the scent of roses he had worn that morning had been traded for dirt and sweat. "Nothing's wrong at all."

I will spend my human life with you.

26

The way home was hot, the sun burning in the sky above them. Alexander told her of Helios, the god who drove the chariot of the sun, and how some days he drove his horses harder than others, though the journey was ever the same. On those days, he said, though the journey was the same length, the overworked horses made the earth swelter, too. It was only when Demeter mourned the loss of her daughter Persephone to the Underworld that autumn and winter came. Elysia listened with rapt attention, though she knew none of it to be true; her father had taught her the reasons for winter and summer, for dawn and dusk long ago, when she had been old enough to turn the globe in his study on its axis – and he had also taught her that the humans did not know these things, not yet. Someday, they might learn, but until then, there was nothing they could do to help them down the path of knowledge. They must stumble along for themselves, and they had their own explanations, explanations that were beyond fascinating. The stories they came up with, the creatures and beings bigger than themselves and yet locked only in their imaginations – all of it was a wonder.

More than once, Alexander caught her staring at him with a slack jaw as she tried to process everything he told her. He'd smirk at her, though once he asked if she had never been told any of this. All she could do was shake her head.

Still more wonders were found outside their minds: architecture, both poor and rich; the fountains, the squares, the agora; their skill with animals, their skill with harnessing the materials given to them; all of it was incredible.

And Alexander was ready to share it with her.

The more stories he shared, the more stories she begged of him. By the time they got to the gate, Elysia was near certain he was half-sick of her, but he laughed with her reaction to every story told. "Someday," he told her, as they neared the house, "all of this will seem…" His eyes cast upward, to the blue of the sky, searching for a word as if he might find it written in the clouds. He looked back down at her. "Someday, all of this will seem mundane." He stopped them at the corner, and Elysia knew that around the bend was her house, and in it a bath, waiting for her.

Taking her hands, Alexander looked her in the eye. "My mother is well-meaning, if a bit misguided. Under normal circumstances, we would be married long before we had laid a hand on one another."

Elysia's face heated, and she knew that beneath the grime and sweat, a blush colored her face. "Well," she murmured, "we have been doing *that* since the day we met."

He laughed, short and soft. "That is not *quite* what I was getting at. I meant… Well, I want to say… I want you to know that I will never treat you in a way that would shame you, even if we are not married." Letting go of one of her hands, he ran his fingers through his hair – and Elysia realized that she witnessed a flustered Alexander for the first time since she'd met him. After a second, he reclaimed her hand and gazed at her with a new determination. "You are in charge of us. I will make no move if you do not give me permission, married or not."

Half of her mouth went up in a smile. "You mean you will not treat me as a whore."

Alexander's eyebrows shot up and his eyes widened. He took a step back. "You know what a whore is, but not who Helios is."

It was Elysia's turn to laugh – he was right. Her knowledge of the world was more practical, learned from the mouths of criminals and the devout in the chamber of judgment. While she knew little of legends, she knew every way a man could harm another man, and far too many ways a man could harm a woman. She had met, albeit briefly, practitioners of every profession she could imagine, including temple prostitutes. "I do know of whores, even the ones who belong to Aphrodite on top of the mountain. I have since I was twelve. I also know of Helios, since you have so kindly told me about him." Pulling him closer, Elysia wove their fingers together. Their hands were the only thing between them. "You did not answer me," she said, though her words had been less a question and more a statement.

"No, I will not take advantage of you," said Alexander softly, raising their joined hands to brush the edge of her chin. Heat flared beneath her skin again. "Even entertaining the idea is revolting."

"Good." Leaning up, Elysia kissed him and lingered – but then remembered where she stood. And the *time.* She took a step back from

Alexander, looking up at the sun. It was beginning to descend into the western sky, turning it to oranges and pinks above the distant sea. "I've missed my lessons – we should have returned hours ago," she whispered, trying to peer around him. "Father's going to be far from pleased."

"It'll be fine, I'm sure," he said, pulling her around the corner.

It was not fine.

When they walked through the front door, Elysia spotted Philip pacing the breadth of the room. As soon as he saw them together, his face became a snarl and he shoved past them out the door, pushing Alexander roughly. Elysia's eye lit on her father, and the look he gave her had her quailed from the moment she met his gaze. *I'm as good as dead,* she thought. What would he do? Take her from the city, put an end to her training, make her take her test early? Keep her away from Alexander?

Elysia planted her feet, standing between her father and Alexander. She had promised herself to keep him safe from the divine aspects of her father – and this would be her first test.

Her father stood up from the kitchen table. His fist rapped on the table, making her jump. "You," he began quietly, dangerously, voice a growl and eyes glowering, "were supposed to be home hours ago."

"I-"

"Do you know how long I looked for you?" Khronos skirted the table to stand before her.

"No, but-"

"But nothing, Elysia. I have been looking for you almost since you left for practice."

Elysia fell back a step as her father's voice rose, until she felt the phantom of Alexander's warmth in the air behind her. "All that time?" she whispered.

"I had meant to watch your training today," Khronos said, taking a step toward her. Behind his lips, his teeth gritted together. Elysia was all too aware of Alexander and every way he shifted; his hand curled into the back of her dress, holding her steady. "Imagine my surprise," her father continued, "when I could not *find you there.*"

"Father," she said carefully, imploring him to drop the ferocity, but he did not relent. He stared her down, fury burning in his gilded green eyes. Taking a breath, Elysia nodded curtly and squared her shoulders. "Herod taught me how to fend off an attacker with a weapon today."

"Did he now?" Khronos said, and his gaze lifted from Elysia – but the moment of relief was short-lived, for his eyes flicked instead to

Alexander. "And what, pray tell, were *you* doing, taking my daughter up to the mountain without asking me?"

"It was spur of the mo-"

The scowl he sent Elysia silenced her, and Khronos turned back to Alexander. "Why did you take her to the mountain?" he asked again, his question closer to a demand than an actual question.

Give him the truth. He will know a lie.

Alexander cleared his throat; the fist clenched in the back of her dress tightened, pressing warmth against her skin, but she was far from melting in front of him – she could not afford that, not here, not in front of her father. It was her job to protect Alexander, even if it was an assignment she had given herself, and she would not be distracted by that hand, no matter how hotly it burned at her back. *He is only finding strength in you*, she told herself, though part of her wondered if he just wanted to touch her, too. After all, if warmth was as heady a drug to him as it was to her, it would be hard to resist. Alexander finally spoke. "It *was* spur of the moment, Khronos," he said, and Elysia knew he tried to placate her father just as she had tried, though she had failed. Khronos said nothing in return to him, though, and so Alexander continued, carrying himself along on a current of conversation all his own. "My intentions were to put her up against the boys in training for the Guard, and you should have seen her, fighting back like they were no more than sticks in the sand. After that, I decided that she ought to meet Euthymios."

The red-gold lines of Khronos's eyebrows rose, but he made no remark.

Elysia frowned. *He knows who Euthymios is, what he is to Alexander's family... But he says nothing about what it must mean for me to meet him.* After all, that was the thing that was the most special about her meeting with Euthymios; it had taken Alexander's involvement with her for her to even be told that he still existed beyond the memory of their childhoods. If she had not taken things a step further, she might never have met that man who seemed so bright despite his brokenness, so ready to accept her. Not only that, but Branimira had once doted on him. Surely that ought to warrant a reaction?

None came.

Alexander continued, filling in the blanks with their walk home beneath the evening sky. He told Khronos the stories he had told her, told him of their visit with Delia, however brief. Finally, he got to the moment where they would have rounded the corner but stopped to have a chat. It was all Elysia could do not to squirm as he skimmed over that part, leading them to the doorway and where they stood now. "That was our afternoon," Alexander finished. His voice was quiet, calm, but something about him was shaken; perhaps it was the way he used her as an anchor, holding onto her like she might suddenly leave with a gust of wind.

"You say these things," Khronos said, and Elysia fell back until she leaned against the warmth of Alexander's chest. Not only was her father still angry – he was steaming, furious enough to fling them across the room should he have the mind to. "And yet, you give no reason," his voice lowered to a whisper, and Khronos nudged Alexander with a finger, "as to why you led her off up to Acrocorinth in the first place. It is quite a walk, as I am sure you know."

Shaking her head, Elysia crossed her arms. "You act as if the fault is to be laid singly at Alexander's feet," she said firmly.

"Is it not?" Though she had been bold, brave even, to challenge her father, Khronos still glared at her with the smoldering green galaxies in his eyes, bearing down on her. He seemed to grow a little taller, his shadow a little bulkier, until it seemed as if he might fill the whole room. Elysia did not back down.

"No, Father," she replied, and to her own surprise, took a step forward. Pressing a hand against her father's chest – beneath which she could feel the heat and beat of his heart – Elysia backed Khronos away from Alexander. "The blame, whatever it is, is as much mine as it is Alexander's. I wanted to go see the boys again as much as he." *Euthymios was a boy once, when he was not in his dark little world,* Elysia reasoned. After all, it had not been the little boys whom they had gone to see; Alexander's brother held that honor. And as such, every word she spoke to her father was a lie, if only by omission. *A lie by omission is still a lie.*

"Whatever the blame is?" Khronos shook his head, his red-gold hair seething above his shoulders like waves thrashing themselves against rocks. A cloud of frustration filled his voice, straining until it sounded stretched, like he had too little air for the volume he tried to push out. "I almost had half the city looking for you. If not for Zeus and Philip, I would have. They sent the household out looking. Zeus barely took me seriously and Philip wanted to hunt you down for the very same reason. Do you know what it was?"

"They weren't sure if I was ready to defend myself?" she asked, praying he would not speak the true answer, not here in front of the man whose name it was. But still, Khronos said it.

"*Alexander.*"

She felt Alexander flinch, and then her link to him was gone; she couldn't see him with her back to him, and their connection disappeared when his hand dropped from her dress. She was blind to his actions.

Khronos continued, and what little headway she had gained was destroyed by the step he took forward. Elysia paled. *He will not be easily calmed, not this time.* "*Zeus* thought you would be safe in his company, no matter what happened. *Philip* thought the opposite, swore that if he did not go after you, Alexander would get away with *abducting* you. Now, while I did not think Alexander would kidnap you, I did not think you would be gone for *eight hours.* I told Philip he could find you himself if you were not back by nightfall. Do you know what that would have meant?" Her father leaned down to look her in the eye, inches from her face. "Do you know what he would have *done?*" he asked.

Elysia blinked, uncomprehending. And then dread filled her. *His irrational mind thought I had been kidnapped.* "He would have killed Alexander," she murmured, so quietly she barely heard herself.

"Louder, Elysia!" her father shouted.

Flinching under the wave of honey-scented breath that hit her face, Elysia curled her hands in her dress. Her palms sweated, her hands shook. "He would have killed Alexander," she repeated, though her voice was only a bit louder; the words were too horrifying to give more volume.

"Alexander, leave." Her father's words were cold, nothing like the tone he had used to address him the other day, when he had called him *friend.* A phantom of warm fingers brushed down her arm, and then the door clacked shut behind Alexander as he left. Khronos's eyes never left Elysia's. He put his hands on Elysia's shoulders. "Do you know what I would have had to do if he killed Alexander?"

"No." *Nor do I want to know.*

"I'd be forced to haul him home and judge him a murderer. He would have been executed."

Her mouth dropped open. Revulsion swam in her gut like snakes skimming across her belly, and Elysia pulled herself from her father's hands. "No." Her father was the judge of the dead, not the living. *No,* her common sense said, *he is the judge of souls.* Her body took another step back, and she was against the wall beside the kitchen table. There was nowhere left to run, except out the door, and Khronos would surely catch her before she made it that far. Not only that, but she was not sure she had it in her to run; she was finally home. To run now would be cruel, and the sky darkened outside – soon the streets would be unsafe. And she was tired.

"Yes," her father replied, but thankfully, he did not take a step toward her. "It is a regrettable thing, but he is one of my own. If he commits a crime, I will punish him accordingly."

Elysia shook her head. "He is *alive.*"

"Murder is an offense worthy of an execution. Even the Greeks know that."

"You raised him – raised *us*. How could you even consider that?" Elysia cried. *Tell me that you did not raise him. Tell me you are unattached.*

"I love him near as much as I love you, Elysia," said Khronos, and her heart sank. "But if he commits a crime worthy of execution, he will be put down just as any other animal would be. If a dog mauled out of turn, it would be put down. It is the same."

"It is *not* the same!" She pushed off the wall, jabbing his chest with a finger. "He is not a pet. He is a man." But something stopped her, terrified her. "If I killed another, would you execute me, Father?" she asked, quiet again, staring up at him. Something foreign edged into the lines around his eyes, something she had not seen before, something that did not belong there.

He is afraid.

"That is different," said Khronos, crossing his arms. "You are my daughter."

"How is it different?" Her volume rose again, carrying desperation with it. "You love him near as much as you love me, but he is an animal that can be put down? Am I not? In what way is it different?"

Khronos shook his head and turned, running a hand through his hair. Returning to his stool, he rested his elbows on the kitchen table and rubbed his eyes. It was then that Elysia saw the food laid out on the table, pita and honey and fruit, all untouched. Enough for three. *He was going to have us to lunch.* Regret filled her lungs, and she tried to breathe it out with a sigh. Instead, she sat across from him.

"You are my daughter, Lys," he said, putting his hands down on the table to look at her. "The circumstances of you killing another person would be wildly different from Philip killing Alexander. It would be in self-defense or in judgment, as those are the only two reasons for which I could ever fathom you committing such a sin." His eyes implored her for understanding, wide and bright in the dimming light of the house. Reaching over, he touched her hand.

"I hope those are the only two reasons I am ever faced with," she muttered.

Khronos sighed across the table. "After you have passed your tests and earned your eternity, I will not be able to judge you, as I would a human. Even if you did kill someone, and not for those reasons but for something more malicious, I would not be able to execute you. Only your body would die," he said.

Elysia stared at him. "Only my body would die," she repeated.

Nodding, her father continued. "After you have passed your tests, your soul will be eternal. Nothing will be able to extinguish it – not even me." He paused to gaze pointedly at her, as if in warning. "Your human form, however, is as mortal as the rest, though it will not get sick or age unless you wish for such things. Wounds, on the other hand, will be as damaging as they are now. You ought to be careful."

Elysia nodded slowly in return. *The rules that apply to him now will apply to me then.*

"I will not be able to control your eternal soul as I control human souls – again, unless you want me to. You will be completely and utterly your own."

"All right," she said, and her stomach rumbled.

"And so will your hunger be your own. Let's get some food in you." Gesturing to the food that had been meant for their lunch, her father smiled. Relief flooded through Elysia, though she remained wary. When had she last seen him so angry, *truly* angry? He had never been remotely close to furious when she had refused to play along and go to the city to begin her tests; he had never so much as raised his voice to her, that she could recall, before she was sixteen, unless she was in immediate danger or putting *herself* in immediate danger. His anger today was born of the worry from her disappearance and what happened afterward – and that was just because she had a few hours unaccounted for, which had given him a battle-ready Philip to deal with; what would happen if something more pressing arose?

Would she incur his wrath?

Uncertain, Elysia reached for a piece of pita. The rest of the evening seemed too short: they finished their meal, Aliya drew her a bath when she returned with the nightfall, and Elysia readied herself for bed.

Lying beneath the warmth of the blankets, Elysia could not sleep. Tomorrow would be the last day before her test, the last day she would have before her days and nights would be spent alone in this city. And dread crept into her stomach, twisting in her gut.

She would be alone.

27

Elysia woke once more before the dawn. She and her father broke their fast in silence, but when they heard whistling outside the window, he spoke. “I will be accompanying you today,” he said, stern.

Elysia groaned.

“I meant to be there yesterday, remember?” asked Khronos, eyeing her. “I will be there today, instead.” Giving her a small smile, he added, “I want only to see how you’re doing.”

“All right,” Elysia replied, brightening as an idea struck her. “You can help carry water.”

Khronos suddenly seemed less enthusiastic. “The… water?”

“Yes, the water. The well in the neighborhood is polluted.”

The walk to the neighborhood was quiet and quick; with Khronos accompanying them, Elysia and Alexander did not dawdle, nor did they hold hands: all three of them carried jugs of water, clear and fresh, from the spring in the garden. Elysia had not counted on the weight of the jugs, though she should have. After all, water was not particularly light. The handles on either side of the jug bit into her fingers, but she did not have to stop to rest.

Upon reaching the neighborhood, Alexander dedicated the day to reviewing each technique, one after another. With Khronos there, they did not pause to talk and there was no reason to compose themselves; everything was business. Though he did not correct her in anything (he did not need to, much to Elysia’s glee), Alexander made her practice cupping her hand the same way she had on the first day: by slamming it into his shoulder. And then they practiced her form in stomping, and after that, her form with the eye jab, between techniques in the order she had learned them. Occasionally, Elysia looked to her father, who wore an expression of surprise, though she hoped it was pride, too.

Soon, they were done with the review. Elysia was surprised not to be fatigued – not yet, anyway, even if she had begun to sweat. They paused for a drink, but as soon as they had had one, Alexander drove her right back to work. He did not go easy on her; the sparring was hard, harder than it had been before. They started and stopped and started again, same as ever, but he kept her going for hours: the sun rose behind the wall and was well into the sky by the time Khronos called for a finish, just before noon. Only half a jug of water remained, and when Khronos volunteered to carry it, Elysia and Alexander exchanged a glance.

They held hands back to the house. Her father did not seem to mind, or if he did, he said nothing. He said goodbye to Alexander and headed into the house, and Elysia heard him call Aliya to draw a bath. Her attention turned to Alexander. "Tomorrow," she said, taking his hands.

With a nod, Alexander smiled that boyish grin that defined her memories of him. "Tomorrow." Raising her hand to his lips, he kissed her scraped knuckles. "Until then, I'll be thinking of you," he said, and slowly pulled away from her, his fingers sliding from hers.

Elysia grabbed his hand, pulled him toward her. Leaning up, she pressed a kiss to his lips, and something in her shifted. She felt wild; her hands tangled in his hair with a fervor she had known only once before, and her mouth opened to his. Arms wrapped around her waist, pulling her close and into his warmth. Heat engulfed her, running in currents and spikes down her arms, in her lungs, in her belly. She kissed him harder.

Alexander pulled gently away, resting his forehead against hers and separating their lips less than a finger's breadth. He closed his eyes and groaned. "Tomorrow," he said, opening his eyes and brushing a strand of her hair back into place. Running his fingers down her chin, he kissed her forehead. "I will see you tomorrow."

"Yes," Elysia replied, and this time, when he pulled away from her, she let her fingers slip from behind his neck. Watching him go, she sighed. *Tomorrow.*

Her bath was quick and thorough; she did not want to be late to her weaving lesson after her absence the day before. After a small lunch, she knocked on her grandmother's door and was glad to see she was the first to arrive. Metrodora, to her surprise, did not ask for an explanation, but Elysia provided one, anyway; her self-defense training had taken her to Acrocorinth. It was all her grandmother seemed to need, and just as she had not asked for an explanation, she did not question the one that Elysia had given her.

Before the other women arrived, Metrodora showed Elysia how to wrap the weft thread around the shuttle and tie it onto the loom. After that, she passed the shuttle through the warp, used a comb to push the thread up and make the weave tighter, and pulled the heddle. Once she learned, she was off. Metrodora was her partner on the other side of the loom, just as Roxane and Theodora were partners on the other loom. Eventually, the five other ladies arrived: Khloe, Khrysanthe, and Ianthe with their spindles, and Roxane and Theodora empty-handed but for the olives, cheese, and wine they brought as refreshments.

The evening flew by in chatter and tedium. Weaving turned out to be as mind-numbing a work as cutting threads and arranging them on the loom; though there were parts of it that demanded attention and dexterity, Elysia spent her concentration on conversation. The women spoke mostly of their families: each, excepting Khloe, had a household to run and children to look after. Khloe spoke little, and when she did, it was to ask advice on her spinning, usually from her mother. Elysia found herself wishing she had had a relationship with her mother beyond the day they had met for the first time; that day was sore in her memory. Mira was not the same woman with the warm voice who had picked her up and carried her away from the weaving room. She was not the same woman who Elysia recalled with paintbrush in hand, trying to wash the scent of her own sickness from the rooms with honey and rosewater.

Elysia left through the back door when the lesson was over, ready for dinner – but when she got there, she found Zeus in the front room. Khronos, on the other hand, was missing. "Dinner is on the gods tonight," said Zeus, and as quickly she had entered the house, she was out of it again, ushered through the front door and into the street.

"Whose temple are we visiting tonight?" she asked, eyebrows drawing together with the question. *And why did you not come back to see me last night?* He had been looking for her, or barely looking, anyway; he had thought her safe in Alexander's hands. Maybe he had heard the argument through the wall and decided not to return.

"Zeus," he replied, and Elysia did a double take. Zeus laughed. "Not *me*," he said, pointing upward. "King of the gods, god of thunder. *That* Zeus. And after that, Ares, god of war. I'm told your test is tomorrow."

"Yes," Elysia affirmed.

"Then you ought to pray to Ares for luck and strength of arm."

The statues of Zeus and Ares were as grand as the statues of the rest of the gods she had seen, carved of white marble and taller than three grown men. Zeus looked nothing like her uncle, who was clean-shaven with the same long, straight hair that Elysia bore; instead, Zeus the god had a curly, full beard and a head of hair that was just the same. Her uncle told her that it was black in the myths, to go with the storm clouds he was so famous for conjuring. Ares, on the other hand, was as clean-shaven as Zeus, bearing a helm under his arm and not much else; Elysia blinked and blushed just looking at the statue. Zeus ushered her to the back of the room, behind the screen where the women were meant to pray. From there, she could see only the naked back of the statue – his face, which had been so like her friend Ares's own, was not visible to her. There was nary a woman around, though, despite the section for them. She supposed they probably would not pray for war, or if they did, it was for the lives of the men they cared for in the privacy of their homes. "Pray," Zeus said quietly, "and then we'll have dinner."

Kneeling, Elysia adjusted her weight to keep pressure off her bruises. But there was no statue of Ares back here, as there had been statues of Athena and Hera in their temple. There was nothing to pray to but the back of the statue's head, and Elysia felt none of the inspiration she had felt when she had seen those two goddesses. Her thoughts were stunted, ungraceful. *Lend strength to my arm, as my uncle suggested,* she thought at the statue. *Keep my assailant from getting the upper hand.* She paused. Did she have more to say? Was that really it? Elysia got to her feet.

"Perhaps I should have taken you to Athena again?" Zeus asked as they left, though the question seemed mostly for himself.

Elysia looked askance at him.

"While she is the goddess of wisdom, she is also a goddess of war," he said, and frowned. "But her domain is not battle, violence, or valor itself – she is the goddess of strategy." They descended the steps quickly and the roar of the crowd and the priest enveloped them as the masses said their evening prayers, this time to Zeus. The sacrifice was dozens of meat goats, roasted in rows over fires that sizzled and popped. The agora was as packed as it had been the night of prayers to Poseidon, but nowhere near as silent; it seemed that Zeus was not afforded the same quiet reverence as his brother. The people out tonight seemed far poorer than the ones who had attended Poseidon's gathering, too: Elysia saw not one shred of purple, even among those gathered in front. The closest she saw to anything rich were the few impressively woven and dyed patterns near the sacrifices and the golden robes of the priest himself. All others wore either common checked patterns, solid-colored, or undyed woolens, some so old and stained as to be nearer muddy gray-brown than their original yellow-white. Zeus and Elysia, in their blue clothes, took places near the front. Once among the crowd, Elysia found the priest's voice hard to make out, but eventually, she was handed a plate of seared goat meat. It had not near as many spices as the beef she'd had, but it tasted similar.

Finally, Zeus took her home, towing her through the crowds. He was not near as careful as her father had been, but he was in a hurry; she could not blame him for wanting to escape the press of people. The scent alone near drove her to her knees.

"Good luck tomorrow, little niece," Zeus said when they reached the door, patting the hand he still held. His fingertips were red with the juices of meat, as hers were. "I doubt you will need it. Pray to Athena, if you like. She might protect you as you go into battle." He smiled his smile at her, the infectious one that made her smile back.

"I think I will," Elysia replied. He said his goodbye and ducked into the house he shared with Metrodora, and Elysia sighed. The day had gone by far faster than she had thought it would, but still, she was exhausted. Alexander had pushed her almost to her breaking point, and she had gotten perhaps two inches of fabric woven; the visits to the temples and the prayer had only served to top off her limbs, which seemed to brim with fatigue to the point of limpness.

Pushing through the door and into the house, Elysia listened carefully – and heard her father's gentle breathing. Once the sun sank behind the garden wall, the house was pitch dark. Elysia made her way to her bed, blindly reaching out with feet and hands to ensure she did not run into anything; the kitchen table and the legs of her bed were not things that would be pleasant to meet with so late at night. Her little toe slammed into something as she took a step, sending her stumbling as pain shot through her foot. Her father caught her by the arm. "Easy there," he said, guiding her to sit on her bed. "It would not do to go into your test with a broken foot."

As she lifted her foot to rub it, Elysia caught the light of her father's eyes; in the dark, they glowed golden, casting their light onto his cheeks and making his irises shine like fathomless, translucent emeralds. Her breath caught. Someday, her eyes might do that.

"No, it wouldn't," Elysia replied slowly, rubbing the pain from her toes.

"Go to sleep," Khronos said, and when he blinked, the light of his eyes extinguished for a moment. "You'll need your rest for tomorrow."

Sighing, Elysia scooted back on her bed, pulling blankets over herself. The air had cooled, though not enough to predict a rain or frost – just enough to herald night. Curled in her bed, she watched as her father blinked his golden eyes at the ceiling, her own little night light, and then closed his eyes. Soon, his breathing deepened in sleep once again.

Tomorrow I will pass my first test, she thought, and then remembered Athena. Turning onto her stomach, Elysia leaned up on her elbows and clasped her hands, casting her eyes toward the dark ceiling. *Goddess of wisdom – I thought that was the only reason people prayed to you, to help them make good decisions. Battle strategies might be the same thing, decisions, but they are webs among webs of decisions... So help me make the right choices tomorrow. Help me to act quickly, to stay calm, to keep my strategies close. Set me on the right path, down the right roads and alleys.* She paused in her prayers and rolled onto her back. And then she addressed not the humans' idea of the goddess, but the woman she had known as a judge. *And thank you, Athena, for watching over me.*

Elysia found herself in the alley again, the one filled with pottery. Dread filled her. Where was Alexander? He had been just behind her, hadn't he? With the certainty of a dream, she knew that if he was not behind her, he must have gone on ahead, through this alley he had said was a shortcut home.

At first, she had to skirt the pottery, but soon, she clambered up a mountain of it – and then a wall stood before her, bricks as chilled as ice. Hands were on her, hands whose callouses she knew as well as her own scars. Turning, she found Philip before her, his stone-dark eyes cruel and hard. He pressed her into the wall with his whole body, fingers clawing and digging into her skin despite the short nails she knew he kept. Elysia closed her eyes as his words washed over her. *Don't you want love? Don't you want to pass your test?*

She woke breathlessly and found her own fingers digging into the flesh of her thigh. Looking around and finding her breath, she rubbed the pain from her skin. It was morning.

I will pass my test, with or without your love.

28

Dawn broke clear and bright over the forsaken neighborhood where Elysia and her father met the judges of her first test – and embraced them, excluding Herod.

Hera earned her hug first, and theirs was almost a tearful reunion: Elysia practically launched herself at the judge, who squealed with glee and hugged her so tightly Elysia feared she might break bone. Apollo eventually tugged her away from the *I missed you*s and gave her a squeeze of his own, and from there, she was passed to Athena, Aphrodite, Eris, and Alexander, whose hug was a bit longer than those before it and included a brief kiss on the cheek. Lastly, she was handed off to Ares, who gave her such a wolfish grin she was hesitant to step into his arms. He beckoned her, though, and when she did, he hugged her close, far more delicately than she had expected.

Behind her, Herod's walking stick stamped the ground. Elysia stepped out of Ares's arms. "Today, you will take this test, which I still question every time we give it…" Herod said, eyes on Alexander, who cleared his throat and crossed his arms. Herod's attention returned to Elysia, and he began again. "Today, you will take a test that will put ya up against an opponent. If ya pass, ye'r done with your training. If ya fail, you start over. Simple as that." Herod's brown eyes surveyed the Six. "Why yer father has decided to bring six more heads into this than's necessary is beyond me, but he's insisted," he added gruffly, and pointed to Ares with the end of his walking staff. "You'll be facing that one there."

Elysia paled. Ares, Judge of Battle and Valor, was to be her opponent?

She was not prepared.

Khronos approached her from beneath the pomegranate tree. "They will judge, and based on their judgments, I will decide whether or not you have passed or failed. Have no concern for Ares. He will recover from whatever damage you do him."

Elysia could not help a frown, and she saw one flit over Alexander's face, as well. *He might not recover if I accidentally break his neck.*

"You will have a route that will take you through the city, and it will give us time to get into place," her father continued, ignoring her trepidation. "Use the paths we usually take to the agora, then come back. We will be waiting, watching you. Ares will not go easy on you, so do not go easy on him. Am I clear?"

Swallowing, Elysia nodded.

Khronos held a hand toward the road that led from the neighborhood. "Go."

Taking a deep breath, Elysia let her eyes rest on Alexander. With his nod, she walked away from the people gathered to judge her.

The way from the neighborhood was as quiet as the way to it; only after she reached her house and headed toward the agora did she see people about. Most of them were women carrying jugs of water or spindles, many with children scurrying ahead of them. Thankfully, none seemed to mind when she darted between their houses or over their fences. Most just gave her a passing, pinned-on smile or took no notice of her.

Every step she took made her instincts prick to higher alert, as for every step she was not attacked, she took one step closer *to* an attack. If anything was terrifying, it was that. When she got to the agora and its morning buzz, it far from put her mind at ease; the walk back, she knew, would be more intense. As soon as she took a step back in the direction of home, she took an extra look at her surroundings – and then shook her head at herself. They would not attack so near people. Anyone could hear her shouts, could intervene. This was not the place.

The closer she got to the halfway point, the closer she came to the perfect place for an ambush: where the houses were thickest, but also filled with women and children. The men of Corinth had already headed to their workplaces for the morning, or else to the agora to sell their goods; the women and children were all that was left in the neighborhoods, and all would turn a blind eye to an attack. They had not been trained the way Elysia had, and they had known their places since birth. They were women, no doubt brought up in Corinth. Elysia shook her head at the thought. *If only all women could be raised as Apocorinthians.*

It was just as she stepped into an alleyway with a low fence at the other end that Elysia saw the people crowded behind it – and recognized her father's red-gold hair among them.

At the scuff of sandals in the dirt, Elysia turned and found Ares practically on top of her. Her instincts had failed her. His hands closed around her throat, squeezing hard enough that she lost her air, her windpipe. Throwing her arm up beneath his, she lifted it and turned with such a force that her shoulder throbbed from the impact of her arm against his, and then one of his hands was gone from her throat, the other loosened and clawing at her, trying to find a hold. Even as the marks from his fingernails ached sharply, Elysia made her turn into a full circle, one hand already cupped and ready to give his ear a ringing smack – but even as she tried, Ares ducked, her hand skimming his brown curls.

Her feet flew from beneath her, and she was on her back. She lost her breath. Her mind screamed at her. She scrabbled away from him, but he half-crawled after her. Elysia saw her opening. Raising up her leg, she kicked his knee as it straightened. A harsh, sickening crunch filled the air. Ares screamed and fell forward.

Oh gods.

He landed on her chest, just as Alexander had, and what little air she regained left her once more. Wheezing, Elysia took inventory. Her legs were useless; his legs were curled on them, pinning her. Her arms and head were free, but he was flat against her – the dirty tricks were off the table, which left only biting and his face.

Trying again, Elysia aimed a slap at his ear, and made contact. Ares bellowed wordlessly and braced an arm against the ground to stop himself from rolling off her. Something in her growled. Gripping his ears, she dug her nails into the place where they joined his head and dug her thumbs across his eyes. Blood sprang from beneath her fingertips, and his bellow turned to a screech. His legs spasmed, and Elysia slammed her knee into his groin.

Ares seemed all too willing to get away from her, keeling over to the side and curling in on himself. Elysia scrambled over to the wall, clawed her way up it, and stood, staring him down. She started to take inventory of herself – drops of blood gleamed wetly on her throat, warm and coppery – but stopped.

She needed to run.

Chest heaving, she took one look back the way she had come, but she could not go that way: if she did, she would be forced to come back through here, as she knew no other way to her house except the one they had taken in the chariot, and she wouldn't remember it. Her head turned back toward the people on the other side of the fence. She ran, lifted her skirts, and vaulted the fence, right into Alexander's arms.

He hugged her tight, holding her off the ground and taking quick steps backward to avoid falling over with the force of her impact. His hand wrapped firmly around her waist, the other clutching at her upper back, her shoulders, her hair – checking for wounds there, Elysia thought. She sucked in a breath as his fingers found a sore spot over her shoulder blade.

She lowered her legs, trying to touch the ground, but his arms held her up; her own, clamped around his neck and shoulders, only served to hold her steady. "I'm fine," she said automatically as she tried to catch her breath. "I'm fine." But Alexander's face was buried in her neck, and he did not seem to hear.

A few seconds later, he let her down and smoothed his hands over her shoulders – and Elysia realized that her shoulder clasp was missing. Eyes widening, she hugged herself closer to Alexander. *Don't look down,* she willed him as she pulled up the side of her neckline that had collapsed without the support of the shoulder clasp. She knew that the other half of it, the piece in the back, must have fallen, too, but her only concern was the front. Thankfully, she had it pulled back up into the proper position before Alexander frowned and looked to see what she was doing. Then he blushed. "Sorry," he said, and looked determinedly upward, looping his arms about her shoulders.

"It's fine," she squeaked, and then called, "Hera?"

"My lady," Hera said, and seemed to understand; there was a little scuffling behind her, and soon enough, delicate fingers pulled the back of her dress up. Elysia winced – it was the same side as the cut on her shoulder blade, and it ached so sharply that she pressed her mouth into Alexander's shoulder to stop herself from crying out. "That will need to be looked at," said Hera softly, and the fabric stopped its painful shifting as the judge pushed the shoulder clasp back into place.

"Thank you, Hera," Elysia whispered through gritted teeth, and after catching her breath, she looked up. The blood that had been on her neck and the front of her dress, on her face, had left crimson smears on Alexander's clothing, on his skin, and, much to Elysia's regret, in his hair. When she looked up, he looked down again, relief flashing across his features. He gave her one of his little crooked smiles. "Thank you," she said.

"Not a problem," he replied, "but people are staring."

Of course they are, she thought. Taking a deep breath, she nodded to herself and turned.

Their expressions were not what she had expected. She had expected somewhere between elated and completely disgusted from different people, but the expressions she expected from certain people seemed to be switched: where she had expected her father to be happy – she had just finished a *test*, after all – he looked utterly scandalized; where she had expected something grim from Eris – she had just wounded a friend – the judge appeared to be the only gleeful one of the group. Aphrodite was missing altogether. Elysia's eyes found her on the other side of the fence, where she helped Ares sit up against the wall, pressing a wineskin against his lips.

Both her father and Herod wore the same strange look, but Herod shook it off. "Now that you are covered," he said gruffly, and Elysia's thoughts reeled. When had her shoulder clasp come undone? During the fight? When she had leapt the fence – when Alexander had caught her? Maybe it was not her clothing malfunction, but that Alexander had been the one to hide her. When she had decided which way to go, she was certain her dress had been in order; she would have noticed anything amiss, would she not? She had felt and seen the blood on her chest. Herod continued despite the panic he must have seen on her face. "We will have the judgment."

Eris piped up first, nearly jumping in her eagerness to answer. "Passed. She fought him off."

Shaking off his own strange expression, Khronos fell into his routine, but skipped Ares and Aphrodite in the order of judgment; they were occupied on the other side of the fence, she talking quietly to him while he sipped from the wineskin. "Hera."

"Passed. She escaped, even if it was not completely unscathed."

"Athena."

"Failed." A pit dropped into Elysia's stomach as she stared at the judge. "She allowed him to take her to the ground. She is more likely to have been violated or killed than she is to have escaped."

Beside her, Alexander reached for her hand. She clutched it so hard her bones ground together.

"Herod."

"Failed. Same as our uncannily named brunette," he replied, eying Athena. She just stared back at him.

"Alexander."

"Passed," came the deep voice beside her, and something inside her squealed in glee. It did not make it to her face, though, nor did she look up at him; she would not have them thinking this was any more favoritism than they already might. "She escaped despite her position."

Khronos turned toward Aphrodite, who was helping a shaky Ares to his feet. The creator was silent as the judge helped her lover limp to the gate, and then spoke her name. "Aphrodite."

"Failed," she said harshly. "If she was found to have so thoroughly defended herself by the Greeks, I can only imagine she would be executed."

Elysia backed up an inch, and Alexander let go of her hand to pull her closer, his hand resting on her hip. Her eyes searched Ares. He limped, his knee bent at an angle that told her he would not be walking on his own for a time. But he blinked in the sunlight, though blood covered his cheeks and eyelids and ran down his neck from behind his ears.

Finally, Khronos said, "Ares," and the single word felt to Elysia like it would seal her fate.

"Passed," Ares croaked, and his wolfish grin was back. He stared at her with clean, white sclerae when they made their appearance at last from beneath the bloody scratches that dominated his eyes. "Because if a woman did this to me, I would not be admitting it to anyone, least of all the law."

A breath of relief left her, and she gripped a hand in the back of Alexander's tunic.

Khronos turned to her. "Then I, Khronos, your father –" *And all those other things,* thought Elysia, "– declare that you have passed this test." And then he smiled, that smile that he kept just for her, bright and shiny and brilliant. He took her from Alexander's embrace and spun her around.

It was worth it, all the training, all the pain and bruises and nightmares – all of it was worth it, just for that moment.

She had passed the first test.

Over her father's shoulder, as he put her down, Elysia's eyes found Alexander's, and he smiled, too, but not just at her; he smiled at both of them.

"Now," croaked a voice from behind them, "can I go home?"

Elysia looked at Ares, who still stood behind the fence with Aphrodite at his side. "Yes," she replied. "Let's go home."

29

Alexander walked home with his father; with her test complete, Herod reasoned, she did not need them anymore. Though it was painful to part from Alexander without explaining her plan, Elysia was ushered home by her father and the judges. Apollo joined Aphrodite and supported Ares's other side, but before they reached the house, Ares was well enough to walk on his own. No new blood flowed from his face or behind his ears; the rest browned as it dried. Elysia had never seen anything like it, even in her years living with the Six.

"A benefit of being a cursed soul forever," Ares explained, rolling his eyes at her gaping expression. "Hits don't tend to stick."

"Good to know," she replied, frowning as Aphrodite glared at her, despite Ares's healing wounds.

Hera distracted her, demanding to know what she had missed and who the blond boy was. Elysia laughed; she had fled to Alexander, and she had done very little to hide it. Her father, emerging from his conversation with Eris, supplied an answer. "Last I asked, there was nothing to know."

Eyebrows raised. Elysia waved them off. "And you pretended to believe me, Father," she replied. Hera gave her such a look that she relented, though. "His name is Alexander. He taught me to defend myself, as Ares so thoroughly learned," she said, grinning at Ares, who winked at her. "He respects me as a person, not *just* as a woman, and I respect him."

"A forward-thinker," Hera said, nudging Elysia's shoulder. Though Hera hadn't meant to touch the wound there, it twinged painfully. Elysia rolled her shoulder. "Sorry," muttered Hera. "Let's get home and get that looked at."

Warmth spread through her. *I* am *home.*

She reached the house without speaking another word, but the judges made up for her: they laughed, poked fun at each other, and reminisced until Elysia wondered how she had gotten by without them. Then again, it had never been like this in the valley. Their interactions had been limited to the chamber and hallways, always in passing. Now that they were in the city, Elysia was surprised to learn just how much they remembered of her: Aphrodite told of Elysia's first taste of wine and the face she'd made; Eris remembered her playing in the judgment chamber when she was too young to know better – she'd sat on the thrones and done her best imitations of each judge. Somber Athena reminded Eris of the next time Elysia had been in the judgment chamber – and the new seat that had been placed there, much to her amazement. *A seat of my own,* Elysia recalled, *and I was finally part of the family business that went on there.*

Just like any family, though, the judges had their quarrels, and one surfaced as Hera cleaned Elysia's wound. It came in the wake of Khronos's announcement that they would be back on the road home within the hour. As soon as he said it, there was an uproar, and Eris was loudest amongst them. "I am not a toy to be shoved into a box as soon as you are bored of me," she said above Ares's obscenities.

Hera remained silent, but her fingers pressed harder into the cut on Elysia's shoulder, making her suck in a breath. "Easy, Hera," she muttered, and the judge's fingers relented.

"You serve at my pleasure," Khronos said to the few who argued with him.

"It's not *our* pleasure!"

Elysia blinked at Apollo's raised voice. Apollo, the golden boy, the one who *pandered* to her father sometimes – he argued? Khronos seemed to still on his stool beside the table, staring at his judge of morality. "Does it matter if it's not your pleasure?" he asked, and while the question was cold, detached, it had a high note.

"Yes, it matters," said Athena from her seat on the lounge beside Eris. "We may serve at your pleasure, but you receive your judgments at ours. Do not forget this, Lord Creator."

Elysia's gaze darted between the judge and her father, and for the first time, she wondered what he would do if the judges refused to give him their judgments. There would be a backup of souls around the globe, she knew, as if there wasn't already – but without the judges, it would be hour-long interrogations to learn the truths of their lives instead of the minute-long ones they had now. On good days, if souls were quiet, the judges could rattle through two in a minute, and that was only when Elysia was present; when she was gone, she knew, they did things at inhuman speeds. That speed kept the afterlife mostly empty and gave souls their second chances almost as soon as they were struck by death… But the length of Khronos's stay in Corinth could only have lengthened the line.

"You may stay until the morning," said Khronos, standing. "After that, you will help me pack what Elysia won't need, and we will return to the valley. No grumbling. Are we clear?"

"Yes," said the Six as one.

"Good. Now, do as you will. You have free reign for the day."

Aphrodite squealed so loudly that Ares clapped hands over his bloodied ears, and before Elysia registered that the judge had risen, Aphrodite was on her feet, pulling Ares out the door. Apollo rolled his eyes and followed them, but Athena and Eris stayed put, mirroring each other as they lounged. Behind her, Elysia felt Hera shift, and something that cooled her wound and set it aflame burned into her skin. Elysia growled something that was half a curse and half unintelligible.

"Wine," Hera supplied.

"Wine," growled Elysia. "Of course."

The wound, Hera said, was small enough not to require stitching or anything aside from attention; she had to check it and clean it often to avoid infection, but that was all. Hera informed her that a nasty bruise formed around it, already a purple near to black, and Elysia nodded. That was where the pain originated – the pressure of the judge's hands. And, of course, the alcohol. "What will you do for the rest of the day?" Elysia asked, facing her. She looked just as Elysia remembered: chestnut curls trapped in braids atop her head, brown eyes glowing amber in the light, rosy cheeks.

"I'd like to see the garden," said Hera, smiling wickedly.

Taking Hera's hand, Elysia pulled her from the bed and through the back room, where Hera gave the bathtub a cursory glance. "I wondered if that thing would fit in here," she said, but Elysia just shook her head and lifted the bar on the back door.

The garden was warm and fragrant in the noon sun, the scent of roses and fresh water wafting through the air. The marble bench and fountain glowed bright in the light – as did Zeus's hair from his seat on the bench, where he ate a pomegranate. Elysia felt Hera still.

When Zeus looked up at the sound of Elysia's footsteps scraping on the flagging, he froze, a few pomegranate seeds halfway to his mouth on the flat of his knife. As the silence between them stretched, Elysia tried to gauge what passed between them, but Hera stood behind her and Elysia couldn't see her face.

Finally, Zeus lowered his knife back to the pomegranate in his hand, scraping the seeds back into it. "Hello," he said, voice low, careful.

"Hello," said Hera in a tone Elysia had never heard before. Hera's face was bright pink, her hand over her mouth.

"Hera, is everything all right?" she asked, loosening her hand from her friend's to put it on her shoulder.

When Hera lowered her hand, she revealed a smile of such radiance that Elysia took a step back. "Yes," she said, and the judge left her side to introduce herself to Zeus.

It was as if Elysia had stopped existing. Deciding against a goodbye, Elysia headed back into the house, shutting the door behind her.

Something had gripped Hera, like she saw the world anew… Like she'd witnessed something miraculous. Elysia leaned against the wall of the tub, thoughts whirling. Had Hera met Zeus before? But it wasn't possible; the Six were never allowed to visit the city with her father, and they had not accompanied Elysia to Corinth.

A half-formed idea struck her.

Hera had once said that reincarnation was not perfect. *Some soul always slips through, taking with it the names we've used. And they inevitably recall a face here, a feature there, and call themselves blessed to have seen the visage of a god.*

Did Zeus recognize her?

Did she recognize *him?*

Elysia spun, facing the door. Her father had had other judges before – always six, but not always the Six she knew. Some grew tired, weary, others grew rebellious or sloppy. Had Zeus's face been one that Hera remembered from her incarnations? But no, that didn't make sense, she told herself as she calmed her breath. Zeus hadn't even been *born* yet; Hera had served for longer than that, and it was not often that humans looked the same way twice.

If that was true, if she *couldn't* know him, had never met him, what explanation was there for her recognition?

Elysia still reeled, supported by the bathtub, when Hera came back in. The second she saw her, Elysia grabbed her shoulders.

"He is the love of my life."

Though she managed to keep a grip on Hera's shoulders, Elysia's fingers went slack. "He…" She felt herself staring, and Hera's cheeks reddened. "That was fast," she squeaked.

"I have waited to see him for eons, Elysia," Hera said, smiling a shy little smile. Half a moment later, her expression clouded. "But I am leaving at dawn."

"Leaving or not, you've seen him – again?" Brows knitting together, Elysia steered the judge into the front room. Khronos, Athena, and Eris had left, though to where, she did not know. She had paid too little attention to hear them leave. "You've met him before?" she asked, sitting them down on the bed.

Hera nodded, twisting her hands. "He was my husband."

Wordless, Elysia pointed in the direction of the garden.

With a short little laugh, Hera shook her head. "Not *him.* His name was Tirigan when I knew him. He was rough and harsh, even to our children, but there were times… Times when he would gaze at me, just as Zeus did. He did that movement with the knife sometimes, the times when I managed to enchant him somehow. After a while, I learned his moods, learned that there really was something beneath his shell. I grew to love him." Hugging herself, her shy smile grew wider. "He – Zeus – he thinks I'm a goddess."

"The people love you in Corinth," said Elysia. The statues in the temple sprang to mind; even there, Hera had worn her braids atop her head behind her crown. Her face had been as near a copy as Elysia supposed the humans could make with their stone and chisels, but the resemblance was unmistakable: the delicate, barely hooked nose, the set of her mouth, the width of her forehead and the bit of crookedness in her hairline.

"I hope sees more in me than a statue," Hera said, the lines of her mouth drawing downward. "I don't see him as Zeus."

"Zeus doesn't look like the god. The god looks like Father with long hair."

With a sigh, the judge shook her head. "When I'm gone tomorrow, he will think he was visited by Hera, goddess of marriage, his namesake's queen. Or, perhaps, he will think he merely dreamed of me."

Elysia took Hera's hands. "I will make sure he does not," she said. But as she squeezed Hera's palms, she didn't see how she could – if she had nothing to tell Zeus except that the Hera he'd met was human, not divine, he might not believe her; he would say that her likeness was too similar to be disproved, and his faith was strong. "Tell me more of your life with Tirigan," she said softly.

The rest of the night, Hera spoke of her last life, the life she had lived with a husband, three sons, and a daughter, the life she had lived next to a river, the life she had lived in peace. When she thought her gods had forsaken her by saddling her with an unfortunate marriage to a brute, they had given her hope with the small things he did – hope that shined in the face of beatings when she did not mind her place, or else roared when she made a mistake. Tirigan cleaned up his own bowl after they had eaten and, occasionally, hers. He watched her over the fire as she spun the wool of the sheep they raised together, helped her carry water when she was great with child, even if it was only then. And in time, even if he had never shown his own love through anything more than tiny actions, Hera had grown to love him.

Eris, halfway through the story, sauntered through the front door and sat down on the lounge opposite them; when she heard what was being told, she remained quiet, propping herself up with her elbows on her knees. At the end of the story, she shook her head. Her raven mane swayed. "Romance that blooms from a plant of abuse is not all too romantic, if you ask me."

Turning slowly, Hera locked her gaze on Eris. "I did not ask you," she said. The chill in her voice made the hairs on Elysia's arms rise.

Hastily, Elysia tried to turn the conversation, because while Hera looked ready to fight a duel, Eris looked cozy. "Did you know some other kind of romance, Eris?" she asked.

Eris's eyes, so deep a brown they were near black, flicked to her face; Elysia was reminded of a cat, toying and pawing at her. "No."

Disappointment, deep and hollow, resonated in her chest. "Oh."

A smirk twitched at Eris's lips. "I would not stand for it. If a man touched or spoke to me a way I did not appreciate, and made the mistake more than once, he would find me vanished the next morning. In the wake of that philosophy, I suffered just about every injustice a woman can endure, but I did not suffer them long."

Elysia sat up straighter. *The world is not made for women such as* us *just now.* "And you kept running? How long?"

Eris's head tilted, her hair shining in the light from the windows, and Elysia felt her predatory presence in the room, sinuous and snakelike, ready to strike, to entrance. "Well, I could work in a town for a few months, sometimes, without a man making his interest known to me," she said. "Those were the best times, when I was free from everyone but my employers. I thought of them as employers – they fed and sheltered me, after all. But I was just a slave girl to them, or else a tavern girl, or a girl in a weaving room. And I would leave after a while, hiding and covering my tracks well enough that they didn't find me. One day, though, during a winter in my thirties, I found myself back at a town I had already visited. I had married a boy there, but he had grown into a man. A most unhappy man, because I had gone missing and left him wifeless but not a widower. His mother poisoned me at her table."

Hands squeezed Elysia's, and she squeezed back. Hera was as shocked as she, it seemed, but the unaffected way that Eris spoke, as if none of this had happened to her – as if it was a happy tale instead of one that ended in the destruction of her own life. *The Judge of Sin and Strife, what did I expect?*

"When I came to the chamber, your father told me my running was over. I could be done. He told me I could serve the justice I had never gotten for the things that had been done against me, and I was glad to take his offer. He told me that I had searched for a home for twelve years after I ran from my marriage."

Elysia let out a breath. There was not another soul more fit to judge sin and strife, then, if Eris had suffered what Elysia thought she must have suffered; there could be no one better at judging lies and half-truths than a woman who had lived to examine all the ones spoken to her.

"But he was wrong."

Elysia's eyes snapped to the woman sitting before her, the woman with the black hair and scarlet dress who had worn both for as long Elysia could remember. Something about her struck Elysia as off, something that had always been there but which she had never seen until now, now that she listened to something other than her judgments. Eris was different from the other judges: she isolated herself. She had not attached herself to Khronos, as Apollo had; she had not formed a friendship with other judges, as Athena and Hera had, and she had certainly not become anyone's lover, as with Ares and Aphrodite. Elysia's eyes widened. Eris was alone. Years – hundreds, thousands – had passed her by, and yet all she had become was the Judge of Sin and Strife.

What is she waiting for?

"I do not need a home," Eris continued, "nor have I been searching for one. If any place is my home, it is my own skin, but I obviously did not have need of that, either." Grinning a little grin, Eris shook her head. "No, a home is a complex thing. I am much more a simple creature than to want that. My only desire is excitement."

Crawling forward, Hera sat down on the bed beside Elysia, crossing her legs before her. "This is something I have not heard," she said.

Eris's dark eyebrows raised. "Is it not? I thought you knew by now. Judgment is entertaining. It's why I'm still around. Of course, you are the youngest judge. It may not have come up in your – how long has it been? Only a thousand years of service? But then again, it isn't something I talk about too often." Reaching forward, the judge placed a gentle hand on Hera's knee. "You still have so much to learn."

Hera pulled her knees to her chest, letting Eris's hand fall back into her own space. Something beneath Elysia's skin prickled.

"Don't touch me," hissed Hera.

"I wouldn't dream of it, my dear," replied Eris, her voice growing as she stood. "But I have better places to be. Only a few hours in the city, and there are so many things to see." The smile she bestowed upon them gave Elysia goosebumps. "Have a good, boring evening here. I doubt I'll be back until morning." And with that, Eris strolled out the door, the slit in her dress swaying to reveal skin up to her hip.

Elysia let out a breath that had hidden in her lungs and exchanged a glance with Hera. The judge was pale, staring at the door as it swung shut behind the woman in the scarlet dress. Putting a hand on her shoulder, Elysia soothed her.

There's something wrong with that one, and it goes beyond not wanting a home.

Just what that something was, Elysia wasn't sure.

30

Morning came too quickly after an evening that had passed just as fast. Elysia had fallen asleep between Hera and Athena in the garden, fighting off their attempts to extract information from her. Distraction had been her best tactic, but she was certain she had fallen asleep halfway through asking a question – and after that, her game was up. When morning came, they badgered her once more.

"Did he kiss you?" asked Hera, both hands on her shoulders. They sat on the bench, all three of them pressed together, enjoying the perfumes of the roses and avoiding the thorns.

Athena, on Elysia's other side, shook her head. "That's not important. What's important is that, if anything did happen, it happened for the right reasons."

Holding up her hands, Elysia leaned into the rosebush behind the bench, trying not to crush the flowers and ignoring the thorns digging into her skin. "If I tell you *anything,* you'll just go home curious, and it'll annoy you for weeks until Father drags you back."

Hera's eyebrows rose. "He *did* kiss you!"

Throwing up her hands, Elysia gazed at the lightening sky. "I kissed him."

A firm hand tugged her chin down, and Hera steered Elysia's eyes to her own. There was a smile there, sparkling mischievously in her amber eyes. "You really are a Corinthian girl."

Behind her, the back door let out a squeak against its hinges. "Time to say goodbye, Lys," said her father's voice, and as she turned, Elysia knew it was too soon.

It was too soon to say goodbye, too soon for them to leave, too soon for her to be alone. Something sank in her belly, an anchor weighing her down as she turned to face Khronos. "Father," she murmured, but she could not move.

He came to her. His arms wrapped her up tight; he was never as concerned about her fragility as everybody else. His arms didn't gingerly encompass her as Apollo's or Philip's did whenever they hugged her. His hugs were snug, warm, and near-bone-crushing, and that was just why they were perfect.

Looping her arms around the back of his shoulders, Elysia buried her head in Khronos's chest. "I'm going to miss you," she said, low enough that only he would hear. Her voice *felt* thick, her throat constricting. "When will you return?"

"Five days," he said, his breath warm on the top of her head, soaking into her hair. "Metrodora and Zeus are right next door, and Aliya will remain with you. Come to the agora on the fifth day, and I will replenish your food." Pulling away and holding her at arm's length, Khronos pushed a strand of white hair behind her ear. "If you want food that isn't smoked fish, you have to go to the prayers. All right?" His green-gold eyes brushed over her face, and she knew she would miss them. They were her light in the dark, her guidance. But someday, she might have eyes of her own that glowed.

"All right," she said, doing her best to put on a faltering smile. It was not easy. Her cheeks hurt from holding it up while tears grew warm around her eyelids.

Holding his hand toward the door, Khronos waved her through. "You still have to say goodbye to everyone else. They're waiting for you."

With Hera and Athena following, Elysia wove her way through the house. At the front door, she took a deep breath and swallowed her tears once more; finally, she pulled it open.

And they were waiting for her.

The women were lined up on a wagon, sitting on the canvas that would cover the goods when it was full; the judges had chariots to themselves, paired off together. Horses that Elysia had never met stood in the traces, but her sorrel was there, as were the whites and her father's stallion. Philip's bay gelding was the only one missing, but she could only assume that it was with him somewhere, waiting for the train of empty wagons.

"We'll see you when you are ready for the judgment of your next test," said Aphrodite from the chariot she shared with Ares, her voice cool. Someone somewhere had crafted the cart to match their thrones; it was red-dyed wood, wheels and walls decorated with pale pink, blue, and beige shells.

Ares, on the other hand, was far from calm – he jumped from the chariot to clap her on the shoulder. "You'll be fine," he said, and his hand reached up to rub her head.

Elysia leaned out of his reach. Ares just laughed. "Just keep on like that. You did better on that test than they would have you believe."

"Thanks."

"Not a compliment," he said, stepping into his chariot. Aphrodite scowled at him. "It was a fact." Wicked smile in place, Ares clucked to the horses, and they rattled off down the street.

Athena gave her a brief smile and stepped up beside Apollo. Before he could say anything, though, Athena put a hand over his where it rested on the frame. Sighing, he gave her a nod. "We'll see you soon, Elysia."

Lastly, Hera stood before her and took her hands. Her own words rang in her ears: *How do I say goodbye to someone as good as you?*

And even though Philip was gone, with Hera, the answer was the same: *You don't say it.*

Unshed tears made her breath hitch in her throat, and her body threw itself into Hera's arms. Warmth and the smell of something sweet, foreign, and distinctly Hera enveloped Elysia as the judge wrapped her arms around her. "It might only be a week or two," murmured the faithful one. "Or it might only be a month. It won't be long."

"I know." Her voice cracked; her vision blurred and swam – her tears were ready to start rolling from her lashes. Closing her eyes, Elysia tried to hold them back as Hera pulled away. It was not much use.

Khronos stepped forward for one last hug, but Eris cleared her throat. "You're just making it harder for yourselves," she said, voice deep, raspy, throaty, as if she had spent the night screeching. "And for me to watch. Let's go." Her eyes were dark slits, squinting in the dawn rising in the east.

Though Khronos shot Eris a look that made Elysia's stomach go weak, he settled for resting a hand on his daughter's shoulder. After giving it a squeeze, he turned back to the train of empty wagons and helped Hera into her chariot. Vaulting into the saddle of his own stallion, Khronos took the reins from Aliya and saluted Elysia. "I'll see you soon, daughter," he said, turning the uneasily prancing horse in circles; it was as though he was a dancer on a pivot, balancing, and she was his focus. "And when I do, we'll sit in that chamber together as equals. All right?"

His voice resonated within her, bringing out something giddy. Elysia swiped at her tears, ignoring their dampness as it clung coolly to the backs of her hands, and let out a little laugh. "All right," she answered.

"But before you can come home, you must do something for me." His eyes bored into her, so intense she almost felt their gaze pressing into her skin. Khronos held his horse well in hand, and even the creature's eagerness for the road stilled as Khronos stared down at her. "Live a human life, Lys," he said, "and all that comes with it."

A *smack* on the animal's rump rang through the morning air and the horse sprang into an uncomfortably fast trot. Just like that, her father disappeared around the corner; only hoofbeats in the distance bespoke that he had ever been there at all.

A rush of breath fled Elysia's lungs, and she woke to the sound of her heart, pulsing in her chest to a pace quicker than normal. Leaning back against the door frame for support, she watched the wagons pull away, led by Hera and Eris in their chariot. A cynical clarity struck her. The sight of Strife and Sin next to the Judge of Faith made her cringe, made her shiver: those two were never on the same side of the chamber together, let alone in a chariot. Something about that left her almost nauseous.

Aliya took her hand. The last wagon had disappeared around the bend, much to her disappointment. She had been off in another land, another valley, her eyes unseeing as the only family she knew fled from her like the sun from the night.

And now we are alone.

"What do you have in mind for the day, my lady?" asked Aliya, her voice soft. Quiet as an owl on the wind, Elysia thought she heard a sniffle from the girl beside her.

Elysia turned, eyes grazing the scar that marred Aliya's lovely skin, and closed her eyes. Opening them again, Elysia squeezed Aliya's hand between hers. She sighed. "I think spinning will be first," she replied. "And, later, perhaps a weaving lesson with my grandmother."

The morning passed slowly, too slowly. Elysia spent it standing, her spindle at her knees, studying each tapestry in turn. Now that her family had left, she had nothing to do but wait for the afternoon – wait and think. When she found the weaving of a tumble of stones looking out at the sunset, where she had once kissed a man she wished to marry, her thoughts turned to her nightmare.

Don't you want my love? Don't you want to pass your test?

Yes, I want to pass my test, her mind replied. Her fingers stopped the spindle, pinching the thread and gathering it so she could touch the fabric. Her fingers brushed over the rock with the flat top, but here it was nothing but wool and dye. *But I passed the one I thought you meant.*

She had passed, and yet that inkling he had given her, that *doubt* – it had not resolved itself. Something was missing, and she did not know what it was.

To judge the souls of humans, you must know what it is to live a human life.

What would it take for the judges to declare that she had lived a human life? Frowning, she moved to the next tapestry, where the fountain of the maid glowed white with gilded edges in sunlight. She was learning to weave, and as soon as she could do it well enough on her own, she might as well have a profession, just as the rest of the Corinthian women did: making cloth and thread for those who bought their own, rather than crafting it themselves. She had a house to live in, and she had made friends – what else might constitute a human life?

Gazing at the maid, she waited for an idea to come to her, but none did excepting the vulnerability she had realized a few days ago. Humanity was vulnerable, and so was she; she was flesh, bone, and blood, just like everyone else. Something about her perspective was missing, and she knew it: she was searching the shallows for Poseidon's dolphins when she ought to be searching the depths. But what would they show her if she found them? Hadn't she learned what there was to know in her time in the chamber?

She moved down the line, squeezing behind the lounge and tracing the outline of the house she had grown up in. It looked so much like the temples in the agora, like the mansions on top of Acrocorinth…

Elysia sucked in a breath.

She had told herself she would figure out a human life with Alexander. And yet here she was, spinning – or not spinning – the day away, waiting for her weaving lesson to begin.

Pushing her way past the baskets at the end of the lounge, Elysia swatted the curtain aside and opened the door to the garden, where the sun told her there was no way she would make it to the mountain and back before her weaving lesson.

Tomorrow, then, she decided. *Tomorrow, my human life will begin.*

And, hopefully, she would find whatever was missing.

Until then, though, she had her lesson to keep her busy, and it turned out to be a rather hectic affair: Theodora and Roxane finished the length of cloth they had been working on, and as they unrolled it from the bar at the top of the loom, Elysia saw that it was much longer than she had first thought. Yards and yards of fabric gathered heavy in Elysia's arms as they unrolled it, and then in Khloe's arms, and then in Khrysanthe's. The fabric could have stretched from the loom and out the door to the other end of the garden – forty feet, at least. And all of it was richly dyed, perfectly even stripes and zigzags that made Elysia's vision swim with illusion. Standing there, with it gathered in her arms, she glanced at her own project – a measly half a foot – and inferiority sank in her stomach. *I'll get there, someday,* she promised herself, but then her mind turned to the weaving room in the valley. How could she get there if she was not allowed in the room? If she did not have a loom to weave on?

Trying to hide her frown, Elysia helped the other women fold the fabric and set it on a stack of baskets in a corner. It was heavy enough that it took four of them to move it as Khloe, Ianthe, and Metrodora set up more threads on the newly freed loom. As soon as they were done, Metrodora dismissed them, waving them off to feed themselves or take care of their families. When Elysia tried to leave through the back door, however, her grandmother stopped her with a hand on her wrist. Before Elysia knew what was happening, she was locked into Metrodora's gaze, staring into eyes that should only belong to a goddess. Now that she was close in the dim light of the house, Elysia saw the silver light that limned her cheeks. And as her grandmother opened her mouth to say something, Elysia cut her off; the words came out of her mouth before she had a chance to stop them.

"Who are you?"

Metrodora's head twitched to the side, and Elysia saw genuine surprise in the O her mouth formed. "Who…" she began and trailed off.

Pulling her arm from Metrodora's grip, Elysia crossed her arms. "Who are you?" she said, this time more softly. "Your eyes are not the same as everyone else's."

Metrodora took a step back, and her own arms crossed, mirroring Elysia. "That's not true," she said. "Khronos's eyes have the same trait. It is more common than you might think."

"Is it?" Elysia asked, taking a step forward. "Then why is it that none but the pair of you has them? Zeus doesn't, Delia doesn't, and I certainly don't. I have looked." As Metrodora took another step back, Elysia stopped following her. Much further, and the woman would run into the loom, and she could not imagine that would be good for the set up – the weights would certainly set themselves to swinging. "You know who my father is, don't you?" Elysia had to know. There was only supposed to be one god; the rest were human fables. And yet here was perhaps another, with eyes that shone like the moon, whereas her father's shone like the sun.

Before her, Metrodora stilled, and then she took a deep breath and stood tall, shoulders back and chin raised. Elysia forgot about the short, doughy woman who was her grandmother. The woman who spoke seemed ancient, changed from the warmth she had shown Elysia and into some cooler, calculating creature. "Yes," she said, her voice deepening even further than it had, the smoke of a thousand fires making it lower than any woman's voice Elysia had ever heard. "He spun the universe."

Elysia's breath left her. Her feet took her a step back. Her head was light; it seemed to swim with thoughts and yet have none. Uncrossing her arms, Elysia drew her breath back in. Fists clenched at her sides, hidden in the folds of her dress, she stared down the woman who would be her grandmother. "If he spun the universe," she said, her voice low and as wary as she felt, "who are you?"

Metrodora reached for a loose strand of thread, and Elysia flinched back again. "I am your grandmother." Holding the thread straight between her fingers, she tugged on it. "And I spun the thread that brought your father into being."

"You..." Her fists loosened in the folds of her dress, and her jaw felt slack. Her hand raised to point at Metrodora. "There is only one god."

"Is that what he told you?" Metrodora asked, and suddenly her movements abandoned the robust, jiggly motions of an old woman and were traded for a sinuous grace as she found a seat on Ianthe's bench. "I suppose he might think that." Her eyes, with their silver rings and spindles, darted up to find Elysia's again. The quicksilver within them seemed to spiral and whirl in the dim light, dancing bright. "I have been gone to him for an eon and a day, since he unraveled the thread and made the universe."

Elysia hand still pointed at her grandmother, but her thoughts were elsewhere, back when her father had told her about the first golden stars. "What is your true name, then?" she asked.

The response of the woman – the goddess – drew Elysia out of her memories.

"I am Ananke."

"I do not know this name," Elysia replied, her arms crossing.

"You don't?" asked Metrodora.

Ananke, Elysia corrected herself. She had just begun to think of Metrodora as her grandmother – how long would it take for her to grow accustomed to thinking of her as a goddess?

"Ananke is a rather minor goddess in the Greek tradition, it is true, and you were not raised to the Greek tradition, either," Metrodora continued, her voice growing distant as she spoke. Suddenly, she clapped her hands together. "It makes no matter," she said. "In the Greek tradition, Ananke is the goddess of destiny, and that, at least, they got right."

"Destiny?" Elysia's brow furrowed. "Destiny, and my father is time."

"We were made for each other, but really, I made him. And I set him loose on the universe. Or with the universe. Whichever you prefer," Metrodora said, folding her hands neatly in her lap.

My grandmother created my father who created the universe. Her head spun.

Her grandmother rose from her bench and took hold of Elysia's hand. Warmth enfolded her fingers, and Elysia's eyes met Metrodora's. "Now, I want you to promise me that you will go to Acrocorinth tomorrow and see your Alexander. I have a feeling he misses you as much as you have yet to notice yourself missing him."

"I promise?" Her voice wavered, a question, but she said the words.

"Good. You may go."

Dismissed, Elysia tried not to stumble on her way through the back door. On the other side, she heard the bar thud into place, and without thinking, she leaned back into the door, knowing full well it would hold her weight. Sliding down its front, Elysia stared into the garden.

All she had done was ask a stupid question, a question that didn't make sense at the time – it did now, of course. But then? She should have let Metrodora keep her identity. Now she was Ananke, some goddess in human form, as Khronos was, only now... Did that make her Elysia's grandmother twice over? She shivered at the thought. *The grandmother of all, and especially me.*

Picking herself off the flagging outside Metrodora's door, Elysia crept back into her own house. Aliya had bread, cheese, and fruit and olives set out on the table, and that was fine, because Elysia was not sure she could stomach meat just now.

No, she thought. *But seeing Alexander tomorrow might make it better.*

After all, Destiny herself had suggested it.

31

Dawn saw Elysia trekking toward the mountain with a satchel over her shoulder. The bag contained her spindle and distaff, which had a cloud of fluffy wool attached. She was following through on her promise to her grandmother, though she could not say whether to Metrodora or to Ananke she'd made the promise. They seemed two different people, one kind and the other stern, though Elysia had no doubt that both could be each of those things. Metrodora had shown her sternness well enough before.

All the same, she was off to see Alexander. Her feet were light and quick on the road.

Her step became almost leaden, however, when she saw who waited for her at the gate, who made her glee dissolve as spices into sour wine. Adrastos stood in the shade of the statues, soaking up the attention of his fellow guardsmen, and Elysia wanted nothing more than to throttle him. Instead, some part of her that was still meek took over. While she stood out in a crowd, with white hair and blue eyes so unlike those of the Greeks, she might avoid attention if she didn't draw any to herself.

As she passed beyond the gate and statues, out of Adrastos's line of sight, a surge of relief rushed through her. Not one guardsmen had said a word to her, not even Zeus. But, she supposed, they were focused on incoming traffic, not outgoing. Where visitors journeyed after leaving Corinth was no concern of theirs, as long as they did not depart with any obviously stolen goods. She kept on, leaving behind the cool shade of close buildings and towering statues, venturing into the pale sunlight of the new day.

Without Alexander to talk the time away, the walk to Acrocorinth dragged on with her feet, crunching in the dry dirt... But soon, the dirt was no longer dry. As she walked, the white clouds blanketing the sky overhead turned grey as a dove's plumage and sent a mist down on the earth, as if they would mire the land in clouds, as well. The mist gathered in tiny, cool droplets on her skin, and her dress became heavy with it in minutes, chilling her. As she neared the mountain, the droplets grew bigger – and fell faster.

By the time she reached the bottom of the mountain, she ran from the rain, her skirt held up to keep it from muddying and from tripping her. Her hair dripped down her neck, loose strands sticking to her face, and the only thing she was grateful for was the fact that her bag at least kept her spindle and wool partly dry. She hiked up the hill, completely bypassing a visit with Delia – reaching Alexander's house was her priority, and while she would love to see the woman, delaying any longer would mean that the way up would be muddier than it was already... And considering that she had gotten there twenty minutes after the fierce rain, the hill was already messy. She slipped seven times on the way up, muck staining her knees and dress, practically coating her legs before she got to the top.

Finally, she reached the house in the niche and found it a flurry of activity. Alexander and Korinna were outside, soaked near through, their clothes clinging to them as they hauled golden sheets of thick-woven straw up the back of the house. She called out, but they didn't hear her; the splashing of water cascading from the cliff above was too great.

Putting her bag in the shelter of the doorway, Elysia followed them to the back of the house, where she had gone rock climbing, where Alexander had kissed her. It was there they spotted her coming around the corner.

Korinna was the first to respond to her presence, while Alexander stared at her, a sheet of thatching held midway to his sister's arms. She was perched on a ladder at the edge of the roof. "What are *you* doing here?" she asked, a snarl in her voice as she beckoned for Alexander to hand her the thatching. "Go home. This isn't a good day for you to play with my brother's head."

Scowling at his sister, Alexander shoved the thatching at Korinna. "It's not a game we're playing." Picking up another sheet, he heaved it onto his shoulders. "Elysia, this really isn't the best day for anyone to be on the mountain. You should go home."

Elysia shook her head and took a step forward; water flooded her sandals, carrying silt and rocks with it. How long had it been since it had rained? "You're here, aren't you? How can I help?"

Though Korinna still looked like she had eaten sour cheese, Alexander pointed back the way they had come. “There are sandbags in the house. Euthymios can show you.”

Nodding, Elysia slipped back around to the front of the house. She tried to shuck off as much mud as she could, but then thought better of it; their house had a dirt floor, just as her own house did. A bit of mud wouldn’t do it much harm.

Taking the stairs three at a time, Elysia looked around. Neither Ligeia nor Herod lurked in the corners of the main room, which left only Euthymios, who she could only assume was in the sleeping room to her left. “Euthymios,” she called. “It’s Elysia. Where are the sandbags?”

His voice echoed from behind the curtain, thin and pained, more a whisper than the timbre of his father or his brother. He sounded as sick as he had looked the last time she had visited. “Behind the baskets by the stairs. There’s just wool in the baskets – don’t worry about moving them.”

Sure enough, bags bulging with sand lay behind the baskets; setting the baskets on the bench, she picked a sandbag up – and barely got it off the ground. She grunted, heaving one up to waist level and trying to get a better grip on it. There was no way she could carry more than one, let alone carry multiple down the stairs. Shaking her head, she made due with the one, hauling it outside. Euthymios was quiet as she left.

She had to take a break on her way up the hill. The sandbag was too heavy to carry even twenty feet, but even so, she managed to keep it aloft most of the way. She stopped when she reached the rock Korinna had tied herself to when they’d gone rock climbing, setting the bag down on it. Korinna and Alexander were still about their business with the roof and the ladder. Alexander caught her gaze as she stood there, trying to catch her breath; the cold and the weight had stolen it. Elysia was thankful Korinna faced the other way and could not see her huffing and puffing as though she might blow the house down.

Alexander beckoned her. “Put it over here, against the back wall.”

Even though she nodded her acquiescence, it took a moment of glaring at the sack before she managed the resolve to pick it up again.

“It keeps the runoff from melting the foundation,” he said, giving her a tired smile as he heaved another sheaf of straw up to his sister.

“Now go get another!” Korinna called down from the roof, and if Elysia had not known that she frowned as deeply as only Korinna could, Elysia would have thought there would be a wicked smile on her face for providing her with more torment.

Alexander rolled his eyes at his little sister. "That's the last of the roof, Kore." Brushing his hands off, he draped an arm over Elysia's shoulders and guided her back down the hill. Despite the coolness of the rain, his core was still warm, and Elysia squeezed as close to him as she could; she was frozen, her body temperature long extinguished. His arm cradled her, brushing over her collarbone, and this time, it was not from the cold that she shivered. "There are more sandbags to be added to the pile, I'm afraid," he said, his voice a purr beside her ear.

Over the sound of her heartbeat fluttering in her ears, Elysia spoke. "Should you leave Korinna on the roof, alone like that?"

"She's better on the roof than my mother and I put together. She can handle herself," he replied, steering her through the doorway. Fetching up her bag with his free hand, he led her up the stairs, though there was barely enough room for them to fit up the stairwell side by side. "What have you got here?" he asked, and she caught his playful smirk.

"Spindle and wool. I thought I might spin with Korinna and your mother."

"And me!" called that thin, strained voice from behind the curtain. The fabric wrinkled as it was pushed further down the clothesline, revealing Euthymios's wan face. "Don't forget me."

In all truth, Elysia *had* forgotten about Alexander's older brother – at least, the fact that he could spin. It was not something she had ever heard of a man doing; her father always used the thread that she or the judges or the women spun for him, though she supposed that once upon a time, he might have spun his own thread. Still, by what Metrodora – or Ananke – had said about him, she had been the one to do the spinning, and he had merely unraveled the thread. Elysia gave Euthymios her best smile. "I won't," she reassured him. "Perhaps when this business of repairs or improvements is over –" She looked up at Alexander, wondering what was *actually* happening out in the rain, and where his parents were, "– we'll spin together."

"Until then," said Alexander, peeling his arm from her shoulder; their skin stuck together from the pressure and rainwater between them. "We have sandbags to lift to keep your home from washing away beneath you, brother."

Euthymios waved them off, and Elysia thought she saw a whirling spindle peeking out from behind the cloth of the curtain. Before she knew it, Alexander had handed her another sand bag, and then grabbed one for himself, his veins bulging with the weight. "I wish this was not such dead weight," she grumbled as she started down the stairs behind him, but he just flashed her a wicked grin over his shoulder.

This time, when she made her trek up to the back of the house, Elysia did not stop to put the sandbag down, though she was as tired – if not more so – than she had been when they had started. Alexander did not stop, so she could not stop, no matter how she wanted to. It was a challenge. Her heartbeat throbbed in her ears. Soon enough, she found herself right behind him, putting her sand bag down beside the one she had wedged against the house earlier. "Why have you waited for the rains to come to do this?"

Alexander's answering smile made her feel frivolous. "If we did not, the new straw would grow weak in the sun, when it is really meant to guard our heads from rain. The sandbags..." He paused, looking up at Korinna, who toed her way down the ladder. "That is another matter."

"Rains don't usually come this hard or this fast, fortunately," said Korinna, her incivility seemingly forgotten. Plucking a straw splinter from her palm, she flicked it away. "And it has been dry for so long that the wet season's beginning is more of a misfortune than a blessing."

Elysia pointed at the younger girl. "See, now she sounds like a student of Metrodora."

Korinna's hands balled on her hips. The snarl she wore made Elysia take a step back.

Between them, Alexander gestured down the hill. "Three sandbags won't do the job."

For what felt like the next hour, Korinna, Elysia, and Alexander hauled sandbags up the hill and wedged them behind the house. By the time they had finished, water skated past them, funneling down the hill on each side of the house – and Elysia shivered to beat a hummingbird's wings. Huddling under Alexander's arms and a blanket in the house, Elysia absorbed as much of his warmth as she could.

"You should stay until the rains cease," he murmured. His chin rested on her head, his back against the wall. "You might actually be warm by then."

A short laugh escaped her throat. "I think the only thing that will get me warm again is a hot bath," she replied, reluctantly sitting up and leaning out from under his chin to look at him. "Which means I should go, rains or not."

"And if she stayed until the rains stopped, we might not get rid of her for a week," said Korinna from her spot on Euthymios's bed.

"Korinna," said Alexander and Euthymios as one.

Standing and shaking it off, Elysia handed the blanket back to Alexander. "I really should go. Aliya will think I've drowned out here."

"If you must," Alexander allowed. "I'll show you out."

At the bottom of the stairs, Alexander pressed a hot kiss to her forehead and smoothed as much hair back into her braid as he could, though white straggles insistently stuck to her neck. Sighing, he shook his head. "Maybe a bath will do you good."

Elysia gave him as big a smile as she could, though her eyes strayed to the pounding rain beyond the door. "It will. I'll be back tomorrow." *Because today was definitely a lesson in living a human life, if ever there was one.*

"I'll look forward to it," said Alexander, but he didn't let her leave just yet – he pulled her in for a kiss, long, sweet, and leaving her breathless. Then he shoved her into the rain, still gasping.

"Alexander!" she screeched.

He grinned at her, white teeth flashing through the rushing water. "Go home. I'll see you tomorrow."

Crossing her arms, Elysia made her way down the hill, but eventually she held her arms out for balance – a broken ankle in the mud and rain would do her no good. She'd be stuck here for weeks unless someone brought her sorrel.

The way home seemed longer than the way there had been, slogging through mud and puddles that went halfway up her calves. She almost didn't notice as she passed the gate; in the rain, thick as it was, the white statues were near invisible against the clouds. The only clues were the increase in population and Zeus's sudden appearance at her side.

"I was beginning to worry about you, little niece," he near-shouted against the torrent of rain. Above her, a white flash lit the sky and set the shadows of her uncle's face to starkness. "Adrastos pointed you out as you were leaving, else I would have thought you missing when I got home for lunch. Are you all right? You're shivering."

"I'm fine," she answered, rubbing her arms. Alarm shot through her, putting her instincts on such a high alert that shudders shot violently across her skin; the hair on her arms that was already standing on end from goosebumps prickled more. "I'm going home to have a bath." Thunder rolled as she spoke, rumbling across the atmosphere.

Zeus grinned at her and pointed at the sky. "My namesake ends the dry season."

Elysia hummed an agreement. With a clap on the shoulder, Zeus sent her down the road.

In the city, the roads were far less muddy: the houses sheltered most of them, but the ditches that ran down the center of the roads were filled with waste, and the stench made it hard to breathe. Pulling up the edge of her dress, Elysia breathed through the cloth; even wet wool smelled better than sewage.

Tap tap tap.

Stopping in the street, she turned, half expecting to see a child or a woman trying to find shelter from the rain.

There was no one there.

Elysia stood frozen, peering at the houses that surrounded her. They were the houses of the poor, just beyond the rotted-cloth shelters that made up the Merchants' Gauntlet. They were mud brick, just as the houses in the abandoned neighborhood had once been, and the rain obscured even the doorways without curtains. The street seemed deserted; no lights glowed within the houses, nor were people fussing about the roofs as they had on Acrocorinth. Despite the poverty here, all the houses had tile roofs, impervious to the rain.

Perhaps it was a stick rolling down the street. She wouldn't doubt it, with the manner of things floating in the middle of the lane. Pulling her neckline up to her nose again, Elysia continued down the street.

She was in a richer neighborhood when she heard the sound again: *tap tap tap.* Her first instincts made her freeze again, though this time she dreaded what she might see behind her – that sound, it was not footsteps. Of that, she was certain, which meant there was no woman or child behind her, searching for shelter from the rain. Besides, in this neighborhood, all the people had roofs over their heads. She was the only one without one. Still, when she looked behind her, she saw no one.

Swallowing hard, Elysia took a deep breath. She gave her surroundings another glance as her skin pricked, but all she saw was white marble, rose marble, black marble. She saw green and smelled figs, damp and pungent in the rain, but there was no one. The walk to her house would only take a few minutes more – she would be there in two, if she hurried.

And when she saw a scrap of black cloth peeking from behind a rich house's pillars, she knew she had to hurry.

Panic spiked through her as she turned. Someone was behind her, someone who walked like a cat. Whatever that tapping sound was, it wasn't from their feet – Elysia knew the sound leathern sandals made against stone. Her own feet made the same sounds.

Taking a deep breath, Elysia ran. Alexander's voice sounded in her head. *You walk quietly, but can you* run *quietly? Listen to what your body tells you.* Lifting her feet, she ran on the balls of her feet, practically jumping with every stride.

Tap tap tap.

No, she thought. *No, no, no, no. Not today, not in the rain!* Someone followed her, and they closed in – that sound had been closer than the rest. Mud slimed its way between her toes as she rounded the corner to her house, and as she turned the bend, she nearly slipped, nearly careened into the wall of a house on the other side of a street –

Tap tap tap.

She slammed bodily into the creamy-colored wood of her door, and the tiny squeak it made was the most comforting noise she had ever heard. Slamming it shut behind her with as satisfying a *clap* as she could make, Elysia swung down, heaved the bar up, and dropped it into place with a *thud.*

Her heart pounded in her ears, throbbed in her head. She heard the blood beating in the veins beside her ears above the patter of rain outside, smelled pita in a basket nearby, and she gave into the temptation to slide down the door.

She was halfway down the smooth-sanded wood when she remembered the back door.

On the other side of the wall, she heard a squeak.

Her mind screamed as she flew to her feet and leapt over the end of her bed, smacking the curtain out of her way. *Not today, no, Metrodora must be around.* But still, she heard nothing, no shouts of protest from her grandmother about a stranger entering her house.

Just as Elysia picked up the bar, the back door swung inward.

"You," she whispered.

32

Adrastos had a staff in his hands, clutched between fingers gnarled as the knots in the stick itself. Three of his fingernails were blackish blue, as if he'd hit himself with a hammer. "Hello, Crone," he said, taking a step into the house. "Or should I call you Lys? I'm never sure which you prefer, and I'd like to choose the one you like least."

Mute, Elysia stepped backward and met the rim of the bathtub. She scooted around it, consciously holding the beam in her hands between them. Her throat swallowed convulsively.

"You do remember what ya've done, don't you?" he asked her, smacking the stick in his hand against his palm. "Stripped me of my work, my house, my slave. And I worked for it all, ya know. Not that you would know, I'd wager ya've not worked a day in your life." The gravel in his voice lowered as his volume did. He closed in on her, and she skirted around the backside of the bathtub, keeping it between them, as well.

Keep him talking, her common sense told her. *Keep him talking, no one's coming to rescue you.* Something about that thought put her between flaming rage and hysterical tears, but she didn't have time for either. She had to get out of the house.

"Do you know what I'd like to do to you, *Crone?*" he asked. The pink of his tongue ran over his teeth.

Oh gods, no. Her whole body shuddered.

"Yes, I could pay you back nicely for what you've done to me." Adrastos tapped the end of the staff on the bathtub as he rounded one end of it, and Elysia rounded the other.

She stopped when he stood on the other side. A grin spread across his face.

Heaving the beam at him, she aimed it right for that smile. The door was in her hand before she knew it, and she was in the garden – but then she had nowhere to go.

Calming her frantic breath, Elysia gauged her surroundings. Roses bloomed everywhere, but the petals had gone limp in the rain, and the bushes weren't as leafy as they might have been; there was nowhere to hide. Her gaze found the maid.

Picking up her skirts, Elysia sprinted to the fountain. The rain plastered her hair to her face. Her dress clung to her, made her clumsy, but she made it to the fountain without falling. The rain covered her splashing a little bit, but not near enough. White light flashed overhead, illuminating the doorway in the half-light the thick clouds let filter through. She saw nothing, even as she peered from behind the maid's elbow.

Closing her eyes, she let her ears take over.

The patter of the rain on flagging, in the pool, on the roses she heard at first, and then the rumble of thunder following the lightning. It was then that Elysia knew she had chosen the worst place to hide. If she was not struck down by Adrastos, she would be struck down by lightning. She leaned her forehead into the maid's marble thigh.

And heard a splash.

Before she could step back, rough, bruising fingers clamped onto her arm, pinching her skin. She screeched, trying to wrench away from him, to find a weak spot in his grip where his fingers met his thumb, but it didn't work. He pulled her closer, leering black eyes burning into hers.

"Hello," said Adrastos, and Elysia thought she might be sick. His hand crushed tighter around her arm, and he dropped his staff in the water.

She tried to pull away, even as his hand closed around her throat, cutting off her air. He slammed her into the garden wall.

Her vision went black before stars of reality shot across it again, and she remembered how he held her.

Pushing her left arm against his grip around her neck, Elysia spun into the roughness of the stone wall and felt cuts open across her cheeks. She must have surprised him well enough that he let go with his other hand, too, because suddenly she was without of his monstrous touch, staggering in the pool. Her head throbbed and spun. Blood trickled warmly down her neck.

Adrastos stared her down with dangerous amusement. "Well-played, Lys," he said. "But I don't want this to be a game. It's not a game if, in every scenario, I win." He lunged at her.

Her head slamming into the wall dizzied her, because Elysia was not fast enough to dodge him. He took her to the ground – and on the ground was a foot and a half of water.

Before she could stop herself, Elysia gasped. Water flooded her mouth, burned down her throat and into her lungs. She coughed it out again, but she choked. His hands were around her neck; the water blurred her vision, his face above her. The pool rushed around her, a silence, blocking her ears of all but the sound of its waves as they brushed past.

Blind, Elysia reached a hand up, even as she felt cruel fingers scraping up her thigh. Breaking the surface, she found an ear and dug her fingers in, yanking down.

It came off in her fingers with a spurt of warmth.

All the pressure on her body released at once.

She broke the surface coughing and retching. She flung herself to the side, crawling away from Adrastos, wherever he was – she hadn't paid attention after his sudden absence, hadn't needed to; she only needed air, and she gulped it like nectar. Distantly, she heard an ungodly screeching, but it blended with the rain and thunder and the water she splashed through.

Just as she pulled her torso onto the rim of the fountain, something grabbed her dress and ripped her backward. Her chin hit the rim. Heat and pain flashed through it, and suddenly she was on her back in the water again, Adrastos astride her. "No," she said, but her voice was a mumble of blood and breathlessness.

"Yes!" His shout was so loud that her ears rung – and when she tried to set his own ear to ringing, he caught her wrist and bent her arm back. "You've done that before, remember?" he asked, grinding his weight into her hips.

You're hurting me, she wanted to whimper, but Adrastos was not Philip. He wouldn't be horrified even at the prospect of hurting her. He didn't want to protect her.

She spit a spray of blood in his face.

Brown teeth smiled at her, stinking even from the few feet between their faces. He leaned down, and Elysia took her opportunity – but when she tried to shove her fingers into his eyes, she hit his jaw instead.

His head snapped back with a *crunch* that sent a jolt through her gut. Blood poured onto her, red, thick, and hot, trickling in a stream from his mouth. Adrastos's body toppled forward onto her, forcing her under the water again. Screaming for help, for anything – for the sake of screaming

– Elysia wriggled free of half his weight, freeing her chest enough to lean up and gasp for more air. It seemed like hours before she wrenched her legs from under his torso, but when she finally did, she realized that Adrastos hadn't moved.

He hadn't made a sound.

"No!" Her voice broke as she scrabbled at his shoulders, turned his body upright in the water. His face was quiet and pale, lips swollen and still streaming blood, black-gray eyes wide open. A coppery stench covered the scent of his breath as blood dripped and diluted into the fountain's pool; his ear was gone, floating somewhere in the water, a red angry hole and torn skin all that remained. His head lolled, his eyes open.

"Adrastos," she said. Her hand halfheartedly slapped his cheek, stinging at the contact, spraying blood. His body merely bobbed in the water. His eyes did not blink. "Wake up."

Her fingers locked in his tunic, dragged him with her to the edge of the pool, sat him up against it. Fingers trembling, she shook him. "*Wake up.*" Something hot mixed with cool rain on her face, and Elysia dissolved as the cloth tore in her hands. She let him fall back against the bowl, her hands held midair. "*Wake up!*" she screamed.

His body slumped to the side, the whites of his eyes shining in the dim light of afternoon.

Scrambling backward through the water, Elysia lost her air as her back rammed into the pedestal upon which stood the maid. Water cascaded onto her hair. She stared at the man halfway across the pool, pale in the half-light of the storm, and retched into the pool as the weight of dread and death landed on her shoulders.

I killed a man.

She tried to reason with herself, but her brain was not for thinking. She stared at Adrastos, the way his neck was bent. Sobs wrenched their way up her throat, but she could not stop them, and she could not close her eyes.

I killed a man.

Not only had she killed a man – she had killed a Guardsman, a soldier, a man who was supposed to *protect* people. He hadn't done his job. All she had done was defend herself. All she had done had been to defend herself.

I killed a man.

Slowly, her head began to turn back and forth. It always stopped right before his body left her vision, and then it would turn back so she could see him again, see the whites of his eyes and the angle of his neck and the way he stared up at the sky, leaning against the rim of the fountain. Elysia was silent and screaming inside at the same time.

I killed a man.

How long she stayed there before someone scooped her up into warm arms was a mystery to her. It was long enough that she was stiff and shivering, unable to move on her own. Someone spoke to her, a voice she distantly recognized, frantic and fast, touching her shoulders, pulling her clothes up into their rightful places again, brushing her hair out of her face. When she was set down on her bed and a blanket was wrapped around her, she caught a glimpse of blond hair and closed her eyes again.

Her breath left her in a rush. "What are you doing here?" she croaked, her throat raw from screaming and sobbing.

Warm fingers probed at the cuts on her face, searing against the chill, near-numbness of her skin. She sucked in a breath as they lit the pain in her wounds anew. "Returning your spindle," said Alexander. "Where is Aliya?"

Elysia's eyes flew open. The girl had not been here when she had arrived. The bruises on her neck made her wince as she looked around. "Not here."

"Good. But you need a bath and your wounds need to be cleaned," he said, not taking his eyes off her. They were gray as the clouds outside, sending their rains tapping on the roof. "You haven't said anything about the man in the pool," he said, lifting her chin to study her neck.

"Adrastos," she whispered. "He…"

"Attacked you?" asked Alexander. Suddenly his hands were off her, space between them.

Elysia nodded, folding her arms in front of herself.

"Do you not want me to touch you?" he asked, sitting back on the lounge across from her.

Staring down at the floor, Elysia caught the sparkle of water on his legs. She shook her head. "No," she said, taking a shaky breath. It took her two more to look him in the eye. "He didn't… I'm fine, just… I killed him." Elysia stood – only for a second, though, because her legs faltered. She caught herself on Alexander's shoulder. Standing did not make the revulsion in her gut go away. "He's dead. He's *dead.* I killed him." Sitting down on the couch, Elysia nested her fingers in her hair. "He's dead. I'm a murderer," she whispered. "My father will kill me."

Alexander knelt before her and clapped his hands firmly on her shoulders, sending pain into her neck. Even when she winced, he held her at arm's length and stared into her eyes. "It does not matter what you have done," he said. His thumbs pressed warmth into each end of her collar bone. "Your father could never harm you."

Elysia stared back at Alexander, reliving her nightmare. Trees burning, boulders chasing her, the earth shaking. Those were only the things she could imagine. "You do not know him as I do," she said, "and even I don't know him at his most wrathful."

"It doesn't matter," said Alexander. "*Never*, not ever, could he hurt you." Certainty sparkled in the depths of his gray eyes. "You are his daughter. That is all that matters."

Elysia shook her head and closed her eyes, losing herself in the deep red of her eyelids. The conversation she had had with her father about killing in self-defense came back to her, but even that left doubt, creeping into the tenseness in her shoulders, the knot in her stomach.

"You're shaking," murmured Alexander. Warmth lighted in the skin of her arms as his hands skimmed over them, up and down, rubbing the chill away.

"I know." Opening her eyes a crack, Elysia leaned forward to rest her head on his shoulder. Her mind was numb but for the pictures playing behind her eyes: Adrastos in the fountain, his scraggly beard shining with drops of water. Alexander's expression when they would say goodbye as she was hauled off to her trial for murder. Her father's wrath, raining acid down upon Corinth.

She could only imagine what the Corinthians would do to her if they found out about the death of Adrastos before her father did.

A knock came from the front door. "My lady?" came the muffled voice of the girl who had been missing since Elysia had come home with a dog on her trail.

As glad as she was to hear Aliya's voice, Elysia did not feel up to moving, and Alexander made no move except to pause in his massage. "I should let her in," she muttered, but when Alexander made to move, she grabbed him with a hand on each side of his waist. "Metrodora's is open!" she called instead.

Thankful that she heard Aliya's footsteps before she heard screaming, Elysia prayed that the girl had missed the body languishing in the fountain – a fountain which was now polluted. She groaned.

The curtain flapping gave the young woman away. "Aliya," Elysia began, not taking her head off Alexander's shoulder or opening her eyes, "I would like a hot bath, if you can manage it." Receding footsteps made Elysia lift her head. "Aliya!" she called again, and opening her eyes, saw Aliya peering back at her. Even in the dim light, the scar on her chest shined. "Not from the fountain. There is something in it that you shouldn't see." *Something that will make you scream.*

Though the girl gave her a quizzical look, she nodded and pushed past the curtain, skirting Alexander, who knelt in the walkway. After a struggle with the sticking bar, she lifted it and left.

Elysia took a deep breath and looked to Alexander, whose hands warmed her shoulders. "What are we going to do with his bo-" The word *body* stuck in her throat like she had swallowed a thorn. Swallowing, she tried again. "What are we going to do with... him?"

Standing, Alexander took her hands. Elysia stared down at them, wishing she could do nothing today but stare at them, trace the lines in his skin. Between carrying the sand bags and putting up the hardest fight she had ever known, her arms felt like soft yarn.

"Take him out of the fountain, for one thing," said Alexander, squeezing her fingers. "It would be kindest."

"He doesn't deserve kindness," Elysia replied. A scowl twisted her mouth and hardened her voice.

"He might not," allowed Alexander, "but the fountain and the water supply do."

"All right." With the help of Alexander's steadying hands, Elysia got to her feet and took a step without falling. He guided her to the back door with a hand on the small of her back, and Elysia stood there, staring at the door, knowing that when she opened it, she would see the back of Adrastos's head with his pepper-and-salt hair leaned up against the fountain, turned up to look at the maid. "I don't know if I can do it," she whispered.

"You can," said Alexander sternly. Elysia looked at him and met hard gray eyes. "And you will. There is only so much I can do without help, and I won't subject anyone else to this. If Zeus were here, it might be another matter, but he's on duty."

The beige wood of the door stared back at Elysia, forbidding. Taking another deep breath and squaring her shoulders, Elysia pushed the door open.

Just as she had feared, Adrastos leaned up against the bowl of the fountain, his back to them. His tunic had torn where Elysia's fingers had clawed at it, drooping over his shoulders to reveal skin far too pale, paler than the rest of him. Rain splattered down on the flagging and into the roses with their blooms turned toward the sun, wherever it was behind the clouds. Elysia let the door hang open on its hinges, staring out at the scene before her.

I killed him.

A shuddering breath fluttered through her, and she reached for Alexander's hand, strong in hers. Adrastos was not just a man anymore – the consequences of her actions were more than killing a human in her father's eyes. As awful as he might have been, as ill his intent – there were people out there who would miss him. Maybe a mother, maybe a sister. Elysia could only hope that he did not have children, as sick a man as he was.

Sucking in a breath and shaking her head, Elysia stepped forward. "Let's do this," she said. "Get it over with."

"All right," said Alexander's voice, soft and deep.

Closing her eyes, Elysia took in the cool drops of rain on her skin and, with a nod, opened her eyes. She strode across the yard with numb steps, listening to Alexander's behind her. The closer she got to the body of the man who had once been named Adrastos, the more she closed herself off to the idea that he had once been anyone of consequence. He was not a person. It was a corpse.

Wincing and cringing and doing her best to pull her weight, Elysia helped Alexander lift the body out of the fountain and lay it out on the flagging in the rain. She was only grateful that she had gotten the feet to carry; if she had had to carry the body under the arms, as Alexander had, she would have surely been sick again: the head lolled with every movement, dropping against its chest and flopping back to hit Alexander in the stomach. With waterlogged clothes, it was much heavier than Elysia had anticipated, and they had to take more than a few breaks as they tried to adjust it and get it onto the flagging – and then Alexander suggested hiding it behind a few rosebushes in case Zeus came home before they could do something with it. After all, Adrastos had been his partner and some kind of friend on the Guard; finding him dead and rotting on the flagstones would not be the best way for that friendship to end.

When they came in from the garden, Elysia was surprised by the humidity in the house, and saw steam rising from the bathtub. Her sigh of relief was so deep that her heart sped. "Aliya?" she called through the house, but there was no answer. The tub was only half full. Elysia turned to Alexander. "Do you want to stay for a bath?" she asked.

His eyes widened, hands held in midair. "I don't think I should," he said slowly, carefully.

"Why?"

Crossing his arms, Alexander gazed down at her. "Why do you think?"

"Our parents wouldn't approve?" she said, crossing her own arms. "I killed a man today, Alexander. Parental approval has flown out the window. I need you. To. Stay." She looked down at his legs again. "You have to be as cold as I am."

Regarding her warily, Alexander put a hand on the rim of the tub, half-trapping her against it but leaving her an escape route. "I'll stay," he said. "But if I'm going to take a bath, it'll be *after* you, not with you. Are we clear?"

"Yes," Elysia murmured.

"Good. I'll see you after your bath." Resting a palm against her cheek, Alexander studied her. He pressed his lips to her forehead before ducking under the curtain.

Alone, Elysia let her shoulders fall, unaware they had been tense. What was she doing? She might want him to stay, but inviting him to *bathe* with her?

Shaking her head at herself, she unclipped her shoulder clasps and stepped into the tub. Aliya came back not too long later with a bucket of water heated by a fired brick.

As she scrubbed herself clean, Elysia berated herself.

I'll be the death of us both.

33

The rest of the evening passed quietly. Alexander stepped into the back room after she came out swaddled in a long gown and a blanket. She had left him water that was still warm enough to at least be *warm*; a cold bath in this weather would be bone-chilling, more a wearisome chore than something to look forward to.

When he came out not ten minutes later in the same tunic he had been wearing, Elysia was sitting on the bed with Aliya, who braided Elysia's still-dripping hair. Elysia frowned at him as he made for the door. "Where are you going?" she called.

He turned back around, eyebrows raised. "You said to stay for a bath. I've done that. I ought to leave – you're preparing for bed," he said, though the more he went on, the less certain he looked.

Finishing Elysia's braid with a leather tie, Aliya got up and left to the back room, pulling the curtain across the doorway behind her. Elysia turned her gaze on Alexander, who had not moved. "Will you please stay?" she asked, and her words came out much quieter than she had intended. Meeker. *I killed a man today.* Something in that surely meant she shouldn't be alone. Even with Aliya... There was no way that she would sleep through the night, and there were boundaries that the women of the household did not cross; judges might cross them, but not the rest. Aliya would not wake her up from a nightmare, should she have one. She would probably quail in fear, herself.

Alexander's gaze softened from the calculations he had been trying to make of her, and his hand dropped from the bar on the door. "Elysia," he murmured.

Holding up a hand, Elysia closed her eyes. *It should not feel so wrong and so right to hear my name in that tone.*

Warm fingers wove themselves between hers, and her eyes opened to find Alexander hovering over her. *And still he walks like a cat.* Lifting her chin with his other hand, he nodded. "I'll stay."

"Good," said Elysia, pulling him down to sit next to her. "Will you talk me to sleep?" she asked, and suddenly it seemed like a much stranger request when spoken aloud. Grateful for the dim light of the failing sun and the clouds, Elysia tried to cool her blush. "I won't fall asleep on my own."

"Of course," he said.

Once she had gotten comfortable and buried herself in blankets and pillows against the chill of the evening, Elysia closed her eyes and listened to his voice resonate from where he sat on the end of her bed, carrying her into the clouds to where the gods lived. He told her stories she had never heard before, of a boy named Icarus and his father Daedalus, who made wax wings and flew on them to escape a prison that they built. He told her of Orpheus, who rescued his beloved from the Underworld. And lastly, he told her of Hades, who kidnapped Persephone and how loath the girl became to visit her mother every six months above the Underworld because she had come to love Hades. He had not been so bad a kidnapper; after all, though he ran the places of terror in the Underworld, he also ruled over places of beauty greater than even the homes of the gods on Olympus: the Isles of the Blessed.

Listening to him describe the lands of milk and honey that awaited heroes after death, Elysia dropped off to sleep.

Morning came far too late. Though Elysia had not woken screaming in the night, she had also not been free of nightmares – they had just been quiet ones. Quiet ones where Adrastos's head snapped back over and over again, where his black-gray irises drained of color and turned white as she watched, where the maid poured not clean water from her pail but blood.

When she finally awoke, after Adrastos's face had flashed once more, pale before her eyes, it was to the sound of her own ragged breathing and beating heart.

And the neigh of horses and clopping hooves.

Elysia sat bolt upright and accidentally dropped Alexander's hand from her grip; he had moved above her head as she slept, curled in a ball on the bed in the narrow space between her head and the wall, holding her hand. Scooping pillows and blankets off herself in great heaps, Elysia made for the windows to find out what caused the din outside.

The door crashed inward on its hinges, the bar ripping its brackets from the walls with a screech so ear-splitting Elysia thought the roof might come down on her head, too.

When a looming figure stepped through the doorway in the dust of shattered stone and mortar, Elysia wished that the roof *had* fallen on her head.

"Father," she squeaked.

The air around him sizzled, his face as red as his hair, his eyes glowing so brightly they looked like the eyes of an animal in the night. Elysia wished she could run.

Khronos banged a fist into the side of the door frame. Around her, stone clattered against itself as the house shook, and she heard more than one tile scrape down the roof and shatter on the ground outside. "What," he began, voice so low it was more a growl than anything. "Have you," he slammed his other hand into the side of the doorway and dust showered from the ceiling. Elysia covered her head with her hands and closed her eyes, crouching down on the ground beside the kitchen table. She might have screamed, but if she did, she couldn't hear herself above the din of the house. "DONE?" he roared, and the next thing she knew, she was in the air, up against a tapestry. It was the only thing that kept her from breaking her ribs or her spine against the sharp stone beneath it. Her father's fist, wrapped in the fabric of her gown, held her up against the wall.

Elysia couldn't make a sound.

"Khronos!" shouted Alexander.

While Elysia closed her eyes and tried not to imagine what Khronos would do to the poor boy who had just borne witness to his godliness, she felt her father turn to look at Alexander.

"Unhand her," said Alexander.

The air felt so electric around Elysia she thought it might zap her in return for the lightning she had missed yesterday. Still, she opened her eyes.

Her father had turned back to her, apparently neither heeding Alexander's words nor paying him enough attention to address him. When he spoke again, his voice was loud in her ears, but it was not only his voice that Elysia heard: it was Ares's timbre, Hera's chill, Eris's rasp. It was Apollo's solemnity, Athena's cruelty, Aphrodite's jealousy, dark and hard and unyielding, and all pointed at her. "You've killed a man," he said, and though his voice was low again, she felt it like a blow to her chest.

Swallowing hard, Elysia leaned her head as far as she could into the tapestry, putting distance between them, but there was only so much space the stone would allow her. He was close enough that Elysia felt the light of his eyes on her cheeks, warm yet so cold she thought her skin might freeze beneath it. "He attacked me," she replied, ignoring how her voice broke. If he was going to show her his wrath, she couldn't blame herself for not being able to speak. *I'm lucky to still draw breath.*

Her father's lip twitched up in a snarl, and he leaned closer. "He *attacked* you?" he asked. "Was that when he groped you?" Something dangerous and cold filled his voice as he leaned closer, an inch from her face. Automatically, Elysia jerked backward, only to fill her head with dizziness and blooming pain. She'd hit the stone again. "He seemed to think it was revenge you killed him for."

He's sentenced Adrastos, she realized, and horror filled her, swooping down into her gut. *He knows the worst side of the story and none other.* "Father," she said, trying to mask the desperation in her voice. The place under her ribs where he held her ached. "Think about this. Think about *me.* I wouldn't kill a man except in self-defense." She would have lifted her hands to touch his shoulder, his face, but her fingers scrabbled at the wall, trying to find purchase, a hand hold – anything that would let her hold herself up and take weight off her ribs. Her legs were useless, doing the same but finding nothing; her heels could not stick in anything. She tried for a deep breath and couldn't find the air, so her next words were fast and breathless, running together. "He stalked me, ran me down, went through Dora's when I locked him out."

Slowly, Khronos let her slide down the wall and released her. Elysia bent over, sucking in air. "And who taught you to break a neck?" he whispered low over her head.

Eyes widening, Elysia straightened just in time to see him turn to Alexander, who stood beside her bed. His blond hair stuck up in every direction, obviously slept on, still damp from his bath in places. "Father, no!" Even though she reached for his cloak, her grip did not stop him from crossing the room, and it ripped from her fingers.

When Khronos got near Alexander, the younger man didn't take a step back. Were it not for the fear that had squirreled its way into her gut, Elysia might have been proud. As Khronos stepped up to him, Alexander stood taller, straighter; though her father was inches taller than him, he was not cowed. Images of the house shaking flitted through her mind, along with Khronos's eyes and the way he had held her up against the wall without muscles trembling or exertion. Alexander had to know he dealt with the divine, and he had not stepped back.

"You taught my daughter to kill," said Khronos, standing over Alexander so the younger man was forced to look up at him. Khronos's fists balled. A jolt went through Elysia: her father only stopped himself from curling his hands in Alexander's tunic by digging his own nails into his skin – and that meant he knew Alexander might disable him. Elysia shrunk down against the wall. Just what her father was capable of, she didn't know. But she knew she ought to be afraid.

Alexander crossed his arms in front of him, forcing more space between himself and Khronos. "If she learned to kill, it was by gouging eyes or taking a groin shot. She did none of those things to Adrastos."

"I was trying to damage his vision, Father," Elysia said, warily rising from where she crouched on the floor. "I thought if he couldn't see me, I could run. I missed. I hit him in the jaw, instead." Taking a step toward them, she met Alexander's eyes before looking back to her father.

Her father seemed on the verge of calming. But he glanced from Elysia to Alexander and back again.

Elysia froze on the spot.

"What, *pray tell*," Khronos said, glaring at her and pointing to Alexander, "is he doing here?"

Knowing she held a spark to a bag of flour, Elysia held her hands up placatingly. "I left my spindle in their home yesterday, and he came back to return it. He... He found me, in the fountain."

"And why *in all of damnation* would you go to *Acrocorinth?*" shouted her father. Elysia's ears rang.

"Because!" she screamed, closing the distance between them. Dragging her father around by his tunic and away from Alexander, Elysia put herself between the pair of them. Letting go of his clothes, she put a finger on his chest. "You left me *alone*. You *left* me, and you left me with an impossible task. *Live a human life?* How?" Her voice rose in pitch and volume, straining her vocal chords and her lungs. "*How?* I don't know anything about them except their crimes. And Alexander is the only one I know who I trust."

"You know your grandmother," said Khronos, disdain in the set of his mouth.

"Do I?" she asked. "Do *you?* Do you know *who she is?* She's more confusing than these tests, more confusing than you. More confusing than *you,* Father."

"Live a human life?" whispered Alexander.

Elysia closed her eyes. Khronos ignored him.

"It doesn't matter," he declared, taking a step forward. "That was yesterday. What's he still doing here?"

Her eyes opened, and she took a step forward to meet her father. "I asked him to stay. I didn't want to be alone."

"You," growled Khronos, "are not alone. Where is Aliya?"

The curtain between the rooms fluttered, but Elysia did not break eye contact with her father. "Here," said Aliya, her voice high and meek.

"Aliya, good, you *are* here." Khronos turned from glaring down at his daughter to give the young woman the falsest smile Elysia had seen since Adrastos's. "How long has Alexander been here?"

"Don't drag her into this," muttered Elysia.

Khronos ignored her, prompting Aliya with raised eyebrows. Swallowing, Aliya answered him with eyes on the floor. "Since last night, milord."

"And why is his hair wet?"

Horror filled Elysia. She looked to Aliya, who looked up at her, the same fear in her eyes that Elysia felt in her own. Aliya swallowed again, silent.

Khronos looked between them and snapped his fingers at Aliya. "Do not look to her. She will only get you in trouble." Slowly, Aliya's gaze tore itself from Elysia's face and moved to Khronos's before dropping to the floor again. "Why is his hair wet?" Khronos asked again.

"It rained," whispered Aliya.

Relief flooded through Elysia's stomach.

"What's that?" asked Khronos.

"It rained," said Aliya, louder.

"It rained," said Khronos. His gaze turned back to his daughter. "It *rained.* But if it rained, surely his hair would have dried within a few hours of being inside a warm, dry house. Isn't that right, Aliya?"

"Father," Elysia said desperately. *Don't make her do this.* Something pulled at the back of her gown; just as he had the last time they had argued with her father, Alexander had hooked his fingers in her dress, a comforting weight, even if it surprised her.

"Yes..." Aliya's voice was so low that Elysia heard only the hiss at the end of the word.

"Speak up, girl, these ears are getting old."

Seeming to choke on her words, Aliya took a moment to respond. Finally, staring at the floor, she nodded. "That's right, milord."

"What other explanation is there, then?" asked Khronos. Slowly, his gaze turned from Elysia and to Aliya, and though she didn't look at him, Aliya still shivered under the weight of his glare. "Aliya?"

"Milady had me draw her a bath," she murmured, and what relief Elysia had felt evaporated. Alexander's grip on the cloth of her dress tightened, and she sucked in a breath.

"She had you draw her a bath," said Khronos, and with a nod, he pointed to the door. "There is a chariot outside, Aliya. Wait for me there."

"*Don't* drag her into this," said Elysia again, and Aliya stopped halfway through the house.

"I'm not *dragging her into this*, Elysia," said Khronos. His face reddened again, his eyes glowing brighter. "I am dragging her *out* of this. You have subjected this poor girl to something no Greek lady should ever have to witness. It goes against the way she was raised and the way she has lived her life."

Aliya scurried out the door.

"No Greek lady?" Elysia hissed. "*I* am a Greek lady. What has she been subjected to that could be so offensive?"

Leaning down over her face, Khronos stared into her eyes, and Elysia was surprised that she did not feel her own burning under the heat in his; a live golden flame burned within them. "You shared a bath with a man to whom you are not married. You slept and dined in the same room as a man to whom you are not married. You slept in a bed with a man to whom *you are not married.* And she had to watch and serve you nonetheless. You have shamed yourself and me, and I have every right to execute this man behind you."

"Those are Drakon's laws," said Alexander, "and we have not done-"

"It does not matter. I am leaving." Khronos turned on his heel, leaving Elysia staring after him, wordless. At the door, Khronos paused. "You might pass your test, Elysia, but even your mother, with *her* ideals, would have been ashamed of you." Pulling the door open, he turned around one last time. "Grooms will come for the body. Do not drink or bathe from that beautiful fountain you have so tainted. When it is time, I might send someone else for you. I'm not sure the stain on my honor will have faded by then."

Her pride swelled from the wounds it had been given and fury filled her.

This is not over.

Just after the door closed on her father, a pair of grooms meandered through the house and came back moments later, struggling with Adrastos's stiff body. They did not nod to Elysia and Alexander as they passed, nor did they acknowledge Alexander when he rushed to pull open the door for them once they realized that they could not open it themselves. Adrastos's clothes, his ripped tunic hanging from his shoulders, dripped water on the floor; drops fell from his fingers and at the bows of the muscles in his arms and legs.

It was then that she noticed it was still raining – and only barely light out.

Her father had left before the dawn, in the thunder and lightning, to find out what had happened, only to be disappointed.

Disappointed and ashamed.

When Alexander closed the door, they were alone again for the first time since Aliya had come back from the agora the night before. Hugging him close, Elysia let out a breath and soaked up his warmth. Her father would come back for her, scold her again before he let her have her throne, and it would not be a light scolding.

This is only the beginning.

34

They stood in the quiet, her head against the warmth of his chest, letting the soft sounds of their breath fill the air.

Finally, Alexander spoke. “Live a human life?” His voice was hoarse, and beneath her skin, Elysia felt the muscles in his abdomen tighten, like he prepared for a blow.

“My father...”

“He is actually Khronos, isn’t he?” Alexander pulled away from her, holding her at arm’s length. Something in her gut *ping*ed with alarm. “You aren’t a girl from the hills?”

“I am, actually,” she said, raising her eyes from the ground. “He is Khronos.”

The look he gave her wasn’t one of complete skepticism, and for that, she was thankful. Still, he sat down on her bed, bouncing a little. “How are you a girl from the hills if your father is a god?” he asked, though he seemed to stare past her, at the curtain between the rooms.

“I wasn’t born different from any other human. I’m just a girl,” she said. “A girl who apparently doesn’t meet the most basic of Greek standards, but that’s beside the point. My mother wanted my father to set requirements for me to become a goddess. I’m trying to fulfill them.”

“Just as Herakles did,” Alexander muttered.

Elysia stared at him.

He looked up at her, then sighed at whatever was written on her face. “You do not know of Herakles, do you?”

She shook her head.

Taking her hand, Alexander drew her down to sit beside him. “Herakles was the son of Zeus,” he began, and Elysia was jolted again by her uncle’s name as a god’s. Alexander kept on with his tale. “Herakles wasn’t the son of Zeus by his wife, but by another woman. When Zeus’s wife grew jealous, she made Herakles kill his wife and children.”

“Gods can do that?” whispered Elysia, but she could not see her own father doing that, nor any of the judges, who had been immortalized by the humans as gods. Then again, as she had learned from Eris, she did not know everything about the Six. And there was Ananke to consider.

“Yes. Hera was always jealous of Zeus’s liaisons outside of their marriage, and she did terrible things to his children. He did to one of theirs, too, though she was always faithful – he threw their infant son off a mountain because he thought the child was ugly.” Alexander gave her a small smile, a twitching of one corner of his mouth. “They are not perfect. Their divinity makes them feel things more vividly than mere mortals do.”

Whatever the case, Elysia reeled from the fact that the Hera and Zeus of the Greeks were married. She thought, just maybe, that she saw Destiny’s hand in it.

“Anyway, when he killed his family, Herakles tried to do penance for his actions, atone for the wrongs he had committed, even though they had been initiated by Hera. He was sent to a king, who gave him ten tasks. When he completed them, the king told him that two had not counted, because Herakles had done them the wrong way. He gave him two more to make up for the ones done incorrectly, and when those were finished, Herakles was given divinity, as well as forgiveness,” Alexander finished.

Elysia shook her head. “I only have three.”

“Live a human life?” he asked.

“That’s the second,” she said, standing and smoothing the wrinkles from her gown. Her father’s fist and the heat of it had left wrinkles gathered across her abdomen, and they did not go away even when she tried to pull the fabric flat across her stomach. “The first is learning to defend myself, which I’ve done. That was why the test was so important. The third they have refused to tell me.”

Humming his acknowledgement, Alexander got up off the bed. For the first time in their weeks together, Elysia heard him swear. Just what the words had been, she wasn’t sure, but he had taken several gods’ names in vain. “I have to get home,” he said, turning from where he’d looked out the windows. His eyebrows went up, though, surprise in his gray eyes.

“Metrodora,” he said.

Elysia whirled.

Sure enough, her grandmother stood in the curtained doorway, apparently having appeared there with footsteps as quiet as Alexander’s. When Elysia turned, Metrodora’s face changed from simple, pleasant surprise to something darker, and she came toward Elysia with hands fluttering. "Your face, my dear," she said.

Closing her eyes, Elysia took a deep breath. Bitterness filled her. *I went to Acrocorinth like I promised, Grandmother. I was rained on, frozen, stalked, nearly killed.* She opened her eyes. "My face is fine," she said. "Alexander and I were just leaving."

"Oh?"

Even Alexander looked at her with a brow raised. "You have to get home, right? I'll go with you."

"If you want to," he said slowly.

"I do."

"Perhaps you ought to stay here," said Metrodora, and Elysia glanced at her grandmother, frowning. The woman had put one plump, calloused hand on her shoulder. "We could weave. I really do wish you would stay – I was late at Khrysanthe's and missed your homecoming last night."

"As much as I would like that, I think I had better go." Elysia took Alexander's hand and almost headed for the door, but the vengeance in her made itself known. "And besides," she said, "the last time I did as you asked, I was attacked. I think you know that."

Metrodora blinked shimmering silver-gray eyes at her. "I have no idea of what you speak, but I will be certain to block the door when you have gone." Her gaze found the bar; it lay to the side of the frame, brackets clinging to its bright wood. "Or not."

Shrugging, Elysia led Alexander out the door.

"Did she deserve that?" he asked.

"Possibly," she replied. *Probably.* What Metrodora had hoped to gain by sending her to what might have been an early grave, Elysia could not fathom.

The way to Acrocorinth was filled with the tales of Herakles's tasks, which Elysia asked Alexander to tell her. He told her all twelve of them – from Herakles's killing the Nemean lion, who impersonated girls to kill heroes, to his meeting and slaying the queen of the Amazons, who was also tricked by Hera: the warriors had been made to disbelieve Herakles's intentions. Elysia asked as many questions as she could ponder, and Alexander had just finished the tale when they passed Delia's.

"Back again, are ya?" came a rough voice from beyond the threshold.

Exchanging a glance with Elysia, Alexander said, "Yes."

The curtain in the doorway moved aside, and dark eyes peered at them. "Better hurry, then. Yer sister's like to beat ya if yer father don't for not coming home last night, could hear his shouting clear down the mountain. And my knee says these rains aren't over."

They were halfway up the hill when one of Delia's predictions came true; the grey-white clouds above them opened and turned the hardening muck back into a red-brown mire. By the time they reached the top, the hem of Elysia's skirt was sodden and stained, the rest of her soaked.

If only there wasn't the stupid dress code.

The house at the top of the hill was much the same as it had been the day before, sandbags lining its foundation and a shiny layer of yellow thatch on top of gray, weathered ones. The curtain in the doorway had been pushed aside, and on the steps sat a girl with spindle and yarn in hand, her face relaxed as she gazed at the whirling weight.

Korinna noticed them as they struggled up the last ten yards, and it was likely only Korinna's disdain for mud that kept her from dragging her brother bodily into the house. Instead, she stopped her spindle, methodically wrapped up the thread, and waited for them with arms crossed.

When they reached her, she blocked the doorway. "I wanted to disbelieve our mother," she hissed, "but I think I was a fool."

Elysia's stomach dropped with the look the younger girl gave her.

"What has Mother said?" asked Alexander, releasing Elysia's hand under the weight of his sister's gaze.

"That you would rather be with this... *woman*," Korinna spat, "than help us take care of our family." She stepped up to him, wrapped her hand in the front of his tunic. "Is that what you were doing, Alexander? *Knowing* your woman, this girl who won't marry you? Her father could kill you."

"Korinna," Alexander said, folding a hand over the girl's wrist.

She yanked her hand back, holding it in front of herself. "Her father," she said. Her voice shook. Anger coursed through her small form, and Elysia saw it everywhere: in the brightening of her Mediterranean skin, in the tendons that stood out in her hands, in the snarl of her mouth. "Could kill you, and you don't touch me," said Korinna. Her hand turned into a pointing finger – one pointed straight at Elysia's chest. "Her father could *kill* you."

"I know," said Alexander. He stepped toward her.

Korinna, despite being at least half a foot shorter than him, stood up straighter the closer he got, until she stood directly beneath his face, glaring up at him with their father's brown eyes. Elysia stepped back against the wall of the stairwell, trying to fight down the rage and revulsion she felt when Korinna said *knowing*. Her father had assumed the same thing.

"You *know*?" Korinna shoved her hands between them and pushed him back into the rain. "Do you know what that would do to our family? Do you know what that would do to *Mother*, or Euthymios, or me? What about Father? He'd bring the house down over our heads. He'd hunt down this *girl's* father, kill him, face prosecution. The Highs would kill him because you can't keep your paws off some *girl*. Drakon would prosecute him himself. We'd see what it means for a High girl to be protected." She spit, and something warm and wet landed on Elysia's sandaled feet. Looking back to Alexander, she shoved him again, though this time, he caught her wrist.

"Drakon's laws protected *you*, Korinna. Father had the same rights that Khronos did when he hunted down that High," he growled, glowering over her. "Khronos has chosen not to exercise his. Do not forget that."

Ripping her hand from his grasp, Korinna gave him a last melting look and headed up the stairs. Over her shoulder, she said, "There's a leak in the roof. Take your *woman* out there and fix it, because I am not going out there again today. Not with you."

When the leather of Korinna's sandal disappeared above the last stair, Elysia turned her gaze on Alexander.

"Outside," he said, sighing. "Now."

Elysia went.

They trudged up the hill behind the house, where Elysia turned around and crossed her arms. Fire built in her gut and chest, and she felt ready to spit flame. *And she was raised to be a lady by Metrodora.* There were so few of her grandmother's teachings in the girl, at least from the behavior she'd witnessed by Metrodora's ladies – even Theodora and Roxane, raunchy and randy at their best, did not bristle the way Korinna did. And Korinna's anger was always aimed straight at Elysia. "First of all," Elysia said, pointing at Alexander's chest from where she stood under the shelter of the cliff face, "explain to me who Drakon is."

Alexander ran a hand through his hair, mussing the clean center part. "Drakon is," he began, dropping his hand from his head and waving it in the air, looking for an answer. "He's a man from Athens. Or was, anyway. He has to be dead by now." Pacing over the narrow strip of mud between the house and the cliff, Alexander shook his head. His hand went to his hair again, clawing through it. "His laws are hard, but some of them are good. One places women of a man's household under his protection." He looked at her, his gray eyes dark in the dim light the rain clouds cast. "If a man of a household finds his unmarried daughter, niece, or ward in bed with a man, he has a right to execute that man. It's made rape, at least in home intrusions, less common, but it's also gotten many an innocent lover killed."

Elysia's fingers went to her mouth as she processed this. Eventually, she looked up at Alexander again, shock ringing through her. "Innocent lovers like you, who haven't actually been lovers."

Alexander nodded.

"But… That doesn't make sense," she said. "You said that my father *had* a right to kill you under Drakon's laws." Brows furrowing, Elysia crossed her arms tighter. "Like he doesn't have a right to kill you now."

"There's another lawmaker, Solon. He's been repealing the laws, I think, but I don't know." He gave her a crooked smile, half his teeth showing beneath quirked lips. "It's been a while since I've been to –"

Alexander stopped short, his smile disappearing. "Did you feel that?" he whispered.

"Feel what?" Elysia asked.

From somewhere beneath her, deep within the earth, came a groaning. The earth lurched beneath her with such force Elysia lost her feet. She found herself on her hands and knees, staring at a quivering mud puddle.

"Get back!" yelled Alexander. Hands grabbed her under the arms, shoving her into the cliff. Her world became rain, mud, cloudy sky, and rough rock against her skin.

Something huge and white slammed into the ground in front of them – a column, toppled down the hill. The world slowed and stopped as she watched the pillar lean forward into the roof of the house, caving it in.

The sound came back to the world. The first thing Elysia heard was her own scream.

Sheltered in a niche in the cliff, Alexander held her back as the mountain shook. Mud, water, and marble fell in a cascade, sliding down the hill with the houses in their paths. Her ears filled with screams – the screams of people above, below, of Alexander, herself. Mud slapped, marble thundered as it hit the earth. The scent of rain trapped itself in her nose. Elysia fought to stay in the niche; the mud beneath her feet was slick, and the earth did not want her to keep purchase on it.

The house left them, drifting – the column had bowed its roof concave. Mud bricks dismantled themselves, dissolving and tumbling down the hill.

The first falling body made Elysia jump back into Alexander's arms, made her breath catch. The girl's hair was as curly as Theodora's, bound up in gold bands, a purple dress with a golden belt barely wrapped around her small form. She could not have been older than five.

A wooden doll was clutched in her arms.

The shock broke. Alexander compulsively brushed her hair back from her face, touching as much of her as he could reach, holding her close, away from the shower of muck that rained down in front of them.

More bodies fell. They must have been shaken from the back of the mountain with their homes. None wore a cloak against the rain, their tunics' reds, purples, and goldenrods torn and muddied by the time they fell down the cliff. Some sprayed blood, and sooner than later, Elysia found herself with her face pressed against the front of Alexander's tunic, holding onto the wall behind him, trying to keep the chill out of her skin.

Eventually, the ground stopped bucking, but they could not leave. Mud and marble still fell from above, and the longer they waited, the farther the houses slid down the hill. Beyond the rain, Elysia saw them – brown bricks and golden thatch with marble columns bearing down. Mud marred the fluted and intricate surfaces of what had once been High houses.

"Gods," said Alexander.

Closing her eyes, Elysia tried to breathe, turning her head back into Alexander's chest. *Gods.* How many people had fallen from the cliff? Twenty? Fifty? *And this is only one side of the mountain.*

Gods.

Elysia took a deep breath. *Gods.*

She remembered the boulders chasing her down the valley's walls in her dream. How often had she been told of the rogue waves that swept cities into the oceans, of the great flood that had forced mankind to start anew?

"My father," she whispered.

"Your father's home by now, Elysia. He's fine."

"No!" Elysia cried, backing up, out of the niche now that things had stopped falling. Closing her eyes for a second, she turned, opened them, saw the damage she had done, all the homes and lives destroyed – and that was only what she could see. *My father did* this. *He* did *this.* How could he not have? Surely, he would have expected Alexander to go home alone, to check on his family. And he had decided to do the most damage.

This is my scolding.

He taught me to kill, and so Father killed him.

"We have to find them."

Her eyes flicked back to Alexander, and his expression made her stomach drop like a stone. Elysia offered him her hand.

Threading his fingers through hers, Alexander set off down the hill with her.

It was not easy going. Mud sucked at their feet, and there was no safe way through the debris. They clambered over marble pillars, past wailing people, adults and children alike. Screams still echoed around them, and rain pattered down, washing blood and tears into rivulets.

The house at the top of the debris was Alexander's – the golden thatch, hardly damp, shone from beneath the mud like a beacon. The rest was just a pile of mud bricks and rock with marble pressed up against it. The column that had demolished the house had rolled further down the hill.

When he saw the thatch, Alexander dug his fingers into it and pulled. Three layers came off in his hand. "Go find wherever the door was," he said. "Might be –"

A scream cut him off, high, wailing, and calling his name.

Elysia jumped at Alexander's answering roar, so loud her eardrums rang, so loud that the word he called almost blended with the rush of rain and another shaking from deep within the earth. Elysia held onto a nearby post impaled in the ground. Alexander kept moving – he clawed another layer of thatch from the roof, so old it disintegrated in his hands. "Korinna!" he called again.

"Please," came the reply. Elysia's stomach convulsed. The girl's voice was half pain, half air.

"Elysia."

She found his eyes – still gray, but darker. His eyelashes stuck together.

"Find the door," he commanded. "If you find them, yell."

She nodded.

Fighting her way down the hill, Elysia clambered through the wreckage that had once been a small village. Mud bricks dissolved in the torrent that flowed down the mountain, exposing the straw within. The house that had belonged to Herod, his wife, and children had no recognizable shape: nothing distinguished its end from its neighbor's beginning.

A labored moan came from her right, and Elysia wheeled.

Korinna lay beside the muddied curtain that had once hung in the doorway, a shard of gray-weathered wood protruding from her shoulder. Sandbags were piled on top of her legs, pinning them. Her eyes found Elysia the moment she stepped within five yards of her. "You." Her good arm moved against the dirt beneath her, trying to push herself away, while her other arm made no move, skin pale against the crimson blood streaming from her wound.

"Korinna," murmured Elysia, but her body did not move toward the girl. Alexander had told her to yell when she found them, but Elysia could not make her mouth open.

The mud was cool on her knees when she knelt beside the girl; Korinna squinted up at her, eyes and lashes dark against skin draining of color. "Let me help you," she said. "I did this, let me help you."

"You did this?" Korinna laughed, but puffs of air came from her throat, then coughing. Her muscles tensed around her wounds. "You're just some girl from the *hills*, remember? Or are you some rare bird with your white hair?" She coughed again.

"My father is Khronos," Elysia said, feeling the warmth of Korinna's blood on her fingers; the wound in her shoulder was huge, rectangular: the board that impaled it sheared off where it must have once connected to a post. "And Khronos is not happy with me or your innocent brother."

Korinna's sneer turned her blood to ice. "So you are a rare bird," she said. "A rare, whorish bird who has flown my brother too close to the burning sun. Get your fingers off me."

"Let me *help* you."

"All you've done is hurt me." Korinna coughed, and a film of blood coated her pale lips.

Something cold shot through Elysia's gut. "Alexander!" she screamed. Korinna flinched and winced, and coughed again, and what had once been a fine spray on her lips turned to dribbles from the corner of her mouth. "Korinna," Elysia said, but the girl didn't look at her anymore; her brown eyes had turned skyward, reflecting the white-gray clouds above. "*Korinna,* stay with me."

The girl's chest lurched upward, as if her lungs were trying to get closer to the air.

"*Korinna!*"

For a moment, just one moment, the girl's eyes found hers again, despite the way they seemed to want to roll upward. With her next breath, shuddering, Korinna spoke.

"No."

Her chest did not rise again.

How long she sat with Korinna, Elysia did not know, but eventually, she became aware of the marked chill in her left hand; Korinna's cold hand was clutched in it, icy, lying in a pool of cooling blood. Pulling their fingers apart, Elysia leaned up and closed the girl's delicate eyelids with shaking fingers. Elysia stood.

Wreckage surrounded her: mud bricks piled ten feet high, foot-thick thatch roofs standing vertically, pale skin shining beneath the sun.

She found Alexander when she climbed through the hole he had dug in the thatch. His hands were scraped and bloody, beginning to bruise, his hair muddied and stringy.

He rocked his brother in his arms.

Euthymios had landed among the baskets, their mother nearby with her arms wrapped around Herod's shoulders. The quiet in the room was broken only by the soft sounds Alexander made. Something foreign filled Elysia, something so intrusive that her only reaction was to stand there with her hands over her mouth.

Eventually, she fell to her knees, and tears ran hot and fast down her cheeks. Her breath wrenched from a high place in her chest.

Ligeia and Herod had been on their way to the stairwell; he had his staff clutched in one hand. His wife's arm must have supported him under his other shoulder, because she still held him there.

It was the first and last time she had seen them together.

A sob wrenched up her chest.

I did this.

Not only had she done this, she had not stopped her father from leaving, had not stopped him to explain their situation, had not talked him down from his wrath. And now, for the first time, she had seen his wrath come to life – against a people who had taught her everything. They had given her life, so she might keep it when someone tried to steal it from her.

Alexander was all she had left of them.

Taking a deep breath and closing her eyes, Elysia got to her feet, trying to wipe Korinna's staring brown eyes from her mind. Elysia's chest, her diaphragm still quivered, and her lips, too. Someone else had need of her now.

Opening her eyes, she went to his side. "Alexander," she said, resting her hand on the sodden shoulder of his tunic.

He stopped rocking, and his lashes brushed his cheeks as he blinked. He ran his hands over Euthymios's hair. What had once been blond had been stained rust, orange, deep red through the translucent strands. The back of his head was a ruin, his face untouched; from his expression, he might have been sleeping. "He didn't see anything coming," said Alexander, his voice thick. "Mother and Father did, and Korinna was halfway down the stairs, on her way out to apologize." Carefully, Alexander let Euthymios's body lean back down on the floor. Adjusting his brother's tunic, Alexander took a shuddering breath. "That's all she would say, my mother. She sent Korinna out to apologize. My father... Gone. Thymios, too. Not Mother, though." A little laugh escaped him, and he looked up at her. His eyes shone in the dim light, but it was not a dancing sort of shine. The lines around his eyes, in his forehead, by his mouth – all pinched in pain. Elysia tried to keep her breath in her lungs.

I have done this to him.

"My mother wanted to make sure Korinna apologized. That was all she said. *She's supposed to say sorry. Sorry*." Alexander shook his head, touched his brother's cheek one last time. "We should look for survivors," he said.

Elysia stepped back to let him pass. On his way by, he grabbed her hand, leading her across the small room made smaller by the thatch that had caved into the middle of it. The room, once ten feet tall, had shrunk to barely five as it slid down the hill, leaving bricks and floor behind when its foundation had collapsed.

They climbed out of the hole in the roof one at a time, Alexander and then Elysia. They stood at the top of the hill, staring down at the chaos below them.

"How..." Elysia began, but her voice trailed off, drowned in the pattering of the rains.

"We search. It doesn't matter how long it takes, Elysia," Alexander said, his voice demanding her attention. And by the look on his face, she had to wonder if it was only determination that kept him from flying apart at the seams. "They are all that matters."

They are all you have. Elysia took a deep breath.

The search must have lasted for hours; it certainly lasted until Elysia was muddy up to her thighs and elbows, and Alexander even further. They dug out a dozen people from the top of the hill to the bottom, mostly children who had been small enough to fit into tiny spaces without getting hurt. Those who were able helped them search, and those with broken limbs gathered in a huddle at the bottom of the hill after they were helped down it.

An hour into the search, Elysia met a woman she could not save.

She was dressed in purples, her hair every color between snow, silver, and coal; she was not far from a dozen pillars that had once been the entrance to her home, according to her claim. When Elysia found her, her skin was chilled, her heartbeat impossible to find. Elysia clutched her hand, kept her a little warm as desperation sank in. "What's your name?"

"Berenike," was the woman's hushed reply.

"Can you move?" asked Elysia.

"I think not, my dear. I'd like to die right here, under Zeus's rain. A pity there's not thunder, too."

Unable to come up with a response, Elysia sat with her. The woman's breathing sped as minutes passed. Eventually, Berenike spoke again. "Have you found my grandson? His name is Leon."

Tears welled in Elysia's eyes. "Yes," she said, but emotion blocked off her throat. They had found the smart-mouthed little boy, the one who had been determined to stick it to the Corinthians. He had been pale and going cold already, stuck between a pillar and what had once been his house. Elysia had done her best to smooth down his short, thick black hair, wiry beneath her fingers. They had found his mother alive but stuck, sheltering beneath her thatched roof. The noise she had made when they recovered her son had split Elysia's soul.

"I wish he had been in the city today. We knew it had been too long since Zeus showed us ill favor, and we were right. His mother disgraced us, you know," said Berenike, her dark gray eyes sad and squinting at the edges, pain in her bearing. "That is why they were Apocorinthians, rather than Highs. If they had been with us, perhaps..."

Elysia nodded. "Us?" she asked. "Should I look for your husband?"

Berenike smiled up at her. "My dear, he is with us now. He waits with Charon beyond the veil, to meet me and guide us to the Isles of the Blessed. Khronos will judge us as the good souls we have always been." Berenike's clammy hand skimmed across Elysia's cheek. "And perhaps this time, we will need not set foot back on earth as new souls. Perhaps this will be the last time we need suffer this world."

Swallowing, Elysia tried to nod and not think. *Another person who thinks they will be judged for the Isles of the Blessed.* Her father had told her of them once: they were a paradise, with streams that flowed of milk and honey, the air perfumed with roses, nectar, and ambrosia, where all men were at peace and could rest for eternity. The isles were a glory, the humans' wish for what waited for them beyond life for their good deeds.

They also did not exist.

Something about that, as she squeezed Berenike's pallid hand, seemed a terrible wrong.

It was, perhaps, a wrong that needed righting.

35

Berenike drifted off not long later, but Elysia stayed with her until her breath stopped. Once she stilled, Elysia stood and looked for Alexander.

She found him at the bottom of the hill with twenty others, helping Delia out of her ruined hut. The woman limped heavily, and there was a lump in her calf that ought not to be there. "We have to get her to Corinth," Elysia said, supporting Delia under her other arm. Alexander frowned at her over the woman's head. "Her sister is there."

"Oh, no, I'm not goin' to the city ta see *her*," Delia growled between them. The onlookers around them scattered, a few trekking back into the chaos of the slope.

"This is not something worth arguing," said Alexander. To Elysia, he nodded. "Your sister will take care of you, Delia. She has a good life. She can afford another mouth. We would not be able to help you the way she could."

"It's a league to that rotten city ye've grown so fond of, and something tells me that the pair of you might find it difficult to get me there, what with my hobbling and the rains. And I've more than 'alf a mind not to go. What say you then?" asked Delia, glancing between them. She was shorter than them, stout, with as many cuts on her face as Elysia had earned herself the night before. Her eyes glittered.

Elysia took a breath. *Everything is closer in the city.* Without the hunting party, which must be near destroyed now, there would be no way for Delia to get meat. The produce the Apocorinthians bought came from the agora; it was one reason Alexander was always in the city – he bought food and wool for his family. With her pottery and supplies destroyed, Elysia saw no reason for Delia to stay besides familiarity. "You should come with us," she said softly. "You might not like it, but it will be easier in the future. Someone might be able to set your leg."

The look Delia gave her was one of the most skeptical she had ever seen, all raised brows and pursed lips. "My life's not been easy since I was a young, young woman."

"Delia," said Alexander.

"I'll go," she said, raising one hand. "But I'll protest loud the whole way. Can you 'andle that?"

"I think we'll make due," replied Elysia.

Once Alexander organized more searches and told the remaining Apocorinthians what to do with the injured, he handed the lead off to the ebon-skinned woman, Olympia, who wore what remained of her yellow dress. Her daughter was nowhere to be seen, but the bloodshot eyes and tear tracks on her face told Elysia where she might be: in the netherworld, with Khronos, being judged on the few years of life she had gotten the chance to live.

The way back to Corinth took longer than Elysia thought possible. Though Alexander took Delia's heavier side, the one she was forced to hop on, the hobbling of the three of them seemed to take three times longer than walking normally, and probably did. The puddles in the path slowed them more, but finally, they reached the gates.

The statues had not moved an inch. When they approached, Elysia spotted Zeus's white-blond head, turned dark as ash under the rain and pale sunlight – he spotted them just as quickly, rushing to their aid. Motioning for Elysia to move, he took her place under Delia's arm.

"Zeus 'as turned his wrath on the mountain, nephew," said Delia.

"We felt the rumbling from here, but only a little. Poseidon and Amphitrite trembled."

"As they should." Delia nodded vehemently. "King o' the gods could 'ave them cowed in a moment."

"I'll tell Metrodora of your coming," said Elysia. At Alexander's nod, she turned and ran between the statues.

The farther she ran, the weaker her limbs felt. When she was halfway to her grandmother's house, Elysia slowed. For the first time since she spotted Adrastos and his friends in that crossroads, Elysia knew she was safe in the city's streets. Adrastos was gone, carted off to she knew not where; the only evidence he had existed at all were the marks he had left on her skin: the bluing bruise around her neck, the finger-shaped marks on her thigh, the cuts on her cheek, chin, and shoulder. Zeus had not spoken of missing him, and no one had raised alarm. It had been a day, and still she was safe. If anyone else tried the same... She would be able fend him off, though perhaps less lethally. A lesson had been learned there; her father's wrath had been incited half by Alexander's presence in her house and half by her killing of a man who would have been served the same fate by justice.

Elysia paused in her step. Was that truly the reason he had been angry with her? *No. It was because both were a stain on our honor*. She nearly scoffed at herself. Her father had an age beyond measure – what need had he of honor?

None. He has no need of honor. It was all a show. But if that was so, what was it for?

Metrodora – or Ananke, or whatever name she went by now – was home when Elysia got there. Her eyes glowed silver even in the dim light of the house, and Elysia frowned at them. "Can't you put those things out?"

"What?" Metrodora asked, looking up at her with eyebrows arched, apparently surprised to see her granddaughter standing in the doorway.

"Your eyes."

"Oh – in a way. I hide them from those who should not see them," she replied, standing and taking her spindle with her. It spun and swayed as she moved from her kitchen table and into the back room, Elysia trailing behind her. "A distinction of divinity, if you will. Why are you here, Elysia?" Her eyes flicked up from the loom she stood before, piercing Elysia like the chill rage she had felt in Korinna's voice, though Metrodora's was much more calculating, measuring her. "You were going to Acrocorinth."

"A mistake, Grandmother, but I am glad I went with Alexander, instead of letting him go alone." *He might have been on that roof when the column bent it into a dish instead of a cone.*

"Is that so? Look at the state of you." Her grandmother's voice went high with a hint of retribution.

"You know it's so," Elysia said. "And you knew it would be so this morning. What's my father's plan?"

"I'm afraid I don't know, child." Blinking slowly at her, Metrodora wrapped her thread around her spindle and set it on a bench, turning instead to the shuttle on the loom. She passed the shuttle through the warp, but never looked away from Elysia, even as she changed the heddle's position.

"I think you do, Grandmother."

"Then I am not at liberty to say. If your father found out you knew, one of his conclusions might be that I told you. He cannot know that I am around to tell you."

Elysia crossed her arms. Her father had known Metrodora for more than twenty years; if her eyes had not given her away yet, there was no way whatever her grandmother couldn't tell her would.

"It's the tests."

Metrodora put down the shuttle. "The what?"

Elysia found herself a seat on the bench. "It's the third test," she murmured, gazing at nothing as she riddled it out. What was her father's game? *Kill people* so she could pass her test? In an earthquake, of all things? In what world would her mother have asked for that? But his anger was *real.* He thought Alexander, whom he'd thought of as a friend, had slept with his daughter, taken advantage of her when she was vulnerable. Elysia closed her eyes and put her head in her hands, groaning.

The door to the front room swung open, and Elysia was distracted. "Delia's coming to stay," she said in a rush.

Metrodora's eyes darted first to her and then to the trio of people pushing their way through the doorway. "*What?*"

Wincing, Elysia nodded, moving a few cushions to the bench in the front room to accommodate Delia's broken leg. Zeus patted her shoulder as he helped his aunt onto the pillows. "The pair of you should probably leave," he said. Nodding to his mother, with her wide staring eyes focused on her younger sister, he added, "Now."

Elysia and Alexander did not need to be told twice. As the door shut behind them, Elysia heard Delia rasp, "The children insisted..."

Standing in the street, Elysia looked up at Alexander. He did not look at her; he gazed down the street to the house at the curve of the road, focused on nothing at all. "Alexander?" She touched his arm. Her fingernails collected a layer of caked mud from his skin. "You need a bath."

He turned his head, brow furrowing, and suddenly Elysia wished she knew the long oath he had muttered earlier. "Gods," she murmured. *I'm going to lose him in his own head.*

He gave her a curious look but kept his silence.

"Bath time," she muttered. Pulling him along by the hand, she led him past the door to her own home and instead to the third house in the row of Khronos's properties. Unlike Elysia's and Metrodora's houses, this one did not adjoin the other two. Its door was cloth and wicker, crackling noisily when Elysia swung it open.

The room within was bare, empty but for a stack of sleeping pallets stacked in one corner. The walls bore no tapestries, the shelves no cutlery nor utensils. Towing Alexander through the room, she ducked around the ragged curtain separating the front and rear halves of the house. The back room held even less, simply four walls and a dirt floor.

The house's yard, however, was a different story.

The courtyard behind the house was walled off, inaccessible to the neighbors whose homes it abutted. Where her own garden was mostly decorative, with its winding rose beds and marble fountain, this one struck Elysia as utilitarian: its fountain was small but clean, its garden arranged in neat rows of not only roses, but herbs. Against the wall opposite the fountain were stacked long, hollow cylinders of clay. Elysia recognized them as beehives; her father had attempted building several contraptions to house his beloved pollinators over the years, but it was likely he'd left his more advanced versions at home.

Beside the fountain stood the same vessels Aliya had once used to fill the bathtub. Letting Alexander's hand slip from her own, Elysia picked one up and dipped it in the fountain. Ripples fanned out from the disturbance, interrupting the thousands produced by the pelting rain. Hugging the jug close to her body, Elysia waited as Alexander picked up the second vessel, filling it with stiff, sluggish arms. Her own arms burned from digging through the rubble, and the weight of the water in the clay pot only made them ache worse. The water sloshed as Elysia carried it back to the house, Alexander right behind her.

The water would be cool, perhaps uncomfortably so, but it would be clean.

Once they had made enough silent trips to fill the tub with two feet of clear water, Elysia set her vessel down at the end of the baked clay monstrosity. Alexander followed suit, and when he looked at her, he held out his hands, emptied once again. She wrapped her fingers around his and squeezed. "Give me a moment," she murmured.

At his nod, she pushed past the curtain to search among the basket of clothes her father had left behind.

When she returned, she draped a fresh tunic for him over the mouth of a vessel. She'd torn herself free of her dress, with its skirt drenched in rain, mud, and blood. Instead, she wore her training tunic. The fabric brushed cool and smooth over her skin, and she breathed in the rose scent someone had dripped over it. Nothing clung to her legs; she was free of the manifestation of what had happened today. The rest of the evidence could be washed away.

Alexander had not moved while she had been in the other room. His breath was shallow, as if his body barely remembered even its involuntary tasks.

Kneeling, Elysia pulled his foot toward her, untying the straps of his sandal. Coated with muck, it had adhered to his sole and needed to be peeled off. When Elysia finished with it, she tossed it aside. His other sandal came off next.

Fingers found her chin, turning her gaze to his. He bent to her level, eyes inches from hers. Their depth made her pause and take a breath, close her eyes so she did not lose herself in them.

"Step into the water," she whispered. Opening her eyes, Elysia reached up to touch the hollow where his neck met his collarbone, studying the threads of gray and black in his irises, where she saw herself reflected. Something about not seeing bright swirls and a glow tattooed there made him so very, very precious to her.

He lifted his foot over the edge of the tub, water tinkling as he broke the surface. Dirt curled like smoke in the water, falling away from his calves. At her direction, he sat, his only reaction to the chill water to grip her hand a little more tightly. She ran a thumb along the line of his jaw and down his neck, testing a streak of brown to see how easily it would come off. Stubbornly, it stayed put, even with the friction of her thumbnail against the stubble he bore.

Still kneeling on the dirt floor, Elysia pushed him to lean against the wall of the tub. Gently pulling his arm toward her in the water, Elysia started with his fingers, rubbing mud carefully from his fingernails and then fingertips, knuckles, his palm. There were so many tiny cuts, pale and bloodless, beneath the layers that she looked up at him, but he stared at the wall ahead. "Tell me if this hurts, Alexander," she said, running a hand across his forearm to the elbow, where the pink joint peeked from beneath layers of grime.

"You're not hurting me," he said, but the note of strain in his voice kept her from continuing. "I'm fine," he added, and though Elysia wasn't sure she believed him, she started again, rubbing first the palm and then the back of his hand with her thumb, releasing clods of mud from his skin. They swirled, melting in the water.

She did first his left arm up to the elbow and then his right, careful not to stress his muscles or touch the cuts scattered over them any more than necessary. She paused to look at him, but his was not the same gaze she had met earlier: something in his eyes had died. A star had gone out. Closing her eyes, she tried not to think of what he must be seeing: the red ruin of his brother's skull, his parents clinging to each other in death. And Korinna – *did he find her?* Her conscience peered in at her, reminding her that he had not come when she had called for him. He had not been there as his sister had died in front of Elysia, coughing red lifesblood from whatever reservoir filled inside her body.

Sighing, Elysia moved to the narrow end of the tub. "Lie back."

Alexander moved from kneeling to sitting, stirring up the dirt that had settled. Gouts of mud fell from his legs as he adjusted.

Finally, he leaned back, and Elysia caught him just above the water with a hand between his shoulder blades. "Far enough," she murmured, letting his head rest in the hollow between her neck and shoulder as she leaned forward. She set out to rub away the mud from his upper arms and worked her way upward, pressing her fingers into his skin.

He groaned, and she stopped, hands hovering over the curve where his shoulders met his arms.

His eyelashes brushed against her cheek as he turned his face to her, and Elysia realized his eyes had been closed. "Don't stop," he whispered, and she felt his breath along her jaw, warm where the water was cold.

Elysia closed her eyes and took a breath. Alexander could not handle his emotions and hers just now, no matter how her heart beat against her chest, demanding to be heard. She had to keep herself controlled, be a constant.

Exhaling the breath she had taken, Elysia started up his shoulders again, pouring water over them where they were exposed above the waterline. He scooted forward, bringing his knees farther up in the tub so she had room to rub his neck. Her fingers found their way into his hair, sticky and clumping with sludge that dissolved at her touch, falling with the rest of the sediment to the bottom of the tub. Elysia kept her breathing controlled, despite her racing heart. If there was one thing she could control, it would be her breath.

Her fingers got lost in the fine strands of his hair; it glimmered like well-beaten gold as it fanned out in the water. She studied his face and its shadows in the dim light. With his eyes closed, she saw the indentations above his eyelids, where his eyes met the bone behind them. His eyes were unmoving beneath the minute veins of his eyelids – relaxed, or so she hoped.

Elysia was suddenly aware that her fingers had stopped again, this time over his ears, where she had been massaging his scalp.

Alexander's eyes opened, and the control she had had over her breathing ceased with her breath. His eyes were dark, deepened by the shadow her face cast down on him. Elysia felt the way they wanted her like a hook around her heart.

Sitting up and sending water flying, Alexander turned to her. The water in the tub swished around him. He simply looked at her as he knelt, the clay of the tub wall between them. Raising a hand, he grazed a knuckle across her cheek. "I love you," he said.

Her thoughts erased themselves as Elysia stared at him, lips parted.

His eyes closed, a small smile at the corner of his lips; the smile didn't feel quite real, like he almost didn't believe himself.

"I love you."

His eyes opened at the same time Elysia pulled him close, her arms around his neck; he braced a hand against the tub, so she didn't pull him down on top of her. Her fingers tangled in the long hair at the back of his head, which still streamed water, clean and cold. "I would be dead without you," she whispered, "but it's not debt I feel when I look at you, when I touch you." Her hand came down, running through the water droplets that dotted his skin like so many little crystals. Her fingers traced the line of his neck and the tendons that stood out to tell her he clenched his jaw. They relaxed beneath her touch. "It's something warm, like sunbeams or a flame, even when we are cold." *As we are now*. "I love you, Alexander," she said, leaning her head back so she could meet his eye.

She felt safe.

"I'm going to kiss you," he said, voice hungry, but with a note of something unfamiliar.

"Good." Pulling him toward her, Elysia met him halfway. His lips were hard on hers, cool from the chill in the water. His mouth was warm, though, and the air she breathed was his, heated and humid and hers. Her lungs ached, as if she was so close to Alexander that with her next breath, she could breathe him in – and she wanted to. She wanted all his heart, all his grief, and all his honor, wanted to take from him the burden of what had happened today, so she could bear it alone.

Something warm landed on her cheek, but the tear wasn't hers.

Pressing her eyes tightly closed, Elysia stopped herself, pushing her thumb into his collarbone to put an inch of space between them.

Alexander let his forehead rest against hers as more tears fell from his eyelids. He wiped the tear from her face. “Sorry,” he mumbled.

“Don’t apologize,” she said, running her hand down his arm. Dread forged a lead weight in her stomach. “But don’t use me.”

His brows came together, a crease between them. “Use you?”

Brushing his hair behind his ears, Elysia put a hand firmly on his shoulder so she could push him away if she needed to. “To hide these,” she said, kissing his cheek and a trail of a tear, salty on her lips.

He let out a little *hah* sound and scooted back, wiping a few more tears away. He held out a hand. Elysia gazed at it, then glanced up at him. “Your turn,” he said.

Her arms were still coated in mud well up to the elbow, though her hands were clean. Tentatively, she gave him her left hand, letting him help her over the edge.

The experience was near celestial. The warmth of his fingers beneath cool water felt like he melted the ice of her skin, and she felt every bubble rising from the swirling water. Elysia found herself closing her eyes; she did not need to see him. Alexander’s knees touched hers beneath the water, and his fingers massaged away the muck on the inside of her wrist, her forearm, over the vein at the inside of her elbow. He let her arm drop, and she groaned. It was short-lived, though, because after he snickered at her, he picked up her right hand and started over again.

Eventually, his hand drifted to her shoulder and guided her to turn around. Elysia’s eyes snapped open, despite being somewhere between transcendence and sleep. “Can I trust you with my hair?” she murmured.

“I trusted you with mine,” replied Alexander, pulling the leather tie at the end and dropping it on the floor outside the tub.

True, Elysia thought. When he gave her braid a tug, she leaned back until her ears were below the water. White noise and the water’s swishing and trickling filled her ears, but soon, she felt Alexander unravel her braid. She drowned in bliss, just a creature with breath and a heartbeat. If she had thought Aliya’s fingers in her hair had been welcome, Alexander’s were better. The mud, sweat, and stickiness around her shoulders dissolved away, and before she knew it, she was half asleep in the slowly warming water.

36

The warmth of lips on her shoulder woke her.

Moaning a protest, Elysia turned her face into the crook of Alexander's elbow, but when she opened her eyes, everything was dark. Conscious of Alexander's face above her own, Elysia resisted the urge to bolt upright. "How long did I sleep?" she murmured. The water was lukewarm now, or perhaps her body had grown used to the chill against her skin.

"A while," said Alexander. "I might have, too." As he leaned back against the tub, Elysia sat up, stretching out her strained muscles. Her knees, bent to accommodate the length of the tub, were sore; she couldn't imagine how Alexander's legs must feel, crossed in front of him the way they were. The skin of her fingers was shriveled, wrinkled from their long submersion.

"We should go to bed," she said. He hummed his assent.

Pulling herself up at the rim of the tub, Elysia rubbed the last bits of mud from her calves and thighs, ignoring the red patches where her skin must have scraped over the roughness of the baked clay as she slept. As she stood, water streamed from the bottom of her skirt, the drops tinkling as they fell back among their brethren in the tub. Squeezing out her skirt, Elysia stepped out of the tub, aware of Alexander watching her. Dipping her fingers into a pot of rosewater propped up on a stool in the corner, she ran the scent down her hair and her neck, along her wrists. "Your clothes are here," Elysia reminded him, touching the blue and white striped tunic in the dark. "I'm going to change in the other room." Giving him a little smile she wasn't sure he could see, Elysia felt her way past the curtain and to her baskets, where she knew a blue gown waited on top of the stack. She pulled her wet tunic over her head and draped it over the lid of the basket, then donned her dress.

Elysia sat on the end of the bed to wait for him, and her thoughts turned back to the test. She chewed her lip, trying to understand. *Father tried to kill him, and for what?* Khronos had slaughtered innocents, those who stood between his wrath and Alexander. He had slaughtered his friends, the only community that could possibly understand the way he had raised her: to be his equal in most things.

For some reason, her grandmother had supported him, because if she had stayed home, as Ananke had wished... Alexander would have died. She knew with complete certainty that he would have been on the roof when that column crushed it.

Why does everyone want this?

If Alexander died – if he *died* – she didn't know what would happen to her. Her hands went to her mouth and her throat spasmed at the unwelcome thought. She had lost Philip, and the judges were at home. If she lost Alexander, if her father somehow succeeded in killing him, or if Ananke did it now, herself... The combination of their cruelty and his loss would break her.

Is that what they want? For me to be broken? Her mother had told her that the test would be wonderful and terrible. But... It didn't seem right. The other two were phrased to have a benefit on her judgment, to teach her what it was to be human, to live a life beyond her father. And humans were not broken. They were vulnerable, not broken.

Elysia thought of the woman she had met in the carnage, Berenike, whose husband had passed, whose daughter had been disgraced, whose grandson had been Leon, the little boy who had been so bright he had been determined to outshine the Corinthians. Berenike had lost them all, but she had known her family awaited her because of the love she had borne them.

Something clicked into place.

Elysia sat back on the bed. *Humans outlive the ones they love most.* Her mother might have been an exception, but her father was immortal. The rest – Alexander's family had died, swept away before his eyes; Berenike had lost her husband, her daughter, her grandson. Metrodora had lost her daughter, her husband. Hera had lost her husband and found him again in Zeus, probably lost her children.

And now, it was her turn.

Elysia looked up at Alexander as he strode past the curtain and took her hand. He, too, smelled of roses, though the new clothes were a little big on him, baggy at the sides, puckering out beneath the arm holes. "What's wrong?" he asked, pulling her other hand away from her mouth.

"Nothing," she said, trying to believe it. She had two gods against her, one so bent on her ascension that he had shaken a mountain. That made her want to reassess her decision to try her hand at the tests, because no matter what the third test really was, she was not going to sacrifice Alexander to pass it. The world would not be whole without him. "Let's sleep."

Alexander sat down on the bench across from her, their hands linked between them.

"Don't even think about it," she growled, tugging on his fingers and scooting backwards.

"Elysia..." The sun setting outside behind the rain clouds glinted off his eyes, turning him into a wary animal.

"There's room enough for both of us, remember?" Fitting her fingers into the spaces between his, she tugged at him again. This time, he stood. "You slept here last night," she whispered, scooting over so there was room beside her for him to lie down.

He trailed a hand through his damp hair. The light shining in his eyes went out as he shut his eyes against his thoughts. "Last night," he murmured, sitting down on the edge of the bed beside her. Elysia heard him swallow. "I thought you had been raped."

The word raked over Elysia's skin. She pulled his hand into her lap, studying it.

"I was afraid you wouldn't want me to touch you, that any kind of contact would disgust you, but you would have frozen to death if you remained in that fountain."

"My body wouldn't let me move," she muttered.

Alexander sighed. "I know." Moving closer to her, he put a hand on her neck. Elysia sucked in a breath as her bruise twinged. "Easy," he said, moving a hand down to her shoulder, where her cleaned cuts were. "Every inch of you he touched makes me wish I had walked you home."

"Let me sleep, Alexander," she mumbled. "You're here now."

"I am," he replied.

They slept beneath the warmth of her blankets and the tapping of the rain, but neither slept through the night. Alexander woke twice with strangled screams, hands held out in claws in front of him, as if he held something he could not put down. By the words she heard as she held him close, the phantom he saw was Euthymios as he held him in the aftermath.

Elysia met Korinna in her dreams, spitting blood and words at her like a snake spitting venom. *Some rare whorish bird with your white hair, flying my brother too close to the burning sun.* Elysia woke shivering and shaking, gasping for air. Alexander smoothed her hair, but she did not fall asleep again until well after dawn.

They stayed in bed until the afternoon. Metrodora came knocking halfway through the day, but when Elysia got up to turn her away, Alexander grabbed her wrist. "You should go to your lesson," he said.

"I'm not leaving you," she hissed. He had been a wreck after they had fallen to sleep, far worse than her, collapsing in on himself after he awoke from his nightmares. The red rims around his eyes made her cringe.

"You need something normal to do."

"*Normal?*" she asked, sitting down next to him on the bed, ignoring the insistent rapping on the back door. Her hands framed his face, his jawline scratchy against her palms with three days' stubble. "There is no normal, Alexander." Elysia kept her voice low, barely more than a whisper lest Metrodora should come around the front and hear their voices through the narrow windows. "My father threatened to kill you. Your family is gone." *Because my father* did *kill them.* The sound of his sharp inhalation told her she had been too blunt. "I'm sorry," she mumbled.

"It's the truth," he muttered.

Metrodora's voice came muffled through the front door, making Elysia jump. "Do not make me come in, Elysia. I know that man never left, and neither did you."

Alexander swore under his breath.

Getting to her feet, Elysia adjusted her dress. She grabbed a sash and tied it around her waist, quickly draping the fabric so she appeared at least half-decent. "Stay behind me," she said, leaning down to kiss him. "She can't hurt you if I'm between you."

He gave her an odd look, and Elysia realized that he didn't know Metrodora was Ananke; she hadn't told him. There hadn't been time. "She's my grandmother," she added, and though his brows remained furrowed, recognition appeared in the lines around his eyes.

Taking a deep breath, Elysia left Alexander where he sat on the bed and crossed the room, padding on bare feet. The beige wood of the door was warm beneath her hand, sunlit for the first time in days. Letting the breath out, she opened the door. The brackets clinging to the bar rattled as it swung open. "Grandmother."

The plump woman in the doorway tried to peer around Elysia, but she was too short. "He is still here?" she asked.

"He will be living with me for a time. His home was destroyed." She tried to say the words without emotion, but a vision of the house sliding away from them filled the space behind her eyes. Elysia blinked a few times to erase it.

Her grandmother's mouth became a firm line. She put a hand on the door that Elysia held open just far enough for herself to stand in the doorway. The door creaked beneath her touch, bowing beneath Elysia's fingers. "I don't think that I, as your grandmother, can allow that, young lady. You are still a woman, no matter who your father is, and you must observe propriety. It is what will keep the city from coming after you with stones."

"Must I observe propriety?" Elysia asked, raising her brows. "I'm afraid I was never taught any. You see, I was raised outside the city, where none of those things matter. Even my heritage did not seem to matter, because I never learned of it and no one saw fit to *tell me*." *My parents ran away from you and you never bothered to tell them, either.*

Metrodora's swirling silver eyes burned into hers. "You speak of things you cannot understand."

"Maybe I will, someday." Elysia gazed right back into her grandmother's eyes. "Someday, I will earn eyes like yours, and once I have done that, we can have all *kinds* of conversations. Until then, let us have comfort, even if it goes against the rules of propriety."

Her grandmother studied her, and then seemed to come to a decision. "I came only to invite you to a midday meal and a bit of weaving," Metrodora said. "The invitation stands."

A smile plastered itself onto Elysia's mouth like a house getting a new coat of whitewash. "Good. Alexander ought to come too, you know. He can weave and spin."

An expression between a pursing of Metrodora's lips and a false smile spread across her mouth. "If he can, he is welcome. I'm sure Delia would like the company of someone she knows so well."

"We'll be over in a moment." Her hand pushed the door closed in her grandmother's face. She let out another breath. Alexander stared at her from his spot on the bed, gray eyes horror-stricken. Grimacing, Elysia put a hand over her eyes. "I'm sorry."

"Maybe Zeus will be there," he said hopefully.

"Something tells me he's still on duty."

Alexander groaned.

Their visit to Metrodora and Delia's went better than Elysia expected: Metrodora allowed Alexander to stand on one end of Elysia's loom and catch the shuttle as she passed it through. He repositioned the heddle for her as she pushed the weft up close to the rest of the weave. The work kept them busy as Metrodora and Delia exchanged stories. Occasionally, Alexander would contribute his own, but Elysia stayed silent, content to listen. The words carried her away, to when she was a little girl and her only wish had been to spin smooth thread and ride her sorrel well. But, after a while, she remembered she had dreamed of marrying Philip even then, when she first found out what marriage was. Suddenly, her childhood left a bitter taste in her mouth.

It doesn't matter. I am not a child anymore.

The rest of the night was quiet. After Elysia and Alexander went home, they went to sleep at sunset, either full of their midday meal or not hungry. Elysia was not sure which was the truth. It did not matter, though, because she woke crying and retching halfway through the night, dreaming of hands around her throat and Korinna's voice in her ears. She made it to the ditch in the middle of the street before her stomach emptied itself. Alexander followed her out not long later, his cheeks shining in the moonlight. They sat on the stoop, breathing in the cool night air.

"Korinna told me I would fly you too close to the burning sun," she blurted. It came out on impulse. Elysia was unable to stop it as the words that had been circling her head like a hawk dove out her mouth.

Alexander's palms rubbed warmth over her shoulders. "I thought she might have said something," he muttered.

"Why?"

"You called yourself a whorish bird in your sleep."

Elysia blinked and then closed her eyes, shaking her head.

"She spoke of Icarus," he said, voice strained. Elysia looked at him, and his grey eyes shone like the stars far above them. His gaze turned heavenward.

"Icarus and his father? I thought they flew out of the maze the king forced them to build." Her voice came out high and puzzled.

Alexander nodded but turned his face back to her. "They did, but their wings were made of wax. Icarus flew too high, too close to the sun." His hand brushed over the rough scab on the bottom of her chin, where her jaw had been cut on the fountain as she fought with Adrastos. "His wings melted."

“So he fell,” she murmured. “And Korinna cast me as the wings that have flown you too high.”

Alexander laughed a little. “She always was dramatic, but we gave her leave to be so. It was something she needed.”

Elysia hummed her acknowledgment, but something felt strange about the way he talked about his sister, like she was something that needed protection always. And yet, she knew how to defend herself – and had learned after a High had gotten his hands on her. Alexander had said that Drakon’s laws had let Herod go after the man who had supposedly been fought off by Korinna.

“She didn’t fight off the High, did she?” she found herself asking.

“No,” said Alexander. “She was in love with him, but he wouldn’t marry her. He took advantage of her admiration for him.”

“Did Herod catch them together?” she whispered.

Alexander shook his head. “He noticed when she was with child, though.”

Elysia’s voice left her.

“Euthymios, Mother, and I tried to stop him, but he beat her until she lost the baby. He loved her, but there is not much more disgraceful than an Apocorinthian falling pregnant outside the marriage bed. The Highs can join us if it should happen to them, but an Apocorinthian? Korinna had nowhere to go.” Alexander shook his head, drumming his fist against his knee. “We might love our girls and our women, but each family has its own definition of honor, and my father’s was strict. Korinna had her dishonor beaten from her, and then he went after the High man who had brought her dishonor. He was easy to find.” Sighing, Alexander looked at her. “He was Leon’s father, and the father of a few little girls, all fallen like Leon’s mother.”

A noise came from Elysia’s throat, one of recognition, of horror. She was suddenly thankful her father had no need of honor. It might mean that he could keep Philip around without regard for her feelings, and it might mean he would turn his wrath on whomever he pleased, but she knew he would never beat her if she “dishonored” him.

“We were no strangers to beatings, mind you,” said Alexander. “But that was one that made me wish I could hit him back without retribution.”

“How old was she?” Elysia asked, fingers over her mouth as if they could stop the words.

“Fourteen.”

And the High... Her skin shivered. He had to be at least thirty, she was certain.

"Korinna became bitter toward everything from then on. Everything except Euthymios, anyway. We let her have him."

"A light in each other's darkness," she muttered.

Alexander nodded.

Elysia sighed. *Even where women belong, they are outsiders if they make a mistake.*

The night went by slowly after that. Alexander fell back asleep, but Elysia lay awake in his arms. At first, he had insisted on putting pillows between them, but that ceased the second he'd realized that, even in her sleep, her arms slipped beneath the pillows and snaked around his waist. She was awake as the pale gold light of dawn danced beneath the curtains, and she was awake when Alexander woke an hour later.

Her thoughts had not left Korinna, and Elysia prayed her father had judged her justly and sent her on to live a better life, somewhere where she would not get beaten half to death after being taken advantage of. Maybe she could find a place as a daughter of the Amazons Alexander had mentioned, if the tribe still existed in the islands that surrounded Greece. Wherever Korinna's soul ended up, Elysia prayed she had brothers in her next life who loved her as much as Alexander and Euthymios did.

The next two days went by much the same as the one before, working with Metrodora on her weaving projects. The other women did not appear, and Elysia was grateful; she was not sure how well she would hold up to questioning. Delia shared stories about the hunting trips she had been on with the other Apocorinthians to bring home meat when they ran out. Metrodora did her best to hide her horror. For a woman who had lived in the cold north, Elysia's grandmother seemed far too squeamish at the prospect of killing creatures for food. *Perhaps it is that they came from her creation,* she thought wryly, trying to equate the Metrodora who did not like the killing of animals with the Ananke who had been all too willing send Alexander off to his death.

Zeus came home halfway through the second day after the earthquake, insisting on taking them to the temple square to get food from the gods' sacrifices. "You're paler than the full moon," he claimed, and as Elysia exchanged a glance with Alexander, she sighed and agreed. Alexander held her hand on the way to the square, his fingers loose and gentle between hers. She stood farther back in the crowd than she ever had before, without her father or the curiosity to see what happened up front. She and Alexander sat on the edge of the fountain, next to a woman drawing water to do her washing. Elysia's eye was drawn to the horse, wild and free but calmed beneath Poseidon's touch. Distantly, she heard Alexander tell her that Poseidon had created the horse, which made him well beloved to men through the world. It was only when meat scalded her fingers that Elysia woke up to the world again, lifting her head from Alexander's shoulder. The idea of food was an unwelcome one, but she ate nonetheless.

The sixth day since her test dawned clear, cold, and bright, the sky a cloudless blue with peach and cream clouds on the horizon. With the dawn came the day she was supposed to go to the agora and retrieve her food for the week.

No matter how hard she tried, she could not convince herself to leave the house. At first, her hands wanted only to pick up her spindle and start on her thread, but then she remembered that no one needed her thread – she did not spin for her father anymore. Metrodora had four women already on the task when she herself was not attending to it. So, for a time, Elysia sat on the edge of the bed and turned her spindle in her hands. It was well used, its weight worn smooth and the shaft even more so. Alexander still slept; his calf pressed into her hip where she sat, his bare foot dangling off the bed. She pulled a blanket down over his toes. The house cooled with the season, but it was not yet uncomfortable. That would come with the end of autumn.

Despite her gentleness, Alexander groaned, propping himself up on one elbow. "Is there a plan for today?" he asked, his voice soft and hoarse with sleep.

Elysia stared at her spindle. "I am supposed to fetch food from my father in the agora, but I don't think I can face him."

"Why?"

Because he tried to kill you and I know it. "I have disobeyed him in everything."

"Elysia," said Alexander, scooting down the bed. He took the spindle from her hands and set it on the bed on his other side. Without it distracting her attention, she was forced to look at him or else pretend to study her fingers. She was not quite so pathetic this morning. "He may be disappointed in you, but that will pass with time."

His eyes were so earnest and clear that Elysia felt herself take a deep breath. *All things will pass in time.* Time was one thing she would have a lot of, as soon as she could find a way to complete the third test, whatever it truly was, without sacrificing Alexander. *I must lose someone I love because humans do all the time.* But who did she love whom she was willing to lose?

Sighing, she shook her head. "It is more complicated than that, Alexander," she said. She couldn't tell him what she knew. It would break him more than he was broken already, and he had just begun to sleep a few hours in the night. She did not need to add the weight of her father's menace to the leaden burden he bore.

"I'll go, then."

Elysia's eyes widened. "No," she said, grabbing an empty basket up from the corner next to her bed. "I'll be fine." *I'm not going to send you traipsing into a trap.*

"Really, Elysia, let me go." A smile nudged up the corner of his mouth – the first one he had smiled since their bath. Elysia's resolve melted. "I should see my friends, anyway, and it might be that I could explain to your father my intent." His smile grew broader, until it almost looked natural on his pale, drawn face, until he almost looked like himself.

"Your intent?" Elysia asked.

Alexander took a knee. "I would have your hand, if you would consent to give it to me."

Elysia gaped at him. "Alexander..." she began, but she didn't know what to say. They had been playing at the Greeks' version of married life the last week, at least in others' eyes. She would love nothing more. But her father –

Her father was married. Her father had even held his wife as a captive for sixteen years after her death. He couldn't forbid her from marrying anyone, whether she lived a human life or an eternal one. He couldn't justify it. And marrying Alexander... That might just mollify whatever dishonor her father pretended. Once they were married, Alexander would be as his son. That might just keep him safe.

"Yes," she whispered.

The light returned to Alexander's eyes like flames dancing in them, the way his eyes had sparkled when she had first met him, but brighter. Smile lines crinkled the corners of his eyes, and before she knew what was happening, he lunged for her and pulled her onto the bed. He just looked at her, arms looped around her waist. Taking the basket from her hands, he pulled away from her. "I'll see you when I come back," he murmured, the heat of his eyes still pinning her in her position, sitting beside him.

Elysia took a beat and a deep breath, drawing him closer by the front of his tunic. He still wore her father's blue and white stripes, and Elysia did not want him to go to her father wearing Khronos's own clothes. "Let me find you something else to wear first."

Philip's clothes were in the house – she knew at least a few tunics had to be lingering somewhere. He had taken nothing with him after she had banished him the first or the second time, and she had found nothing on her father's side of the room. As she searched through the baskets on her own side of the room, she realized she should have known better.

Philip had once been hers, or so she had thought.

She pulled the lid on the second to last basket, one closer to the front of the house than the others. Beneath the lid was plain cloth, the undyed yellow-white of clean wool. "Found it," she said, pulling the one on the top of the stack. Throwing it to Alexander, she waved him off.

The thing was half an inch shorter than her father's had been on Alexander, still a bit large. Philip was built like a bull, and though he was a bit shorter than Alexander, he had his clothes made long so that he could tear pieces from the bottom of the skirt in an emergency. It was something he had requested from the first time Elysia had fallen from her horse and scraped her palms and elbows, and he had had nothing to wrap them in. Nevertheless, it was as near a fit as Alexander was like to get from any clothes in her house. Unless Philip looked closely, he would not recognize cloth so like what he was accustomed to seeing Alexander wearing.

"I'll be back soon," he said, still grinning. "If your father sees fit to let me keep drawing breath."

"Don't jest about that," she muttered, fisting her hands in the fabric over his chest. It was made with thread spun by her hands with love for Philip. And while Alexander was not Philip, Elysia did not think Alexander wore it any worse than Philip had. If she had the power to identify which threads had come from her own spindle in the cloth, she was sure she would find them positively glowing.

Pulling him close, Elysia kissed him, letting the fire his lips gave her spread through her skin. His lips were soft on hers, softer than they had been in a while, missing the urgency she felt. So she pulled him closer, her hand running up his chest and into his long hair.

"Elysia," he said against her lips.

She broke away, burying her head in his chest. “I’m sorry,” she murmured.

His palm pressed below her shoulder blades, and Elysia took a breath that had his scent wrapped up in it, roses and earth and some scent she had learned was distinctly Alexander. She let go of him, clutching her still half-clawed hands together to hide the indentations of the weave of the fabric. “I’ll see you when you come home,” she said.

Nodding, Alexander pressed his lips to her forehead. “An hour at most, unless a friend decides my betrothal is something worth celebrating.” Giving her a wicked smile, he pulled the door open and slipped through it, narrowly avoiding the bar that stuck out.

With a shaky sigh, Elysia pulled the lids off a few baskets. The food in them was still good, though the bread was stale. The pomegranates in the garden were fewer now that Zeus was home from his shift for a week; he went through them the same way Elysia had once known Philip to go through figs.

With luck, they’d be able to provide for themselves soon enough. That was part of a human life, she was sure: gaining independence. She already had more than she thought she ever would, living away from her father in a city thirty thousand times more populous than her home. Even if Alexander lived with her, she’d had the run of her own household – at least, when the household had included Aliya and numbered more than two. Now, with just him, they spent whole days together, which was nothing to complain about.

Living a human life will be easier than you think, she told herself. She did everything a woman ought to, according to the Greeks: weaving, spinning, getting meals out when she had to. Sitting herself down on her father’s stool, Elysia closed her eyes.

She hoped she was doing it right.

If she missed something, she didn’t know how she would pin it down. Alexander was as human as she was like to find: happy, hurt, irritated and intense, bright as the sun. And he was all she had, here in this city.

She put her head in her hands.

And he’s put his life in my father’s hands without realizing it.

37

The door squeaked twenty minutes later.

Elysia was organizing baskets in the back room, trying to figure out what was in them – from what she could tell, they were lengths of cloth with designs so faded she could not discern even the smallest of details about them. Her eyes could not detect a pattern, though there were colors beyond count.

Putting aside the heavy cloth in her hands, she brushed her hair behind her ears. *He's home*. It had been an unaccountably quick trip – it took ten minutes to walk to the agora. *Maybe he decided not to go, after all.* Whatever the reason, Alexander was home, and that was something to celebrate.

Brightening, Elysia pushed past the curtain.

She lost her breath as something slammed her into the wall.

Bleak brown eyes stared into her own, framed by black lashes so close she could count them. His hand clasped around her throat, but not even tightly enough to make her bruise twinge; the hand that had gripped her hip and slammed her into the wall had stolen her breath. His skin was dry and rough, even with the light touch that held her throat. She swallowed as carefully as she could, breathed as evenly as she could.

"What have you done?" he whispered, voice desperate; the breath that rode it smelled more of sharp red wine than figs.

"Unhand me, Phil," she said, staring back at him, wariness in her gaze.

"I don't think I can. Not until you tell me what you've done."

Closing her eyes, Elysia breathed as deeply as she could with his hand over her windpipe, its heat pressing into her. His hand on her hip was a claw on her bare skin, right where her dress split beneath her belt. She had not paid it any attention as she explored the baskets, and the triangle of skin between the middle of her thigh and her hip had slid out from beneath its usual cover. "I've done nothing, Philip. Nothing that wants this treatment from you."

Philip stilled, his hand at her neck not hovering so much as resting. Elysia opened her eyes and saw shock written on his face, loosening the lines around his mouth and forehead.

"Unhand me, Phil," she said again.

His hand slipped from her throat to her shoulder. Elysia breathed easier, her hands still raised instinctively in surrender. Philip was not someone she wanted to fight. He was her friend, or had been, once. Though she could hurt him with words, she was not sure she could raise a hand against him.

"You deny permitting Alexander to stay in your home?" he breathed.

Elysia shifted. His short nails dug harder into the delicate skin over her hip. Gritting her teeth, she said, "No."

"Then you *have* done something wanting this treatment, Lys. I told you I would protect you. That is what I'm doing."

"You're hurting me, Philip," she said, clasping her hand around the wrist of the one that held her hip. "I thought you could not stand to see me hurt."

"I never could," he said, holding her shoulder tightly to the wall as his other hand rose to her face. She stared down a softer version of Adrastos with twenty times the volatility. Elysia let out a breath as his fingers brushed over her chin, her cheek, where the cuts she bore from days earlier grew smaller at last. Pinching his fingers at the corner of one, he peeled the scab from her face as she squeezed her eyes closed and tried to breathe. "But when I think about him holding you late at night, him *knowing* you, the sweet girl I taught to ride a horse..." Philip wiped away a warm trickle of blood.

"He has not *known* me, Philip," she hissed.

"Has he not? Your father told me you had Aliya draw the pair of you a warm bath, the poor girl. And just after some poor bastard tried to have his way with you. I knew you had an appetite, Lys, but not quite that big of one."

"Aliya drew me a bath. I offered him the warm water when I was done. And do not say such things, Philip." Her voice pitched low, Elysia stood up straighter. "You might become the next poor bastard."

"I'd heard you killed him," Philip said, pulling at the next scab the garden wall had wrought in her face. "He might have deserved it, but tell me, doesn't Alexander deserve the same?"

Elysia froze against the wall, even the muscles beneath her ribs tensing. "No," she said certainly. "He has been an honorable man."

The look Philip gave her, an eyebrow raised, looking down his nose at her, was one that she knew meant she ought to know better. She had seen it so many times that she knew it better than even her father's face. "Honorable is not a man who shares a woman's bed for five days before asking to marry her. Honorable is not a man who guides a girl out of a fountain when she is most vulnerable and takes advantage." Philip blinked at her. "I did not."

"Not taking advantage of me when I am vulnerable does not make you honorable," she growled. "You would be honorable if you respected me as something beyond property."

"I do respect you as something beyond property, Lys," said Philip. Elysia's instincts buzzed so loudly she thought her stomach might turn. "And as you are a woman of my household, I will be invoking Drakon's laws to reclaim your honor, as your father seems so lax about doing."

"My honor has not been deflowered," she said, turning her nails into his wrist. "You are the closest anyone has come to doing that. Perhaps my father should take your head."

Philip hissed and yanked his hand from beneath her nails. Elysia took her chance. Throwing up her arm, Elysia spun out of his grip, but Philip grabbed her braid. Her scalp panged as she turned back to him, her mind reeling. She couldn't hurt him – her father might judge her for that. He still thought Philip couldn't hurt her, even after the words they had exchanged. The cuts flowing freely on her face and the red crescents branded into her hip told her that her father would have his proof, even if he would not accept it.

Philip grabbed her jaw and pulled her toward him, pressed his lips to hers.

He tasted like a wine sink.

Enough.

Elysia slapped him across the face. Her ears rang with the sound of it.

She knew instantly it was a mistake.

The slap he gave her in return took her to the ground, the stinging in her bloody cuts such that it stole her breath, burning against the earth of the floor. Elysia pulled herself up by the edge of the lounge. Philip's shadow made everything feel dark, though it was just an hour past dawn. The heat in her cheek pulsed with her heartbeat. "I'm going to marry him, Philip," she said. Some vengeful beast took hold of her, grinning up at him in the darkness he cast. "I would have married you," she whispered, "but I'm going to marry him."

The fury in Philip's eyes lit hot. His fists trembled, but he did not move to strike her.

"I love him," she said, pulling herself farther up, pulling her legs in so he could not step on her. "I would still love you, if you had not wasted the respect I deserve. If you had just seen fit to treat me as an equal, it might have been different. I'm glad it's not." Elysia glared up at him. "I am too much property for a man such as you. You are small," she spit. Elysia thought maybe it was not a vengeful beast that had taken hold of her. She felt the rawness she had seen in Alexander's sister, the girl who had been beaten until she lost her only child at fourteen, who had lived for her brothers, who had forgotten to cover her deep, seeping wounds because she did not care anymore. "You are mean," she said, "and I would not name a fruit fly after you."

Philip's hand had just pinned her throat to her father's couch when the front door slammed open behind him, and then suddenly, Philip was gone.

Elysia breathed deep the newly rose-scented air, letting it fill her lungs again as she regained her surroundings. Philip's shadow had been replaced by that of a blond man. Her vision swayed as she sat up; the skin that had been pinned between her spine and the wooden lounge ached. It had not seemed all that long his hand had been around her throat, but she had been elsewhere – anywhere else, as long as she did not have to think about the man she had once loved who crushed the air from her lungs.

But someone else was here now. He and Philip exchanged words, words so heated Elysia was certain they would singe her ears. Clumsily, she felt along the edge of the couch for the end and dragged herself to lean against the arm, pulling in the air she had lost.

"You will kill her," said Alexander's voice. Elysia pictured him, hands held at the ready to catch Philip should he come charging like he was wont to do.

"You don't think you will?" Philip's voice was so incredulous that the disbelieving laugh that followed it did not surprise Elysia. "Teaching her to fight? She's highborn. She'll be a goddess someday. You teaching her to fight will welcome attention she doesn't need. They'll find out she rides horses like a man, they'll find out she's killed a guard, they'll find out her household is secular at best. She'll be brought down like the lowest cur."

Lowest cur, she thought. *Says the man who tried to strangle me twice and kissed me between.* Air worked its way back to her brain. Dizzily, Elysia got to her feet, holding onto the couch for support. It slid with her as she swayed, but she managed to stay upright.

They paid her no attention. “That will not happen,” Alexander replied, “and those are outside circumstances. You’d have killed her with your bare hands.”

“She is mine.”

“She belongs to no one. She is a woman with as much self as you have.”

“It’s an expression, *boy.*” Elysia scooted behind the couch, ready to take shelter as Philip’s voice grew colder, dangerous. “Haven’t you heard her call me hers before?”

“It’s not an expression when you think she is a possession,” Alexander said. His fists clenched as Philip lunged for him.

Alexander’s fist sank into Philip’s abdomen. Elysia heard the air leave his lungs all at once, like a tightly sewn pillow compressed. As Philip gasped, Alexander swung around behind him, hooking his arms in front of Philip’s and locking them in place. He pressed his woven fingers against the back of Philip’s skull. “Surrender,” Alexander said.

“Never,” growled Philip.

Alexander’s fingers pressed harder, and Philip’s neck bowed. “Surrender,” repeated Alexander.

Philip’s eyes darted to Elysia’s face, half terrified, half rabid. “Alexander,” she whispered.

“Surrender,” Alexander shouted, Philip’s neck bent further downward.

“*Let him go!*” she screeched.

Gray eyes met hers, as fearful as Philip’s. “Not until he surrenders. I will not have him hurt you again. Surrender, Philip,” he commanded.

Philip’s mouth twisted into something that spoke excruciating pain. “I answer only to Khronos,” he choked out. “And my lady, when she sees reason.”

Elysia clutched her fingers to her mouth. “Surrender, Philip,” she murmured.

He gazed at her with such clarity she knew his answer before he spoke. “Not if I can’t have you.”

A crack sounded, the same one that had resonated from Adrastos when her hand struck his jaw.

The air froze.

“*No!*” she screamed, but Philip fell forward, his eyes open and fallen toward the floor with the rest of his body. Alexander let him fall, his hands up as if in surprise, as if in innocence.

Scrambling around the edge of the couch, Elysia caught herself on her bed when she stumbled. She slipped to the floor, fingers hovering over Philip's hair. It was the same as it had always been: the deep, rich black of coal with diamond flecks. She knew if she ran her fingers through it, it would tickle her skin like a thousand tiny feathers. She couldn't stand to touch him, though, because she was certain if she did, she would feel the lifelessness beneath his hair, the warmth leeching from his skin. She heard herself mutter Philip's name, and then her hands hooked beneath his shoulders, turning and pulling him into her lap. Brown eyes gazed emptily up at her, unnaturally still. Taking a deep breath, Elysia closed his eyes, his lashes soft against her skin. She leaned down and kissed his forehead, tracing the lines that had formed there after years of raising his brow at her.

Finally, Elysia looked at Alexander, who still had his hands raised, staring down at them like he could not believe himself. His fingers trembled as he spoke. "I did not mean for that to happen," he whispered.

Elysia stared at him, uncomprehending. Her fingers at last pushed into Philip's hair, letting it fly back beneath her fingers. "He was a friend," she murmured, dropping her gaze back to Philip. Her hand traced his ear.

Elysia sucked in breath, and it came out a sob.

"I'm sorry, Elysia."

He was my first love, you know, she wanted to say, but she could not say that to Alexander. It would hurt him more than anything, and there was no helping Philip now. He was at home with the Six, just where he belonged. Death might be as final for Philip as it had been for her mother. "He'll be fine," she muttered.

"You know that?"

Elysia looked up at Alexander. His eyes spoke more fear than she thought he had the ability to possess. "Better than anyone," she assured him.

At last, Alexander let his hands fall.

Clearing her throat, Elysia tried to compose herself. Philip was at *home.* He'd just be wondering how he had gotten there, and perhaps he would figure it out.

Hooves clopped in the road outside. Dread swooped down to land on Elysia's shoulders like a hawk.

"Hide," she said to Alexander.

"*What?*" he asked, brows coming together.

"Hide!" she yelled.

The door slammed open against the wall.
Elysia met her father's golden eyes.

38

If her father's eyes could shoot flames, Elysia was sure they would. She prayed, as she sat with Philip's head in her lap, that that was one way in which his human form limited him.

Khronos's eyes pierced her, searing through her to search her soul, moved from her eyes to her cheek. Elysia remembered the sting of fresh blood flowing from the wounds there. After surveying her, his eyes moved to Philip on the ground. "Tell me what has happened here," he said, and gravel slid into his voice. "Or so help me, I will try you both for murder."

"Father," she said hoarsely. *You said you knew I would only ever kill in self-defense or judgment.* "Philip tried to kill Alexander."

"He tried to kill Alexander, and yet you hold his body, daughter," said Khronos, watching her with an eye so critical she could not hold his gaze. "So tell me what has happened here, because I doubt you would hold the man who tried to kill your betrothed."

Elysia's eyes shot to Alexander, who nodded. He had told her father – who had not struck him down in the agora. Perhaps Alexander had been too surprised that he survived to stop Philip before he ran back to the house to belittle her. Slowly, she turned back to her father. "Alexander pulled him off me." *I think.* "He was so angry with my answers that he tried to strangle me. I antagonized him into doing it a second time." Elysia swallowed and looked down at Philip. His body heat was beginning to fade, his head lolling limply in her lap.

"I put him into a lock," said Alexander's voice above her. "I asked him to surrender, and he said he would not without your word or Elysia's. He refused her. I... I pushed a little too hard, and he broke."

Elysia closed her eyes and sighed. "He was wild, bent on killing us both. If Alexander had not stopped him, he might have succeeded."

"The Six will be the judge of that."

Elysia's eyes snapped to her father.

"Get in the chariot," he said. He walked out the door, shoulders slumped.

A pair of grooms walked in seconds later, the same pair who had carried Adrastos's body from the garden. This time, though, they stopped when they stepped over the threshold.

"I'm sorry," Elysia said to them. Carefully, she held Philip's head in her hands as she scooted from beneath him, and gently set it on the floor, brushing his hair back into place over his forehead, smoothing his hairline. With his eyes closed, something about him looked peaceful that had been missing from him in life.

The grooms pardoned themselves as they moved past her, countless *my lady*s dropping from their mouths. They held Philip with much more tenderness than they had managed for Adrastos, the one at his head supporting it with as much grace as he could muster while holding Philip beneath the arms. They ferried him from the house in silence as Alexander moved to take Elysia's hand and help her to her feet. "What happens now?" he asked, holding her hands.

"Now," she said, "the judges of the afterlife will decide if we are murderers."

The chariot ride was just as jouncy as she remembered and far more crowded. Though there were wagons behind them, Khronos insisted that Alexander ride in the chariot, lest he run away. Elysia, too, was forced to stand in the small space the cart afforded the three of them, squeezed into the front corner. Alexander stood behind her, her father to her left, the reins clutched in his white-knuckled fingers. Alexander kept his hand fisted in the back of her dress until they reached the gates. Without Zeus's presence to lighten them, the statues seemed strange, forbidding. Corinth's outskirts looked like nothing but a stretch of brown, gold, and white beyond the dry, infertile Gauntlet.

I came here for the promise of eternity. I leave as a killer.

Philip was hidden beneath the white sheet the women used to ward off the Gauntlet's thieves. More than one girl had wailed when they saw him. Khronos had sent a groom to gather them from the agora before he left, though he left two men to mind the stand.

After they left the shadow of Poseidon and Amphitrite, Khronos said not a word until they reached the valley. Elysia heard only the creaking of the chariot and felt the warmth of Alexander's hand at her back. Eventually, she closed her eyes.

She did not open them until she was home.

She knew it by scent: the dust of the road and the dryness in her mouth were replaced by the smell of green things as they passed the boundary. She knew the sweet scent of grass, the cool shade the olive trees cast on the road. She knew the scent of life, of water, sun, and earth.

Elysia opened her eyes and found herself halfway down the road, the white mansion growing in the distance. The slackness of Alexander's fingers at her back told her he couldn't believe his eyes. She almost couldn't, either.

Home.

Mild green fruit hung from the limbs above her; her father had maintained the harvest bounty in their absence, and for some reason, it surprised her. The valley had been almost empty: the only inhabitants had been a few servants and the Six, who were hopeless with farm work. Nothing had changed in this place, yet everything inside of her had.

I am here to be judged. Elysia was not certain this house would still be her home once she'd sat in that rickety chair. She'd sit in the center of the circle of thrones, the one that was meant to be hers directly behind her, judging her in its own way. No matter how flowery her father had made the throne, no matter how beautiful it was, and no matter how she wanted it, she wasn't sure it could belong to her after that.

"Olympus," Alexander whispered behind her.

"Not quite, son," said Khronos. "Olympus is a mountain. This is a valley, even if it is home to gods."

Gods, thought Elysia. *He counts me among them.*

When the chariot stopped outside the stables, Elysia took Alexander's hand and led him to the house in silence. Her sandals rang on the marble floors, scuffing occasionally, a sound she'd learned to ignore when she'd heard it every day. Now, it seemed impossibly loud as she led him from one floor to the next, until finally she reached the third. Down the hall, the entrance to the chamber stared innocently at her. Beside her hung the curtain that hid the loom her father had used to weave the valley.

"What do you know of the judges of the afterlife?" she whispered into the quiet, open air of the house. To their left, the hallway opened out into the cool, sunlit air of the morning, the columns shining pale and casting white light onto everything behind them.

"Not enough," he replied, but squeezed her hand. "Cronus, Zeus's father, judges souls for the Isles of the Blessed. There are a few other judges who sit in judgment on the masses, but I have not made a study of them. Some even say it's Corinth's hero who waits for them at the door of the Underworld, with Pegasus and Kerberos by his side."

Giving him a little smile, Elysia squeezed his hand in return. "It's not Corinth's hero," she said. "It's the Six, the people who were named after the Olympians? The ones my father brought to judge my self-defense test."

"I stood in the presence of gods?" Running a hand through his hair, he shook his head. "I need to be informed when these things happen."

Elysia laughed, but it was short-lived, for her father swept up the stairs behind him. "The Six are souls," he said, voice gruff and short, "and they await." His green and gold cloak rippled as he strode past them. Elysia took a deep breath.

"They will know your every action and deed, Alexander." He would get nowhere but deeper in this pit of trouble if he tried to hide anything. "They will know mine, too."

Flexing his fingers against hers, Alexander nodded.

When they came around the illusory wall, Elysia blinked in the light of the torches, the only light allowed in the windowless room aside from her father's eyes, bright and bolder than the flames. To Elysia's horror, two chairs had been set in the middle of the room.

"Sit," said Eris, her voice throaty even in that single syllable.

If I sit, I won't be able to leave.

Watching Elysia's indecision, Hera spoke. "Sit, Elysia," she said, holding out a hand toward the chairs.

Elysia sat in the chair on the left, trying to hold her father's gaze. Alexander sat beside her, his hand still clutched in hers between them.

"The judgment of the souls of the woman Elysia and the man Alexander will commence," said Eris. Elysia's heart sank.

We are just as any other humans, in the end.

39

“Are there any words you wish to preface your judgment?” Eris asked, sitting in her black throne. The red dress she wore and the torchlight on her skin turned her into a flaming shadow, a specter against the pearly whiteness of the rest of the room.

Pressing her fingers into Alexander’s hand to suppress whatever urge he might have to speak, Elysia nodded. She had heard many a fool lie their way through judgment; it had only hurt their cases. “Any actions we took were either in self-defense or framed by profound loss,” she said, meeting her father’s eyes.

“That is all?” asked Eris.

“Yes.”

“Very well,” said Khronos, waving his stylus at Eris. “Begin with Elysia, Eris.”

Eris stood. Flames shone in her black hair. “In the ways of sin and strife,” Eris began, “Elysia has caused much.”

Elysia’s heart skipped a beat.

“She has had men pursuing her since she has been in Corinth and has allowed them to act in her name. She did, however, punish those who acted criminally. She banished the man Philip when he instigated a fight in her name. She banished him again when he would not recognize her as equal, albeit with cutting words. When the man Adrastos groped her, she deafened him in one ear, but then acted vengefully and removed his privilege via her father, Khronos the Creator. In this, she created a cycle of vengeance, in which Adrastos felt he had the right to assault and kill her for her crime. Elysia ended the cycle when she killed him in self-defense, an accident justified by the man’s intent.”

The breath Elysia held rushed out of her, filled with relief.

“In the matter of the death of the man Philip,” Eris continued, “she is less blameless.”

Her fingers slid between Alexander’s in panic.

"When he confronted her for what he saw as a slight to his own honor, having done his best to claim her, as well as a slight to her father, Elysia answered his first questions truthfully. Philip made clear his intent to kill the man Alexander when he returned home. Elysia escaped his hold when given the chance. He found a hold on her again, however, and kissed her."

Alexander's fingers tightened around hers.

"After she slapped him for kissing her without leave, he slapped her in return, and from the ground, she antagonized him." Eris's black eyes glimmered in the torchlight. "She called him small, mean, and told him she would name a fruit fly after him."

Khronos looked up sharply from his tablet. Elysia shrank in her seat.

"Philip strangled her until the man Alexander knocked him away from her. Words were exchanged between the two men, each attempting to speak their own ideals on Elysia's behalf, and Philip lunged for Alexander. Alexander broke the man's neck when he held him helpless."

Fury lit in Elysia's gut. The judge put on a show. But as soon as she had said Philip had tried to strangle her, Khronos's eyes had gone back to his tablet, apparently disinterested in Eris's judgment of his daughter.

"Had Elysia spoken on Philip's behalf, he would have been spared, but she did not. All in all, she has caused much strife and committed perhaps a sin or two, even if she is no hardened criminal. She has fulfilled two of her three tests to my satisfaction."

Fulfilled...? Blank space filled her mind, and then Elysia glared at Eris as she reclaimed her seat. *My tests are being judged amidst this? What does she think I have not done?*

"Ares," said Khronos, glancing up.

Ares rose from his seat of red sandstone, and the smile he wore for Elysia was warm. "In the ways of battle and valor, Elysia has learned much. She has learned to fight to protect herself. She has learned to care for others on the battlefield as only one who has seen such can, and she has learned to respect those who see her as an enemy, as well as those who know her as a friend. She has learned to understand which of her claimed friends are her enemies, and she can put puzzle pieces together."

Eris raised an eyebrow at him. "Ares, I hardly think that counts."

Raising his hands in surrender, Ares took his seat.

"Your judgment of the tests, Ares," said Khronos, making a mark on his tablet. *Let it be a good mark*, Elysia prayed. She had never been able to decode his method for marking his tablets – they were simply tallies.

"Passed on all counts."

Elysia gave him a grin so huge her cheeks burned. He smiled right back.

"Aphrodite."

Aphrodite stood, her blond hair falling in a wave that matched the ones carved in the blue-green glass of her throne. "In her relationships," Aphrodite began, "Elysia has failings and successes, like most. Her relationship with the man Philip, precious to her for most of her life, failed the moment she learned what he truly thought of her, something she had been blind to. She has learned to seek out those who will make her stronger and left behind those who sought to make her weak. Passed on all counts." Looking like she had eaten bitter fruit, Aphrodite resumed her seat.

"Hera."

Hera stood, her grey gown so long that her sandaled toes were lost among the folds gathered on the floor. "In the way of the faith," began Hera, "Elysia has had no need to seek it out, but she has when she thought guidance could be offered, and in this, her human life has been fulfilled in my domain. Passed on all counts."

As Hera sat, Khronos called Athena's name, and the blue eyes that Elysia met were astonishingly cold.

Bracing herself, Elysia awaited Athena's judgment.

"In the way of wisdom, Elysia has lost some of her rash ways, but gained others," Athena said. "She has found insight but sought revenge. She has made right choices unknowingly and wrong choices knowingly and considered her future from only one perspective. Two of the three tests have been fulfilled to my satisfaction."

Elysia turned to gaze at Apollo as Athena took her seat. *Two and three.* Her tests fell to Apollo. Should he accept her, she would be allowed to ascend sometime, but if he did not, it would become someone else's decision – her father's or another's.

Apollo stood, his golden hair bright in the torchlight. "In the way of morality," he began, a ghost of a smile twitching up the corners of his lips. "Elysia has learned what society dictates and the difference between its ideals and her own. She has acted morally, according to her own code, but she has passed only two of her tests to my satisfaction."

Panicked eyes shooting to her father, Elysia tried to slow her racing heart. With Apollo's speaking of Khronos's name, the Six rose with a rustle of movement. Khronos raised his head slowly, as if it were heavy.

Surveying the room, Khronos nodded to Eris. "In the matter of the death of the man Philip, I find the woman Elysia guiltless except in that she was a fool for cajoling him when he meant her harm. In the matter of her ascension, I will reserve judgment."

Speechless, Elysia stared at her father.

"The judgment of the man Alexander will commence," said Eris, and the rest reclaimed their seats. "In the ways of sin and strife, Alexander has caused little."

Elysia squeezed his hand, and Alexander returned the squeeze a moment later. Something akin to hope danced in his eyes when she cast a glance at him. His gaze was glued to Eris.

"Though he had various fights with his parents and siblings as children are wont to do, he rose to violence only once, when the man Herod beat the woman Korinna near to death."

"Eris," Elysia said, frowning. The judge looked to her, brows raised. "You cannot judge Alexander on his life when you are here to judge him for the death of Philip."

"Am I?" Eris asked.

Elysia's gut twisted. She didn't know anymore.

"Two years passed before the man Alexander rose to violence in rage again, this time at the goading of the man Philip, who had been intent on beginning a fight with the woman Elysia's defense trainer since before he had even set out to meet him. In this fight with the man Philip, Alexander was mostly –"

"I was there, Eris," said Khronos, making Elysia jump. "You may continue to the next event worth remarking."

"The next strife the man Alexander caused was between the woman Elysia and her father, Khronos, when Alexander took Elysia to the mountain Acrocorinth without Khronos's leave. Though the pair of them claimed it was because the man Herod had wanted to teach her to fend off an attacker in possession of a weapon, the visit was truly to meet the man Euthymios, brother of Alexander, a visit Alexander decided on spontaneously after he and Elysia kissed."

Horror rang high through Elysia's gut as her father looked up and stared at her, his mouth pressed into a hard line. Elysia watched as the stylus made a tick mark in the wax and tried to hide the way she shrank in her seat. *He is judging Alexander on his behavior toward me.* The only relief she could muster was that they had not gone further.

"Alexander acted honorably as Elysia's shield after her dress was dismantled during her first test, though she acted more familiarly than any of us expected."

"I seek your objectivity, Eris," said Khronos, pointing to her with his stylus. "The others will share their opinions."

Though the judge nodded, Elysia's eyebrows came together. She had never heard Eris so blatantly include speculation in her judgments. The sly smile hiding in the corners of her mouth made Elysia wary.

"My apologies, my lord," said the judge, and Elysia felt her simpering across the room. "The man Alexander showed Elysia much of what she has learned of living a human life when he allowed her to help make improvements to the home he shared with his family. When she left her spindle in his house, he sought to return it to her, though he acted with much encouragement from his brother Euthymios."

Elysia raised her eyebrows at Alexander, and as he met her gaze, he smiled ruefully. *Euthymios my champion and Korinna my critic,* she thought. *At least they kept him balanced in his opinions.*

"When he found Elysia, she sat in the middle of the fountain with the dead man Adrastos, shock and exposure imminent in her cold skin. He carried her into the house and was extremely careful with her. Elysia had the woman Aliya draw her a warm bath, which she offered to the man Alexander after she bathed and dressed. Elysia requested that he remain for the night, and they slept apart, though they were on the same bed."

Thank you for that token of goodwill, Eris, she thought, trying to balance this judge in her mind.

"In the morning –"

"I know what happened, Eris," Khronos said, nodding to Alexander. "You have my apologies for my reaction."

A jolt of fury shot through Elysia's shoulders. Her teeth ground together. He owed her an apology, too. Taking a breath, Elysia squeezed Alexander's hand. He nodded to Khronos, who watched his daughter with curious eyes.

"Begin after the earthquake."

"After the earthquake, Alexander and Elysia helped the woman Delia back to the woman Metrodora's home."

Elysia's eyebrows went up in surprise. Even Eris, in her omniscience, had not seen that Metrodora was not, after all, named Metrodora, nor that she was inhuman. *She must shield herself somehow.* After all, her father, in all his years, had never detected her.

"Elysia and Alexander drew a bath and bathed together."

Elysia sat in shocked silence, her brain utterly devoid of every thought except the curses running in circles around her mind. Even her father stared at Eris. His gaze returned to Elysia, and she counted the strokes as he drew five new lines on his tablet. Beside her, Alexander looked as stoic as she was mortified; his face had become a mask of careful blankness.

"The next four days and nights are utterly without remark, except that the unmarried woman Elysia and man Alexander shared the same bed every night."

Elysia closed her eyes, unable to watch anymore as her father seemed to draw a mark for every word Eris spoke.

"This morning, the man Alexander proposed marriage to Elysia without her father's permission, which he asked later in the agora of the city Corinth. When the man Philip reacted to the news by running from the agora, Alexander followed his trail, finding him at Elysia's just in time to witness Philip strangling Elysia with his hands. Alexander knocked Philip away from Elysia and stood between them. Words were exchanged, and Philip lunged for him. Alexander found a hold on him, and when Philip would not surrender, Alexander broke Philip's neck."

With a triumphant smile on her face, Eris took her seat. Beside Elysia, Alexander's face had gone ashen despite his blank expression.

"Ares," said Khronos, and Ares stood.

"In the ways of battle and valor, Alexander has known little except in the protection of others, especially the defenseless. As a young man, he attempted to protect the woman Korinna from the man Herod when Herod was intent on beating her until she lost an unborn child. Alexander failed in this attempt but redoubled his efforts to protect the women he loved when the woman Elysia was threatened, killing her assailant. He has learned how to care for both friends and enemies on the battlefield." Ares sat again, and Elysia took a deep breath to calm herself.

"Aphrodite."

Aphrodite's words, at least, were kinder. "In relationships, Alexander has shown great honor, fighting for those he loves, sometimes to the death. He has never stopped protecting them, some even beyond death." As she sat proud and straight, Aphrodite offered Alexander the warmest smile Elysia had ever seen the judge bestow on anyone, even Ares – something that earned a scowl from the brown-haired judge sitting to Aphrodite's left.

"Hera."

"In the way of faith, Alexander has kept faith with the gods more often than with men, as is shown by his attempt to stop his father from harming the woman Korinna. That, however, was not a bad thing, as his father's decision was a horrifying tragedy, resulting in the damaging of his daughter's body and the loss of a life, young though it might have been. He prayed frequently but rarely asked for favors and was humble in his requests." Hera's face was as impassive as Alexander's as she took her seat, and that made Elysia's stomach clench.

"Athena."

Graceful as the owls that supported the arms of her throne, Athena stood. "In the way of wisdom, Alexander has shown enough to be called adequate. He often waited an appropriate amount of time before acting and thus made a good decision. A notable exception was in his killing of the man Philip."

Elysia's fingers, which had been loose in Alexander's hand, gripped his tightly, the tips of her fingers pressing into the tendons in the back of his hand. His clutched hers in return, until she could no longer remember which fingers belonged to her.

"Apollo."

Elysia could not turn to watch Apollo rise, not this time. Instead, she closed her eyes, waiting to hear that smooth voice that had once sung her to sleep.

"In the way of morality, Alexander is unquestionable."

Relief flooded through her like a wave breaking through a storm wall, reaching to every corner of her being. Elysia's fingers relaxed against Alexander, and she opened her eyes, letting out a quiet breath. For just a moment, she exchanged a hopeful glance with Alexander – one that he returned, his face no longer as stone.

"He remained honorable with the unmarried woman Elysia as a man of Greece is expected to, and he served his family to the end." After a moment's pause, Apollo spoke Khronos's name, and Eris, Ares, Aphrodite, Hera, and Athena rose.

Though he judged Alexander, Khronos's eyes met only Elysia's, and with the look he gave her, her stomach dropped through the floor. "In the matter of the death of the man Philip," he said, "I find the man Alexander guilty of murder –"

"*No!*" Elysia shouted, and when she tried to stand, found herself stuck to her seat, just as the petty soul had been three weeks earlier. Unable to stand, she banged her fist on the chair and her feet on the floor, making Alexander jump beside her.

"– and sentence him to die at sunset –"

"*Father!*"

He did not hear her, for his lips continued to move.

"– by the stopping of his heart."

Beside her, Alexander was pale as the marble floor beneath his sandals.

With her father's silence, Elysia could no longer scream at him. To do so would be to fill the room with ringing sound, and should she do that, she felt as though she might shatter like glass. "Father, please," she whispered. "You told me that mercy was as divine as justice."

"And so it is," said Khronos, standing and setting his stylus on the tablet. His gaze turned to Alexander, who sat frozen in his chair. "You have eight hours of daylight remaining to you, Alexander. Use them well. And I will find you, Elysia," he said, his eyes returning to his daughter, so sharp she thought he would drive a knife into her soul with them. "I will find *him*, no matter where you try to take him. It will do you no good to run."

Without so much as another glance to them, Khronos strode from the room, the Six filing out behind him.

Sitting in the stillness of the empty room, Elysia swallowed and closed her eyes.

Justice is as divine as mercy.

40

Still staring at the blue-black crystal of her father's throne as it shone in the torchlight with its beautiful and terrible faces, Elysia took a breath. "I should never have let you leave the house this morning," she whispered.

"Elysia," he said, hooking his fingers under her jaw, turning her face toward him. The gray eyes she knew to dance with light were still and steady, even in the torchlight. "I have eight hours remaining to me. I do not want to hear how it is your fault."

"You can't just let him kill you, Alexander," she said, closing her fingers around his wrist. "You can't just give up."

"Would you believe me if I told you I wasn't giving up?"

Elysia shook her head.

Alexander sighed, running a hand through his hair, eyes cast down. He looked up at her again. "I will see my family in the underworld, Elysia," he said, and Elysia closed her eyes.

There is no underworld. She could not bring herself to speak the words aloud. When he reincarnated, when his soul found new life, he would have a new family. He would not know the difference. She would no longer hear him waking in the night screaming, would no longer find him leaning over the edge of the bed, struggling for breath as tears ran down his cheeks.

Tears slipped down her own cheeks at the thought of him reuniting with his family in some happier place he imagined. She knew she could not give it to him. All that waited for him was a fresh start. Once he had gone, he would not know he had left something behind. He would not know he had left her grieving.

"Hey," Alexander said, wiping her tears with his knuckles. His voice was hoarse, and Elysia wondered if she was making him cry, too.

Opening her eyes, she let the cool air of the chamber fill her lungs to the bottom, refreshing her. She slid her fingers down his wrist to twine with his. "There is a place I want to show you," she said. Getting to her feet, Elysia ignored the scuffing her sandals made over the marble. Alexander looked hesitant, wary even, but she tugged him to his feet. Without a look back at the throne that was supposed to be hers – that pale white, flowery thing – Elysia led him from the room. Down the stairs they went, and as they walked, Elysia sped up, until she swung herself around the banister at the bottom of the stairs. Alexander laughed, and they ran. Wind rushed warm and sunlight poured over her skin. Her braid bounced against her back with each step.

She would be free in her last moments with him.

When they reached the ground floor, Elysia turned right, toward the hills in the east. To the west were the stables and the spot she and Philip had claimed as theirs, but to the east – the east was unexplored. It had always been crops and forest and rocky soil, too far for her to walk on her own without someone to talk to. With Philip, she had always gone west, but today, she would go east.

After a while, Alexander no longer followed behind her, but walked beside her. The sun rose higher over their heads, and they walked through fields burgeoning with ripe burgundy grapes, so round they nearly split. They walked through a grove of pomegranate trees, throwing light onto the ground in dapples and filling the air with their sweet scent, but Elysia walked past them.

"Where are we going?" Alexander asked her once.

"I don't know," she replied.

And she didn't, but she kept walking. They came to a field of golden wheat. Elysia learned for the first time that the fuzzy heads of grain on the long, slender stalks were spikier than they were soft, and that running her fingers through them made her palms tickle and itch, like skimming her fingers over a bristly brush.

At the end of the field, the first of the steep, rocky hills rose up before her. Alexander helped her climb, but soon, she tied her dress up in a knot beside her knee, and there it bobbed against her leg until they reached the top of the hill.

They stood on top of the world, breath raw against dry throats.

"We forgot the water," said Elysia.

Alexander laughed. "That we did," he said, walking to where a shelf of rock hung over the hillside. Though Elysia half expected him to lean over the edge as he once had on the cliffs of Acrocorinth and play at being a bird, he didn't; the wind was too weak to even make her hair sway. Instead, he sat at the edge, one leg dangling and the other raised, his knee clasped between his hands. The shadow he cast was near invisible, the darkness marching off the rock and into the abyss below them. The sun beat down from on high, readying to pass its apex and begin its descent. Alexander patted the rock beside him, and the clap echoed. "Our shadows will be bigger than any god's," he said, grinning up at Elysia as she came to stand beside him. Her chest seized for a moment, thinking of Poseidon and Amphitrite and the shadows they cast over Corinth at every time of day. From up here, any shadow Alexander cast into the valley would be ten times as tall. But something else about Poseidon and Amphitrite struck her. She knelt beside Alexander, the rock and soil digging into her knees like so many tiny daggers.

"Marry me," she murmured.

Alexander's eyes snapped to her, their clear gray depths shadowed by his brows.

"Marry me, Alexander," she said quickly. Something in her made her reach out and touch his arm, lighting up when he did not pull away. "If we are free to do what we will with the time we have left, marry me. Let us find what my father has taken from us."

"Elysia." He blinked at her but stopped himself short. Turning back to look at the valley that stretched out before them, Alexander shook his head. "You will not be a widow for eternity," he said to the fields below.

Elysia took hold of his chin and turned it to her, studied his face with the long nose and the clear eyes, the lips as chapped as hers from hot sun and the dry salt air of the city. "Whether or not I am a widow for eternity isn't the point," she said, holding his face between her hands. To her surprise, they matched his skin – her skin had grown tan. "My heart will be widowed whether it is an official title or not, and even if we are married, there will be no one to witness it." Elysia leaned in until her lips were an inch from his, her forehead resting against his, warm from their trek beneath the sun. "It is a bond between you and me, and no one else. There are no gods to sanction us, nor any gods that would, given the chance." Voice lowering to a whisper, Elysia let her fingers comb through his smooth hair. "We are our own, and we always will be."

Alexander let out a breath and closed his eyes; his lashes fluttered against her cheek. Finally, he said, "I love you." His eyes did not open, though, and Elysia waited for him to finish. Minutes of silence passed between them, and Elysia felt the sun grow warm on the back of her neck. Panic sang in her veins when Alexander opened his eyes at last. "You are your own, my love, and a Greek marriage would take that from you. You would be mine, and you have felt how that goes."

A sigh swept out of her lungs. "I don't want a Greek marriage," she said. "It doesn't even have to be a marriage a Greek would find stomachable." Though a wry smile twitched at his lips and he shook his head, Elysia kept on, hands moving down to squeeze his shoulders. "It just has to mean something to *us*. Can we do *that*?"

Alexander ran a hand across the top of her head, smoothing her hair down with warmth. "If you can think of something that will make you mean more to me than you already do," he whispered.

As she sat in silence, Alexander smiled. "I don't think you'll find anything, Elysia. There's a certain kind of meaning that comes with being the only thing in the world a man has left."

Elysia lunged for him, clinging to him with arms around his neck. She bowled him over, taking him down inches from where the shelf ended, and Elysia remembered the time she climbed a mountain. Her instincts were as alive as they were now, lighting her limbs on fire with awareness of every touch. Alexander rolled them away from the cliff. "I'm not taking you with me when I go," he said, running his thumbs beneath the circles under her eyes. Her skin warmed at his touch.

"No, you'll just leave me missing you for eternity," she mumbled, nestling herself into his side. The sky was so intense a blue above her that her eyes flickered closed.

Alexander turned, and his face wore a frown. "You will be a goddess, able to visit the underworld whenever you please."

Elysia closed her eyes and felt tears gather in her lashes. *It doesn't work that way.* "I love you, Alexander," she whispered.

"I love you, Elysia," he murmured back, though she could hear his puzzlement.

An hour passed as they lay beneath the sun, and when Elysia felt her legs cool in the shadow of Alexander's, she knew the time was nearly upon them. She could not stop her tears.

"Easy now," said Alexander, running his hand down her arm to weave between her fingers. Elysia pulled his fingers to her lips. She could not stop herself as her lips traveled up his arm and left droplets of saltwater in their wake. She heard his breath hitch in his chest when her lips brushed his wrist, his elbow, the hollow where neck met shoulder, and by the time her lips had reached his throat, Alexander's hands tangled in her hair, pulling her braid apart.

Her lips found his, her hands found his. Elysia raised their joined hands into the light of the setting sun.

They will never take you from me.

Alexander broke free of her when he had to catch his breath. Elysia looked out over the valley, trying to catch her own. Her heart raced in her chest, beating fit to fly from beneath her ribs.

She looked back to Alexander, who wore a smile so broad his cheeks showed dimples she had never seen before. “I lo-”

His chest made a movement like his lungs were sucking for air and finding none, and Alexander stopped midword.

“Alexander?” she said, but her volume rose from a whisper to a shriek as his hand clutched at his chest and his eyes moved downward. She remembered her father’s sentence.

The stopping of his heart.

Alexander’s eyes found hers. There was a mix of panic and clarity there, stillness and insanity, terror and peace. “I love you,” he murmured. The hand that had been on his chest moved toward her, and then it was as if she had vertigo.

He fell away from her, his hand dropping to his side and his eyes drifting upward. He spread-eagled on the flat rock, eyes open and skin tinted the color of the sunset above him.

Elysia’s chest seized painfully, and seized again, and again and again and again as her body tried to find a sob but her mouth wouldn’t let it out. She dissolved in silence, clutching the hand he had held out to her. His skin still smelled of the rosewater he must have run down his wrists. She clutched his fingers to her lips and rocked, breathing in the warmth and the scent, the roughness of his callouses against her mouth. After a while, she didn’t know how long, she pressed the back of his hand to her forehead. Sharp pain stabbed through her when he did not flinch at her head hitting his chest, as it was supposed to when she surprised him.

I will find him, no matter where you try to take him.

41

When next she opened her eyes, stars shone above her. They were bright little white pinpricks in the ceiling of the world. Elysia wondered if that meant that somewhere, there was a world as bright as they, and it shone down through the holes to taunt her because she could not have it.

Alexander remained still. His heart was silent beneath her head. His lungs did not draw breath. She had not listened to the strength in his heartbeat, had not heard the blood pulse in veins. She had not heard every note his voice could reach and what each sounded like, and she had not felt his fingers over every inch of her skin. They had not become husband and wife, and they had not made a life for themselves independent of her father.

But he had taught her to live.

Elysia counted to sixty after she opened her eyes, and then again, and then again, until she finally propped herself up. Alexander's eyes shone in the starlight.

Somehow, she stood. She forgot how she managed it and how she moved, but she found herself with hands dirty and scratched, rocks gathered in a pile near Alexander's knees.

Elysia drew an outline in stones around his body. She allowed herself as much precision as she could handle, turning the rocks so that the flat edges were turned toward Alexander and the round ones faced away from him, the reasoning of which was unknown to her. It felt right, so she did it. More carefully still, she rested stones across his body. She left his eyes open, because he needed to see the light. There was some better place out there, and his soul would find it when it was given its chance to start anew.

Before she covered his middle, Elysia took the knife from the sash of his tunic and placed it beside the rocks. And then she balanced them until he was hidden beneath the weight of stone, his body safe where it could see stars and sunrises and sunsets for as long as it would last.

When she laid the last stone, Elysia pressed a kiss to the cold rock, picked up the knife, and climbed down the hill, the knot in her dress still bobbing against her leg. Her hair was free, its leather cord lost somewhere up on the stone with Alexander.

As she walked through the field of wheat, gray in the darkness, Elysia raised the knife to her white hair.

Dawn found her in the garden, the knife tucked into her own belt. Hera found her there and could not hide her gasp. Without a word to the judge, Elysia headed up the flagged path and into the house, taking the stairs three at a time, her shoulder-length hair bobbing with her step.

The chamber was as cold in the dawn light as it was in the afternoon, lit only by the torches in their sconces. They had already lit themselves when she entered, and in the chamber, her father and the rest of the Six waited for her. Hera slipped past her and behind Eris's throne to sit in her own.

"Take a seat, Elysia," said Khronos, and though his hand was held toward the chair in the center of the room, Elysia sat in her throne. To her left, she heard Apollo shift.

"Judges," said Khronos, and they stood. He looked to them one at a time, green-gold eyes bright in the torchlight. Elysia thought they looked more like a hot fire than the cold light of the stars she had seen, furious and consuming and pressing their prey up against a wall before they devoured it. "Have you changed your verdicts in the matter of the woman Elysia's ascension?"

"We have," said Eris, Athena, and Apollo as one.

"Elaborate."

"In the matter of the third test," they said, and Elysia took a deep breath at the sound of Eris's rasp, Athena's solemnity, and Apollo's smooth tenor wrapped up in one voice. "Elysia has completed the requirement."

Khronos nodded, waving his hand. Whatever she felt was not surprise. It was something like a change in the seascape: a single whitecap amid blue-green emptiness. "Pray tell Elysia the requirement so she might know what she has done."

"In order to judge the most profound moments of a human life, you must know great love and great loss."

Something in the pit of Elysia's stomach clenched, but she sat in her chair with its hard, marble seat and stared at her father.

I will find him, no matter where you try to take him.

"Elysia," said her father.

He seemed to expect a reply, so Elysia said, "Yes?"

"In my power as the Creator of our universe, I will raise you to divinity from your human form. Is this your wish?"

"Yes."

"You understand that as a being with divinity, you will have eternal life and immortality?"

"Yes."

"Then it will be that you are eternal."

The fire in her father's eyes consumed her, white-hot in her bones and skin, separating joint from ligament and tendon from muscle, popping and snapping like pine needles thrown on the pyre of what had once been her being.

The next breath she took drowned her, and Elysia felt a hollow form in her soul.

I will find him, no matter where you try to take him.

Her world went white.

TO BE CONTINUED

ACKNOWLEDGMENTS

As they say, it takes a village, and writing a book is no exception. Without the help of my family, friends, and fellows in the writing pursuit, this novel would not have felt the warmth of sunlight on its cover. I must first thank Jo Kaiser, my critique partner, who is likely the only reason *Eternal* was completed at all.

My initial readers have been an integral part of the process. Desiree, Melissa, Andrew, Nina, and Spencer – thank you for your invaluable feedback! Marian Blue, Lorie Langdon, and Heather Webb have all been wonderful writing mentors over the course of workshops.

My beautiful and tolerant cover model, Haily, gave me more to work with than I could have ever wished. Elysia's personification could not be complete without her and her sass. Thank you to Michael K. Eagan and Alex Gavac for their help navigating the troubled waters I encountered with my adventure into cover design. An enormous thank you to Shelby Lee Lubchuk for my author portraits!

To my fantastic writer friends: I couldn't have done it without your unwavering support! Stephen, Myk, Lou, Alex, Leslie, Nicole, and everyone else – you're awesome, and I look forward to supporting your works in the future!

To my friends at home, thank you for believing in me. Sean and family, Michelle, Trevor, Richard, and Jason, thank you for pestering me. A big thank you to Don and Noel, who wouldn't let a visit end without an update.

To my teachers and guides: Mr. Bergquist, Mr. Hall, Mrs. Bakeman, Charlene Ray, and Fiona Claire, you are the reason I believe in myself. Without you, I wouldn't know just how much I am capable of. Thank you.

Last but certainly not least, thank you to my family, who has waited ever-so-patiently for the last four years to get their hands on this. Thank you for loving me as I am and for helping me strive toward the future.

ABOUT THE AUTHOR

Cassandra Thomson was born on Whidbey Island in the Pacific Northwest. Instilled from a young age with a love for nature, Cassandra has dreamed of creating new worlds since the age of seven. While *Eternal* is not her first attempt, it is the first to see the world beyond her desk drawer.

Cassandra remains a resident of Whidbey, along with her dog, a spritely terrier mix named Daisy. She is a student of literature, pursuing a BA in Creative Writing and English. You can find Cassandra online on Twitter, Facebook, and elsewhere.

Cassandrathomson.com
Twitter: @CAT_wrote
Facebook: https://www.facebook.com/CATwrote